Th

Tota**y**

Three powerful romances from three
fabulous Mills & Boon authors!

Totally Tempting

ANNETTE BROADRICK

MARY LYNN BAXTER

PEGGY MORELAND

All the characters in this book have no existence outside the imagination of the author, and have no relation whatsoever to anyone bearing the same name or names. They are not even distantly inspired by any individual known or unknown to the author, and all the incidents are pure invention.

First published in Great Britain 2011
Harlequin Mills & Boon Limited,
Eton House, 18-24 Paradise Road, Richmond, Surrey TW9 1SR

TOTALLY TEMPTING © by Harlequin Enterprises II B.V./S.à.r.l 2011

The Man Means Business, Totally Texan and *The Texan's Forbidden Affair* were first published in Great Britain by Harlequin Mills & Boon Limited in separate, single volumes.

The Man Means Business © Annette Broadrick 2006
Totally Texan © Mary Lynn Baxter 2006
The Texan's Forbidden Affair © Peggy Bozeman Morse 2006
(*The Texan's Forbidden Affair* was previously published in the UK as *The Forbidden Affair*.)

ISBN: 978 0 263 88341 1

05-0311

Printed and bound in Spain
by Litografia Rosés S.A., Barcelona

THE MAN
MEANS BUSINESS

BY
ANNETTE BROADRICK

To Ralph and Betty Carruthers,
who believe that family comes first,
for which I'm extremely grateful.

One

"**M**an your battle stations! Incoming! Incoming!"

Jodie Cameron grinned at the innovative way the receptionist notified her that the man she worked for had finally arrived at the office on this gloomy winter day in Chicago.

"Thanks, Betty." Jodie cleared her computer screen, brushed a wisp of hair that had escaped the tidy knot at the back of her neck away from her face and waited for him.

Jodie knew something was up with Dean Logan. In the five years she'd worked for him Dean had never come to work this late in the morning. He generally was already there when she arrived.

Earlier she'd checked his calendar to see if he was scheduled to go out of town, but he had nothing written down. She had wondered if he'd decided not to come in since it was Friday and he planned to go on a week's vacation starting on Sunday. But that didn't seem likely. He would have called to let her know.

This would be the first vacation he'd taken since she'd been his secretary, and she looked forward to having the time to clean out files, set up subfiles and work uninterrupted.

At least Betty had warned her that he wasn't in the best of moods. Dean was moody at the best of times, but no matter how cranky he was this morning, she could put up with him for one more day.

She waited at her desk for him to enter her office.

Dean was an astute businessman and he'd worked hard to build his electronic security business. She had no idea why he didn't appear content with what he'd accomplished during the past fifteen years.

The man looked more like a football player than the head of a multimillion-dollar corporation. Too bad he rarely smiled. As far as she could recall, she'd never heard him laugh.

He was not the jovial type.

His face looked as if it had been carved out of granite and his nose had been broken at some point. His heavy brows and piercing silver-blue eyes would never get him selected to a list of America's sexiest bachelors.

Not that his looks stopped the bevy of beauties who flocked around him. Each hoped to have the distinction of becoming Mrs. Dean Logan.

From what Jodie could tell, he neither encouraged them nor discouraged them. Rachel Hunt was his latest arm candy. He'd been seeing her for almost three months now, which was close to a record for him.

Jodie knew when he started seeing someone new because he had her take care of sending flowers, ordering gifts, obtaining tickets for various events and, at times, listening to his comments about the women who came and went in his life.

He knew that most of the women were more interested in his money and connections than in him. He listened cynically to confessions of undying love and a yearning for a commitment he refused to give.

Hence the number of women who came in and out of his life.

There were times when Jodie saw the loneliness in his eyes. At some point, long before she'd come to work for him, Dean must have made the decision not to allow anyone to get close to him. She found that to be very sad. Not that she'd ever let him know that she pitied him. No, she listened when he needed to talk and kept her opinions to herself.

Of course, her sister would never believe that, since Jodie was known for expressing her opinion on myriad subjects at any given moment. She smiled at the thought.

Dean moved silently, and she had grown used to his suddenly appearing in her doorway. As he did now.

"Good morn—"

"No, it definitely is not a good morning." Dean stopped in front of her desk, pulled an envelope out of his coat pocket and handed it to her. "I won't need these." He started into his office. "Would you mind getting me some coffee, please? I have a hellacious headache."

"Sure," she replied absently. She picked up the envelope and looked inside. The envelope held the airline tickets to Hawaii that she'd ordered for Dean and Rachel. Had Rachel changed her mind about going?

She stood and walked over to the coffeepot, filled one of the large mugs she kept nearby and followed him into his office.

Dean stood with his hands in his pockets looking out the window. She set the cup on his desk and sat in her usual chair.

"What happened, Dean?"

He didn't answer right away. Instead he stared out at the spitting snow and occasional ice blowing against the glass. She waited.

After several minutes of silence, he turned and sat down behind his desk, reaching for the coffee. "Do you have any aspirin?"

"Certainly." She went to the small bar behind a sliding door and poured him a glass of water before she picked up the aspirin bottle and set it in front of him.

He really was in a ferocious mood. His frown, always intimidating, was firmly in place. No wonder people were wary of him. She didn't think he realized how gruff he sounded…and that was on one of his good days.

When she'd first gone to work for him, Jodie knew she had replaced a string of four women who had attempted to work for him and left after only a few weeks. So she'd been warned.

However, she was made of sterner stuff. She'd been raised with three brothers and she and her sister had learned to hold their own with the boys.

After several minutes of silence, Dean looked at her with a puzzled expression. "Why are you here?"

"I work here," she replied with a straight face.

He closed his eyes. "Sorry. I'm not in the best of moods."

No kidding. And he'd actually apologized! She must mark the day on her calendar.

"How long have you worked for me?"

"Five years."

"Why?"

"Why what?"

"If I'm such a disagreeable person, why do you put up with me?"

"Who said you're a disagreeable person? I find you extremely agreeable as long as you get your own way," she replied lightly.

"Rachel says that everyone in this office is intimidated by me. But you aren't."

"I wasn't aware that was part of my job description. Is that what's bothering you this morning?"

"No."

"Do you care what people in the office think of you?"

"No. Well, except for you. What do you think of me?"

She sat back in her chair and considered her answer. Finally she looked him in the eye and said, "I think you're a brilliant man who is impatient with people, a man who has single-handedly built this company into a thriving corporation by ignoring the naysayers and following your own vision."

"Hmph."

He took the aspirin and drank the water. Then he picked up his coffee and sipped.

They sat in silence for several more minutes.

Finally Dean said, "Rachel broke up with me last night."

She couldn't hide her surprise. That must be a first for Dean. He was generally the one who broke things off any time a woman wanted more from him than he was willing to offer.

"Because you wanted her to go to Hawaii with you?" she asked, her disbelief plain.

He grimaced. "Actually she didn't give me a chance to surprise her with the tickets before she informed me that she never wanted to see me again."

Jodie was caught off guard by his admission. "Oh? I didn't realize you'd planned the trip as a surprise."

"Well, I did. Turns out I was the one surprised."

"What in the world happened?"

"I forgot we had tickets to the opera last night. I worked late to clear my desk and I'd forgotten to put the opera on my calendar."

"Oops."

"By the time I checked my cell phone messages on the way home, I was an hour late picking her up."

"Uh-oh."

"She was furious when I arrived at her place. I pointed out that we could still get there before intermission. It wasn't as if we didn't know the story, after all. However, the opera no longer mattered as far as she was concerned." He scrubbed his face with his hand. "She handed me a sack with the things I'd left in her apartment since we've been seeing each other and told me to get out."

"Rachel was obviously upset at the time," Jodie said. "Why don't you call her today and tell her about the trip you've planned? I'm sure you'll be back in her good graces once she discovers your surprise."

He was shaking his head before she finished. "I'm not going to do that. She made it plain she wanted no part of me, so why should I bother?" His mouth turned up at the corners. "I'll admit my ego might have been bruised a little and I went home to sulk, but she made it clear that we were through. I can accept that."

He nodded toward the envelope she'd placed on his desk. "So," he said with a shrug, "I won't be needing those."

Oh, dear. She'd promised herself never to offer her opinion unless he asked for it—and then any question he asked invariably had to do with business.

She wrestled with her conscience for a long moment but could no longer remain quiet. "I disagree," she said bravely, bracing for his response. "I believe you need the time away whether Rachel is with you or not. You know you love Hawaii and it's been three years since you acquired the condo there. I think you should go and spend some time on the beach. Forget the business for a few days. Catch up on your sleep. Once you're there, I know you'll enjoy it."

He leaned back in his chair and stared at her. She waited for his salvo telling her to mind her own business. Jodie was surprised when instead he asked, "Do you think I'm married to my job?"

She eyed him uncertainly. This man had never questioned himself in front of her before. Now that he'd asked her opinion, she wondered how candid she could be while he was in this unusual mood. "Maybe," she said cautiously.

He lowered his brows and stared at her. "Gee, thanks."

She might as well continue. "Look at it this way. You needed to put in long hours when you first started the company and you got into the habit of spending most of your time here. Now you've hired people you can rely on to take care of the day-to-day business. Maybe it's time for you to discover other things you might like to do with your life besides work."

He rubbed his chin. "I suppose." He shook his head. "I still can't get over how angry Rachel was when I arrived. What did I do that was so bad, please tell me? She could have called a cab when she couldn't reach me and been able to see the whole thing."

"Did you by any chance call her after you listened to her messages?"

"Why? I was on my way to pick her up by that time."

She coughed to hide her amusement. "My guess is that her irritation was the result of an accumulation of times when you've been late or forgotten to call or gone out of town without notice. Some women can find that sort of behavior off-putting."

"You don't."

"You pay me quite well not to notice. Besides, I'm your secretary, not your girlfriend."

He studied her in silence for a moment. "That's only going to last another few months," he said, not sounding at all pleased. "You'll be moving over to Frank's department in June."

She grinned. "All thanks to you."

"You caught me in a rare moment of gratitude for your hard work. You graduate with your degree in business this spring, don't you?"

"That's right. I wouldn't have been able to take the night classes without your paying for my tuition."

"I didn't pay it," he growled. "The company did. It was strictly a sound business decision. With your knowledge of the company and your quick grasp of things, it would be foolish to hold you back from exercising your full potential."

He rubbed his forehead as though the headache was hanging on. "Of course, that means I'll go through hell finding someone to work for me."

"No, you won't. I'll do the screening. If I think someone—male or female—will be able to work with you without running the first time you raise your voice, I'll set up an appointment for you to meet them."

"I suppose that might work." He didn't look happy at the thought.

His decision to promote her had been quite a sacrifice for him and she knew it. Beneath that tough, gruff exterior was a very fair man.

Of course, he was clueless about women, but what man wasn't?

"Do you socialize much?" he asked, surprising her again. He'd never shown any interest in her personal life. He was definitely in a strange mood today.

"I date occasionally. Of course, going to school three nights a week and studying takes up most of my spare time."

"I work you too hard."

She offered him a cheerful smile. "Comes with the territory."

"The only reason I planned the trip was to appease Rachel, even if I was a little late in doing so. However, there is a man I'd like to meet in Honolulu. Steve Furukawa owns several businesses in the islands, and I'd like to offer our services to him." He studied her for a moment. "In case he's interested, I'd need you to help me make a presentation to him. I think we should both fly out there. We'll spend a day or two on business and the rest of the time we'll be on vacation."

"Me?" She almost strangled on the word. "I can't do something like that!"

"Why not?"

She stared at him in disbelief. Didn't he understand? Obviously not.

"I'm in the middle of classes, for one thing. And it just doesn't look right, our going to Hawaii together."

"It will be a business trip."

"You've never needed me on one before."

"Jodie, you're a very competent secretary and level-headed. As for school, I doubt missing a week's worth of classes will cause you to flunk. Will it?"

"Well, no, but—"

"Then I don't see a problem." He ruffled through the stack of files on his desk. "Would you check with accounting and see if they have the latest figures on the Malone file? I'd like to see them before lunch if possible."

Two

"**W**hat did you say to him?" Jodie's sister, Lynette, asked her that evening after dinner.

Jodie had a standing invitation for dinner at Chuck and Lynette's home every Friday, but she'd never had such earthshaking news to share as she did tonight.

Chuck had called earlier to say he'd be home later than normal and for them not to hold dinner for him. Jodie hadn't mentioned Dean's plan when she'd arrived. Instead she'd helped with dinner and then made certain that her nephews, Kent and Kyle—seven and six respectively—got their baths and were ready for bed.

It was only after she'd joined Lynette in the living room while she nursed eight-week-old Emily that Jodie dropped her bombshell.

"I think I muttered something but don't remember what. I was reeling."

"You're going, of course."

"He practically ordered me to go," Jodie wailed with a laugh.

"When are you supposed to leave?"

"The tickets are for Sunday morning. Early Sunday morning."

"So his latest darling finally had enough of your romantically challenged boss, did she? She lasted longer than the others, though."

"I think what got to him was that she was the one who broke things off. He usually has the privilege of doing that. At least he got a taste of what rejection feels like."

"I can't believe she turned down a trip to Hawaii. I would have gone and then broken up with him," Lynette said with a grin.

"She didn't know about his plans. He'd kept the trip a surprise."

Lynette shook her head with disbelief. "Doesn't the man know anything about women? The anticipation of going is part of the excitement."

"We're talking about Dean Logan. Of course he doesn't know anything about us. For a brilliant businessman, he's unnervingly obtuse about the opposite sex."

"Well, who cares, if you get a free vacation out of it?"

"I'll be missing three classes."

"So? You've aced all your tests, you can easily catch up."

The door opened between the garage and kitchen, and Lynette peered over her shoulder. Chuck was home.

"Good evening, all," he said, sauntering into the room.

He was a police detective for the city and looked good in his sports jacket and slacks. "How are my three favorite women doing?" He leaned over Lynette and gave her a leisurely kiss that made Jodie's toes curl to watch.

When he straightened, he brushed his lips across the top of Emily's head. Emily ignored him. Dinner was more important at the moment.

"Your dinner's in the fridge. Just put it in the microwave."

"How are things going for you, Jodie?" he asked casually as he turned to go back into the kitchen.

Before Jodie had a chance to answer, Lynette said, "Her boss has invited her to go with him to Hawaii for a week."

Chuck stopped in his tracks and spun around. "Are you serious? Logan asked you to go away with him? Wow. Aren't you the sly one? I had no idea you two were an item."

"We're not! Believe me, there is nothing going on in a romantic sense. The girl he's been seeing broke up with him. He had the tickets. I suggested he should take the vacation anyway, and he decided to meet with a prospective client while he was there. He said he could use my help. So it will be a working vacation."

Chuck grinned. "And you believed him."

"Of course. Why shouldn't I?"

Chuck, his dinner forgotten, sat down next to Lynette. "Jodie. Honey. Let's get real, okay? A man doesn't invite his good-looking secretary to go away with him to a tropical isle without some strictly male motive. He's going to do his best to get you into his bed. Count on it."

"Chuck!" Lynette kept her voice soft but emphatic. Jodie wondered how she did that. "Not every man has sex on the brain like you do."

He gave her an intimate smile. "Oh, yes, they do. Some just hide it better than others."

Jodie said, "You're probably right, Chuck, but Dean is a definite exception. I've worked for him too many years not to know that he doesn't notice me as a woman. I'm an efficient machine to him and that's fine with me."

"If you say so. When do you leave?"

"Sunday morning."

"Have you ever been to Hawaii?"

"No."

"Then go and enjoy yourself. I would guess he's picking up the tab for your accommodations."

"Actually he acquired a condo there a few years ago. It was part of a business deal he made. He went over to check it out and that's the last time he was there. There are three bedrooms and three baths. I think the company he bought it from used the condo for the executives to, quote, get away, unquote, for some relaxation."

"So he'll have you right where he wants you for a leisurely seduction," Chuck replied, twisting his imaginary mustache with a grin.

"Nothing wrong with your imagination, that's for sure," Jodie replied, laughing. "If you'd ever met him, you'd see how far off base you are."

"Why? Is he some kind of monster?"

"Let's just say he takes some getting used to. Once his business is completed he'll probably forget that I'm there."

Lynette said, "Now that's carrying the platonic bit too far, sis. There's bound to be a middle ground between what you've imagined and what my crazy husband came up with."

"So you two think I should go ahead and plan to go?"

They answered in unison. "Yes."

"But what about the talk around the office?" Jodie asked. " Won't that give everyone the wrong idea?"

"So what?" Chuck answered. "It will give them something to gossip about. Probably improve morale. The office employees will start a betting pool as to when you'll announce your engagement."

"You're a big help," Lynette said, shaking her head at her spouse. "The idea here is to give her reasons to go, not make up stuff."

"Well, since it looks as though I'm going, I'll need to go shopping for beachwear tomorrow."

"Great idea. Buy some things that are colorful and tropical. No business suits." She eyed her for a moment. "You've said you never have time to get your hair cut. Why don't you get it trimmed tomorrow, as well?"

Jodie nodded. "I could do that."

"And get plenty of sunscreen. You know how easily we burn, thanks to our Scandinavian ancestors."

Jodie looked at her arms and ruefully shook her head. "I hope to come back with at least a little more color. I'll slather myself with the stuff and see what happens."

Lynette lifted Emily to her shoulder and rubbed her back until she gave a very unladylike belch, causing the three of them to laugh. "I need to put her down," Lynette said. "I'll be right back."

"I need to go, you guys. It's been a long week," Jodie said, rising. "And it looks like I'll be spending tomorrow shopping."

"Poor baby," Lynette consoled with a grin. "That's your favorite hobby in the entire world, and we both know it."

"True. And buying summer things in the dead of winter will be just the thing I need to get into the spirit of the trip."

Later that night while Jodie prepared for bed, she thought about the comments she'd heard tonight from Lynette and Chuck. She scrubbed her teeth and removed her makeup before looking in the mirror.

"Are you going to be brave and treat this as a chance in a lifetime to see Hawaii with all expenses paid?"

Here image stared back at her with sparkling eyes.

After a long pause, she sighed and said, "You're no help. You want to see Hawaii. Will the trade-off be worth it? Hawaii with all its pleasures weighed against a week with a man who's a workaholic? Knowing Dean, he'll have us working the whole time we're there.

Then again, we're bound to find some time to enjoy the sun and sand.

She smiled as she crawled into bed.

Three

Dean stood in front of the mirror shaving early Sunday morning and wondered what he was doing. Had he lost his mind?

What had possessed him to invite his secretary to go with him to Hawaii? She was a great secretary. In fact, she was a great human being, but he didn't need to spend a week with her to be reminded of the fact.

Of course, if he planned to meet with Furukawa, he could use her presence there to help him make a presentation and to help formulate a contract. She was very conscientious and did her work without a complaint.

But to take her to Hawaii with him?

Had his midlife crisis arrived sooner than expected? Why else would he have considered taking her? He knew nothing about her outside of the office. Well, he knew she was single, but that was about it. Did she have family close by? Would they warn her about going with him?

He could get in trouble for harassment.

Well. Maybe that was a little extreme. She'd had the option to say no. When he'd called her at home last night she'd sounded agreeable enough. He certainly hadn't coerced her. At least, not much.

He finished dressing and picked up the bag he'd packed. He'd had trouble knowing what to pack besides his business clothes. The only other time he'd been there, his business suits had been expected, but then he hadn't been on vacation. He'd spent the three days in meetings, ironing out the conditions of the merger with the parties involved.

He'd tossed in a few shirts and khaki pants this morning and even remembered to stick in a pair of tennis shoes, which was a laugh. He hadn't played tennis in years, but it was the idea that counted.

Maybe he *was* a little too focused on business. Working hard had become a habit, and he wasn't certain that he could break it.

Or that he wanted to.

He'd really let Rachel's comments get to him, which was ridiculous. What did he care what she thought about him? He'd just been surprised, that's all.

He and Jodie would get along well enough for the few days they'd be there, he was fairly certain. He'd treat the trip as a bonus for Jodie in appreciation for her years of service.

He smiled at the thought, pleased that he'd found the correct category for the trip.

* * *

Jodie had almost reached the door into the airport before Dean recognized her. She looked different, but why? Then he realized that she was wearing her hair down. He'd never seen her wear it any way but pulled back into a knot on the nape of her neck. It danced around her neck and shoulders in the wind. She certainly looked different this morning.

He glanced at his watch and frowned.

As soon as Jodie stepped out of the cab, she spotted Dean waiting for her just inside the door to the airline check-in counters. She hurriedly crossed the sidewalk toward him.

The wind-chill factor must be in the teens. Hawaii sounded better and better to her. At least she'd be getting away from the wonderful winter weather of dear old Chicago for a few days. She looked forward to soaking up some sun.

Just as she reached the door, he opened it and took her bag. "You're late," he snapped. "Security is tight and I don't want to miss the flight."

Actually she was forty-five minutes earlier than the airline recommended, but she wasn't going to start their trip together disputing his words. Instead she smiled at him and said, "I'm here now and good morning to you. Have you checked your luggage?"

"Yes." He glanced down at her suitcase. "Is this all you're taking?"

She looked down at her bag and then back up at him. "We're only going to be gone a week," she replied.

"I thought women packed three or four suitcases wherever they went," he mumbled.

"Not me."

"Well," he said awkwardly. "That's good."

She walked over to join the line to the counter and he followed her. "I might as well stay with you. No sense losing you in this crowd."

Jodie realized that he was nervous! She found that hard to believe, considering how much traveling he did. Was it because she was along?

She hadn't spotted it at first, probably because she'd been shaken by his accusation that she may have caused them to miss their plane. There was no way she would lose him in the crowd. As tall as he was, she'd spot him in any group.

She circumspectly checked out what he'd chosen to wear for the trip and was pleasantly surprised to see him in black pants, a black turtleneck sweater and a black leather jacket that fit snugly at his waist.

The wind had ruffled his dark hair and the leather jacket made him appear dangerous and very masculine.

He looked downright swashbuckling.

Now if he'd only smile once in a while, he could be attractive.

They reached their plane with time to spare, which Jodie wisely did not point out. Dean stopped and bought himself a paper and a couple of magazines. Jodie found the newest book out by one of her favorite authors, as well as a crossword puzzle book in case she got tired of reading.

She watched Dean as he paced the concourse. Was the man ever still? She placed her parka on her lap and started reading.

When it was time to board, first-class passengers were seated first. Not too bad. Dean waved her to the window seat before settling down beside her. A flight attendant checked to see what they would like to drink and handed them menus for breakfast.

Once they gave their orders, Jodie settled comfortably into the luxurious depths of her seat and looked around her.

The only time she'd seen first class on her flights was when she'd walked through to the tourist section. What a way to travel.

"Are you nervous about flying?" he asked after several minutes of silence.

She'd been peering out the window when he asked, and she straightened. "A little perhaps. Why?"

"I noticed your fingers gripping the armrests, and the plane hasn't moved."

She jerked her hands away and folded them into her lap. After a moment she dug into her purse and pulled out the book she'd been reading but gave up a few minutes later because she couldn't seem to concentrate. Maybe she'd work one of the crossword puzzles.

After another prolonged silence—were they ever going to leave the terminal?—Jodie asked, "How long is the flight, do you recall? I've forgotten what the reservations said."

"About thirteen hours, depending on a headwind. We change planes in Los Angeles."

"Oh."

"We should reach Maui by midafternoon local time."

"But we'll still be on Midwest time."

"True."

Well, she'd exhausted all her skills at social chitchat

with him. Jodie picked up the airline magazine and began to thumb through it.

After what felt like hours, the plane finally taxied out to the runway for takeoff. Then it stopped. The captain apologized for the delay. There were nine jets ahead of this one. Great. That gave her plenty of time to rethink this whole idea.

Dean cleared his throat. "Jodie?"

She'd just peered out the window again. "Yes?"

"I'm a little embarrassed to mention this after you've worked for me so many years, but I really don't know much about you besides your work ethic, which is outstanding, and your determination to get your degree, which is admirable. I'd like to learn more about you. Why don't we use this time to get acquainted?"

"I'm sorry, but I really don't want to talk right now. I need all my concentration once we're ready for takeoff to make absolutely certain the plane's wings are firmly attached." After all, there was a lot of thrust by the jet engines, and everyone knew that takeoffs and landings were the most dangerous times during a flight. Unless they happened to fly into the side of a mountain. They had to cross the Rockies, didn't they?

Or if they went down over water…say, maybe the Pacific Ocean?

"Jodie?" She jerked her head away from the window and looked at him inquiringly.

"We're perfectly safe, you know."

"Of course we are," she promptly agreed. "As long as we sit here on the runway." She glanced back out the window to continue to check the wings.

Dean made some kind of noise that sounded as if he was either choking or coughing. She looked back at him in concern. His lips were compressed and he wore a frown. His shoulders shook and suddenly, like Mount St. Helens, he erupted into laughter.

Laughter? She had rarely seen him smile, much less heard him laugh, and she stared at him in amazement. What a difference it made in him. He looked much younger than his thirty-eight years. Who would have believed it?

He immediately attempted to quell the sound, but then he looked at her again, recognized her bemusement, shook his head and continued to laugh—a deep-throated sound that finally made her smile.

He reached for his handkerchief and wiped his eyes, blew his nose and finally, after what seemed like forever, managed to stop.

But he continued to smile and she still hadn't recovered from the change in him. Dean was smiling and, miracle of miracles, his face hadn't cracked into a thousand little pieces. Who would have believed it?

"Care to share the joke?" she asked. She smiled her pleasure at this unexpected peek into the man she thought she knew so well.

He touched her arm and slid his hand down, lacing his fingers between hers. "I'm sorry. I shouldn't have laughed at your nervousness. You're going to be just fine, I promise."

"From your lips to God's ear," she muttered.

He chuckled again. He was certainly getting a great deal of amusement out of her fear of flying. Then again, maybe it was worth it to see that the man had a human side. A decidedly masculine side at that.

The brackets around his mouth had revealed dimples. She bet he hated them.

In fact, the man bore little resemblance to her stone-faced boss. Same hair and eyes, same strong jaw, and yet with his silver-blue eyes sparkling and his teeth flashing he was actually handsome.

Okay, she was losing it. When she looked at Dean Logan and saw a handsome man she knew she'd lost her grip. Fear could certainly do crazy things to a person's perceptions.

"I was born in Indiana," he said in a casual voice as though answering her question. "Came to Chicago to attend Northwestern and never left. How about you?"

She cleared her throat. "We're from Wisconsin originally."

"Who is we?"

"Mom, my three brothers, my sister and me. My parents got married way too young, but they were in love and didn't want to wait until after they finished school to get married. My brother came along not long afterward, and Dad dropped out of college to get a job. He took good care of all of us, but I think he pushed himself too hard for too many years and he died of a heart attack when he was forty-five.

"Mom had to get a job but had trouble finding one since she'd never worked before. Without training or an education, it was tough going for her. She ended up as a waitress. Both Mom and Dad really stressed the importance of an education when we were growing up. All three of my brothers worked their way through college so they could take care of her."

"Where does your family live?"

"All over the place. Mom's in Phoenix. That's where

they lived when Dad died. One of my brothers is an attorney in Oregon, one is career Navy and based out of Bremerton, Washington, and one lives just outside of D.C. doing who knows what. If anyone asks, he says, 'I work for the government' in a vague way and changes the subject. My sister, Lynette, and I live here in Chicago."

"Do any of them have children?"

She smiled. "Chuck and Lynette have two boys and a brand-new baby girl. The boys are pleased as little boys can be that they have a baby sister. My sister had two miscarriages before Emily came along."

"Are any of your brothers married?"

"Not a one. Too busy with work or too busy playing the field." She waited, and when he didn't ask any more questions, she said, "It's your turn. Tell me about your family."

She wasn't sure at first that he was going to answer her, but eventually he said, "My mother lives in a nursing home here. I had an older brother, but he and my dad were out on Lake Michigan at the wrong time years ago. A storm blew up and they didn't make it back."

"How awful. How old was your brother?"

"Twelve. I was eight and had a cold, so my mother wouldn't let me go with them." He looked away. After two or three minutes he added, "I haven't talked about them in years."

She wondered about the emotional scars he carried from that time. No doubt he'd been upset, probably angry, that he didn't get to go. Then to lose them like that. Survivor's guilt probably played a part. She knew him well enough not to say any more by way of sympathy for his loss.

"Why aren't you married?" he asked bluntly.

She looked at him in surprise. "Isn't that a rather personal question to ask?"

"Probably. But if I'm going to drag out all my personal stuff, I figure you can, too."

"Mmm. I don't think it's quite the same, unless you want to discuss why *you're* not married."

"That's easy enough. I have no intention of getting married. I was engaged once, but she found someone who had more money and broke the engagement six weeks before the wedding." He shrugged. "She's on her third marriage now, so she did me a favor. After that I decided to devote my time and energy to building my business, which was much more important to me than getting too involved in a relationship."

"You know, Dean, one of these days you're going to meet the woman you've been waiting for your whole life. And when you do, you'll be a goner."

"Somehow I doubt that very much." He studied her for a moment in silence. "So," he finally said, "have you ever been married?"

She shook her head, feeling a little exasperated with him. His persistence was one of his strongest traits. It made him an excellent businessman. But she didn't particularly like it when he aimed his curiosity at her.

Before she could decide how much she wanted to share with him, the captain's voice came over the speakers and said they were next to take off.

She immediately tightened her seat belt.

"Any tighter and you'll cut off the blood flow to the rest of your body," he said drily.

She took a deep breath, held it briefly and slowly ex-

haled. She was being an idiot. She adjusted the strap
around her and forcibly relaxed her shoulders.

"No," she finally said in a strained voice. "I have never
been married."

"Why not?"

"Because I haven't wanted to be, obviously."

"Any particular reason?"

"I feel like you have me under a microscope."

"Why? We're going to be together for the next week. I
just want to get to know who you are when you're away
from the office."

"Oh, all right. I had one serious relationship when I
was nineteen. I shared a tiny apartment with one of my coworkers. We were both secretaries in a law firm and that's
where I met him. He was a law student working at the firm
part-time.

"We dated for more than a year and we talked about marriage once he finished law school. We spent most of our free
time together. Everything was perfect…until I came home
early one night and found him in bed with my roommate."

"Ouch."

"Yeah."

"Did he explain why?"

"To hear him tell it, he'd left school early and thought
I might be home. When I wasn't, my roommate suggested
he wait there for me. I'm sure she planned everything to
work out the way it did. His explanation was that she was
there and one thing led to another and it didn't mean anything. He apologized. Said it would never happen again."

"And you said?"

"I was very dignified. I told him if he ever made an attempt to see me again, I'd severely injure a delicate part of his anatomy."

He made a strangling sound but didn't comment.

"He pretty much left me alone after that. He and my ex-friend/roommate got married a few months later because she was pregnant. I don't know what happened after that because I accepted the job I have now and moved closer to work."

"You took it hard."

"That I did. There's something about finding out that someone you considered a friend and the man you thought you were going to marry betrayed you that dampens the spirit."

"But that was—what?—five years ago?"

"About that."

"And you haven't had a relationship since?"

"Not a serious one, no," she said, knowing she sounded defensive. "I just don't intend to get hurt again. So I don't allow anyone to get too close."

He looked at their hands, still entwined. "Then I feel honored."

She lowered her brows and glared at him. "We are not close. I work for you. Just because you think I'll try to get out of this plane before we take off doesn't mean we're close." She pulled her hand away just as the plane began to roll.

"Actually you work for the company."

"You are the company. Like I said, I work for you." Faking nonchalance, she picked up the book and determinedly began to read, hoping his questions were at an end.

Four

Jodie was glad to get off the plane in Los Angeles and walk around. She'd finished her book and decided to get more reading material.

"We have time to get something to eat if you'd like," Dean said as they walked past several small restaurants located along the concourse.

"I'm not really hungry. They'll feed us on this next flight, won't they?"

"Yes."

"Then I'll wait."

She glanced out the glass walls and saw sunshine, blue skies and palm trees. What a difference from Chicago. "I've never been to L.A. before. I guess this doesn't count since all I'm seeing is the airport."

"Don't you like to travel?" he asked. He motioned for her to go into one of the coffee shops with him.

"I haven't done all that much. I've flown to Phoenix several times to see my mother. One Christmas the family gathered in Oregon at my brother's place. Otherwise, my schedule keeps me too busy."

They got their coffee and found a small table near the glass wall overlooking one of the runways. "Then I'm glad you've come with me this week."

"Thank you."

"I hope this isn't out of line, but I can't get over how different you look with your hair down."

"Ah. You have no problem asking why I'm not married but hesitate to make a comment about my hair?"

"You have a point. Is it too late to apologize for my earlier questions?"

"Much too late since you listened to the entire tawdry story." She spoiled her solemn reprimand by chuckling at the expression on his face. "Do you like my hair shorter?"

"Oh. You had it cut."

"Yesterday." She ran her fingers through it. "I'm still getting used to it myself."

"It's, uh, you look very, uh—" He stopped. "Yes, I like it."

"Why, thank you." She looked around them. "Are you ready to find the gate for the next leg of our trip?"

He stood and stretched, briefly causing a gap between his sweater and pants. His stomach was flat and toned. She wondered what he'd look like in a bathing suit.

On the way to the gate Jodie picked up a couple of magazines. She was a little more relaxed for this second flight.

In fact, she was getting sleepy despite the coffee. Perhaps she'd be able to nap once they got into the air.

Jodie stirred as the captain announced that the plane would be making its descent into Kahului Airport, Maui, and that they would be landing in forty minutes.

She couldn't believe she'd slept that long. She glanced at her lap and saw the magazine she'd been reading when she'd fallen asleep.

She looked over at Dean. He wore his horn-rimmed reading glasses and seemed engrossed in a technical manual. No murder mysteries and thrillers for that man.

"I see you found something light and entertaining for your vacation reading," she said.

He lowered his chin and looked over his glasses at her. "Each of us relaxes in his own way. Did you sleep okay?"

"Surprisingly so." She covered her mouth and yawned. "I could get used to traveling in style." She waited a beat and said, "If you'll excuse me, I'd like to go freshen up before the seat-belt light comes on."

Dean moved promptly out of his chair and stepped back. She walked to the front and saw that the lavatory was unoccupied, thank goodness. She went in and locked the door. After she washed her hands, she found her comb and ran it through her hair.

The haircut really did give her a different look. The waves fell around her face and called attention to her eyes. She was surprised that Dean had not only noticed but commented on her appearance.

She felt that she'd been on the plane for at least a week and wondered if she'd ever get the constant drone of the engines out of her head. When she opened the door, she found another first-class passenger standing there. She smiled. He returned her smile with interest.

Jodie felt herself blush and hurriedly returned to her seat. Dean had seen her coming and was standing in the aisle out of her way when she arrived.

"Thank you," she said hurriedly and slipped into her seat.

He sat down beside her and closed the manual he'd been reading.

During the next fifteen minutes he asked her a few more questions about her life—her hobbies, favorite movies and television shows—and she gave him brief answers, at least enough to satisfy him. After that he left her to read her magazine.

She still felt strange about traveling with him, but she'd no doubt get over that once they arrived at the condo and she set up a routine of sorts.

Once they landed, she and Dean methodically checked around them for their belongings before getting off the plane. Anyone seeing them would think they were a couple who'd been married for years. She had no idea why the thought made her nervous.

Once in the terminal, Jodie noticed that many of the people on departing flights wore leis. She smiled, looking forward to getting one for herself. Dean found an available taxi and he and the driver put their bags in the trunk of the cab.

Dean settled into the seat next to her. "So what do you think?"

"I'm amazed. The scented air is refreshing."

"Beats the heck out of car exhausts and diesel fuel."

She glanced at Dean while he gazed out the window and asked questions of the driver. He already looked more relaxed than she'd ever seen him. That was good. She had hopes that the rest would do him good.

The scenery was breathtaking, with towering mountains on one side and the ocean on the other. They followed the coast for several miles until the taxi slowed and turned onto a lane that led to security gates.

Dean gave his name and the gates swung open.

Once inside the gated area, the lane wound through tropical foliage that looked green and lush. When they reached the building, she felt that they'd burst into sunshine with a panoramic view of the sea and the sand.

She sighed with pleasure.

Dean helped her out of the taxi, and while he went to get their bags and pay the driver, Jodie looked up at the building. Balconies jutted out, all facing the water. There would be a fantastic view from each one. The scent of lavish blooms wafted all around her, and she took several deep breaths for the pleasure of soaking up the aromas.

"Ready?"

Jodie turned and saw Dean waiting by the door, their bags in hand. "Sorry," she said. "I'm awestruck." She walked over to the door, opened it for him and then followed him across a large lobby to the elevators.

She pushed the button and the doors silently opened. Once inside, she asked, "Which floor?"

"The top one." She nodded and pushed the fourth-floor button.

When the doors opened, Jodie discovered there was only one set of double doors on the floor. Dean put their bags down, reached into his pocket for a key and opened one of the doors.

He stepped back for the bags and nodded. "After you, Ms. Cameron."

She hurried inside only to come to an abrupt stop, causing him to drop the bags just inside the door. "Oh, Dean, I've never seen anything like this. It looks like the set of a Hollywood movie about the rich and famous."

He closed the door and followed her into the room. "Pretty impressive, I'll admit. Would you like a tour?"

The condo encircled the elevator shaft, with windows looking out in all directions. She saw the well-stocked kitchen, the formal dining room with a mahogany table that could easily seat twelve people and three spacious bedrooms, each with its own bathroom and balcony. She thought the word for them in Hawaii was *lanai* but wasn't certain.

"Pick whichever bedroom you like," Dean said after their tour.

"Which one would you like?" she asked, feeling overwhelmed with choices.

"Doesn't matter."

"Mmm." She paused in the doorway of one. The room seemed the size of a basketball court. The view drew her to the window. "This will be fine," she murmured, opening the door to the outside.

She could hear the sound of the waves rolling onto the beach, the rhythm soothing to her ear. When she turned around, Dean was no longer there. He'd placed her bag on the bed.

Jodie wandered into the bathroom, which was larger

than her living room in Chicago. She smiled. She could quickly become used to living like this. All she could think was, Wow.

Suddenly feeling energized despite the long trip, she quickly unpacked, changed into a pair of cotton slacks and a sleeveless blouse and went back to the main room.

Dean was at the bar, pouring himself a drink. "Want one?" he asked as she walked in.

"Water will be fine. I'm not much of a drinker. I thought I'd go down and wander on the beach for a while."

"Aren't you hungry? I thought we could go eat first."

She thought about it. "Yes, as a matter of fact, I am. I suppose there will be plenty of daylight after we finish eating."

The restaurant was next to the complex. One side was open with tables and chairs inside and out. Jodie noticed there were only a few people at the tables. She glanced at her watch. "I suppose it's a little early to be eating according to local time."

"Doesn't matter. They're used to customers coming in at all hours. They're open twenty-four hours a day."

Once seated, Jodie picked up her menu and started reading the items listed. She yawned and hastily covered her mouth.

Dean watched her for a moment in silence before speaking. "You're going to want to go to sleep early tonight despite your nap on the plane, but if you can manage to stay awake, you'll adjust to the time change quicker."

"The steady sounds of the surf are so soothing. I hope I don't fall asleep with my nose in the salad."

Dean picked up his water glass and held it out. "Here's to our working vacation together."

Jodie picked up her glass and lightly tapped it against his. "I appreciate the invitation." She yawned again. "The way I'm feeling now, I could sleep the entire week away."

Once their food arrived, there was no more conversation. Jodie didn't want to chatter; that wasn't her style. Since they'd already commented on the beauty surrounding them, she could think of nothing to say to him.

By the time they finished eating, the sun was low in the west. Dean walked beside her in silence, his hands in his pockets, as she made her way to the sandy beach.

As the sky darkened, they watched the lights appear along the shoreline before turning back toward the condo. Walking in the sand would be an adjustment, but if she walked like this every day, she'd be in great shape when she returned home.

She smiled at the thought.

"What do you find so amusing?" he asked, stopping as she did to empty the sand from her shoes. He followed her example.

"I was thinking what a workout walking in the sand is. If I'm not in shape now, I will be by the time we leave."

"Probably."

A man of few words. Not that she cared. Tomorrow she would be up with the sun and she intended to enjoy every minute she was here.

After Jodie went to her room, Dean took a shower, dried off and stretched out on the bed.

He thought about Rachel. His anger at the abrupt way she'd dismissed him had caught him off guard. He'd learned many years ago to keep his emotions locked down.

He considered himself to be a thinking man who wasn't swayed by irrational feelings. But when Rachel had blown up at him—*inconsiderate* and *unfeeling* were the nicest things she'd called him—he'd felt an anger he hadn't experienced in a long time.

She hadn't given him a chance to explain. And she'd made it clear she wanted nothing more to do with him.

He had no problem with that and he was thankful he hadn't told her about his plans. Jodie had been right. He'd needed to get away for a few days. Seeing her excitement and enthusiasm this evening had caused him to look at everything through her eyes.

He couldn't remember a time when he'd been that joyous about anything.

Yes, having Jodie here with him might teach him how to enjoy life a little better.

He bet she'd been protected from the harsher realities of life until her—what? boyfriend? fiancé? she hadn't said—pulled his stupid stunt.

He smiled at the way she'd handled the situation. She'd faced the clod and gotten rid of him. But she'd suffered. Why else would she now be too busy to date much?

He turned and adjusted his pillow, willing himself to sleep. Instead his thoughts circled around Jodie. She'd looked so different today when she'd arrived at the airport, wearing formfitting jeans, a sweater, ankle boots and a parka.

The cold had turned her cheeks and nose a rosy hue, and he couldn't help wondering why he'd only noticed today how attractive she was. She was more than attractive, actually. *Beautiful* was an overused word and it didn't quite fit her, but it came close. He liked her looks. He liked and had always appreciated her frankness and her refusal to be intimidated by him. Jodie worked hard and earned every penny of her salary. She was smart and he valued her judgment.

He'd be lost without her.

At least she'd still be with the company. He hoped she could find someone as efficient to replace her.

He wanted this trip to be special for her. He'd get in touch with Furukawa tomorrow to set up a meeting. Once they met, he'd know if he had a chance of setting up some security systems for him.

He settled into sleep, planning the next day's activities.

"So much for plans," he muttered to himself the next morning when he discovered Jodie wasn't still in bed. He'd ordered breakfast from the restaurant, and when it had arrived, he'd knocked on her door.

When she hadn't answered, he'd eased the door open and discovered her room to be empty.

He sat at the kitchen bar, sipped his coffee and ate some of the delicious fruit that seemed to come with each meal. He'd arranged to have several newspapers brought to him each morning, so he read them while he absently ate.

Eventually Dean wandered over to the window and looked down at the beach.

The water looked peaceful this morning and there were several people on the beach, some walking and some relaxed in recliners, reading.

He watched as a lithe young woman came out of the water and grabbed her towel. He watched her for a few minutes before he recognized Jodie.

Her blond hair clung to her head in a beguiling helmet. Her face glowed with pleasure as she quickly dried off and placed her towel on the sand.

Dean couldn't take his eyes off her. Why had he never noticed her trim waist and curvaceous backside. In a one-piece bright red swimsuit cut high on the thighs, she could have posed for the cover of *Sports Illustrated* magazine.

She slicked her hands over her hair before ruffling it with her fingers. She had a way of moving that was quite sensuous. Why had he never noticed?

Dean realized that he wasn't the only male taking notice of her. As he watched, one of the men walked over and spoke to her. Dean turned away. It was none of his business what she did or who she met. So why was he bothered by seeing another man come on to her? There was absolutely no reason for him to feel so possessive about his secretary. She was free to enjoy her vacation in whatever manner she wanted.

He looked back down at them. The male said something to her and she laughed and turned away.

She laughed.

She didn't laugh around him.

With fresh resolve, he turned back to the papers on the counter and scanned them. He looked at his watch. He felt restless and unsettled, and it was too early to call his prospective client. He wondered how things were going at the office. His second in command could handle anything that came up. He knew the business as well as Dean did.

Dean paced to the window and looked at the sea, the mountains and finally the beach. She was alone now, but that didn't seem to bother the men who noticed her. He hoped they got their eyeful.

Dean turned away. He could go down there, maybe do a little swimming...except he hadn't packed a suit. Well, he could walk along the beach, but then the sand would fill his shoes.

The clothes he'd chosen to bring weren't suitable here. Of course, he'd be working, so it probably wouldn't matter. But if he wasn't working, what then? He shook his head in frustration. What did people do on vacation? After a moment he picked up the phone and called the office.

The sun was high overhead by the time Jodie gathered up her towels and beach bag to go search for something to eat. She'd go shower and change clothes and wander down the beach. There was bound to be a place other than the restaurant that was nearby.

She'd had great fun this morning and had met several people who, like her, were there enjoying the warm weather and beautiful scenery with no regrets about missing winter on the mainland.

She'd met a couple on their honeymoon, another celebrating their thirtieth wedding anniversary and a young couple with two little girls playing in the shallows.

Two or three guys had stopped and introduced themselves. One of them said he was on the beach each morning and would probably see her again. Another told her that today was his last day there and he intended to enjoy the water to the very last minute.

When she let herself into the condo, Jodie knew Dean

wasn't there. She wasn't certain how he managed to do it, but his charged energy filled whatever space surrounded him. When he wasn't there, the place was peaceful.

She looked around and saw a pile of newspapers beside a chair and the remains of breakfast on the kitchen counter. He'd ordered for both of them, she discovered, lifting a lid. She ate a brioche and then grabbed a banana. Delicious. That should tide her over while she showered and dressed.

Peering into the mirror after her shower, Jodie touched her nose. Yes, she'd definitely gotten some sun. She was going to have to be very careful not to burn.

She rubbed more sunscreen into her skin before she went into her bedroom to dress.

Jodie had splurged on her new clothes, telling herself that a vacation in Hawaii deserved tropical wear. She chose a pair of sandals, walking shorts and a sleeveless blouse that matched her blue eyes.

She left the condo and waited for the elevator. When the doors opened, Dean stood there. He was the first to speak.

"Going down?" he intoned politely.

She laughed. "Yes, please," she said, stepping into the elevator.

"I came up to see if you were here and wanted to get something to eat."

"You read my mind. I thought I'd walk along the beach and get something from one of the little restaurants I saw earlier."

He put his hands in his pockets. "I take it you enjoyed your morning?"

"Very much. How was yours?"

"I talked to Furukawa this morning. He said he could see me day after tomorrow, so I guess I'll be hanging around here for the next couple of days." He glanced at her and then away. "I think I'm going to need some pointers on how to take a vacation. I hope you're up for the job."

Jodie smiled at him. "Oh, I'm sure you'll get the hang of it soon."

The doors opened and they stepped into the lobby.

"I've called the office twice in hopes of learning about some crisis that only I could handle," he said with a slight smile. "Unfortunately everything is running smoothly."

He sounded so disgruntled that Jodie laughed. "It's not that bad, I'm sure."

"I asked around to find out what people usually do here besides visit the beach." He reached into his shirt pocket. "I found there are all sorts of things to see, if you'd be interested."

They walked out toward the water and walked along the edge.

He offered her the brochures and she eagerly took them. She looked over the various places of interest.

"There's so much to do and see."

By mutual agreement they turned toward a small café that caught their attention. Once seated, they glanced over the menu. Jodie ordered a large salad and Dean had a sandwich.

She continued to look through the brochures. "I'm amazed. We could spend a month and probably not see everything." She pointed to one of the brochures. "We can attend a luau," she said hopefully. "Or have you already been to one?"

"'Fraid not. I wasn't here long enough to do any sightseeing. I'm game for whatever appeals to you."

"Mmm," she said thoughtfully, thumbing through the brochures. "We could explore the other islands, charter a helicopter to look around at everything, check out the mountains or turn into slugs and lie on the beach all week."

He couldn't seem to take his eyes off her. She glowed with enthusiasm, something he'd rarely felt. "Sounds like a plan." He glanced at his watch and reached for his cell phone. "I'll make reservations for the luau and then I thought I might rent a car so I can do some shopping."

Her brows lifted. "You want to go to a mall? Dean, you have hidden depths!"

"I'm embarrassed to say that I didn't really pack the right clothes." He glanced down toward his feet. "I'm going to need to go native and get some sandals, maybe a couple pair of shorts, as well. And no self-respecting tourist could leave the islands without owning an authentic Hawaiian shirt."

She laughed. "Good for you. Step number one—dress for the occasion. Do you want me to go with you?"

He froze. Of course he wanted her with him. He realized that he'd presumed she'd go.

He cleared his throat. "Unless there's something else you'd like to do."

"I love to shop. Stick with me, kid, and I'll show you a pro at work."

He touched her hand. "Thank you."

She grinned at him. "You may not feel so grateful after I drag you through a few stores."

"I'll take my chances."

As a general rule, Dean disliked shopping, but then he'd never before gone on a spree with Jodie Cameron. They wandered through one of the malls and listened while groups of the locals played ukuleles and serenaded the shoppers.

"I used to play one of those when I was a kid," she confided as they stood and listened.

"Were you any good?"

"Well, I won't go so far as to say that, but I learned three or four basic chords that worked for most songs. What I lacked in talent I made up for in enthusiasm." She looked up at him and laughed, wrinkling her nose.

She was adorable.

"You'll have to play for me sometime," he said.

"Oooh, nooo, I don't think so. I haven't touched one in years. I don't know what happened to the one I had."

"Then we'll add that to our shopping list. One ukulele for you to serenade me with each evening. There are all kinds of working vacations. Who knows? You may launch a new career."

"You have no idea what you're asking," she replied ominously before she ruined the effect with a chuckle.

Dean followed Jodie in and out of various stores, in awe of her shopping talents. She knew immediately whether something would work for him and wasted no time looking at the rest.

She finally sent him back to a dressing room to try on several of the items she'd chosen. While she waited, Jodie wandered over to the gift-shop section of the store. She cheerfully bought gifts for everyone in the family as well as several of her friends.

She'd just paid for them when she saw Dean come out wearing a pair of shorts that fit him like a glove and a short-sleeved shirt with a tropical print.

"Wow. You look gorgeous," she said without thinking. When he turned an interesting shade of red, she realized what she'd said. "Oh! I'm sorry. I shouldn't have—"

"Oh, no. Don't apologize. You've just made my day. I don't believe anyone has every applied that word to me."

"Turn around," she said, still feeling a little awkward.

She checked the fit of the shirt across his shoulders and tried to ignore the way the shorts curved over his muscular butt. "You'll do," she said in a croak. Jodie cleared her throat. "What about the others? Did you like them?"

"Yeah. I'm getting all three shorts and a few extra shirts." He glanced down at his bare feet. "I, uh, didn't think my black socks and shoes went with the outfit."

"Good thinking. It just so happens the shoe department is right over there. Let's see what size you are and we'll get you fixed up right away."

By the time they reached the condo it was late afternoon and both of them had their arms full of packages. Once inside, they dumped them in the middle of the floor.

"I think we bought out the stores," he said, staring at the pile in wonderment.

"I still can't believe you actually bought a ukulele. You must be a glutton for punishment."

"How can you be in Hawaii and not want to play some of their songs? Now you have the songbook to help you."

"Uh-huh," Jodie replied, sounding skeptical. She looked around. "All right. Let's sort them out."

"What did you sneak off and buy while I was trying on shoes?" Dean asked, sorting through and picking out his purchases.

"A dress to wear for the luau tonight. I thought as long as you're going native, I might as well join you."

They carried the packages and sacks to their respective bedrooms. Before going into hers, Jodie looked at him and said, "I'm going to need a nap if I'm going to stay up late tonight."

"I was thinking along the same lines. I'll set my alarm to ring in a couple of hours."

"Thanks."

Once inside her room, Jodie leaned against the closed door, dropping her packages. What in the world was wrong with her! She felt as though scales had dropped from her eyes. How could she ever have thought Dean wasn't attractive? Maybe it was the environment and seeing him away from the business. He seemed so earnest about learning how to vacation. She wondered if he'd ever done anything like this before. How sad if he hadn't.

What bothered her was the amused affection she'd felt for him all afternoon as they'd looked at clothes. When she'd run her hands across his shoulders, she'd felt the ripple of muscle beneath her fingers and had a sudden longing to continue touching him.

Without a doubt, she was in trouble. They'd been gone two days, and here she was getting all tingly whenever she looked at him.

Of course, she wasn't going to do anything about it. That

would be too foolish to consider. But there was no law against looking—if she could keep herself from doing something obvious, like drooling.

Five

His wristwatch alarm woke Dean and he was surprised how soundly he'd slept. He sat on the side of the bed and looked out the sliding glass doors. The sky was turning to a deep blue as the day faded. Checking his watch again, he went down the hallway and knocked on Jodie's door.

There was no response.

Finally he opened the door and saw her sound asleep, a cover thrown over her.

"Jodie?"

No answer.

He walked over to the bed. "Jodie, it's time to wake up."

"'Kay," she mumbled into the pillow without moving.

Giving in to temptation, he turned on the radio on her night table and turned up the volume, which certainly did the trick. She jerked up on all fours and looked all around in alarm.

"Sorry. Didn't mean to startle you," he said, trying not to smile.

She sat back on her heels. "Oh. Guess I should have warned you. I'm a sound sleeper."

"I gathered that. I'll let you get ready and meet you in the living room."

"Are you going to wear your new clothes?"

"Absolutely," he said and removed himself from the room.

"Wow," she said to him when she joined him later. "You've definitely gone native."

"When in Rome…" he said with a shrug, trying not to stare.

She wore a tropical print with a sea-blue background. It looked to be wrapped around her, revealing her shapely shoulders and hugging her delectable body. There was little evidence of the secretary tonight.

"What do you think?" she asked and slowly turned in a circle.

He swallowed. "Looks good. Fits nicely."

She laughed. "Actually it's a wrap. The clerk showed me how to put it on. I'm wearing an honest-to-goodness sarong."

That's when he knew he was in serious trouble.

She walked toward him. "I also bought this shell necklace to go with it." She took his arm. "This is going to be so much fun, I just know it."

He silently agreed—if he could survive the evening without grabbing her and kissing her senseless.

* * *

Jodie decided that the luau was everything she'd dreamed about and more. Foods—some she liked better than others—and mai tais, a drink she'd never had before and found delicious, all added to the occasion. The native dances called to her. She had no idea how the women moved their hips so rapidly to the beat of the drums.

It was the drums that kept her pulse throbbing. She glanced at Dean beside her, who seemed to be enjoying himself and the entertainment. She glanced back at the young women. They really were something. Every man there watched them with avid eyes.

She leaned against his shoulder and gave him a slight nudge. "Think you could dance and play the drums like that?"

He glanced at her. "I wouldn't attempt to try. Are you enjoying yourself?"

"Oh, yes."

"You might want to go easy on the rum drinks. They have a delayed kick."

She looked at her almost-empty glass. Was that her second one or her third? "Oh. They taste like fruit juice." She glanced over at his glass. "What are you drinking?"

"Piña colada. Want to try it?"

"No, thanks." She sipped on her drink. "There can't be much rum in this or I'd be able to taste it."

"You're not much of a drinker, are you?"

"Not really." She grinned. "But I'm on vacation, so I thought I'd indulge."

The drums came to a sudden stop and Jodie looked around. The dancing girls were carrying leis in their arms and placing them around each guest's neck.

She liked the way Dean looked with the flowers draped over his shoulders.

"Are you ready to go back to the condo?" he asked.

"Sure." They had walked along the beach to this location and would walk back. He helped her up and she realized that she was a little dizzy. Maybe Dean had been right about the drinks.

He slipped his arm around her waist and she naturally did the same to him. He looked good tonight. The shorts he'd chosen to wear showed off his muscular legs. She smoothed his shirt beneath her hand, enjoying the feel of him. She smiled to herself. This was definitely a romantic evening, and Dean was fulfilling her fantasy of a midnight stroll with someone she cared about.

As they ambled along the edge of the water, she looked up into the sky and said, "I've never seen the stars so bright."

"Big cities tend to put off too much light to see the stars."

"That explains it." She rested her head on his shoulder. The sound of the surf added a sensuous rhythm to the night. She'd never been this close to Dean before and she inhaled the scent of his aftershave.

His warmth radiated along her side, and her body tingled everywhere they touched.

"It's going to be hard to top this experience," she said dreamily to break the silence that had fallen between them. They turned toward the path that led to the condos. When he didn't answer, she lifted her head and looked at him. He looked grim as he stared ahead of them. She eased away from him and promptly stumbled.

He grabbed her arm to keep her from falling.

"I think you were right about the drinks," she said rue-fully. "I'm beginning to feel the effects."

He opened the door to the lobby for her and waited until they were in the elevator alone before he said, "I'm afraid you're going to have a bad headache in the morning."

They stepped out of the elevator and he unlocked the door to the condo. Once inside, she replied, "Probably. But it will be worth it."

He nodded. "Hope you feel the same way in the morning." They walked toward their bedrooms. They reached hers first.

"Thank you for tonight. I hope you weren't bored," she said.

"Not at all. I don't think I gave the business a thought for, oh, at least thirty minutes." He grinned at her.

She smiled. "I don't know what I'm going to do about you."

"A good-night kiss would be nice."

His comment caught her off guard. It was the last thing she'd expected to hear from him.

"Of course," she said and leaned toward him. She closed her eyes, expecting a peck on her cheek. Instead he slowly drew her into his arms and brushed his lips against hers. What was happening to her? Was it the rum that sud-denly made her melt against him…and put her arms around his neck?

By the time he loosened his grip, they were both gasp-ing for air.

"I've wanted to do that all evening," he said hoarsely.

"I didn't know," she murmured and rubbed her finger

along his strong jawline and cheek. Jodie attempted a smile. "Well, good night," she managed to say before she stepped into her room and closed the door.

Dean closed his eyes and stood there. What had he done? Was he out of his mind? He'd taken advantage of the fact that she was there with him, which was unconscionable.

And why hadn't she slapped his face!

Now he knew exactly how she felt pressed against him, how she tasted as her soft mouth opened to his like a budding flower. He'd not forget it, nor would he forget the fact that they still had five days together before heading back to Chicago.

He shook his head and strode into his bedroom. He stripped off his clothes and headed for a much-needed shower and some stern self-talk. Getting involved with Jodie Cameron would be the height of recklessness.

Unfortunately for his peace of mind, he'd discovered tonight that he'd been involved with her for years.

The first thing Jodie knew the next morning when she opened her eyes was that Dean had grossly underestimated the effect of the mai tais. She didn't have just a headache; concrete drills were going off inside her head.

The second thing that registered was the heavenly scent of freshly brewed coffee wafting its way into her room. The thought of coffee was the call of the sirens that drew her out of bed. She put on the thick terry-cloth robe that was in the bathroom, carefully brushed her hair—even her scalp hurt this morning—and went in search of the elixir that might help her live.

Dean sat at the kitchen bar, next to the coffeepot, reading the paper. He glanced up when she moved carefully toward him.

"How're you feeling?" he asked, his voice low.

She almost whimpered. Even that much noise made her head hurt worse. "I should have stopped after the first drink," she whispered. She filled the large coffee mug sitting beside the pot to the brim and immediately lifted it to her mouth. It was too hot to drink, but she could live off the aroma for a moment.

"Aspirin will help," he said, nodding toward a bottle there on the counter.

She filled a glass with water, took a couple of tablets and sat down on the bar stool next to Dean.

He wore shorts, a shirt and sandals. He looked rested and fit. She could almost hate a person for that when she felt like something that had washed up on the shore. He continued to read the paper, and for the first time she fully appreciated his taciturn personality.

She sipped her coffee and squinted out the window. The sun had been up for hours, but at this particular moment she didn't care if she ever saw the sun again.

Dean laid the paper on the counter and got up. He walked over to the expanse of windows and drew the drapes closed.

"How did you know?" she asked with relief when he seated himself once again. He flicked on the small light near where he sat.

"I've overindulged myself a few times in my thirty-odd years. I know what it's like."

She placed her mug on the counter and rested her head in her hands. "The drinks tasted so innocent. I had no idea…" Her voice faded.

He raised his hand to rub her back in sympathy but thought better of it. He cleared his throat. "I know the idea doesn't sound appealing, but you'll feel better once you get some food inside you."

"You are absolutely right. The idea doesn't sound at all appealing."

He grinned and picked up the phone. After ordering them both breakfasts, he hung up and looked at her. "Nibble on some toast, drink some juice—"

"Are you kidding?" she asked in horror, dropping her hands from her head. "I'll probably never drink another glass of juice again."

"It wasn't the fruit juice that caused your pain."

She groaned. "You're always so logical."

"So are you, most of the time. You'll feel better as the day wears on."

"That's a relief. Right now I'd have to get better to die."

He chuckled but didn't say anything else.

When their meal arrived, he opened the door and took the tray, giving the waiter a tip before closing the door and bringing the food to the bar.

Jodie eyed the tray skeptically at the same time her stomach growled. Like it or not, she needed to eat something.

Did Dean always have to be right?

Miraculously by midafternoon she was beginning to feel almost human again. Not well enough to go outside just yet, but better. Anything was an improvement.

Dean had left after breakfast and hadn't yet returned. She wondered where he'd gone. Not that it was any of her business. He might have hooked up with one of the women they'd met at the luau last night.

She frowned at the thought.

What was the matter with her? He'd dated a number of women since she'd worked for him and she hadn't given the matter a thought. Until last night, she hadn't figured he had much passion in him.

She'd definitely been proved wrong there. She groaned at the memory of her response to him. If she hadn't felt so awful this morning, she probably couldn't have faced him.

At least he'd been a gentleman and hadn't mentioned what had happened last night.

Jodie finally went in and showered, the water having its usual soothing effect on her. By the time she dressed and returned to the living room, she felt human again.

She heard the key in the door and glanced around as Dean let himself inside. When he saw her, he grinned and said, "Ignore the ransom note, I managed to escape."

Six

Jodie jumped up and stared at him in shock. "You were kidnapped?" she asked, her voice going up.

He paused before closing the door. "Sorry, I was just making a joke. I was gone longer than I expected to be." She lowered herself back into the chair, feeling silly for overreacting. "How are you feeling?" he asked, making himself comfortable on the nearby sofa.

"Much better than this morning, thank you."

"Did you eat anything for lunch?"

"I ordered some soup. I wasn't up to going downstairs."

"I've set up sightseeing tours for the rest of our stay here. We'll meet Steve Furukawa for lunch tomorrow in Honolulu. While we're there, we'll see the Pearl Harbor Memorial and whatever else looks interesting. There are some great places to see while we're here. I think you'll feel well enough tomorrow to enjoy them."

"Oh. Well. That's nice. I mean, I'm looking forward to it."

"Do you think you're up to sitting out on the beach for a while? The fresh air will do you good."

She nodded. "Good idea. I'll go change."

He got up when she did. "I'll do the same."

As she changed into a two-piece suit she'd bought the day before, Jodie realized that she hadn't seen Dean in his swimsuit. He'd reported that it fit, and that was all that had mattered to her.

She just wished she wasn't so physically aware of him.

They rode the elevator in silence. Jodie wore the matching cover-up to the suit. Dean had on one of his shirts but hadn't bothered to button it. They both had large towels with them.

She did her best not to stare at his chest. Instead she trained her eyes on his face, only to discover that he was looking at her with a great deal of interest.

"New suit?" he asked as they left the building.

"Yes." She stopped and put on her dark sunglasses.

Once on the beach, Jodie carefully laid out one of her towels and slipped off the beach cover.

"Very nice," he said and she glanced around. He stood with his hands resting on his hips, obviously waiting for her to finish making her beach nest.

Dean stripped to his swimsuit was a Dean she'd never known existed. It unnerved her to have all her ideas about who the man was turned upside down. When did he have time to work out, which he had to do to be in such good shape?

She sat and he tossed his towel down and sat beside her.

She wished that she could forget the kiss they'd shared. It had been an aberration; certainly not the norm. However, every time she looked at his mouth, she remembered how his lips had felt touching hers.

The man certainly knew how to kiss!

"This is nice," he said several minutes later. "Is the air helping your head?"

"You're being nice to me," she finally replied. "And it's making me nervous."

"Why? Aren't I always nice to you?"

"Shall I be polite or honest?"

"You're talking about the office, aren't you?"

"That's the person I know—or thought I knew."

He leaned back on his elbows. "Well, we've moved past that, haven't we? After last night?"

She groaned. "I was hoping you'd forgotten about that."

He turned onto his side, propping himself up on an elbow. "Why? We'd had fun at the party and we ended the evening the way most dates are ended—with a kiss."

She slipped her shades down her nose and looked at him. "This is not a dating situation, Dean. I happened to be available to come here because my boss gave me the time off."

"Worked out well, didn't it?" He grinned. "You've opened my eyes regarding several things about my life. I'm hoping you can continue to teach me how to relax and enjoy myself. You've done a good job so far."

Jodie sat up and folded her legs into a yoga position. "What's going on, anyway? What do you hope to accomplish while we're here, other than gaining another client?"

"I want to get to know you better. I've already told you."

"Why? You've known me for years and have never looked at me the way you have since we arrived here."

He chuckled, and despite her practical nature, she was charmed by the sound. A week ago she would have sworn he didn't know how.

"I've never seen you in a swimsuit before...or a sarong, for that matter," he offered casually. Then his tone changed. "I find you fascinating. You have so many facets to your personality, and I've discovered that I want to learn each and every one of them."

"Dean. We'll be back at the office next week and none of this will have mattered. I don't want to make anything more out of our time together than it is."

"I guess that means we won't be sleeping together."

Chuck was right. All men thought about was getting an available woman in bed with them! Then she realized he was laughing at her reaction.

"You're teasing, right?"

"Actually I'm enjoying the expressions running across your face. Just so we're clear, I wouldn't say no if you decide to take me up on my offer."

She shook her head and stretched out on her towel once more. Her heart raced so fast she was certain he could see it pounding in her chest. She knew he was teasing.

He had to be teasing, hoping to fluster her.

Well, she was made of sterner stuff.

Her tone casual, Jodie said, "I'll think about it."

He gave a whoop of laughter and said, "You do that," and then trotted to the water's edge to wade out into the water.

She watched him dive into a wave and appear on the other side. Of course she wasn't going to sleep with him.

That would be the dumbest thing possible for her to do. Okay, so he wouldn't turn her down. So what? To him it would be a casual fling. But becoming intimate with him would change her life. Long after he'd forgotten about this trip, memories would haunt her. It would be impossible to work closely with him without recalling what they had shared.

No. The answer was no.

Jodie stood and walked toward the water.

The water felt good to her, cooling her overheated body. Jodie lowered herself into the water and began a leisurely crawl, feeling her muscles work as she glided through the water.

When Dean spotted her, he angled toward her, cleaving the water in strong strokes.

She smiled at him as he drew near. "I decided to see if the water felt as good as it looks…and it does."

"How's your head?"

"Still on my shoulders. From now on, I'll have one drink and stop, no matter how good it tastes to me."

They continued to swim parallel to the beach, Dean keeping pace with her. Eventually they waded toward the shore together and continued walking until they reached their towels. He quickly dried off and waited for her to gather her things.

"What would you like to do this evening?"

There was a provocative question if she'd ever heard one. "You don't have to entertain me while we're here, you know."

"True, but we've both got to eat and I'd prefer not to eat alone."

"That makes sense, I guess," she replied. "Do you have someplace in mind?"

"Actually I do. I ate there the last time I was here and the Polynesian food is well prepared. If you've never tried it, you're in for a treat."

They stepped inside the elevator.

Finally she nodded. "All right. Thank you for suggesting it."

That evening Jodie looked around the softly lit room, the hurricane lamps on each table making an oasis of light. "You're right," she said to Dean, "this is a great place with a distinct atmosphere."

"I'm glad you're enjoying it. Do you like the food I ordered?"

"It's different but really good. Thanks for bringing me." She sipped her iced tea. "How should I behave toward your prospective client tomorrow?"

He studied her for a moment in silence. Finally he said, "No striptease, no hula and no playing the ukulele."

"Striptease? I've never done anything like that in my—" She stopped. "You're teasing me again."

"Can't resist. You're so much fun to watch when you react."

"Fine. Just for that, I'll take my ukulele and sing all through lunch."

"You can sing?"

"No."

"A threat then."

"Very much a threat."

"You'll do fine tomorrow. You know our business very well. Speaking of which, once we get back, I'm going to talk to Frank Godfrey about putting you into his department as soon as possible rather than waiting until you graduate. We're only talking about a few months. So treat tomorrow like a training session as I present what we have to offer and answer Furukawa's questions."

"You're going to promote me now?"

"Not this minute, no. But when we get back to the office I'll start the ball rolling."

"That's wonderful news! Thank you so much."

"Don't thank me. Frank's a good supervisor and he'll work you hard learning how we go about providing the necessary equipment to keep our clients secure."

Over dessert and coffee Jodie asked, "Why are you promoting me now?"

"What do you mean?"

"Well, you don't have a secretary lined up to replace me, for one thing."

He groaned. "Don't remind me. But that shouldn't take too long."

"Well, um…"

"Why do you make such a point that I'm difficult to work for?"

"Because you are difficult to work for. Or have you forgotten how many secretaries walked out on you before I was hired?"

He pulled his earlobe and looked uncomfortable. "I've mellowed since then."

"I'll take your word for it."

"Haven't I?"

"You've mellowed because I learned how you like to work."

"That doesn't sound too hard."

"That's true. It doesn't." She looked around. "Shall we go?"

"Wait a minute. I'm missing something here, Jodie. Tell me."

"You want your office to run smoothly. I know your likes and dislikes enough to anticipate how and what you want, that's all."

"In other words, you can read my mind."

"Not at all."

"That's good to know considering some of my thoughts while on this trip."

A burst of heat engulfed her and she knew she'd turned a fiery red. Jodie picked up her water glass and drank. When she had emptied the glass, she studied it without looking up.

"I'm sorry. I didn't mean to embarrass you."

Why should he apologize when she certainly wouldn't want him to learn of any of her thoughts these past few days?

"It's all right."

He brushed his fingers across the back of her hand. "No, it isn't. I've made you uncomfortable around me and that's the last thing I want. You're right. It's time to go."

They drove back to the condo listening to music. Once inside the condo, Jodie said, "If you'll excuse me, I think I'll go to bed."

"Of course. Sleep well."

Dean watched her walk out of the room, still irritated with himself. What was the matter with him, coming on to her like this? He'd been off balance where she was concerned since he'd first seen her at the airport.

He wandered over to the window and looked out. The view continued to be spectacular, even at night. While he stood there, he thought about their trip to Oahu the next day.

In an airplane.

In a small airplane.

Of course, Jodie knew they would have to fly. From what he remembered, the flight was a short one. They barely got into the air before it was time to land. The small plane could make the experience a little bumpy since the pilot flew at a reasonably low altitude.

Perhaps the flight here from Chicago had helped to allay her fears about flying. He could only hope.

One look at her face the next morning and he knew his hope had been futile. Not that she said anything. However, despite the slight tan she'd gotten thus far on the trip, she was a pasty white. Not a good sign.

Without a word, he poured her a cup of coffee. He'd been up since dawn and had already had several cups.

"Thank you," she murmured, immediately picking up the cup and sipping.

He waited until she set the cup down and then casually asked, "How are you this morning?"

"Okay," she said quietly.

"I believe our flight leaves in a couple of hours."

She didn't comment.

"Jodie?"

Startled, she looked at him. "Yes?"

"Are you nervous about the flight?"

"How did you know?"

"I remembered you were a little nervous—" there was an understatement if he'd ever made one "—on our flights here."

She nodded. "I don't mind it once we get in the air and level out. It's the taking off and landing that bothers me."

"Unfortunately that's what we'll be doing this morning."

"Oh. Well, of course."

"Why don't we go downstairs and get some breakfast. Are you up for that?"

"Okay."

She didn't sound at all certain.

While they ate, he chatted about the office and some projects he was working on, trying to keep her mind off her upcoming ordeal. She responded in monosyllables.

Finally he said, "I thought we might go to the Big Island tomorrow. It will mean another short flight, but I've been told the volcano is something to behold."

She went from pasty white to an interesting color of green.

"Of course, if you don't want to go…"

"That's fine. Really. Whatever you want to do is fine with me."

Sure it was.

Dean checked his watch. "We should head for the airport soon. Do you need to go back to the condo?"

She shook her head.

Today she looked like the secretary he'd known for years. She had her hair pinned up—he hadn't realized how much he liked to see it down until now—and wore

a lightweight suit. She looked like a business professional despite her pallor. Unfortunately for his peace of
mind, he had the vision of her in a swimsuit and wearing a sarong. He would never view his efficient secretary in the same way now that he'd gotten to know her
better.

She must have been hurt badly by the jerk she'd
thought would be her husband. How else could he explain
to himself the subdued person he'd known for the past
five years?

Seeing her literally letting her hair down and enjoying
herself had been a revelation to him.

Once in the car, he tried to make conversation by asking her about various subjects. She answered in monosyllables until he gave up and turned on the radio.

By the time they were seated in the smallish plane, he
knew that the situation required drastic action.

He'd been on flights like this before. The plane took off
at a steep angle. Since she'd admitted she'd never been on
one this small, she probably would be startled.

"Jodie?"

"Mmm?"

He took her hand. "Do you know what I'd like to do
right now?"

She turned and looked at him hopefully. "Get off the
plane?"

He laughed. "Um, no. What I'd like to do is kiss you
senseless."

Well, that certainly took her mind off flying. She stared
at him in astonishment. "Why?" she asked starkly.

"Well, for one thing, you have the most kissable mouth

of anyone I've ever known." He looked down at their clasped hands. With his other hand, he stroked the back of her hand with his finger. "And you fit into my arms as though you were made just for me."

He felt her hand tremble and she turned a charming shade of red, which nicely replaced her ashen color.

The plane started moving. He lifted her hand to his mouth and kissed her palm, his tongue lightly touching her. She stiffened when they took off. He wasn't certain whether it was the kiss or the flight. So he leaned toward her and kissed her on the mouth.

Her lips trembled, and he took his time caressing her mouth with his lips and tongue. Slowly she responded and he forgot his reason for starting this in the first place.

An amused feminine voice spoke near his shoulder. "I'm sorry to interrupt you, sir, but I'd like to offer the two of you something to drink, if you like. We'll only be in the air for another twenty minutes."

Jodie pulled away from him and stared at her. "We're in the air?"

"Yes, ma'am." The flight attendant grinned. "I can understand your distraction."

Jodie looked at Dean. "You did that on purpose!"

Dean told the attendant to bring them some orange juice before he looked at Jodie. "I suppose I did. I've never accidentally kissed anyone."

She glanced out the window and blanched.

"From now on you'll sit in the aisle seat," he said briskly. "We're doing fine."

She turned and looked at him. "You know what I mean! You deliberately distracted me."

Once again he lifted her hand and kissed her palm. "Did it work?"

"I know I'm being ridiculous about flying."

"You just need to do it more often so you can get used to it."

"That's your prescription, Dr. Logan?"

"Absolutely. And here in the islands is a perfect place to practice. We'll make certain to visit each and every one of them."

"Oh, joy," she muttered.

Their drinks arrived and he let go of her hand.

The landing was as abrupt as the takeoff. Jodie squeezed his hand so hard she must have been cutting off circulation. But he didn't mind. She was adorable when she was vulnerable.

Once on the ground, Jodie felt giddy with relief despite her embarrassment. When she had finally let go of Dean's hand, it still had the imprints of her fingers on it.

They took a cab to the address Dean had. Once they arrived, Jodie asked, "Is this his office?"

"No. This is a private club for local businessmen. He said to give his name at the door."

Jodie waited while Dean spoke to the man who met them at the front door. The man looked at a list he carried on a clipboard, found Dean's name and nodded. He escorted them to a double door that was ornately engraved.

When Jodie walked in, she looked around her. There was a large bar made of teak to the right of the entrance. A maître d' met them at the top of the steps.

"We're here to meet Mr. Furukawa," Dean said.

"Right this way, sir," the man replied.

The place was meticulously designed and elegantly decorated. The only sounds were the murmured voices of other diners, their voices muted by the thick carpeting underfoot. Pristine white tablecloths covered each table and they looked like islands floating on the deep red carpet.

The maître d' continued through the room until he reached an alcove that overlooked the water. Once they were seated, he poured ice water into glasses and said, "Your waiter will be with you shortly."

Once Jodie was certain he was out of earshot, she said, "The scent of money is everywhere."

Dean grinned. "I noticed."

She gazed at his mouth. Jodie discovered she had a little trouble breathing whenever he smiled at her. She couldn't forget the touch of his lips on hers.

"Sorry to keep you waiting," a newcomer said from behind her.

Dean stood and extended his hand. "Perfectly all right, Mr. Furukawa," he said.

"Please, call me Steve."

Steve wore a custom-made suit that showed off his trim figure and tanned face. His hair gleamed like polished pewter.

"Steve, I'd like you to meet Jodie Cameron, one of the employees with our firm."

Steve took her hand and bowed slightly. "It is a pleasure."

While they ordered and their meal was served, Jodie watched and listened as the men discussed several topics, none of which had anything to do with a possible security installation. She couldn't help but wonder why he'd brought her, unless the business meeting was to take place after their meal.

Dean included her in the conversation, and when Steve asked how she was enjoying Hawaii, she responded readily enough.

Once their plates were removed and they were left with fresh cups of coffee, Steve said, "I've been reading up on you, Dean."

"And?"

"You and your company have an excellent reputation in the security field. What kind of security do you offer?"

"We make certain that no unauthorized person can enter your place of business without a silent alarm going off, alerting the staff. We offer hidden surveillance cameras that record everyone who goes in or out. Security codes are installed and updated regularly. In addition, we install special software on each computer in your office that will also alert you should anyone attempt to gain illegal access to the company's computers."

"I see." Steve glanced at his watch. "I'd like you to see my setup and give me some idea of what your systems would cost to install and run."

Dean nodded. "Of course."

Steve signed for their meal and the three of them returned through the restaurant. Several people spoke to Steve while they made their way to the entrance.

By the time they reached the street, valet parking had his car waiting.

The men continued to chat during the drive. Jodie, in the backseat, made notes of the conversation that pertained to business, finally feeling as though she could be useful.

By the time they left Steve Furukawa that afternoon, he'd agreed to become one of the company's clients. On the way to the airport Dean called the office and left a voice-mail message for the legal department that he had a new client.

Once on the plane, Jodie—determined to ignore the butterflies in her stomach—said, "Your trip has been a success, hasn't it?"

Dean nodded. "Definitely. Thank you for taking such extensive notes. I'll fax them to the office so Lawrence Kendall will have the information he needs to prepare the contract." He studied her for a moment and then asked, "You doing okay?"

She nodded.

"Good. So shall we visit the volcano tomorrow?"

"I'd like that," she replied, hoping he didn't detect her lack of enthusiasm.

"Or we could stay at the condo and enjoy the beach area," he said casually.

"It's up to you."

"My only reason for suggesting the trip was to allow you to see more of the islands."

"Why don't we wait until the day before we leave then?"

"Whatever you say."

Once back at the condo, Dean said, "We have time to go for a swim before dark if you'd like."

"I'd like that." Jodie went into her room and closed the door. Somehow, some way, she would get through this week with the man she'd gotten to know here on the islands who only vaguely resembled her boss. The fact that she liked and enjoyed this new person unnerved her more than a little.

All she could hope was that once in the office again, he would assume his sardonic personality.

Seven

Saturday afternoon they left the condo for the last time and headed toward the airport.

They'd spent the earlier part of the day on the beach and swimming, chatting about their time there. Jodie hoped her manner hadn't betrayed how sad she was to be going home. Dean had made her laugh that morning. She so enjoyed his wry sense of humor.

She glanced at Dean driving the rental car. He'd already returned to his terse manner and stone face, which would help her adjust to the fact that the man she'd spent the week with was nothing like the man she worked with.

Once on the plane, Jodie picked up one of the magazines she'd bought and waited for takeoff.

Dean touched her hand and she looked at him. "Thank you for being here this week."

"I enjoyed it. I'm not looking forward to Chicago's winter, I can assure you."

She closed her eyes during takeoff and prayed that the pilot could get the large plane in the air without a problem since they were immediately over water.

Once they leveled off, the flight attendant brought their meals and drinks. After she ate, Jodie closed her eyes and willed herself to sleep, determinedly putting the islands and the memories there to the back of her mind.

They arrived in Chicago Sunday morning. Dean gathered their bags and said, "I'll take you home."

"Thank you."

"Wait here and I'll bring the car around."

While she waited, she looked out at the gray skies and the people huddled into their winter coats to get away from the wind. *Yes, Dorothy, you've returned to Kansas and Oz is only a memory.* There was nothing more tangible than the weather to remind her that her fantasy vacation had come to an end.

She saw a late-model sports car pull up to the curb, and Dean stepped out. She picked up her suitcase, and in a few strides he'd come inside and picked up the rest of their luggage. With customary efficiency Dean loaded the bags in the surprisingly roomy trunk and opened the passenger door for her.

Once they were both inside, he pulled away from the curb. "Where to?"

She gave him directions and settled into the comfortable seat. He drove with efficiency just as he did everything else. When he reached her apartment complex, she said, "You can let me out here. I can—"

"I'd like to see where you live," he said bluntly.

"Why?" she asked just as bluntly.

"No reason, really. Do you have a problem with my knowing where you live?"

"Of course not. Personnel has it on record."

"You've been really quiet this morning. Any particular reason?"

"I'm just tired. I had trouble sleeping on the plane."

"Well, now that you're home you can sleep the day away."

She directed him to the entrance of the underground parking and showed him her second parking space. He pulled in next to her red car.

"Yours?" he asked, getting out and going to the trunk.

"Yes."

He picked up her luggage, which included the ukulele case, locked his car with the remote and followed her to the elevator. Once inside, she pushed the button for her floor and they waited in silence.

When she opened her door and motioned for him to go ahead of her, he walked in. She'd hoped he would put the cases down in the hallway and leave. No such luck. He set them in the hallway and continued into the living room.

"Nice place," he said, glancing around.

"I like it."

He walked over to her and without a word took her in his arms and kissed her, taking his time. She didn't want to respond to him; she couldn't allow herself to respond to him and she was unnerved by how much she wanted to.

When he released her, his words were quietly prosaic. "I'll see you at work tomorrow," he said and let himself out.

Jodie stood there and stared at the door. With one kiss he had brought the fantasy home to Chicago. What was she going to do?

After she unpacked and began to wash clothes, she called Lynette. Kent answered.

"Hi, Aunt Jodie. Are you calling from Hawaii?"

"No, sweetheart. I'm back home. Is your mom there?"

"Uh-huh."

"May I speak to her?"

"Uh-huh."

She could still hear him breathing into the phone. She heard Lynette in the background say, "May I have the phone, please?"

Kent sounded fainter as he said, "Uh-huh."

Lynette took the phone and said, "Do you think I need to increase my son's vocabulary?"

Jodie replied, "Uh-huh."

They both laughed. "How was the trip? Did you throttle your boss? Toss him in the ocean? Drop him into one of the volcanoes? Tell me everything."

Her feelings toward Dean had changed so much in the week she'd been gone that for a moment she didn't understand why Lynette would say those things.

"Actually he was fun to be with. I enjoyed being there with him."

After a prolonged silence Lynette said, "Who is this? Hello? Was I cut off from my sister? Hello? Hello?"

Jodie chuckled. "Cut it out. And you needn't worry about my sanity. He was on vacation and I had an opportunity to see another side to him."

"Somehow I never expected to hear the words *fun* and *Dean Logan* in the same sentence coming from you. What in the world happened to turn Mr. Hyde into Dr. Jekyll?"

Jodie sighed. "Doesn't matter. Mr. Hyde was definitely present once we landed at the airport. By noon tomorrow I'll have forgotten completely the friendly, funny man I met on the island." The kiss didn't count.

"Speaking of meeting men, did you spot any good-looking hunks strolling the beaches?"

"Quite a few, actually," Jodie replied, grinning. "Of course, most of them were accompanied by professional swimsuit models. Or if they weren't, they should be."

"You can hold your own with the best of them, kiddo."

"I had at least ten pounds on the heaviest ones."

"And all in the right places. Did you have Dean drooling?"

Her throat tightened and for a moment she couldn't speak. Finally she said, "Not so you'd notice."

"Plan to come over tonight for dinner. I hope you took lots of photos so I can be envious and jealous and all that stuff."

Jodie laughed. "You are so full of it. You wouldn't be away that long from the kids."

"True. But I can dream. See you tonight."

Jodie turned off the handset and said, "Dreaming isn't real." She didn't need to tell Lynette that, of course. She needed to remind herself.

She took a nap before going over to Lynette and Chuck's. She carefully dressed and hoped that they couldn't read her face. Maybe they'd think the glow was all suntan. She could only hope.

Kent and Kyle greeted her at the door that evening with whoops and hollers that made her laugh.

"Boys!" Lynette said. "Hush or you'll wake Emily."

They immediately quieted. "Did you bring us something?" Kyle asked expectantly, eyeing the large shopping bag she carried.

"Kyle!" Lynette scolded. "You know better than that!" She hugged Jodie before she stepped back. "Don't you look great! The tan really emphasizes the color of your eyes."

Chuck joined them. "Looking good, little sis. Vacations obviously agree with you."

Jodie sat down on the sofa and immediately had two little boys eyeing the bag. She began to pull out various gifts, explaining where she'd found different ones. When she finished, she said to Lynette, "Dean bought me a ukulele."

"Did he know you play?"

"I made the mistake of telling him. Actually the chords came back to me fairly easily and I'm not too bad on the thing."

"Did you bring it with you?" Kent asked. "I didn't know you can play."

"No, I left it at the apartment. One of these days when you come to visit I'll get it out for you."

Eventually they sat down to eat. Everyone was full of questions and the time flew by. It was only when she got ready to leave that Lynette walked her to the door and quietly asked, "Something happened over there, didn't it?"

"What makes you think that?"

"Because I know you. There's a shadow in your eyes I've never seen before."

"I'm just tired. Traveling really wears me out."

"If you say so."

"It's probably the letdown of getting back home and picking up my routine again."

Lynette hugged her. "Okay. Then we'll see you Friday night, right?"

"Right."

Jodie let herself out of the warm house and into the cold. She hurried to her car and crawled inside. While she waited for the car to warm and the heater to kick on, Jodie thought about Lynette's comments.

Truly, nothing *had* happened except for a few shared kisses, and she had no intention of discussing her response to Dean with anyone. After all, the kisses had been an impulse of the moment…except for the one this morning. She hadn't needed the reminder that she was strongly attracted to Dean Logan, which wasn't very smart.

She turned on the car radio and listened to music during her drive home, determined to put him completely out of her mind.

Eight

"**W**ow! Look at you!" Betty said by way of greeting when Jodie walked into the office the next morning. "Quite a tan. You certainly stand out among all of us oatmeal-colored people. So where did you go?"

"Hawaii."

"Ooooh, well good for you. Does the boss know you took off the same week he did?"

"Yes. Is he in yet?"

"Haven't seen him, but that doesn't mean much. It's not unusual for him to get here before I do."

Jodie nodded and headed to her office.

Once there, she almost groaned at the sight of her desk covered in papers with notes attached, files stacked high and file drawers half-open. She glanced into his office and saw Dean at his desk, frowning at something he was reading.

She put her purse away and made coffee. While she waited for the coffee to brew, she sat and began to sort through the mess on her desk.

"Jodie? Is that you?"

She stood and walked over to his doorway. "Yes. How did you manage to go through so much work this morning?"

"Oh, that's from yesterday. I spent the day catching up on what's been happening. Is there coffee?"

She glanced over her shoulder. "Yes. I'll bring you some."

"Thanks," he said absently, leaning back in his chair, still reading.

There, you see? she told herself. He's already forgotten last week and has moved on with his life.

Or so she thought until she set his coffee on his desk and he looked up at her. The heat in his eyes made her tremble. He'd never looked at her like that in the office before.

"Was your family glad to have you back home?"

"My nephews were more interested in what I brought them," she answered. "Lynette and Chuck agreed that I looked tanned and rested, which, according to them, was just what I needed."

He nodded thoughtfully and straightened in his chair. "I'd like to meet them sometime."

"My family?" She had to be mistaken. That couldn't be what he meant.

"Yes."

"Oh."

"Have lunch with me today and we can discuss it."

"I, uh, generally eat lunch at my desk."

"Not today."

"Is this business-related?"

His frown deepened. "Of course not."

"Then don't issue orders about my personal time." She turned and went back to her desk. She started filing papers and folders, her back to his door.

After several minutes she heard Dean clear his throat. She looked over her shoulder and saw him standing beside her desk.

"What do you need?" she asked pleasantly.

"Some manners. Obviously. I apologize for ordering you around."

"Apology accepted."

"I, uh, I'd like to take you to lunch. Please?"

She shut the file drawer and walked over to him. "I don't think that's a good idea. I enjoyed the trip and appreciate your giving me the opportunity to get away from the cold weather for a few days. Now that we're back at work, I believe it would be better if we return to our regular routine."

"I don't see what's wrong with having lunch together."

"At the moment the office staff is under the impression I decided to take off a week while you were gone. Once they see us together and notice our tans, they'll figure out we were together."

"Do you care?"

"Yes."

"Why?"

"I don't want to become the stereotypical secretary who's seeing her boss socially."

"I'm not suggesting we date. It's no big deal to have lunch at the same time, is it?"

"You're being deliberately obtuse."

"No, I'm not. I prefer to think of myself as unconsciously obtuse."

"I'd rather not go out today," she said politely. "I plan to study over my lunch hour. I brought a sandwich."

He nodded slowly. "You're probably right," he said.

She picked up some papers and turned away to the filing cabinet.

Jodie waited until he'd returned to his desk and then rested her forehead against the filing cabinet. She hoped he hadn't noticed that she was trembling. His attitude had caught her off guard.

If she consistently turned him down, he would soon give up and get on with his life, which was just the way she wanted things. She knew his dating patterns. The last thing she needed or wanted was to become involved with him.

And…if she repeated that often enough, she might be able to convince herself.

Dean sat down at his desk and looked at the work awaiting him. Most of it was to approve what had been done in his absence and to sign off on it. He leaned back in his chair and swung around to face the windows.

Jodie was right. Of course she was. Just because he'd enjoyed her company this past week didn't give him the right to expect their relationship to continue in the same way here in Chicago.

She was his secretary. That's all. The thought reminded him that he needed to call Frank. He'd leave her alone. They'd probably get back to their routine all right if he could forget how much he'd enjoyed kissing her and seeing her in a swimsuit. How much he'd enjoyed their conversations.

He shook his head to clear it. Getting emotional about the trip was ridiculous. Dean turned back to his desk and reached for his private address book. Now that he was no longer seeing Rachel, he knew of several women he could call. He only had to pick one.

He reached for the phone.

That night Dean's home phone rang close to eleven o'clock. He glanced at the caller ID and shook his head.

"Hello, Rachel," he said when he picked up the phone.

"Oh! There you are. I've been looking for you all week. Your office said you were out of town, and when I asked to speak to Jodie, I was told she'd taken a week off, so there was no way I could think of to reach you."

"Well, now you've found me. Did you find something else of mine that I left at your place?"

"Oh, honey, I am so sorry for the way I treated you. I don't blame you for not returning my calls. I don't usually behave so atrociously. It was just a really bad day for me."

"I noticed."

"Please forgive me. I miss you so much." She lowered her voice. "I've missed making love to you."

He thought about the relationship he'd had with Rachel and realized that he'd put her completely out of his mind. That told him what he needed to know where she was concerned. Whatever they'd had, it was over.

"Did you remember that this is the weekend we were going up to Wisconsin to visit Winnie and Fred?"

"Rachel, I figured that when you broke up with me, we wouldn't be seeing each other again, much less Winnie and Fred."

"I was awful and I know I was. But I didn't mean any of it. I was just angry and I took it out on you."

"As I recall, I was the reason you were angry."

"Well…but that doesn't matter in the larger scheme of things. Let's face it, all couples quarrel. That's the first one we've had in the three months we've been seeing each other."

He didn't say anything.

"Dean?"

"I'm sorry, Rachel, but I've already made plans for the weekend."

"What sort of plans?" she asked suspiciously.

"Nothing you'd be interested in."

"Try me," she said flatly.

"I have a date Saturday evening with someone I've known for a long while. You don't know her."

"You're seeing someone else!" Her voice lost its rounded tones.

"You made it quite clear you never wanted to see me again. I took you at your word."

"I said I was sorry," she wailed. "Please don't do this to me!"

"Rachel, listen to me. There's no reason to continue seeing each other. The points you made were valid. If it took your getting angry to tell me, then so be it. I'm not going to change, you know. You were right. I am married to my work. I forget social events. I'm bad about escorting you to everything you want to attend. Why bother to continue to see me? There are lots of men who would be eager to spend time with you."

She didn't reply right away. When she did, she sounded

as if she might be crying. "I screwed up. I know that. I know your work is important to you. I was way out of line that night and I know it. I just want to see you once in a while."

"I'll call you when I can, but I picked up a new client last week and I'll be putting in long hours coming up with the right combination of security devices to protect his company." He thought about their situation for a moment. "I'll give you a call in the next week or two. Have fun with Fred and Winnie."

He hung up the phone and wandered over to the windows. His condo had a great view of Lake Michigan. As a rule he found the sight relaxing. Tonight he felt lonely, which was most unusual.

He went into his bedroom, undressed and stretched out on the bed.

He was doing what needed to be done. He'd see Susan Saturday night and catch up on her news. They'd lost touch after he'd moved his mother into the nursing home. Susan had been her live-in caregiver and a sweet woman. He'd been surprised that she hadn't remarried by this time. She'd been a widow for six years or more.

As for Rachel…he'd have to think about whether he wanted to spend much time with her. He discovered that although he was lonely, Rachel wasn't the answer. He refused to consider who might be.

Jodie's phone was ringing when she walked into her office the next morning. She dropped her purse on the desk and reached for the phone.

"This is Jodie."

"Hi, Jodie. It's me…Rachel."

"Oh. Good morning. I'm not sure if Dean's here yet. Do you want me to have him call you?"

"Oh, no! No. I, uh, I called to talk to you."

"Really?"

"Yes. You know, Jodie, I admire you a great deal and I know that Dean couldn't get along without you."

When Rachel paused, Jodie didn't know what to say. What was this phone call about?

Finally Rachel said, "I mean, I know you're discreet and I'd rather you not tell Dean that I called."

"All right."

"The thing is that Dean and I had a spat a week or so ago and I think he's still a little angry with me. He didn't return my calls last week, and when I spoke to him last night, he said he was seeing someone else."

Well, of course he was. Dean Logan didn't waste time. He must have found someone who would have lunch with him or was available for whatever else he wanted. Good.

"I see."

"He's just trying to make me jealous and he wouldn't tell me who he was seeing. Do you know?"

"I have no idea."

"Oh." Rachel sounded disappointed. "He said he'd known her for a long time. I thought you'd probably know her."

Jodie chuckled. "He knows so many people that I wouldn't be able to guess. After all, he's lived in Chicago for years."

"Oh, he'll probably tell me," Rachel finally said with a laugh. "Once he's over his anger. We were supposed to visit some friends in northern Wisconsin this weekend, but I guess he's planning to see her instead."

"I'm sorry, Rachel. I know this must be painful for you."

Rachel sighed. "It's my fault. I must have been going through PMS or something and took it out on him."

"I hope the two of you can work it out," Jodie said. She was sincere. It would be easier for her to have him completely unavailable.

"Thanks for listening, Jodie. I appreciate it."

Jodie hung up, dropped her purse in the drawer and peeked around the corner into Dean's office. It was empty. Thank goodness. She doubted that he'd appreciate her discussing him with Rachel, although in the past she and Rachel had talked to each other regularly.

The next time the phone rang, it was Dean.

"Hi, sorry I didn't let you know I wouldn't be in this morning. Something came up that I needed to take care of."

"No problem. Believe it or not, your phone has been quiet. Maybe everybody thinks you're still on vacation."

"Good. I should be in around two o'clock."

"Okay."

As soon as she hung up the phone, the intercom buzzed. It was Betty.

"Your secret admirer has left something for you at my desk."

"I'm sure. I don't have a secret admirer."

"Well, someone just sent you a beautiful bouquet of tropical flowers. They look and smell heavenly. He must be in looove." She drawled the last word.

What was Lynette up to now?

When Jodie walked into the reception area, she found a truly awesome vase filled with lush flowers. "Was there a card?" she asked.

"Don't know," Betty replied.

Jodie looked through the long stems and saw a small white card. She opened the envelope and stared at the message.

Thought you'd enjoy the scent of the islands in your office. D

"Well?" Betty asked brightly.

"Oh! A friend from school."

"No kidding. Have you been seeing him long?"

She looked at the flowers before answering Betty. "I've known him for years."

Jodie carried the large vase back to her office and placed it on top of the filing cabinet. The flowers smelled enchanting, and she wished she knew what Dean Logan was up to.

Nine

When Jodie arrived at Lynette's on Friday, she realized they had company. She stopped in the hallway to hang up her coat. As soon as she walked into the living room, Chuck said, "Look who's in town," motioning to Carl Grantham, who was sitting across from him.

"Carl! What a surprise. What brings you to Chicago at this time of year?"

Carl got up and hugged her. He'd been Chuck's best man at their wedding, and as the maid of honor, Jodie had spent time with him. He was a great guy. He was also gay, which she considered to be a loss to the female population.

"The company sent me. I tried to convince them that Florida would have been better, but they wouldn't listen to me."

Carl could have been a model had he wanted, but he preferred being an engineer.

"How long are you going to be here?" she asked.

"Until Tuesday. Chuck and Lynette insisted I stay here with them. I told them I could get a hotel since it was a business expense, but…" He shrugged his shoulders.

"I know. I've never been able to win an argument with Chuck either, and you've known him longer than I have!"

Chuck chimed in. "We've got a lot to catch up on. The guest bedroom is far enough away from the kids that he won't be disturbed by them."

Lynette came in from the kitchen. "Hi, sweetie," she said to Jodie, giving her a hug. "You're just in time to help me get the food on the table."

"Where are the boys?"

"They're spending the night with Chuck's folks, and Emily is asleep. I won't guarantee for how long, though, so let's eat."

Over dinner Carl told them what was going on in New York and discussed some of the plays he'd seen. His partner was an actor who was presently in one of the popular musicals on Broadway.

"I would love to see him onstage sometime," Jodie said. "His voice alone sends chills through me."

"And when did you hear his voice?" Lynette asked with a smile.

"While you guys were on your honeymoon and I called Carl to tell him he'd left his jacket in my car. Carl wasn't there, so Chris and I had a nice long chat."

"Telling tales about me is what they were doing," Carl said with a mock frown.

"As I recall," Chuck said, "he was touring when we got married and couldn't come to the wedding."

Carl nodded. "He'd just gotten in when Jodie called."

"I didn't see the coat in the backseat for several days. It had fallen to the floor."

"I was wondering if the three of you would like to see the musical showing at the McCormick. I saw it on Broadway and it's really good."

Lynette shook her head. "As much as I'd like to, I can't ask Chuck's folks to keep the boys two nights in a row."

"Which is an excuse," Chuck said. "She doesn't want to leave Emily with anyone."

"Well, that's true."

Carl looked at Jodie. "How about you?"

"I'd love to! I haven't gone to the theatre in much too long a time."

"Great. I'll see about tickets for tomorrow night. If they're sold out, we can catch the Sunday matinee—that is, if you're available."

"I think I can safely say that my social calendar is quite bare either day."

Carl shook his head. "Then the men around here are blind. You look sensational. Where did you get the tan? The contrast with your blond hair and blue eyes is stunning."

"I was in Hawaii last week."

"Alone?" he asked with a lifted brow.

She glanced at Lynette and Chuck. "Well, not exactly."

"Aha."

"No, no, nothing like that. I was with my boss who had business there."

"He must be eighty years old not to have been aware of you."

Jodie laughed and knew she was blushing. "He's a businessman, completely wrapped up in his company." She refused to look at Lynette. Instead she kept her eyes trained on Carl.

After dinner the men went into the other room while Jodie and Lynette cleaned up the kitchen. Jodie was putting dishes in the dishwasher when Lynette said, "I have a question. You don't have to answer it, but did Dean make a pass at you while you were there?"

Jodie took her time straightening and turning to face Lynette. "A pass?" she repeated, stalling for time.

"You know…did he try to kiss you or suggest you could be more than a secretary to him? I couldn't help but notice that you blush every time he's mentioned, which has never been your reaction to him before." She studied Jodie's face. "You're right. It's none of my business. You're a grown woman and I don't need to hover." She touched Jodie's cheek. "I just don't want to see you hurt."

"There's nothing going on between us," Jodie answered truthfully. "He's all business at the office. Nothing's changed. He's already dating someone else."

"Doesn't take him long, does it?"

"I'm sure they're lined up waiting for him to notice them."

They walked into the living room and Jodie turned to Carl. "I need to get home. Call me when you have the tickets."

"Even if we don't get the tickets for tomorrow night, I'd like to take you to dinner."

"I'd like that."

"Good."

"I'll draw you a map to her place," Chuck said. "She's moved since you were here last."

"Great," Jodie said. "I'll wait to hear from you."

Jodie drove home thinking about the evening. She thought the world of Carl. He was drop-dead handsome with a wry sense of humor, graduated at the top of his class at MIT, but most important, he was a warm, gracious person.

Nothing like Dean, who had returned to being a bear this past week, growling at whoever was closest, which was usually her.

The oddest thing, though. He'd sent her a dozen roses today. When she'd thanked him, he'd nodded without looking up and said, "I noticed the others were fading. It's nice to have fresh flowers in the office."

So the flowers weren't really for her. They were for the office.

Once home, Jodie went to bed. While waiting for sleep, she wondered what Dean was doing tonight.

Dean sat at his desk at home and read contracts that had been prepared for new clients. With all the security breaches in the corporate world these days, more and more companies were looking for high-tech solutions, causing his business to flourish. So why wasn't he more excited about the increase?

Was it possible he was bored?

Of course not. That would never happen.

It was almost midnight before he went to bed. Despite the hour, he had trouble falling asleep.

Carl had managed to get tickets for the Saturday-night performance. He picked Jodie up early enough for them to have dinner before the show.

As soon as she opened the door, he said, "You look fabulous, Ms. Cameron."

"Come in, Carl. You look stunning yourself."

"Stunning?" He quirked his eyebrow.

"You look like you should be modeling. Custom-made suit?"

He nodded. "So. Are we ready to go?"

"Absolutely." She put on her coat, picked up her purse and joined him at the door.

By the time they reached the theater, Jodie had laughed so much her tears had wiped off the little makeup she wore. Not that she cared. She couldn't remember the last time she'd so enjoyed herself.

With Dean perhaps?

Don't go there.

Once they were seated, she said, "I can't believe you got such good seats."

"Actually they were a last-minute cancellation. Looks as if we lucked out."

As the lights began to dim, Jodie noticed a couple being seated a few rows in front of them. She recognized the man immediately—it was Dean with his new girlfriend.

She couldn't believe that they had chosen the same night to see the musical. She gave her head a quick shake of dismissal.

"Something wrong?" Carl leaned toward her to ask.

"Not really. I just saw the man I work for. He doesn't seem to be the musical-theater kind, so I was a little surprised." She nodded toward the couple.

"How long have you worked for him?"

"Close to five years. It's a great company to work for.

They've paid for me to take college courses at night. I'll actually get my degree this spring."

"Great benefits."

She watched as Dean leaned over and said something to the woman he was with. She looked to be about his age, and from what Jodie could see, she appeared to be very attractive.

The overture finished and the curtains opened. After that, Jodie forgot everything else but the magical experience of musical theater.

Dean and Susan went into the lobby during intermission. He told her to wait there and he'd get them something to drink from the bar. While going through the crowd, he almost literally ran into Jodie.

"Well, hi," he said with a slight smile. "Fancy meeting you here."

"Hello, Dean," she said. "I'd like you to meet Carl Grantham."

Dean hadn't realized that she was with someone. He held out his hand. "Dean Logan." The man was everything he wasn't. Good-looking—all right, great-looking—debonair and appeared charming.

"Dean is the man I work for," she said to Carl.

"I'm glad to meet you. Jodie was singing your praises a little earlier."

Dean looked at Jodie and she turned a fiery red. He looked back at Carl. "That's always good to hear. If you'll excuse me, I was headed to the bar to get drinks for Susan and me. Good meeting you, Carl. I'll see you at the office, Jodie."

Dean turned his back and walked away before he did or said something outrageous. He wanted to flatten Carl and grab Jodie, proclaiming that she belonged to him and only to him. He'd never experienced such a surge of jealousy and possessiveness. What was wrong with him anyway? He'd never dated Jodie, so why should a few shared kisses last week make him feel so possessive of her, of all people? He wasn't jealous of women he dated.

Dean glanced back at the couple, who appeared to be enjoying each other's company. He frowned. Damn it, he didn't want her seeing other men. When he rejoined Susan, she thanked him and said, "What a striking couple you stopped and talked to. They look perfect for each other. Are they married?"

"No. She's my secretary."

"I see. Jodie, isn't it?"

"You've got a great memory. Yes, that's Jodie Cameron."

"I remember when you hired her. After a few months you couldn't say enough good things about her."

"Well, she's taking another position in the company in a week or so and I'm going to need another secretary. Don't suppose you'd be interested?"

Susan laughed. "I'm afraid not. I'm more comfortable doing private care work."

"How do you like your present assignment?"

"I like it. In fact, the son of the man I'm caring for has shown an interest in me."

"That's not surprising. The question is, are you encouraging him?"

"I believe I am," she admitted with a smile. "He's a single parent with two children. I have no idea where their mother is. She's never mentioned. The girls and I get along famously. They were upset that I was going out tonight with someone other than their dad."

"A ready-made family. Is that what you want?"

Tears filled her eyes. "That's the only way I'll have children. I think this could turn into something serious." She blinked away the tears. "I don't think he was particularly enamored of my seeing you either."

"It will do him good. We won't tell him that you're the sister I never had—"

"And the brother I never had," she finished.

He touched her cheek. "You know I'll always be there for you. Would you like me to meet him and make intimidating noises about his treating you right or he'll answer to me?"

Susan laughed out loud and gave him a hug. "I really don't think that will be necessary, but I'll keep it in mind."

Jodie watched the attractive woman with Dean hug him and turned away. The lights flickered, signaling that it was time to return for the next act. Once seated, Jodie did her best not to watch for Dean.

She also decided that she didn't need to see him with other women either. Next time she'd make certain not to go anywhere where she might run into him.

Ten

There was another bouquet of flowers on her desk when Jodie arrived at work on Monday. This time she didn't bother to thank him since the flowers were for the office. However, she did comment on how beautiful they were.

He looked up from his work. "Did you enjoy the musical?" he asked.

"Very much. I haven't seen a stage production in much too long a time. How about you?"

He shrugged. "It was okay, I guess. If you like that sort of thing. I've never been able to figure out why, when they become romantic, they sing to each other instead of kissing."

She smiled. "So why did you go?"

"Susan mentioned wanting to see it."

"She seems very nice."

He leaned back in his chair and studied her. "I spoke to

Frank earlier. He said he could put you to work in three weeks if that's okay with you."

She nodded. "That's fine with me. I'll call the employment agency and find someone to replace me."

He cleared his throat. "Jodie, there's no one who can replace you. I'd like to keep you here, but I know I'm being selfish. You deserve a chance to put your education to good use and I don't want to hold you back."

She blinked back the tears that suddenly appeared. "Thank you for giving me the chance. I promise I'll find someone who is every bit as good as I am. Within a week you won't notice there's been a change."

He shook his head. "That will never happen." He picked up a letter lying on his desk, a clear dismissal of her, which was just as well.

Jodie returned to her desk. She was going to miss seeing him every day, but it was better this way. The infatuation she seemed to have acquired while on Maui would die a natural death once she wasn't around him so often.

The days went by and Jodie slowly settled into a routine of doing her work and interviewing prospective employees.

Rachel seemed to be back in Dean's life. She called him every day or so, and Jodie happened to hear him making plans with her for a weekend next month.

Jodie spent her evenings working on school projects and studying for finals. She'd be glad when she moved to her new position. Being around the old Dean who never laughed and rarely smiled made her heart ache for him. He'd returned to his hard-crusted shell, and it was as though the man she'd gotten to know in Hawaii no longer existed.

She had hoped that, for his sake, he would look around him and enjoy his life more fully. It was his choice, of course, to revert back to the all-business-all-the-time man he'd been.

Why should she care?

She didn't want to think about the answer.

Sunday turned out to be almost springlike, which wasn't surprising considering that spring would be there in another few weeks. Jodie decided to go jogging. She hadn't been out much these past several weeks. She drove to one of the nearby parks, parked, stretched and started out in a slow jog.

She recognized some of the other joggers because they'd been coming there for years. The sunshine and blue sky must have encouraged them to get out, just as it had her.

Afterward, she stopped into a deli and bought a large sandwich and headed home.

She decided to shower before eating. She'd barely gotten wet when she heard the doorbell. Since Lynette always called first, she didn't have a clue who could be there.

Jodie hurriedly stepped out of the shower and grabbed a bath towel, then hurried to the door.

"Who is it?"

"Dean."

"Dean?" She panicked. "Hold on a sec." She rushed into the bedroom and found a robe to put on and hurried back to open the door. "I'm sorry to keep you waiting. I was in the shower when I heard the bell. Please. Come in."

He walked in and said, "I hope you don't mind my stopping by without calling first."

"I'll forgive you this once," she replied with a smile, "especially since I just got home and you wouldn't have reached me anyway. Would you like some coffee while I get dressed?"

He shook his head. "Had too much already, but thanks."

She waved at the grouping of sofa and chairs and said, "Have a seat. I'll be right back."

Jodie hurried into her bedroom and closed the door. What was he doing there? And why was she letting his presence rattle her so? She didn't have any answers. She dug out an old pair of jeans and a faded sweatshirt, stuck her feet in house slippers and went back to the living room.

He stood as soon as he saw her. "You look comfortably casual," he said with a lopsided grin.

"I am." She stood there for a moment, waiting, and when he didn't say anything, she said, "Let's sit down. I'm sure you have a reason for coming by."

He settled back on the sofa while she sat on the edge of one of her chairs.

"I've been thinking."

That sounded a little ominous. "About what?"

"Us."

She frowned. "There isn't an us."

"Actually there is, whether we do anything about it or not. We became friends while we were in Maui. I'd like to give the relationship a chance and see where it takes us."

Oh, dear. His reason for being there was worse than she'd thought.

After a moment she replied, "I don't think so."

"Why not?"

She rolled her eyes. "Oh, let me count the ways. One, I

work for you, which we've already discussed. Nothing has changed in that regard. Two, I'm not into flings. Besides, you're still involved with Rachel and I don't want to get in the middle of that."

He looked uncomfortable. "We've agreed that the relationship isn't working for either of us. I won't be seeing her anymore."

"I can't imagine her breaking up with you unless she found out you're seeing someone else, and I don't believe that's the case. I always know when you're seeing someone. You send them flowers, you get them tickets..." Her voice trailed off and she stared at him in dismay. "You sent *me* flowers."

"So I did."

She stared at him, feeling confused. "Well...but...you didn't mean them in that way," she said.

"I meant them exactly that way," he murmured.

"Oh, my gosh."

"You didn't guess?"

"Are you kidding? Of course I didn't think that's what they meant." She couldn't believe she was having this conversation with Dean.

He leaned forward, resting his elbows on his knees. "The thing is, Jodie, I'd like to start seeing you socially. I discovered that I enjoy your company. When I'm with you, I see everything through your eyes and I like the new perspective." He kept his gaze focused on her. "Teach me how to relax and enjoy life a little more, like we did in Hawaii."

"You're asking me to tutor you?" she asked, frowning slightly.

"If you want to call it that."

"For how long?"

"I don't understand the question."

"Well, let me put it this way. How long do you generally date one person before moving on?"

"What kind of question is that? I have no idea."

"Well, I do. It averages about two to two and a half months. How long do you expect to see me?"

He threw up his hands. "This isn't the conversation I thought I'd be having."

She crossed her arms. "Really? Did you think I'd rush into your arms when you decided you want to spend time with me away from the office?"

"If I did, that idea got blown out of the water."

"Dean?"

"What?"

"What's this all about?"

He leaned back on the sofa, rested his head against the back and sighed.

"I miss you more than I could have dreamed I would. We were good together. We had fun together. Or I did, at least. What's wrong with extending that?"

"We could try it, I suppose," she said thoughtfully.

"Your enthusiasm is underwhelming."

"I could be your transition person until you find someone else."

He closed his eyes. "Transition person," he repeated without inflection.

"Maybe we could do that. Still nothing serious."

He straightened. "So you'll do it?"

"Within reason. I'm busy with school, as you know, but maybe once a week or so we could spend some time together." She brightened. "We could meet for coffee after my classes. Have dinner on weekends. Is that what you want?"

"Never mind what I want. I'll take what I can get."

"All right then." She stood up. "I brought home a sandwich from the deli. I'm willing to share it if you're hungry."

"As a matter of fact, my appetite is definitely returning." He stood, putting him a step or two away from her. "Shall we seal our agreement with a kiss?"

She looked wary. "We were talking about food."

"Of course. Why don't I take you out for lunch? It's a beautiful day for this early in the year. We might take a drive after we eat." He lifted her chin with his forefinger. "Just know that food isn't the only cause of my hunger," he said and kissed her.

Not fair, not fair at all. He knew how his kisses affected her. There had been too many occasions when he'd felt her reaction.

This kiss was no exception, even though she stiffened at first, determined not to be swayed. It was his gentleness that destroyed her resolve, because she'd never considered him a gentle person until they'd spent the week together.

Now all the emotions he evoked within her poured out and she knew they were more powerful than her determination not to succumb.

The problem was that all her valid reasons still stood.

The problem was that she found him too compelling to resist spending a little more time with him.

The problem was that she was going to be hurt badly when the relationship ended. All she could do at this point was deal with the pain at that time.

Eleven

The following Wednesday Jodie reached for her purse as she prepared to leave the office when Dean called to her. She went into his office.

Without looking up from the schematic drawing covering most of his desk he asked, "What time are your classes over tonight?"

His question was the first personal remark he'd made to her since he'd left her on Sunday. Jodie had begun to wonder if she'd dreamed that her boss had come over to plead his case for seeing her socially or whether it was some fantasy she'd concocted to relieve an otherwise boring weekend.

"Nine."

"Tell me where to meet you," he said, marking something on the drawing.

"Uh, well, there's a coffeehouse a couple of blocks from—"

"No. I'll pick you up at school. Where are your classes being held?" When she didn't answer, he straightened away from the desk and looked at her. He was still in his boss mode, snapping out orders.

After a moment she gave him the address, turned around and walked out.

Dean watched her leave with a frown. He hadn't handled that right. He wasn't sure what he'd done wrong, but he could tell from the stiffness in her shoulders as she walked away that she wasn't pleased with him.

He rolled his head, trying to loosen the muscles in his neck and shoulders. Women were a mystery he'd never been able to solve. Until now he'd never particularly cared.

Ever since they had returned from Hawaii he'd had a tough time concentrating whenever she was around. He'd been disgusted at himself for not being able to clamp down on his emotions. All she had to do was walk into the room and he immediately wanted to make love to her. He'd been forced to stay behind his desk so that she didn't see his physical response to her.

So he didn't look at her any more than was absolutely necessary.

Not that his idea was much help, since he had a similar reaction whenever he heard her voice.

She was driving him crazy.

The problem was that it was too late to do anything about it. When they'd first returned from Hawaii and she'd refused to have lunch with him, he'd tried to force himself to forget about his attraction to her. He'd only been kidding himself.

Now that he'd finally gotten her to agree to see him, he'd managed to offend her in some way.

Great going, Logan.

When Jodie walked out of the classroom that evening, she saw Dean leaning against the opposite wall, his arms crossed. She did a double take. He looked too much like the man she'd gotten to know in Hawaii, not the man she worked for.

She started toward him at the same time he straightened.

"Hi," she said.

He smiled at her. "Hi, yourself. Ready for some coffee?"

"Sure."

"The weather is nasty. Would you like to go to my place?"

She lifted her brow. "For coffee?"

He looked innocent. "Of course."

"All right."

When they reached the doors of the building, she could see that rain and touches of sleet poured from the sky. He opened an umbrella she hadn't noticed and, pulling her close to his side, hurried her to the car.

"Wow," she said, a little breathless, once they were inside the car.

"Where's your car?"

"At home. I took the bus."

"Good thinking."

She watched the windshield wipers ferociously battle the rain and sleet. "I decided before all of this hit."

"You knew I'd get you home."

"There is that."

She'd never been to his home, although she knew where it was: in one of the high-rise buildings overlooking Lake Michigan. He entered the underground parking area and parked by the elevators in a space with his name and the word *Reserved*.

The elevator silently whisked them to his floor, and by the time he opened the door to his home, all Jodie could think was that she was way out of her league.

He helped her off with her coat and said, "Have a seat. I'll go make coffee."

Jodie wandered over to the windows and looked out at the shimmering lights muted by the rain. If ever she'd needed a reality check, his place did that for her. She remembered how she'd gone on and on about the luxury condo while they were in Hawaii. His home was more luxurious.

She closed her eyes. She would be an idiot to think that he could have more than a passing interest in her.

"Here you go," he said from behind her. Jodie turned and watched him put a tray on the coffee table in front of the long sectional furniture arranged to take in the view.

"What am I doing here?" she asked, walking toward him.

He straightened and looked at her. "Having coffee?"

She gave her head a quick shake. "That isn't what I mean," she replied and sat down on the edge of the sofa. "This isn't going to work."

He sat a couple of feet away from her. "I noticed you seemed to be upset with me when you left the office."

She reached for the coffee. "That was something different," she replied and sipped on the drink. She realized she was shaking, as much from nerves as from the weather. She held the cup with both hands, warming them.

"So what happened to cause you to change your mind in three days?"

She didn't answer him. Instead she continued to carefully drink her coffee.

When she didn't answer, he asked briskly, "Am I supposed to guess?" Now he sounded like the man she worked for.

Jodie set her coffee cup back on the tray and turned to him. The problem was that he didn't look like her boss at the moment. With his hair mussed and in his cable-knit sweater, he reminded her of the man she'd spent time with in Hawaii.

She bit her lip. "I know I said that I'd start seeing you, but the truth is that we come from two different worlds and nothing is going to change that. I live a simple life and have simple tastes. I'm not at all your type."

"What exactly is my type?" he asked, his jaw stiff.

She waved her hand vaguely at the room. "Women who are used to all this luxury, who expect it, women who go to operas and symphonies and are photographed whenever they attend some function. That's not me."

He studied her, looking quizzical. "I don't recall inviting you to an opera or the symphony."

"You know what I mean," she snapped.

"I wish to hell I did. What is going on in that busy brain of yours?"

"I've come to my senses. I can't do this. I'm sorry." She stood. "I need to get home. I'll call a cab."

"Not on your life. You're not going to run away from this discussion."

"Please date someone else instead of me. The woman

you took to the musical, for instance. Or…I don't care. Just someone else."

"I believe your prejudices are showing."

"What are you talking about?"

"You can't go out with me because I attend various functions around town? Or are we back to the fact that you work for me?"

"Actually I do dislike you giving me orders when it's not job-related."

"Care to give me an example?"

"This afternoon. You took charge once I agreed to see you tonight. Told me what you were going to do and where we'd meet."

"You could have said no."

"I could have, yes. I should have."

"I get the sense that we're talking in circles without getting to the crux of what's bothering you."

"All right. Then here it is. Hawaii was wonderful. I couldn't have imagined a more perfect vacation. But the vacation is over. Yes, there's a definite attraction between us. You want to encourage it. I want to ignore it, which is why I'm relieved to be moving into another department next week. Let's forget about Hawaii and get on with our lives."

"I believe we tried that, but I, for one, have found it impossible after getting to know you better."

She closed her eyes. "I can't do this," she said quietly.

The silent room seemed weighted with emotion.

He studied his coffee in silence. When he looked up, his face revealed nothing of what he was thinking or feeling. "I'll drive you home," he said quietly.

Jodie waited until she was alone in her apartment before she broke down and cried.

Jodie moved into the engineering department the next week. Dean had hired one of the women Jodie recommended. Her name was Candace Rudin and she appeared to be quite competent. Jodie had expected to spend several days with her, but Candace had quickly grasped the routine, the filing system and the way Dean liked to work.

Once in Engineering, Jodie was determined to learn everything she could as quickly as possible. Several weeks went by, and Frank praised her repeatedly, patiently answering her questions when she couldn't figure something out.

She had been there two months when Frank dropped an envelope on her desk one morning. She looked up. "It isn't payday, is it?"

He shook his head. "No. It's time you learned firsthand about installing our equipment. That's your plane ticket."

A plane trip. Great. "I don't suppose we could do this somewhere that we could drive to, by any chance?"

"Sorry. Besides, I won't be going. Logan said that since you'd already been to this particular office, it made sense for you to see the next step. He'll be going with you to show you the ropes."

There was only one office she'd visited and it was in Honolulu. She peeked into the envelope and saw the ticket, confirming her suspicions. She looked at Frank. "I haven't finished what I'm working on," she pointed out.

"Doesn't matter since there's no rush on that one. Besides, you'll only be in Hawaii a few days—four at the most."

"Oh." She forced herself to smile. "Well. That's good.

I mean, I'll enjoy being part of the installation process. I'm just surprised that Dean would be the one to do it."

Frank shrugged. "I'll admit he hasn't done an installation in a long while. Probably wants to keep his hand in. Don't worry, though. You already know how he can be and won't be caught off guard when he starts snapping at you for not working fast enough. Just ignore his moods."

"I'll do my best."

Twelve

Dean greeted her briskly when she arrived at the airport the next morning. She had a moment of déjà vu when she saw him, except that today he wore a business suit.

She had also dressed for a business trip, in a light-colored suit and matching heels.

"Good morning," she said, walking up to him.

He turned around. "It's nice to see you again," he replied politely. "Have you checked your bag?"

She nodded.

"Have you had breakfast? If you haven't, there's a restaurant along the concourse where we could get something."

"Fine."

He strode along the corridor, a man on the move, and Jodie had to skip a time or two in order to keep up with him.

Once they found the restaurant, sat down and ordered,

Jodie caught her breath. Her shortness of breath was in no way connected to seeing Dean again. He looked like a modern-day pirate in his dark suit. All he needed was a knife between his teeth.

"How is Candace working out?" she asked during their meal.

"She's all right."

She couldn't think of anything more to say to him. She wanted to ask him why he'd decided to do the installation himself rather than send someone else.

But she didn't.

She wanted to ask him why he'd decided to have her accompany him, given their situation.

But she didn't.

Was it because he wanted to prove to her that he'd moved on after she'd turned him down? Perhaps. No doubt he was already involved with someone else by now.

Which was just as well. She wished that she'd been seeing someone these past few weeks, someone who would have helped her forget about her attraction to him. This trip would be much easier for her if that were the case.

"How do you like working for Frank?" he asked after several minutes of silence.

"He's great. I'm fascinated by all that we're doing."

"You'll be able to see how we implement the work your department does in Furukawa's offices." He paused for a moment. "I thought you might enjoy seeing the islands again."

"Are we going to stay in the condo?"

"No. Candace made reservations for us to stay in one of the hotels in Honolulu."

"Oh."

"Are you ready to go to our gate?"

She nodded.

Once on the concourse, he continued his fast pace until Jodie finally said, "Dean, I can't keep up with you in these heels. Would you please slow down?"

He immediately stopped and waited for her to catch up with him. "Sorry. My mind was on other things."

They continued walking for what seemed forever to Jodie before they reached their gate.

They found seats although the departure lounge was rapidly filling up with passengers waiting to board.

Dean spotted their plane, which they could see through the glass wall. "Looks like they're finishing loading luggage and food." He glanced at his watch. "We should be boarding shortly." When she didn't comment, he asked, "Do you have something to read on the plane?"

"In my purse."

Dean was not usually so talkative. Making idle chitchat wasn't part of his personality.

"Dean?"

"Yes?"

"Look, I know this is awkward for both of us. I appreciate your taking me on this assignment. I know you didn't have to be the one to go."

"Actually I felt that Furukawa needed to know that his security was important to me. We've stayed in touch these past few weeks ironing out the contract and determining exactly what should be installed. The fact that I'll be installing the systems is personally important."

"Will we start this afternoon?"

"Not with the actual work, no. However, we'll go to his office, pay our respects and invite him to dinner if he doesn't have other plans. We'll get started on the installation first thing tomorrow morning. It won't take more than a couple of days if everything goes according to plan."

The flight attendant announced that it was time to board and they stood. Jodie had noticed that once again they were flying first-class.

As soon as she'd found out she'd be making this trip, she'd visited her doctor and asked for something to help her deal with her anxiety about flying. He'd given her a prescription for a mild anti-anxiety drug and told her to take it a half hour before flying. She'd taken it with breakfast and was already feeling calmer.

Dean escorted her to their seats. "Would you prefer to sit on the aisle?" he asked.

"Yes, please."

She reached for the airline magazine in the pocket in front of her and began to read.

"Are you okay about flying?" he asked.

"I think so. Yes."

She could tell that he didn't believe her. It didn't matter. She needed to get used to flying now that she was a representative of the company.

By the time they took off, she was getting sleepy. She'd had a restless night, dreading spending time with Dean again. Lack of sleep, together with the prescription drug, had her yawning by the time they leveled off.

Jodie leaned her seat back and went to sleep.

Dean took the opportunity to study her—the way her mouth was shaped, her thick lashes, the slight tilt of her nose. He'd missed seeing her each day. When he found himself going to her department in hopes of seeing her, he knew he had it bad.

His dreams were filled with her...talking with her, making love to her, riding in the car with her. He was never alone in his dreams now, which was tough when he woke up each morning to discover he *was* alone and none of it was real.

Dean couldn't figure out what was going on with him. Was it because he hadn't been with a woman since the first trip to Hawaii? He hadn't been interested enough in Rachel to respond to her sexual overtures, which was the major reason she knew their relationship had come to an end.

They'd spent a weekend together, a last-ditch effort on her part to prove something to him—or herself. Despite all her attempts at seducing him—provocative night wear, a full-body massage—nothing had worked.

He figured he'd been too tired that weekend. His dreams of Jodie were more satisfying than the reality of being with Rachel.

This trip was to prove something to himself—to prove that his fantasies of Jodie were absurd. Candace had booked a suite so that each of them had a bedroom. They wouldn't be spending much time there.

This was strictly a business trip.

He was not lusting after her.

What he needed to do was find someone nice to date— someone with blond hair and blue eyes, someone who looked trim and fit, someone who was fun to talk to, to be with, someone who could make him laugh.

Someone like Jodie.

* * *

Dean had awakened her as they'd approached Los Angeles. There had been little time for them to find their gate for the next leg of the journey and neither one of them had said very much.

Once they'd been back on the plane, Jodie had read a little but fallen asleep within the first hour. Consequently she felt rested and ready to go to work when they landed in Honolulu.

They checked in to their hotel and she discovered that they had a gorgeous view from the balcony off the main room. Their bedrooms were located on opposite sides of this room.

They met Steve Furukawa at his office and showed him the schematics for the job. Dean answered his questions at length, and when Steve was fully satisfied, they set up a time to begin the next morning.

Steve agreed to have dinner with them, but Jodie begged off. Once Dean left their hotel room, she changed into more casual clothes and took a long, contemplative walk along the beach.

She had to face a difficult fact: she was in love with Dean Logan. She wasn't certain when it had happened, but there was no doubt about it. Being with him again had taught her that she'd been kidding herself when she'd decided she was over her infatuation with him. Of course, she had no intention of acting on her desire for him. She wasn't that stupid or self-destructive.

She wondered if there was a group somewhere she could attend to learn how to get over him. If so, she would definitely join.

By the time she returned to the hotel, the exercise had worked its charm. She was pleasantly tired, tired enough—she hoped—to be able to sleep, since tomorrow would be a long day.

When Jodie opened the door to the suite, she was surprised to see that Dean was there. He was on the balcony, sitting on one chair, his feet propped on another, sipping a drink.

"How was dinner?" she asked, walking over to him.

He moved his feet and motioned for her to sit down. "The food was good and I enjoyed getting to know Steve a little better. He gave me a brief family history. He told me how his family came to Hawaii from Japan many years ago. He's an interesting man."

She sat down and propped her bare feet on the railing. "There's something about this place that seems almost magical. The scent of flowers, the soft breeze. It's easy to forget there's another world out there."

"I watched you walk along the edge of the water. I was relieved to spot you. I was worried when I discovered you weren't here when I got back."

"I had no idea you would return so soon."

"Steve wanted to get home to his family. I enjoyed listening to his stories about his sons and daughters. He's very proud of them."

"You constantly surprise me," she replied.

"In what way?"

"Somehow I can't picture you listening to stories about children."

"Why not?"

She shrugged. "I can't see you as a family man." When he didn't reply, she added, "I didn't mean to offend you."

"I'm not offended. I never thought of myself in that light, so I suppose you're right."

They stayed on the balcony enjoying the night air for a while. Then Dean said, "I'm going to bed. See you in the morning." He stood and stretched, and Jodie straightened and got up, as well.

Once inside, Dean switched off the lamp, leaving the room bathed in moonlight.

"Thank you for giving me this opportunity, Dean."

"No problem. I seem to get some masochistic pleasure whenever I'm around you."

"What do you mean?"

"Don't pretend you don't know, Jodie. I want to make love to you so badly I constantly ache with it. And that's when you're not around."

She hoped the darkness hid her flushed face and the trembling of her body. "I didn't know," she said faintly.

"Do you want a demonstration?" he asked. He walked over to her and drew her into his arms. His kiss was gentle at first. If he'd grabbed her, she could have easily pushed away from him. It was his gentleness that undid her.

The kiss quickly heated up and Jodie felt him pressed against her, his arousal very evident.

Alarms went off in her head...or were they bells? She couldn't tell and at the moment did not care. She slipped her arms around his neck and kissed him back with all the pent-up love and passion she had for him.

Dean was the one who broke away. "I'm sorry. That was inexcusable." He turned and strode toward his bedroom. "Good night."

Good night?

He had kissed the living daylights out of her and all he could say was good night?

Every nerve in her body tingled with anticipation. She took deep, steadying breaths, shaking so hard she could barely stand there. How dare he start something he didn't intend to finish.

She should be grateful.

She should be thankful for his restraint.

She turned away and started to her bedroom and then wheeled around and marched across the room to his closed door. Without knocking, she shoved the door open. She didn't see him but she knew he was there.

"That was a rotten trick, Dean Logan! How dare you start something and then walk away as though nothing had happened!"

She slammed the door and marched back to her room, slamming that door for good measure.

The nerve of the man. Just because she refused to date him. Just because she knew that making love to him would be the worst possible thing she could do to herself didn't mean that she could just walk away after the passionate kiss they'd just shared.

So maybe she did want a fling after all! That was all that Dean would ever have with her.

She went into the bathroom and took off her clothes. She'd take a shower until she was calmer.

She turned on the shower and, without waiting for it to warm up, stepped inside, needing the shock of cold water on her heated body. She stood with the spray hitting her face, forcing herself to let go of her frustration and get a hold on her emotions.

Which was why she didn't hear Dean enter the room until the shower door opened behind her and Dean stepped inside wearing nothing but a smile.

Thirteen

Too bad he didn't have a camera to catch the expression on Jodie's face when she saw him.

"You're right, as usual," he said smoothly. "A gentleman should never, ever start something he doesn't intend to finish." He took the washcloth out of her nerveless fingers and said, "Turn around and I'll scrub your back for you."

She looked down at him and blinked. If she thought he hadn't been affected by that kiss—which he felt certain was quite apparent at the time—she could have no doubt about his condition now.

"Dean?" Her voice sounded strangled as he gently turned her away from him. He traced her spine with his finger from the nape of her neck down to her luscious derriere.

"Yes?"

"What are you doing?"

"Isn't it obvious? Scrubbing your back." He took his time sliding the cloth up and down her spine, pausing at her hips to place his hands on either side.

"That isn't what I—" She stopped and dropped her chin to her chest.

"I never want to leave a woman angry at me for not finishing what I started."

She slowly turned and looked at him.

He smiled at her.

"We're really going to do this, aren't we?" she whispered, her breath catching.

He dropped the cloth and cupped his hands around her face. She really was adorable. "Yes, we really are," he replied…and touched her lips with his tongue. Her mouth was lush and smooth to his touch. He settled his mouth over hers, fighting to control his passion until she was as ready as he was.

If he could.

She placed her hands tentatively on his chest and leaned closer, her mouth opening to him like a rosebud blossoming.

He dropped his hands and stepped back, breathing hard. "I think our shower is over, don't you?"

She looked at him and nodded. Dean reached around her and turned off the water. He led her out of the shower, picked up a towel and quickly dried her off. He swiped the towel over himself, dropped it and picked her up.

She leaned her head against his shoulder, closed her eyes and sighed.

He placed her on his bed, slid the covers from beneath her and yanked them off the bed before he lay down beside her.

"I brought protection," he whispered and nodded toward the bedside table. Her eyes widened at the number he'd brought with him. He grinned. "Just in case," he said.

He kissed her again while he explored the curves and hollows of her body with his hands. He wanted to memorize every inch of her. She shifted and reached for him.

Dean quickly caught her hand. "No fair. This is for you, not me." He trailed kisses along her jaw, down her neck, and touched her nipple with his tongue.

She groaned and he glanced up to see her face. Her eyes were closed and her face was flushed, but it was the soft smile of pleasure that encouraged him. He pulled her gently into his mouth while he played with the other tip, then eventually shifted his mouth to her other one, his hand gliding over her stomach and abdomen until it rested in her nest of blond curls.

Jodie pushed against his hand in invitation and he moved downward, feeling her moist heat. Dean shifted and knelt between her legs. She reached for him, and he took her hands in his before he lowered his head and kissed her curls.

She jumped as though she'd been electrocuted, and he murmured soothing words to her while he explored. She quickly climaxed, crying out, and Dean moved over her, sliding deep inside.

Jodie hugged him to her and fell into the slow rhythm that was costing him a great deal. His body hummed with urgency and he finally gave up all pretense of control. They moved together, uttering soft sounds and breathing heavily.

When she tightened around him in a spasmodic rhythm,

he quickly climaxed with her and, in one final lunge, buried himself deeply inside.

He collapsed on his elbows, careful not to put much weight on her, before he rolled onto the pillow next to hers.

They lay there on the bed without speaking, catching their breaths.

Finally Jodie murmured a soft, "Wow."

He turned his head and gazed at her. "At the very least," he replied.

She turned onto her side and stared at him, which made him a little nervous.

"What are you thinking?" he finally asked as the silence went on.

"My brain shut off much earlier this evening," she replied.

He got up and went into the bathroom, wondering if she was already regretting their intimacy.

Jodie watched the bathroom door close behind Dean, forcing herself to face what had happened just now, what she had triggered by her earlier remarks.

If she'd given the matter much thought, she would have known that Dean would be wonderful in bed. When it came right down to it, she realized now, she'd expected sex. What she'd experienced with him was making love.

A little later he opened the door and peered out. "Want to try that shower again?"

She smiled. "All right."

Despite the fact that he'd seen all there was, she felt shy. She slipped her robe around her.

When she reached him, he immediately removed the robe before cupping her breasts in his hands. He kissed each one and looked at her quizzically. "This isn't what I expected."

"What is that?"

"I want you just as badly now as I did before."

She glanced down at him. "So I see."

He moved reluctantly away and turned on the shower. "However, I don't want you to think I'm some kind of animal." He held out his hand and guided her into the shower.

She took the washcloth and carefully soaped him, enjoying his reaction as she slid her hand along his hardened length. Eventually she soaped his back, as well, discovering the view was equally enticing on that side.

When he rinsed off, he quickly covered her with suds and as quickly rinsed her off before he slid his arms beneath her hips and lifted her, guiding her legs around his waist.

The position left her open to him, and he slipped inside her, leaning her back against the wall.

She closed her eyes, her arms around his neck, and gave herself up to the experience.

"Jodie?"

"Hmm?"

"We need to get up. It's almost six."

Her eyelids flew open. "Already? How did that happen? I feel as though I just fell asleep."

"Probably because you did. I'm afraid I kept you awake most of the night." He rolled out of bed and walked to the door. "If we hurry, we can get something to eat before we go to work."

Jodie wasted no time getting out of bed once he closed the door behind him. She quickly dressed, dismayed that her hair stood out everywhere. That's what she got for going to bed with wet hair. She shook her head at herself. Her hair was the last thing she'd been thinking of last night.

She did what she could with it, forcing it back into a tidy bun, and prayed that her hair would not give her trouble today, of all days.

Dean was waiting in the sitting area when she walked out of the bedroom. He wore a sports jacket and slacks, his shirt collar open.

They decided to eat at the coffee shop in the hotel. Once they'd ordered, Jodie sipped on her coffee and stared out the window. When she glanced at Dean, he was watching her intently, making her feel more self-conscious than she had before.

Finally she asked, "What are you thinking?"

"I'm concerned that you're already regretting what happened last night."

"It's too late for regrets," she finally replied.

"But you're sorry that it happened."

"It complicates matters."

"In what way?"

She raised her eyebrows. "You know better than I do that this relationship isn't going anywhere."

"I don't know that at all." He sipped his coffee. "Where do you want it to go?"

He'd given her the perfect opening to tell him that she wanted marriage, a home, family and a husband who loved their life. Dean Logan would not want to be that man.

When she didn't answer, he said, "I would never hurt you, you know. What's wrong with us spending our leisure time together? We're both consenting adults. Neither of us has any obligations to someone else."

Thankfully their breakfasts arrived, interrupting the conversation. While they ate, Jodie asked him about the job they'd be doing and what they would do first.

By the time they finished eating, caught a cab and arrived at Steve's office, each of them was concentrating on getting the job done as quickly as possible.

Jodie couldn't help but notice how well they worked together, speaking to each other in a shorthand that they'd developed when she was his secretary. By the end of the day Dean appeared to be pleased with their progress.

"If tomorrow goes as well as today has gone, we'll be ready to fly back to the States day after tomorrow."

"Sounds good," she said. The day had taken its toll on her energy, particularly since she had not gotten much sleep last night. They took a cab back to the hotel. Once there, Jodie said, "I think I'll order in tonight and go to bed as soon as I eat. I'm beat."

"I really worked you today. You did a fine job, by the way."

She clasped her hands in front of her. "If you'll excuse me, I'd like to take a bath before I eat."

He frowned. "Of course. Did I overwork you today?"

"Not really. I guess I used a lot of nervous energy trying to learn so much so quickly."

"You should have said something."

She smiled. "I am."

"I mean sooner."

"I'm fine, Dean. Just very tired."

"I don't feel like eating out either. Tell me what you want to eat and I'll order for us while you take your bath."

She didn't care. She wasn't hungry. She just wanted to have some time alone. "A chef's salad."

When he walked to the phone, she went to her room and closed the door, leaning against it and looking at her bed with longing. It had taken all of her concentration to stay focused on Dean's instructions today instead of thinking about what had happened last night.

She was well and truly hooked on him. The problem was that he had no intention of reeling her in. If she did continue to see him once they returned home, how long would it be before he tossed her back into the water?

Once in the tub, she was soothed by the warm water. She rested her head against the tub and closed her eyes.

Dean glanced at his watch when their meal was delivered. He hadn't heard anything from Jodie in more than half an hour. He tapped on her door. "Jodie? Your salad is here. Are you ready to eat?"

There was no response.

He opened the door and peered inside. The only light was in the bathroom. "Jodie?" He felt a twinge of alarm.

Dean stepped inside and went to the door of her bathroom. When he looked inside, he found her asleep in the tub. A feeling of tenderness washed over him, although he had no idea what the emotion was since he'd rarely felt it.

"Jodie," he said in a firm voice.

Her eyes flew open and she scrambled to sit up.

"Sorry to come in on you but I wanted you to know supper is here." He turned and walked out of the room.

Jodie stared at his retreating back in dismay. He sounded irritable. And then she chuckled. Dean usually sounded irritable, so what was different?

The difference had occurred in his lovemaking last

night, in his murmured endearments, in his eagerness to make love to her as the night passed.

She had definitely provoked him the evening before, therefore she had no one but herself to blame.

Jodie quickly dressed in pajamas and a robe and went into the other room. She found Dean staring out the window, his hands in his pockets. She could see his reflection and he looked grim.

"I'm so sorry for taking so long. As you saw, I fell asleep in the tub."

He turned and walked over to the table that held their food. "I owe you an apology for working you so hard today. I'm used to pushing myself until I get the job done."

"I didn't mind." She sat down at the table. "You should have gone ahead and eaten. Your food must be cold by now."

"Doesn't matter."

They ate in strained silence. Once they were finished, Dean rolled the table into the hall and returned to the sitting room. "I'd like to discuss something with you, if you don't mind."

Her nap had done wonders for her. "Of course," she said and sat on the sofa.

He pulled a chair closer so that he was facing her. "I need to apologize for last night. I had no business coming into your room and getting into the shower with you. Could I plead temporary insanity?"

So that was what had him looking so grim. She smiled. "After what I said to you, how could any red-blooded male have ignored the challenge?"

His shoulders relaxed and he smiled ruefully. "Well, there is that. However, my conscience has gotten the better of me and I need to confess. I brought you along on this trip hoping that something might happen between us."

"I suspected that. You're very aggressive when you set a goal for yourself, and I must have been on your list. Just remember that I was a willing participant last night."

"But you don't like flings."

"That's right. And I don't think we should continue to see each other once we're home. It would be too awkward for both of us. I admire and respect you—" *and love the living daylights out of you* "—but I can't be what you want."

"Exactly what is it I want?"

"A short-term companion who's there when you have time to see her, who can accept what you want without strings attached. Someone like Rachel."

"I thought I made it clear I'm not seeing Rachel—or anyone else, for that matter," he said, sounding frustrated. Dean got up and started pacing. "You make me sound very shallow."

"I don't mean to. Your commitment to the company is total. You have no room for anything but a casual relationship with someone."

"And you're not the casual type, I take it."

"Unfortunately no. However, you never seem to have trouble finding others who will accept the kind of relationship you want."

He stopped pacing and looked at her. "What do you want from me? Am I supposed to declare that my intentions are honorable? That I want to get married and move to the suburbs, have a family and settle into domestic bliss?"

She gazed at him for a long time before she finally said, "I would never suggest such a thing."

"Good. Because I'm definitely not that kind of guy."

"I know," she murmured.

"So last night was an aberration and won't happen again."

"Yes."

He crossed his arms over his chest. "Fine. I can live with that. Is this where I ask if it was as good for you as it was for me?"

She smiled. "It was sensational."

He suddenly sat down again. "Yeah, it was," he said, sounding a little bewildered.

They sat in silence for several minutes before he said, "We'd better get some sleep. Tomorrow's going to be another long day."

Jodie stood and said, "Good night, Dean," and went to her bedroom.

He sat there for a long time, staring blankly out the window. With sudden decision, he left the suite, went downstairs and walked out onto the beach.

He walked the beach until dawn.

Fourteen

Six weeks later

"Mr. Logan, Mr. Greenfeld is here to see you."

Candace Rudin had taken to her job with alarming ease. She was punctual, efficient, unobtrusive. In all, a well-trained secretary.

Damn, he missed Jodie more and more as each day passed...as a secretary, of course.

"Have Betty send him back, please."

She nodded briskly and went back to her desk.

Candace had quickly learned that he disliked the intercom and cheerfully came to his office door to give him messages.

Candace was a very nice woman. A little formal, perhaps; she'd told him she wasn't comfortable calling him by his first name. She lived alone except for two cats since her husband died two years ago. Her three children were grown. She didn't mind overtime and put up with his moods.

What more could he want?

While he waited for Greenfeld, Dean stood and walked over to one of his windows.

He hadn't seen Jodie since they'd returned from Hawaii. He'd stopped finding excuses to go to her department to see her. She'd made her position quite clear and he would respect that.

He'd taken dates out to dinner, to see a play or movie and once to a Cubs game. At the end of each evening, though, he'd kissed them good-night at the door and gone home.

None of them stirred him at all, despite their intelligence, their looks and their behavior toward him. The dating scene was really becoming a bore.

He heard Greenfeld greet Candace and turned. "Good to see you, Jacob," he said, walking to the man with his arm outstretched.

"You, too, Dean," Jacob replied with a smile as they shook hands. "Thank you for seeing me."

Dean grinned. "Are you kidding? I was glad to hear from you after all this time. You disappeared after we graduated from college. How've you been?"

Once again Dean immersed himself in business and put all thought of Jodie away…until later that night when he fell asleep hugging his pillow and dreamed he was with her.

What was wrong with him anyway? he asked himself, staring out at the lake the next morning. When had he ever taken no for an answer when he really wanted something?

The truth was, Jodie taking another job in the office had left a big hole in his life—and it wasn't about sex, although that had been great.

He missed seeing her. He missed the sound of her voice. He missed the delicate scent of her perfume. Even if he never made love to her again, he knew he would remember everything about the pleasure of bringing her to a climax, of holding her in his arms afterward.

She'd graduated from college and had not sent him an announcement. He'd sent her a gift anyway and received a polite thank-you note that could have been written to his great-aunt Harriet. If he had a great-aunt Harriet.

He'd hoped that over time she might change her mind and be willing to see him again, but he realized that he'd be tripping over his gray beard before that happened.

It was time for drastic action. As his plan began to appear in his head, he nodded. He was a man of action, after all. Hadn't she mentioned that he was aggressive when he wanted something?

Well, he was ready to admit that he wanted her and no one else.

He would wait no longer to get her back in his life, on whatever terms she set.

"Isn't this a beautiful day," Lynette said, stretched out on a blanket in one of Chicago's parks. "I'm so glad we planned this."

Jodie nodded. She had Emily in her lap and was playing with her while Chuck played catch with the boys.

"Me, too."

"How's it feel to finally be through with school?"

"A little lost, actually. I don't know what to do with all my spare time."

"Well, it's been a boon for me. Chuck and I have certainly enjoyed your staying with the kiddos and giving us some alone time." She grinned. "I feel definitely decadent sleeping until late in the morning once a week."

"You deserve it."

Suddenly Lynette shouted, "Way to go, Kyle, good one." When she turned back to Jodie, she said, "You don't talk about work much anymore. Why is that?"

Jodie shrugged. "Nothing to talk about. I'm learning so much stuff that my head spins at times, but I'm enjoying it."

"And we're still not going to discuss Dean, are we?"

"There's nothing to discuss. I haven't seen…" Her voice trailed off.

"What's wrong?"

"If I'm not mistaken, that's Dean Logan coming toward us now."

Lynette sat up. "Really? Where?"

Jodie nodded toward the man drawing closer.

"You're kidding me," Lynette said in awe. "He's gorgeous. And you always said he looked like he should be on Mount Rushmore with his great stone face."

"He could."

"The grin he's wearing could melt rock, honey. And I believe it's directed at you!"

"Hi," he said when he reached them. "I thought that was you." He glanced at Lynette and back at Jodie. "Mind if I join you?"

Before Jodie could find her tongue, Lynette scooted over

and patted the blanket. "We'd be delighted. Wouldn't we, Jodie?" she asked, her eyes wide in mocking innocence.

He didn't wait for her answer but sat on the blanket.

"What are you doing—" Jodie began to ask when the boys interrupted her.

"Hi!" Kyle said. "Do you know our aunt Jodie? We have sleepovers at her house and she's—"

"Hush!" Lynette said, gaining Jodie's eternal gratitude for stopping him. Kyle wasn't known for his tact or diplomacy.

"Dean, I'd like you to meet my sister, Lynette, and her children." She nodded to the boys. "Kent and Kyle." Then she looked down to the infant in her arms and said, "This is Emily."

Chuck joined them. "Hi. Chuck Patterson," he said, his hand out.

Dean shook hands. "Dean Logan."

"Ah," was all Chuck said.

"I don't care what rumors Jodie has brought home to you, it isn't true that I eat young children for breakfast."

"Ooooh, gross!" Kent said with a grin.

Chuck sat down. "Why don't you let me rest for a few minutes, guys? Go toss the ball between you."

When the two of them moved away, he turned and looked at Lynette in disbelief. "Did you see that? They actually minded me. And without argument." He looked at Jodie. "Boy, if you ever decide to hire yourself out as a nanny, I can give you a glowing recommendation."

"If you haven't already guessed, Chuck is my brother-in-law."

Chuck reached for the ice chest. "Would you like something to drink? We have colas, lemonade and water."

"Water sounds great," Dean said.

Chuck pulled out two bottles of water. He gave one to Dean and rolled the other across his forehead. "I'm getting too old for this," he said, grinning.

Jodie cleared her throat. "What a coincidence that you should be at the same park we chose."

Dean smiled blandly. "Isn't it?" He turned and asked Chuck about his police work, giving her no chance to probe any further.

When they were packing things to go home, Lynette suddenly said, "Dean, why don't you come have supper with us tonight? You and Chuck seem to have a lot to discuss."

"Oh, I'm sure he's—" Jodie leaped in to the conversation just as Dean replied.

"That sounds great, Lynette. Thanks."

"—too busy," Jodie ended lamely.

"Don't expect anything fancy. It will probably be left-overs."

"My favorite meal."

Chuck and Lynette laughed.

Jodie glanced away for a moment before she said, "Look, you guys, why don't you go on and I'll get home. I have a dozen things to do and—"

Lynette gave her the famous big-sister stare for a moment before she replied, "Nonsense. We'll meet you over there."

Jodie watched them head to their car in silence.

"If you don't want me to go, I can make my excuses," Dean said quietly.

She shook her head, unable to say anything.

"What's wrong with my getting to know your family?"

"Nothing at all. Why do you want to?"

"Because I've missed you. I thought we were friends. We worked amicably together for several years. Now I feel like a leper where you're concerned."

She took a deep breath. "It's called self-preservation, Dean. I thought we'd come to an understanding. I don't want to get hurt."

"I would never hurt you."

"Not intentionally, I'm sure."

"Let's make a deal. Let's spend the next three months seeing each other as friends. Strictly platonic. I'd like to spend time with you, that's all."

"Friends. You think we can do that?"

He grinned. "I can if you can."

She sighed and then held out her hand. "Well, friend, we'd better get over to Lynette's before she sends Chuck out to find us. I wouldn't put it past him to put out an all points bulletin over the police scanner if we don't get a move on."

Fifteen

"Lighten up, sis, would you, please? I've never seen you so quiet!"

Jodie picked up a large salad and a platter of spaghetti and headed to the dining area. "I thought you'd appreciate the fact that I'm not talking your ear off!"

Lynette followed her with a large bowl of sauce that'd she'd removed from the freezer and heated, together with a basket of French bread drenched in garlic butter.

Jodie could hear Dean and Chuck chatting away in the living room like old buddies.

The sisters paused and looked at the table to be sure everything was ready. Lynette glanced at Jodie. "You've been keeping secrets, haven't you, sis?"

Jodie's heart lurched. "What do you mean?"

"That man is more than a boss to you. The way he looks at you is a dead giveaway."

"Oh, please. We've known each other for several years. We had a comfortable relationship when I worked for him. I rarely see him now."

"Whatever you say, dear," Lynette replied. She walked into the living room and said, "Sorry to interrupt your bonding, guys, but dinner, such as it is, is served."

"Lynette!" Jodie snapped from behind her.

Lynette turned and said, "I repeat. Lighten up."

Within five minutes Dean had charmed the Patterson family. His behavior contradicted everything she'd ever told them about him. Great. Now she looked like a liar.

Dean interrupted her glum thoughts by saying, "Jodie, why don't we catch a movie tomorrow and maybe have dinner afterward?"

Before she could respond, Kent piped up with, "She's your girlfriend, isn't she, Mr. Logan?"

Okay. That was it. Jodie saw no hope for her except to silently slide out of her chair and under the table.

"Well, Kent," Dean replied, winning points for remembering his name, "we are definitely friends—very good friends."

Kyle went into action. "Are you going to marry her?"

Jodie knew her face flushed a fiery red while Chuck scolded the boys. "It's not polite to ask personal questions, boys," Chuck said sternly. "Now eat your dinner."

When Jodie glanced at Dean, he winked at her, causing her to shake her head and shrug.

Thankfully Chuck introduced an innocuous subject that lasted through the rest of the meal.

Once dinner was over, Jodie helped Lynette clear the

table and load the dishwasher. She'd wiped down the counters when Emily cried out.

Lynette looked at her watch. "Right on time. I'd better go feed her."

"And I need to get home. Thanks for dinner again. Two nights in a row seems a little excessive."

"Don't worry about it. You know you're welcome anytime."

Lynette went upstairs and Jodie returned to the living room. "I'm going home now. Thanks for everything," she said to Chuck.

Dean immediately stood. "I need to go, as well." He turned to Chuck. "Enjoyed getting to know you. We'll have to find the time to go to a Cubs game soon."

Chuck also stood. "Sounds like a plan, Dean." He hugged Jodie. "Take care, sweetheart."

Jodie and Dean went outside to where they had parked their cars. She turned to say something when she realized he was right behind her.

"You never answered my question," he said, his hand massaging the nape of her neck.

She took a deep breath before saying, "Thank you for asking, and yes, I'd enjoy going to the movie with you." There. She'd just dived into the deep end.

He grinned. "See how easy that was?" He leaned closer and kissed her, his hand still caressing her neck and shoulders. As usual, the casual kiss turned into much more, and when they stepped away from each other, her heart was pounding so hard she wondered if she was having a heart attack or a stroke.

"That was a little more than a friendly kiss," she managed to say, catching her breath.

He shrugged. "What can I say? All's fair in love and war."

"Which one are we talking about?" she asked.

He gave her a brief hug and turned. "You'll have to figure that one out on your own," he said over his shoulder as he strode to his car.

When Jodie got home that night, she faced her fears. Of course, he hadn't been serious about being in love with her. He'd been up-front about what he wanted from her. Friendship. There was no reason in the world to run away from a friendship. The only way she could get hurt was to hope for some kind of commitment from Dean, which she knew she'd never get. One of the reasons his relationships ended was because the women wanted to marry him. She knew because she'd listened to a few who'd hoped she would put in a good word with him.

Lynette was absolutely right. She needed to lighten up. It wouldn't be the end of her world when he moved on to someone else. She wouldn't let it be.

She spent the next hour trying to figure out what to wear tomorrow.

Once home, Dean wondered why he'd mentioned love or war. Seeing Jodie was neither love nor war. He missed her, that's all. He'd always enjoyed being around her. What was wrong with that?

She'd made it clear she would not go to bed with him. He'd accept that. He didn't particularly like it, but he'd accept it in exchange for having her in his life again.

Dean looked at the stack of papers he'd brought home earlier today. When was he going to have time to go over them? Not tonight, anyway. He'd review them in the morning before he left to pick up Jodie. He'd never let his social life interfere with business before, but what he didn't get done, he'd do at the office on Monday.

He'd enjoyed seeing her again and meeting some of her family. He and Chuck had clicked. Chuck had been friendly without being overbearing, and Jodie's name had never been mentioned between them.

Once in bed, he thought about Jodie until he fell asleep.

"I can't remember laughing so hard in a long time," Jodie told Dean once they left the movie theater the next evening. "My sides hurt."

"I can relate," he replied with a smile. "I'm glad you enjoyed it."

She had, and not just the movie. They'd watched the comedy with fingers entwined like a couple of teenagers. Dean had laughed out loud on a few occasions, and the sound had cheered her. Maybe she did have an influence on him, since she couldn't imagine his going alone to see a movie.

Once seated in a Greek restaurant, they ordered. Over their salads Jodie asked, "Everything still working out with Mrs. Rudin?"

"She's very efficient. What I hadn't realized was how often you and I discussed business matters. You were my sounding board for most of my decisions. I hadn't realized it until after you were gone."

"If I can help, you know I'd be happy to."

"Thank you. I also have a request to make…more like a plea, actually." He looked grim. "There's a dinner and dance I'm expected to attend on Saturday night. I'd skip attending it since I've already made my donation, except that I'm one of the speakers. It's a benefit to raise money for Alzheimer's." He paused a moment. "My mother was diagnosed with the disease a while ago, so if they need me to make a speech, I will. I just hate like hell to go by my-self and I'm not seeing anyone these days."

"Of course I'll go with you, Dean. I'd like to hear you speak."

"No, you wouldn't, believe me. The regularly scheduled speaker was forced to cancel at the last minute, so I'm fill-ing in for him."

Dean still wasn't seeing anyone? How strange. Dean was never one to wait to find someone else when one of his relationships faltered. Of course, they'd never had a re-lationship—except for work…and when they'd visited Hawaii. But other than that, she hadn't seen or heard from him. He was a virile male who never lacked having a woman in his bed.

However, it was none of her business and she didn't comment on that part of his remarks.

They discussed several business matters during their meal, falling into a familiar routine. Jodie felt comfortable with Dean for the first time since she'd gone to Hawaii with him—that is, until they reached her front door.

She turned to him and said a little stiffly, "Thank you for this evening."

He lifted an eyebrow. "Aren't you going to invite me inside?"

"No."

"Even if I beg?"

She chuckled. "Dean, if I invite you inside, we both know that we'll probably end up in bed together."

"And your point is?"

"That's a little too friendly for me, I'm afraid."

"Okay."

She looked at him quizzically. "Okay?"

He shrugged. "You're right, that's all. Our relationship is strictly platonic, I swear." He held up his right hand. After a moment he asked, "Is it all right if I kiss you good night?"

She glanced down the deserted hallway and felt that her self-restraint would be helped by being there. "Okay."

He took his time pulling her closer to him. He started by nibbling on her earlobe before he planted small kisses along her jawline. Just as she knew it would, Jodie felt her control slipping. She moved her hands from his chest to around his neck, and when he finally found her mouth she was more than ready for him.

The kiss went on and on until the sound of the elevator brought her back to reality. She released him, gasping a little. Her body quivered with passion, which he knew darned well.

His smile was slow and intimate.

A couple got off the elevator and turned the other way without seeing them.

"Good night," Dean said gently. "Pleasant dreams." He turned and walked to the elevator, which conveniently opened when he pushed the button. She stepped in quickly, watching Dean until the door closed.

Jodie closed and locked the door and made it to her bedroom on wobbly knees before collapsing on the bed.

Who had she been kidding? Whether she saw Dean or not, her emotions were in a tangle where he was concerned.

Of course she wanted to experience again what they'd shared in that Honolulu hotel. He aroused a passion in her she'd never known existed. Now he was using that knowledge to remind her what they could have if she wanted an intimate relationship with him.

However, she was determined not to give in to her baser instincts. She would not. She could not.

Which meant that another restless night awaited her.

Sixteen

Jodie opened her door on Saturday evening to find Dean Logan looking drop-dead gorgeous in a tuxedo that was obviously custom made. His shoulders looked broader than ever, and since she vividly recalled how they felt beneath her fingers, she found it difficult to speak.

She finally said, "Come in," sounding hoarse. She cleared her throat.

He paused in the doorway for a moment before stepping inside. "I'm early. I apologize."

"No apology needed." She picked up her evening bag and tried not to notice the way he looked at her. During another shopping trip she'd found what she considered to be the perfect little black dress to wear. The style was deceptively simple and she knew she looked good wearing it.

Dean's look made clear that he approved and it made clear that he wanted her.

Some friendship this is going to be. Who was she kidding anyway?

So why are you willing to see him?

Because I have a masochistic streak in me, that's why.

Oh.

She picked up a lacy stole and slipped it around her shoulders.

They were silent in the elevator. Once in the car, Dean turned to her and said, "Is it overstepping the boundaries of friendship to say you are a knockout in that dress?"

She smiled demurely. "Thank you." He started the car after a quick shake of his head, as though clearing his brain. "Have you decided what you plan to say tonight?" she asked.

Once on the street, he replied, "I suppose. I never say what I've written anyway. All I know is that it will be short."

They pulled into one of the large conference centers and turned the car over to the valet. Other people in formal dress converged on the entrance to the hotel, and Dean guided her along in the same direction.

Several people spoke to him while eyeing her surreptitiously. He introduced her briefly to those who stopped to speak to him.

They'd almost reached the ballroom when Jodie heard a familiar voice behind them.

"Dean! I thought that was you. I never expected to see you at one of these things."

They stopped and Dean turned. "Hello, Rachel." He

recognized her escort. "Good to see you, Bailey," Dean said and shook his hand.

In a bright voice Rachel began to say, "So aren't you going to introduce us to—"

At that point, Jodie reluctantly turned to face them.

"Jodie? Is that really you? You look— I mean, uh, it's good to see you again." The look she gave both of them belied the comment. "So," she said to Dean, "I'm surprised to see you with your secretary." Her implication that he'd resorted to attending the gathering with the hired help wasn't lost on either of them.

"Actually," Dean said, looking amused, "she no longer works for me. She's working in Engineering now."

Jodie looked down at her toes. She could imagine Rachel's guess at how she got the promotion. She mentally squared her shoulders and looked Rachel in the eye. "That's true. I graduated from school at long last. Dean told me a few years ago that when I got my degree he'd move me into one of the other departments."

Rachel looked at Dean. "I bet you're lost without her...being your secretary."

"Somehow I've managed to survive," he replied wryly.

Once the two couples entered the ballroom, Rachel looked around and said to Bailey, "Do you recall our table number?" and they drifted away from Dean and Jodie.

Jodie looked up at him. "Rachel's looking good, don't you think?"

He frowned slightly. "I guess she looked okay. I didn't notice." He started toward the front of the room where the dais was set up. "We're at table one."

When they drew closer, Jodie saw that their table was

filled except for the two seats reserved for them. She recognized a couple of the men but only because she'd seen their photographs in the paper.

The movers and shakers of Chicago were there tonight. Dean hadn't told her that the affair would be so well attended. She wondered if the size of the crowd would bother Dean. She'd never thought of him being a public speaker.

Dean introduced her to the table at large. Everyone was gracious and she found herself relaxing—until one of the wives asked, "What branch of the Cameron family are you, my dear?"

"The Wisconsin branch."

"Oh." The woman sounded disappointed. "You're not related to any of the Camerons here in Chicago?"

Jodie smiled politely, wishing for the evening to end. Right now. "Not that I'm aware of."

"Pity. I suppose you've traced your roots back to Scotland."

"Not yet."

"Genealogy is fascinating work. You'll enjoy it once you get started."

Jodie was relieved when the waiters came out with their salads and the conversation became more general.

She hated feeling so inadequate in situations such as this. She thought about telling the woman that her mother was a waitress in Phoenix just to see her reaction.

As the meal progressed, Jodie was surprised to discover that the food was delicious. No telling how much the meal had cost, but it was a vast improvement on the rubber chicken usually served at the events she'd attended.

After dinner the emcee of the event spoke to the gathering, thanking them for coming and introducing Dean as the speaker.

Why she should feel so nervous for him she had no idea, because he appeared composed enough as he strode to the dais.

Within minutes after he started speaking he had the room mesmerized. He drew from his personal experience and the pain involved watching a loved one slip away from reality.

As promised, he kept his speech short and very much to the point and when he finished, he received a standing ovation. Jodie stood with the rest, tears in her eyes. She'd never been more proud of him.

The emcee thanked him and told everyone to enjoy the music and dancing. The dance floor filled quickly with the first song. Everyone at their table was on the dance floor when Dean turned to her. "Shall we dance?"

Jodie nodded and they walked out onto the floor. Once they were dancing, she said, "I was impressed with your speech. Your calm discussion of such a personal and painful situation touched us all."

"I felt it was the best way to explain the need for more money for research."

"You are a man of many talents, Mr. Logan."

He pulled her closer to him and she put her head on his chest. She was surprised to discover his heart racing and lifted her head.

"Sorry. I react this way when I'm around you."

Only then did she realize that he was aroused. She couldn't help blushing.

"Would you prefer not to dance?" he finally asked.

"Oh, Dean, you're making things very difficult for me."

"And you have a way of making things hard for me."

"It's not that I'm playing hard to get…."

"I know. It's not your fault that I can't stop myself from reacting to you." He continued to dance but held her a few inches away from him. "This friendship thing isn't working."

She shook her head, unable to speak. That's when she knew what she had to do. "All right then."

"All right what?"

"I'll sleep with you tonight."

He stopped dead in his tracks, causing another couple to run into them. "Sorry," he said and slipped his arm around Jodie's waist. "Please tell me that you're serious," he said roughly.

She nodded, her gaze direct. "I'm serious."

"We need to go," he said. He took her hand and started off the dance floor before the song finished.

Jodie remained silent while they waited for his car to be brought around, and neither of them spoke on the way to her apartment. She realized that she quivered with need, a need she'd tried to ignore for weeks. She wanted him. She wanted him now.

The door barely closed behind them when he lifted her, pulling her legs around his waist, leaned her against the door, fumbled with his zipper and shoved inside her as he ripped her panties.

Their lovemaking was hot, strong and very passionate, both of them climaxing within minutes. Dean gathered her closer and walked—as much as he was able to with his pants around his ankles—into her bedroom, where he carefully placed her on the bed.

She watched him remove his tuxedo and allowed him to slip her dress and underthings off her. Still without speaking, he joined her on the bed and made slow, sensuous love to her. They responded to each other as they had in Hawaii. Jodie knew that she would never, ever, forget this night.

He left at dawn.

The following Monday morning Jodie handed Frank her resignation. By that afternoon, she was on the road heading south.

Seventeen

Dean called Jodie's apartment several times on Sunday but got no answer. He figured she'd gone to her sister's and he fought the temptation to call her there just to hear her voice.

He owed her an apology for his Neanderthal behavior Saturday night. The problem was, he couldn't promise that he wouldn't behave the same way the next time they were alone.

What kind of spell was he under that she was on his mind most of the time? All right, all of the time. He'd be in meetings with clients and his mind would wander.

This was not the way he'd ever conducted himself and he didn't like it. The problem was that he didn't know what to do about it.

On Monday he had back-to-back meetings, most of them out of the office, and he didn't return until after four.

He decided to check with Jodie to see if she'd like to have dinner with him that night. Nothing wrong with that. He'd make certain they weren't alone, either during their meal or when he took her home. He would show her that he could, in fact, restrain himself around her, but being alone with her would be too much for him.

For that matter, he could bring her back to the office to get her car.

Feeling pleased with his plan, Dean went to the department where she worked. When he didn't see her, he strolled into Frank's office.

Frank looked up. "How did the meeting with Flynn go today?"

"He liked the presentation you made last week and he's ready to sign on."

"Good to hear."

"I, uh, was looking for Jodie. Did she go home early?"

Frank frowned. "Didn't she tell you?"

"Tell me what?"

"She resigned this morning—used her vacation time in lieu of notice and left."

Dean sank into the nearest chair. He felt as though Frank had punched him in the diaphragm, knocking the breath out of him. When he didn't say anything, Frank said, "I figured you knew about it."

"No. No, I didn't." He was quiet for a moment and then asked, "Did she say why. I thought she was happy here. Did she mention another job?"

"Sorry. Actually she said very little, just cleaned out her desk. I'll admit, I hated to see her go. She's good. Sharp. Creative. In the time she's worked for me, I've been very impressed with her work. She was one of the people who worked on the presentation I made."

Dean nodded, although he didn't hear what Frank had said. His mind was racing with questions. Why had she quit so abruptly? And without telling him?

What the hell was going on?

"You all right?" Frank asked after a lengthy silence.

"I'm fine. Just surprised. The news caught me off guard, that's all." He stood up and said, "I'll talk to you later."

Dean didn't go to his office to check messages or mail. He went directly to the parking garage, got into his car and drove to Jodie's apartment.

There was no answer after repeated knocks.

His next stop was the Pattersons' home. As soon as he knocked, the door opened wide. It was Kent.

"Hi," Kent said with a big smile.

Dean returned his smile. "Hello, Kent. Is your mom home?"

"Uh-huh." He turned away and yelled, "Mom, it's Aunt Jodie's boyfriend."

"Have him come in and have a seat. I'll be there shortly."

Dean stepped inside. A tornado had recently come through the living room, judging from the scattered toys, shoes and jackets.

"Can I get you something to drink?" Kent asked politely.

"No, thank you."

"Oh." Kent sat across from Dean and looked at a loss as to what to do next.

"Don't let me interrupt whatever you were doing," Dean said, equally polite.

Kent grinned. "Okay," he replied and immediately slid

to the floor, where he'd been playing with small racing cars on a track that wound around the couch.

Lynette came hurrying in a few minutes later. "I'm so sorry to keep you waiting. I just got home from picking up the boys at school and it was time to feed Emily."

"No problem."

Lynette immediately began picking up toys, coats and shoes. "I'd apologize for the way the house looks except it would be a waste of time, since this is the way it looks more often than not."

"I won't keep you. I dropped by to see if you've talked to Jodie in the last day or two."

Lynette straightened and looked at him, obviously puzzled. She sat down in the chair recently vacated by her son. "She was here Friday night."

"Did you talk to her yesterday or today?"

"No. What's wrong? Has something happened to her?" she asked, making no effort to hide her alarm.

"That's what I'm trying to find out. She quit her job today, used accrued vacation time as her notice and left."

Lynette placed her hand on the side of her neck. "Good heavens. I had no idea she was considering such a thing."

"Neither did I. We went out Saturday night and she seemed to be fine when I left. I thought you might have some idea why she quit and where she might be."

She shook her head. "I'm sorry, but I don't. Have you tried her apartment?"

He nodded. "And I've left several messages on her machine."

"I'll call Chuck and have him check out her apartment. I hope nothing's happened to her."

She picked up the phone and made the call. When Chuck answered his cell phone, she told him what she'd just learned. After she hung up, she said, "He'll go check. Do you want to wait here for him to call back?"

He stood. "That won't be necessary. I'd appreciate your calling me when you find out anything." He gave her his cell phone number and left.

His phone rang as he parked his car at his condominium. "Logan."

"Hi, Dean, this is Lynette. Things are getting more and more curious. Chuck said her apartment looks okay but most of her clothes and personal things are gone."

Numbly he replied, "Thanks for letting me know."

"No problem. I'm sure I'll hear from her soon. She isn't one to want people to worry about her, which is why all this is such a surprise. This isn't like Jodie at all. Anyway, I'll have her call you when I hear from her."

"Thank you."

He pocketed the phone and walked to the elevator.

Was it something he'd said Saturday night? Or done? Or did her disappearance have nothing to do with him?

He had no way of knowing.

Friday morning Lynette's phone rang. When she answered, Jodie said, "Hi, sis. Thought I'd let you know I won't be there for dinner tonight."

"Joanna Louise Cameron, where in the world are you? I've been frantic since Monday when Dean told me you'd quit your job."

"Dean told you?"

"Yes. When he couldn't reach you at home, he came

over here to see if I knew anything. Chuck went to your apartment to see if you had been hurt or worse. Why didn't you let anyone know where you were going?"

"Because I wasn't sure where I intended to go when I left Chicago."

"Where are you?"

"I showed up here at Mom's late last night. I plan to stay a while and will probably look for a job down here."

"Have you lost your ever lovin' mind? What's wrong with the job you had here? You loved it. You were excited about it."

Lynette heard Jodie sigh. Finally she said, "It's a long story."

"I've got time to hear a long story. The boys are in school and Emily just went down for her nap. Tell me."

Jodie wasn't ready to talk about Dean to anyone, but she knew she owed Lynette an explanation. Finally she said, "I had to get away from Dean."

Silence greeted her admission. Finally in a horrified voice Lynette asked, "What did he do? It must have been serious for you to run like this. Did you call the police?"

"It's nothing like that, Lynette. I did a really stupid thing and it's so trite I'm embarrassed to admit it. I fell in love with my boss."

"So? He appears deeply enamored of you, as well."

"Not really. He decided he wanted for us to date and I agreed. I truly thought I could handle my response to him, but I can't. Whenever he's nearby, all he has to do is look at me and I go up in flames."

"Oh, honey. There's absolutely nothing wrong with that. Is that what scared you away?"

"Partly. The thing about Dean—and he's the first to admit it—is he isn't interested in a long-term commitment. And that's the only kind I want. I've been careful not to tell him how I feel, but now he's going to guess that I'm crazy about him. Once a woman tells him she's in love with him, he practically leaves skid marks getting away from her.

"So I decided that it would be better for me to leave before I had to go through that. I've tried to make a clean break with him, but somehow I end up going out with him again. I have no willpower where he's concerned. None. So I realized that I would have to go someplace where there was no chance of running into him. So I resigned."

"Maybe you're different. Maybe he'd be willing—"

"No. It's our ego that tells us that we can cause a person to change if we just love them enough. That's our fantasy, but the reality is that Dean knows what he wants and has no reason to change."

"Maybe so," Lynette replied. "But he was very concerned about you. I told him I'd have you call him. I guess that's not going to happen."

Jodie rubbed her forehead where a headache loomed. "I'll admit, I didn't expect him to contact you. If you should hear from him again—which I very much doubt—tell him whatever you want, but don't tell him that I'm in love with him. I want that to be our little secret, Lynette, okay?"

"I don't keep secrets from Chuck."

"All right. Tell Chuck. That's all."

"Well, honey, you have to do what you have to do, I suppose. I can't bear the idea of you living so far away. How's Mom taking all this?"

"I haven't told her. She had to leave early to go to work at the diner. She'll be home a little after two."

"Maybe you can convince her she doesn't have to work. Each of us is contributing to her support. It's not as though she has to work."

"She knows that, but she said she'd miss visiting with the locals who stop in every day. You know Mom. She loves people. I'm sure she's in her element there."

"Try to get some rest. That's a long trip from here."

"Tell me about it. I'm going back to bed. I'll talk to you later."

Lynette hung up the phone and immediately called Chuck. As soon as he answered, she told him about the call.

"So she ran away," Chuck summed up.

"Yes."

"That's too bad."

"I promised her that I wouldn't tell anyone but you about her feelings for Dean."

"Okay."

"However…you didn't make her any promises. So if you wanted to let Dean know…"

"No way am I going to get involved in any matchmaking. I don't need both of them cursing me. Come on, sweetheart; let her live her life the way she wants."

"Even if she's miserable?"

"Yes."

"Oh, Chuck, why do you have to be such a guy!"

"What? What, may I ask, is wrong with being a guy?"

"You just don't understand women."

"Probably. Especially at the moment. I haven't a clue what you're upset about."

"I'm upset because you have the opportunity to get two people who love each other together. That's not matchmaking. They've made the connection. They're obviously involved with each other. At least give Dean the information, okay? Then whatever he does about it will be up to him."

After a moment of silence Chuck grudgingly replied, "I'll think about it."

"You do that and I'll be eternally grateful—and I will express my gratitude in a number of creative ways."

Eighteen

Candace stepped to Dean's door a few days later and said, "There's a Mr. Chuck Patterson on line two. Shall I get his number and have you call him back?"

Without answering her question, Dean grabbed the phone. "Chuck! Good to hear from you. Hold on a minute, will you?" He raised his voice slightly and said, "Candace, please close the door and hold my calls."

He uncovered the mouthpiece of the phone and asked, "Have you heard from her?"

There was a pause and then Dean heard Chuck's laugh. "You've got it bad, my friend. I called to see if you wanted to go to the Cubs game tomorrow afternoon. My treat."

"Oh. Let me check my schedule." He looked at his calendar. He had two appointments that morning but none in the afternoon. "Sounds good. Where should I meet you?"

"I'll pick you up in front of your building," Chuck replied and named a time.

"Okay. Is she all right?" Dean asked.

"She's fine, Dean. She's visiting her mother. We can talk more tomorrow."

"See you then," Dean said and hung up the phone.

She was in Phoenix? Just like that, she quits her job, walks out on him without a word and goes to see her mother?

It would seem so.

Dean and Chuck arrived at the game early. They'd talked about everything under the sun on the ride to the stadium... everything but Jodie's sudden departure.

At any other time Dean would have enjoyed Chuck's company, but knowing that he was withholding information about Jodie made Dean want to throttle him.

At long last Chuck brought up the subject by throwing Dean a curveball. "So what's going on between you and Jodie anyway?"

"Uh, well, I mean, we've known each other quite a while. She was my secretary for several years."

"I understand that and that's not what I'm talking about. Most men don't respond to a former secretary leaving as you have."

Dean nodded. Chuck wasn't going to accept any vague remarks. If he wanted to know what was going on with Jodie, he'd have to bare his soul. Since he was a very private man, he found the idea excruciatingly painful...almost as painful as missing Jodie.

"I finally faced the fact that I'm in love with her, that

I've probably been in love with her for years and was too dumb to recognize it. I've done some really stupid things in my life, but letting her slip away from me like this has to be the biggest mistake I've ever made."

The sentence hung in the air and seemed to expand on the breeze. There. He'd said it. Too bad he hadn't realized that what he felt for her was love until after she was gone.

"That right?" Chuck asked with a smile.

"Yeah."

"So her leaving like that has been tough on you."

"You could say that." What an understatement that was.

"What did she say when you told her?"

"What? That I love her?"

"I believe that's the topic of this conversation, yes."

"I never told her," Dean mumbled.

"Sorry, I didn't catch that."

Dean cleared his throat. "I said that I never told her, fool that I am, because I didn't realize it until very recently."

"I see."

"So how is she? Have you talked with her? Do you know when she plans to come back?"

"I haven't talked with her, but Lynette said she seems to be doing okay. Jodie told her that she might look for a job in Phoenix."

"What! You're kidding, right?"

"Nope. That's what Lynette reported to me."

The crowd roared its approval about something. Chuck and Dean hadn't been paying attention when the game started, and the Cubs were up to bat.

"Looks like a single," Chuck commented.

"Yeah."

"I don't know if you want to hear any suggestions from me," Chuck said briskly, "but here's one anyway—go to Arizona and tell her how you feel. I'm sure the news would have more impact with her if you're there in person."

"I could do that."

"Good. Now, then. Let's watch the game, okay?"

Jodie had been at her mother's for two weeks and was getting restless. She missed work. She'd been tempted to call Frank to see how things were going until she remembered that she no longer had a job.

She'd set up a couple of job interviews for the following week, but in the meantime there was nothing much for her to do. The house was spotless and her mom's garden had already been weeded within an inch of its life.

This morning she decided to enjoy the early-morning coolness outdoors before the sun got too hot.

She loved her mom's backyard. It was very private, with a six-foot wall surrounding it. Inside the wall her mom had planted all kinds of colorful flowering plants, which reminded Jodie of the lush foliage in Hawaii.

Jodie put on a two-piece bathing suit and, once outside, stretched out on one of the lounge chairs and removed the top to her swimsuit. A small hand towel covered her breasts, leaving her shoulders bare. Next she picked up the book she had started the night before and began to read.

Sometime later the doorbell startled her awake, and she realized that she'd dozed off. She considered getting up and answering the door, but she was too relaxed to move. Besides, all of her mom's friends knew that she worked mornings. It was probably some kind of salesman.

She decided to ignore the door and let her eyes close, basking in the quiet and serenity. She'd had trouble sleeping since she'd been there, and from her reflection in the mirror each morning she knew the lack of sleep had taken its toll on her.

"Ah, there you are."

Jodie's immediate reaction to the sound of a very familiar voice was to scream involuntarily and jerk upright.

"Sorry. Didn't mean to startle you," Dean said. "When no one answered the door, I decided to check back here." He looked around. "The garden is beautiful by the way."

When she could speak, she said, "What are you doing here!" Without waiting for an answer, she grabbed a large towel and wrapped it around her.

"Mind if I sit down?" he asked, his voice bland.

She stared at him as though he were an apparition. Finally she nodded.

Once he sat down, he took his time looking her over, from her ponytail to her freshly painted toenails.

"You're looking rested," he said, which she knew to be a lie. He wore a golf shirt and slacks, the shirt clinging to his wide chest and his pants outlining his massive thighs.

"Did you ever play football?" she blurted out. How did that manage to pop out of her mouth? She was losing it.

The look on his face was indescribable. He finally answered, "Yes, in high school and college. Why do you ask?"

"Just curious," she replied faintly. "If you'll excuse me, I'll, uh, go get us something to drink." She didn't give him time to respond before she fled the patio, ignoring the kitchen and racing down the hallway to her room.

She quickly put on some clothes.

Dean Logan was there? In Phoenix? This couldn't be happening. What was she going to have to do, find some deserted island somewhere to make certain she didn't see him?

She hurried into the kitchen, removed a pitcher of lemonade from the fridge and set it on a tray. She added two glasses filled with ice and returned outside.

Dean watched her walk toward him without expression. She placed the tray on the table between them and poured the juice. Once seated, she glanced quickly at him, then away.

She took a swallow of lemonade to aid her dry mouth. "You haven't answered my question. What are you doing here?"

He leaned back in his chair and looked around the garden. "The same thing you are. Enjoying the sun."

"How did you know where I was?"

He lifted his brow. "Was it supposed to be a secret?"

She shrugged. Lynette probably told him. Jodie hadn't told her not to mention her whereabouts to him for the simple reason that she hadn't expected him to come looking for her.

When she didn't comment, he said, "I decided that I work much too hard. I work ridiculously long hours and have a slave driver for a boss." He paused and drank some lemonade. "I decided to follow your example. I quit my job and came to Arizona."

"What do you mean you quit your job? That's impossible."

"Actually it isn't, because I did it. Others can manage the place as well as I can. I've trained them well."

"You could barely get through a week away from the office when we were in Hawaii the first time. The only way you managed was to call the office several times a day."

"Once I realized that I am, in fact, a workaholic, I decided it was time to change my lifestyle."

"So you came to Phoenix? This isn't the best time of year to visit, unless you're looking for sunstroke. I never stay out later than ten o'clock for that reason."

What was the matter with her? She was babbling. The last thing she would have expected was for him to come there.

He sipped from his glass, looking totally relaxed. "Actually Chuck happened to mention that you were visiting your mother while we were at a Cubs game together." He gave her a steady look. "You left without telling me you were leaving, and I thought I'd find out what I had done to offend you."

This was exactly why she'd left Chicago—to avoid explaining why she couldn't deal with their relationship. "You didn't do a thing, Dean," she finally said.

As though she hadn't spoken, he said, "I've been thinking about our last night together. You gave no hint that you intended to walk away from your career and leave town. May I ask why?"

"It was a personal decision I made. I didn't tell anyone."

"I got quite a shock learning that you'd resigned. You seemed to be enjoying your new position."

"Dean, I really don't want to discuss this."

"The thing is, I feel like a fool," he went on to say. "I've been pretending that it didn't matter to me whether I saw you or not, when the truth is I want to be with you all the time." He paused and scrubbed his hand over his face. "I'm not saying this right. What I'm trying to say is that what we have together is too precious to let go of. I want to share my future with you. I thought if I came here and told you that I finally figured out that I'm crazy in love with you—and have been for who knows how long—that you might consider marrying me."

All right. Now she knew she was hallucinating. Dean Logan proposing marriage? It was almost laughable…if she felt in the least like laughing. Which she didn't.

"How quickly we forget," she said. "It was only a couple of months ago when you told me that a commitment and marriage were the very last things you were interested in." She glared at him. "Remember? No house in the suburbs for you. No tiny people to make claims on your time."

She was proud of her little speech. Too bad her teeth were chattering with nerves during the whole thing.

"That was a dying man going under for the third time, unaware that it was way too late for him to be spouting such nonsense."

"Nonsense?"

He leaned toward her and took her hand, which lay limply on her thigh. "It must already be in the nineties out here and you're chilled." He stood and started toward the sliding glass doors into the house. "I'll find something to wrap around you."

She jumped to her feet and followed him into the house. He didn't pause but continued down the hallway looking into rooms. He saw a crocheted afghan lying on the foot of her mother's bed, swept it up and returned to the hall, where he wrapped it around her. Then he pulled her close, holding her tightly against him.

"I know I've given you every reason to believe that I'm a confirmed bachelor. My only excuse is that I'd convinced myself, as well. My feelings for you have always been there, but it wasn't until we went to Hawaii the first time that they shot to the surface. I just didn't recognize them for what they were at the time."

She pulled away from him and walked to the living room, where she sank into her mom's cushy chair. "I'm sorry, but I'm having a little trouble taking all of this in," she said, feeling light-headed. She must have gotten too much sun.

He knelt beside her chair. "I want what Chuck and Lynette have—a lovely home, three great kids and, yes, a place in the suburbs where we can raise our own."

She covered her cheeks with her hands. "This can't be happening."

"Would you at least consider the idea of marrying me? I don't want to sound maudlin and say that I don't know how I'd get along without you in my life, but there it is. I know I'm not much of a catch. I'm impatient and irritable, I work too much, I don't know how to sit back and enjoy life. But you've shown me a whole new world out there, away from the office, and I'd like to learn more…with you as my teacher."

Dean watched her closely, wondering if he'd made a co-lossal mistake by coming to Phoenix to see her. She'd left everything she'd worked for in Chicago. Was it just to get away from him?

"Why did you leave?"

Some color had come back in her cheeks. Funny, but he'd never thought that his proposing marriage would cause a woman to almost faint.

"Because we can't seem to be together without ending up in bed."

"I'm afraid that's true. I have very little self-control where you're concerned." He took her hand once again. "I suppose that I've gone about all of this backward. Since it's the first time I've ever proposed, I'm not very good at it. The real question here is, do you love me?"

Her eyes filled with tears. He was such an idiot. The last thing he wanted was to make her cry.

She laced her fingers with his. "Yes, Dean, I'm in love with you despite everything I can do not to be."

"Is loving me so bad?"

"It is when you made it clear that you weren't interested in love."

"I was wrong. I can't think of a greater gift than you loving me."

The tears trickled down her face.

He cleared his throat. "As long as I'm already on my knees, I'd like to formally ask. Jodie Cameron, will you do me the great honor of marrying me, of loving me, of saving me from the horrible state of bachelorhood?"

She laughed through her tears. "Oh, Dean." She cupped his face in her hands. "If I'm dreaming, please don't wake me up."

"You can't be dreaming because my knees are killing me." He stood and held out his hand. "Well?"

She answered by throwing herself into his arms, covering his face with kisses.

After a lengthy and very passionate kiss, he pulled away long enough to say, "Is that a yes, by any chance?"

"Yes, Mr. Dean Logan, I will be most happy to marry you."

"And have a few children?"

"If that's what you want."

"That's very much what I want. Speaking of which—" he looked around the room "—where's your mother?"

"At work. She'll be home early this afternoon."

"I have an idea how we could spend our time waiting for her."

Yes, there was passion in his eyes, but Jodie saw something more, something she'd never expected to see—his eyes shining with love and tenderness. He had well and truly convinced her that he loved her. What more could she possibly want?

"Perhaps you'd like to show me what you have in mind," she replied.

With a shout of laughter he picked her up and carried her back down the hall to her bedroom.

He was right. He'd found the perfect way to spend the rest of the morning.

Epilogue

Six months later

"You look like a princess in a fairy tale," her mother said to Jodie. She'd carefully placed the tiara and veil on Jodie's head while they stood before the large oval mirror in a room set aside for the bride.

Lynette added, "And who would have believed that Dean Logan would turn out to be a prince after all? If you'd told me a year or two ago that you would end up marrying Dean, I would have been convinced you were truly marrying an ogre."

"Lynette! Shame on you," her mother said. "Dean is a lovely man…polite, considerate and a joy to be around."

Jodie and Lynette shared a glance in the mirror and smiled at each other. Dean had done a great job of selling himself to their mom. Once Dean and Jodie had returned to Chicago, Jodie and Lynette had convulsed into laughter when Jodie had told Lynette about his visit to Phoenix.

"I've never attended a wedding this large, much less been in the wedding party," Mom said. "As you know, George and I eloped. And Chuck and Lynette had a small ceremony."

"Believe me, the idea of eloping ran through my mind many times these past few months," Jodie said. "I turned everything over to the wedding planner and went back to work."

"Dean said that since this would be his one and only wedding, he wanted a large celebration," Lynette explained. "He didn't care how much it cost. Everyone who's anyone in the business world was invited."

Jodie closed her eyes. She didn't need the reminder. She could see herself tripping down the aisle—literally tripping down the aisle—and skidding to a stop at Dean's feet.

There was a tap on the door. "Come in," she said.

Her three brothers, who were ushers, stepped inside. "Everyone's seated," Dave, the oldest, said.

Randy spoke up. "Wow, sis. You clean up pretty good."

"Gee, thanks, Randy. I'm glad you approve."

Rick, the impatient one, looked at his watch and said, "C'mon. Let's get this show on the road."

The three women followed the men out into the foyer. To save argument, both Kent and Kyle were ring bearers. Of course, that created an argument between them because each of them wanted to carry Jodie's ring. Lynette finally got that straightened out by threatening not to let them be a part of the wedding.

The music started and the young boys started down the aisle, looking sharp in their new suits. They were growing up so fast. Jodie blinked the moisture from her eyes. Get real. These are the same angelic beings who kept her constantly embarrassed with their frank questions to Dean every time they saw him.

Jodie had asked two of her coworkers to be bridesmaids. Lynette was her matron of honor and her mother would walk her down the aisle.

After Lynette reached the front of the church, the music switched to the well-known wedding march and the guests stood. Jodie's throat closed up. She was not going to cry, she was not going to cry, she was not—

Then she saw Dean waiting at the altar and that did it. Tears slid down her face as she started toward him. She couldn't stop smiling.

Jodie didn't remember much about the actual ceremony. She heard the rumble of Dean's voice and had responded when it was her turn, but all she could think about was the fact that she was actually marrying Dean Logan after all these months of answering the wedding planner's incessant questions.

"You may kiss the bride."

The pastor's words jolted her out of her reverie. Jodie turned to Dean, who was watching her with amusement. What? What did he find so amusing?

When he leaned toward her, he whispered, "I thought you were going to fall asleep there for a minute," and he kissed her.

He really kissed her. It wasn't a brushing of lips or a ritual peck on the mouth but a leisurely kiss. When he finally raised his head, her face was flaming and the guests were laughing and applauding.

Music filled the sanctuary as they started up the aisle. Once in the foyer, Dean turned to her. "Hello, Mrs. Logan. I hope you're having a good day."

"I wasn't going to fall asleep! I was just distracted a little."

"You must have been, since the pastor had to ask a couple of his questions to you twice."

"Oh, no." She covered her face with her hands. "And I didn't want to do anything to embarrass you. At least I didn't trip over the gown and fall down coming down the aisle!"

"You could never embarrass me, Jodie. I find you delightful, besides being the love of my life."

By now they were surrounded by well-wishers. After greeting several people, Dean and Jodie hurried outside and got into the limo waiting to take them to the large hotel where the reception would be held.

They settled into their seats, and Dean reached inside his coat pocket and pulled out a small, long and narrow box. "I want to give you your bride's gift before we get to the reception."

A necklace. He'd bought her a necklace. "Oh, Dean, what a thoughtful gift."

He lifted one eyebrow. "Aren't you going to open it?" he asked.

"Oh! I'm sure I'll love it," she said and lifted the lid.

There was no necklace. Only a folded envelope and a key. Bewildered, Jodie looked at him. He smiled.

She opened the envelope and found a note and two airline tickets to Hawaii. "Oh, we're going back to Hawaii!"

"Why not? That's where I really got to know you. This time we'll stay as long as you like."

She unfolded the note and read. "No, this isn't the key to my heart because you already have it in your safekeeping. This is a key to your new home."

"My home? What have you done?"

"Conspired behind your back. I got Lynette to go house hunting with me to find a home she thought you might like. Of course, if you don't like it, I can always—"

She threw herself into his arms and kissed him all over his face, his ears, his jaw and his mouth. "You are the most high-handed man I've ever known," she finally said, laughing with delight. "You bought me a house without consulting me?" She looked at him with mock disapproval, his face cupped in her hands.

"Actually I haven't bought it yet. I waited to sign the contract until you have a chance to see it. The Realtor gave me the key, and I thought we could go over there after we leave the reception. If you approve of it, I'll sign the papers before we leave."

So maybe a man could change a little. She was touched that he was trying. "I can hardly wait to see what you've picked out for us."

She knew that she would love the house because Lynette knew her so well. She would love it even more because Dean had chosen to surprise her with it.

One thing she knew for certain: there would never be a dull moment being married to Dean Logan.

* * * * *

TOTALLY TEXAN

BY
MARY LYNN BAXTER

Dedicated to Walter G Bates,
forester and friend, who once again has gifted
me with his immense talent.

One

Grant Wilcox had just stepped out of his truck when Harvey Tipton, the postmaster, walked out of the Sip 'n Snack coffee shop.

Harvey greeted Grant with a grin through his scruffy beard and mustache. "Hey, about to take a look-see, huh? Or maybe I should say another one."

Grant gave him a perplexed look. "What are you talking about?"

"The new piece in town."

Grant made a face. "I'm assuming you're referring to the new woman in town, right?"

"Right," Harvey responded, with his head bobbing up and down, his grin still in place. He obviously saw no reason to be ashamed or to make an apology for his unflattering terminology. "She's running the shop for Ruth."

Of all people to run into, Grant groaned inwardly; Harvey was the town's most prolific gossip. And the fact that he was a man made it worse.

Grant shrugged. "That's news to me, but then I haven't been in for coffee in a while."

"When you see her you'll regret that."

"I doubt it," Grant said wryly.

"I didn't figure you for dead yet, Wilcox."

"Give me a break, will you?" Grant was irritated and didn't bother to hide the fact.

"Well, she's a stunner," Harvey declared. "Heads above anyone else around here."

"So why are you telling me?" Grant asked in a bored tone, hoping Harvey would take the hint.

Harvey gave him a conspiratorial grin. "Thought maybe you might be interested, since you're the only one around here without a wife or significant other." He slapped Grant on the shoulder and widened his grin. "If you know what I mean."

For a second Grant wanted to flatten the postmaster's nose, but of course he didn't. Harvey wasn't the only one who had tried to play matchmaker for him.

Sure, he'd like a hot-blooded, feisty woman to occupy his bed on occasion, but the thought of anything permanent made him break into a chill. For the first time ever, life was good—especially in the small town of Lane, Texas. As a forester, Grant was doing what he loved and that was playing in the woods, cutting trees that would eventually earn him a ton of money.

More than that, he wasn't ready to settle down. With his roaming past, he never knew when the itch to move might strike; then where would he be? Trapped. Nope, that wasn't for him, at least not now.

"So want me to go back in and introduce you?" Harvey asked into the silence, following with a deep belly laugh.

Grant gritted his teeth and said, "Thanks, Harv, but I can take care of myself when it comes to women." He pointedly looked at his watch. "I'm sure you have customers waiting for you."

Harvey winked. "Gotcha."

Yet once the postmaster was out of sight, Grant found himself walking a bit faster toward the entrance to the Sip 'n Snack.

Kelly Baker scrubbed her hands hard in the hot, sudsy water, pulling her lower lip between her teeth. She had been putting pastries in the front counter and was convinced she had goo up to her elbows.

Since she'd been in this small country town of Lane—three weeks now—she'd asked herself over and over if she'd truly lost her mind. She knew the answer, though, and it was no. Her cousin, Ruth Perry, had needed help, and Kelly had come to the rescue, just as Ruth had come to hers following the tragic event that had changed her life forever.

"Ouch," Kelly mumbled, feeling a stinging sensation in her hands. Jerking them out of the water, she grabbed a towel, then frowned as she looked at her fingers. Gone were the long, beautifully manicured nails and the soft skin she was once so proud of. Now, her hands looked all dried and pruney, as if she kept them constantly immersed. She did, even though she had two daytime helpers, Albert and Doris.

Another sigh followed as Kelly looked around the empty

coffee shop, picturing how it would look in a short time. It would be teeming with people. She smiled to herself at the word *teeming*. That term hardly fit this tiny town.

Still, who was she to make fun? Ruth's newest addition to this logging community of two thousand had been a huge hit. With little invested, her cousin was already turning a profit—albeit a small one—selling gourmet coffees, pastries, soups and sandwiches.

According to the locals, Sip 'n Snack was the place to be. And that was good. If Kelly had to be in this place, at least she was where the action was, until the shop closed every day.

Kelly dreaded the evenings. They were far too long and gave her too much time to think. Even though she walked in the door of Ruth's small, cozy house so exhausted she could barely make it to the bathtub, much less to bed, she still couldn't sleep.

But nights had been her problem long before she came to Lane. And now with the empty afternoons, the past had ample opportunity to rear its traumatic head and haunt her once again. Soon, though, she would fulfill her obligation to her cousin an would be back at home in Houston where she belonged.

However, she reminded herself ruefully, her personal life hadn't been any better there or she wouldn't be *here* now. Inside, at the core of her being, her heart had been coated with cement that nothing could chip away.

"Phone for you, Kelly."

When she picked it up, Ruth's cheerful voice said, "Hi, toots, how's it going?"

"It's going."

"I don't want to keep bugging you, but I can't stand not

knowing what's going on. I'm having major withdrawals from the shop."

"I can imagine."

"Have you met him yet?"

Kelly made a face. "Met who?"

Ruth chuckled. "The town hunk, the only single guy worth his salt around there."

Kelly purposely hid her agitation. "If I met him, I didn't know it."

"Oh, trust me, you'd know."

"You're wasting your time, Ruth, playing matchmaker."

Her cousin sighed. "It's past time you looked at other men. *Way* past."

"Who says I don't look?"

"Pooh. You know what I mean."

Kelly laughed. "Hey, don't stress yourself about me. If I'm supposed to find someone else, I will." Only not in this lifetime.

"Sure." Ruth's tone was a tad cynical. "You're just telling me what I want to hear."

Kelly laughed again. "Gotta run. I just heard the buzzer."

Before Ruth could reply, Kelly hung up. Setting her smile in place, she came from behind the counter, only to pull up short and stare. Later, she didn't know why she had behaved in such a manner. Perhaps it was because he was so tall and handsome.

Or better yet, perhaps it was the way he was looking at her.

Was this the "hunk" Ruth had just told her about?

To her chagrin, the stranger's dark blue eyes began at the tip of her toes and worked slowly upward, missing nothing of her trim frame. He gave a pointed glance at her breasts and hair, making her strangely glad she had recently placed highlights in her short, sherry-colored tresses.

When those incredible dark eyes whipped back up to hers, the air was charged with electricity. Stunned, Kelly realized she was holding her breath.

"Like what you see?" she asked before she thought. God, where had that come from? *Her real job.* Being bold and forward was what had pushed her to succeed in her profession.

The big guy grinned, a slow, sexy grin. "As a matter of fact, I do."

For the first time since her husband's death four years prior, Kelly was completely unnerved by a man's stare. And voice. She sensed, however, this stranger wasn't just any man. There was something special about him that commanded attention. *Rugged* was the word that came to mind.

She wasn't used to seeing men in worn jeans, washed so much that their color had faded, plus a flannel shirt, scarred steel-toed boots and a hard hat in his hand. Even in Lane, this caliber of man was rare.

He was still staring at her. Kelly shifted her feet and tried to look away, but failed. That ruggedness seemed to go hand in hand with his six-foot-plus height, muscled body and slightly mussed, sun-kissed brown hair.

Big and dangerous. A treacherous combination.

God, what was she thinking? No matter how attractive or charming the man, she wasn't interested. If so, she would've encouraged other men's affections—in Houston. He was probably up to his armpits in women, anyway, even in Lane.

No man would ever measure up to her deceased

husband, Eddie. Having drawn that conclusion, Kelly had concentrated on her career and made it her reason for living.

Breaking into the growing silence, she asked in her most businesslike tone, "What can I get you?"

"What's the special today?" he asked in a deep, brusque voice that matched his looks.

Kelly cleared her throat, glad some normalcy had returned. "Coffee?"

"That'll do for starters," he responded, striding deeper into the shop, pulling out a chair and sitting down.

"The specials are on the board." To her dismay, Kelly was rooted to the spot like a tongue-tied imbecile. Then, red-faced, she finally whipped her gaze to the board behind the counter, which always listed the day's coffee and food specials.

"Not this time," he drawled, "unless I've lost a day." He paused. "Today's Wednesday, not Tuesday. Right?"

Convinced her face matched the color of her hair, Kelly nodded. She hadn't changed the sign, which under ordinary circumstances wouldn't have been a big deal. But for some reason, this man's comment made her feel inadequate, a condition she despised.

Shrugging her shoulders, Kelly gave him a sugary smile and said, "French vanilla latte is the coffee flavor for the day."

He rubbed his chin for a moment, then frowned. "Too bad a fellow can't just get a plain cup of joe?"

Realizing that he was teasing her, she kept that smile in place and said, "Sorry, this is not that kind of shop. But then you know that. So if it's supermarket coffee you want, you'll have to make your own."

He chuckled. "I know."

Despite her reluctance, she felt a grin toying with her lips. "I'll take the plain brew that's closest to normal old coffee."

When she returned with the cup and placed it in front of him, Kelly didn't look at him, hoping to discourage further conversation. Despite his good looks, for some reason, this man made her uncomfortable, and she wanted no part of him. Still, she handed him a menu.

He glanced at it, laid it aside, then looked back up at her. "So you're the new Ruth?"

"Hardly."

"So where is she?"

"Out of state caring for her ailing mother."

"You're filling in, huh?"

"For a while, anyway."

His thick eyebrows bunched together as his gaze locked on her again. "By the way, I'm Grant Wilcox."

"Kelly Baker."

Instead of offering his hand, he nodded. "A pleasure."

Every time he spoke, she had a physical reaction to his voice. It was like being struck by something you thought would be severe and bruising, so that you recoiled inwardly. Only it wasn't at all. It was pleasant, in fact.

"You from around here?" he asked after taking a long sip of his coffee.

"No," Kelly said hesitantly. "Actually, I'm from Houston. How about yourself?"

"Not originally. But I am now. I live about ten miles west of town. I own a logging company and recently bought the timber on a huge tract of land. So I'm stuck in Lane. At least for the time being."

The skin around his eyes crinkled when he smiled, and

he was smiling now. "We've just started cutting, and I'm happy as a pig in the sunshine."

Was he deliberately trying to sound like a hick or was he trying to tell her something by using that off-putting terminology? "That's good," she said for lack of anything else to say. Despite her reaction to Grant, intellectually she couldn't care less what he was or what he did. So she asked if he'd like something to eat now.

As if he picked up on her attitude, a smirk crossed his lips, then he said, "I'll have a bowl of soup and a warm-up on my coffee."

All he needed to add was "little lady" to go with that directive. He definitely didn't seem to be the world's most progressive guy. Was it so obvious she was out of her comfort zone? Or was he just intuitive? It didn't matter. What *did* matter was that his condescending manner not only infuriated her, but also made her more determined than ever to serve him with perfection.

Grabbing the pot from behind the counter, Kelly made her way back toward his table, a smile plastered on her lips. She picked up his cup, and that was when it happened. The cup slipped from her hand and its contents landed in Grant Wilcox's lap. He let out a shout.

Speechless with horror, Kelly watched as he kicked back his chair and stood.

"I'd say that was a good shot, lady," he said.

Though her empty hand flew to her mouth, Kelly's eyes dipped south, where they became glued to the wet spot surrounding his zipper.

Then they both looked up at the same time, their gazes locking.

"Fortunately, none the worse for wear," he drawled, a slow smile crawling across his lips.

Horrified, mortified—you name it—Kelly could only stammer, "Oh my God—I'm so sorry." Her voice sounded nothing like her own. "Stay put and I'll get a towel."

Whirling, she practically ran to the counter, When she returned, Grant's eyes met hers again.

"Here, let me," she said, reaching out, only to stop abruptly when she saw the open grin on his face. She yanked her hand back, feeling blood rush into her cheeks.

"That's okay. I think I'll just change my jeans."

"Uh, right," Kelly said after finding her voice.

"How much do I owe you?"

Kelly was appalled that he'd even ask that. "Under the circumstances, absolutely nothing."

He turned then and walked toward the exit. Kelly could only stand spellbound in shock.

When he reached the door he turned and winked. "See ya."

She hoped not. But at the same time, she was sorry, because he *did* have the cutest ass and swagger she'd ever seen—even when he'd just braved hot coffee from her hands.

Too bad they were wasted on her.

Two

He hated paperwork, but that didn't mean he could ignore it.

Grant's gaze cut over to the desk in the corner of the room, and he groaned. Not only were there stacks of invoices that had to be paid, there were folders that needed to be filed.

He'd gone outdoors for a while. Swinging an ax had given him some much-needed physical relief. After spending most of the morning behind closed doors with his banker, reviewing his finances, he'd needed the outlet. Bank sessions nearly always made a nutcase out of him.

A lot of things this morning had made him half-crazy. Following his shower a short time ago, he'd checked his crown jewels for the first time, since their coffee bath that morning, and deduced they were intact and good to go.

Grant snorted. Only problem with the latter, they *had*

no place to go. Better yet, no one to go to. He could barely recall the last time he'd shared a bed with a woman and really enjoyed it. Through the years, few women had had the power to either disturb his libido or hold his interest.

However, he had to admit with brutal honesty that Ruth Perry's replacement, whoever she was, had definitely done both.

Kelly Baker was one fine woman. He couldn't help but notice her fragile porcelain skin with its delicate dusting of freckles. She had wonderful bones, with curves that were just right, and her clothes draped her slender frame to perfection.

Too bad she didn't seem to have a brain to match all those physical assets. A twinge of conscience bit him, telling him that probably wasn't a fair assessment of the woman. They'd spoken for barely two minutes, and he didn't know anything about her but her name. No doubt, though, she was out of her element and didn't have a clue what she was doing in the food business. Under other conditions and circumstances, he might have enjoyed spending time with her.

"Ah, hell, Wilcox," he muttered, reaching for his beer and taking another swig, "give it a rest."

She wouldn't be caught dead with the likes of him. It hadn't taken him but a few seconds to get her number—a city broad with a city attitude. As far as he was concerned, both those things sucked. No way would the two of them ever get together.

Again, that was too bad; she was a looker. He liked women with spunk, and she appeared to have more than her share of that. He'd relish the opportunity to play with a woman like her. For a few days anyway, he mused ruefully. It was okay to dream, just as long as he didn't do something foolish and try to turn those dreams into reality.

He almost laughed aloud at that crazy thought.

No way was he going to mess with that woman. Already there was something about her that was a real turn-on to him. Perhaps it was because she appeared so untouchable, so condescending, that he wanted to explore what lay under that sheet of ice, then prove he was man enough to melt it. First by grabbing her and pressing her against the wall of his chest... He could almost taste her flesh as he imagined himself caressing, nibbling, kissing her mouth, her neck, her shoulders and her back.

What would she feel? Would he make her tingle, make her hot?

Now that was a hoot, thinking she'd ever let him within touching distance. Disgusted with his thoughts of the ice queen, Grant got up, trudged to the kitchen and helped himself to another beer.

It was after he'd killed the contents that the idea struck him. He stood still, feeling heat boil up in him. "Ah, hell, Wilcox. Forget it. That's crazy. You're crazy!"

Crazy or not, he was going to do it. Grabbing a jacket, he headed out the door, knowing that he'd probably lost what mind he had left.

Her face still flamed.

And not from the tub of hot water she'd been soaking in for at least thirty minutes. How could she have done such a thing? How could she have been so clumsy? She never had been at such a loss before. Cool, calm and collected was how she was thought of at the firm, how she generally operated on a day to day basis.

Or at least how she used to, before…

Kelly shook her head, refusing to go there. She had already beaten up on herself enough. To dwell on the now was not only detrimental to her psyche, but stupid. What happened four years ago couldn't be changed. Nothing would ever bring her family back.

What happened this morning, however, was another matter altogether.

"Merciful heaven," Kelly muttered, reaching for the loofah and sudsing her body so hard she left it tingling. Then, deciding she couldn't change the morning's embarrassment no matter how much she might want to, she got out of the tub and dried off.

Later, wrapped in a warm robe, she sat on the sofa close to the fireplace. Even though it was relatively early, she should try to get some sleep, but she knew any attempt to do so would be futile. Her mind was still too revved up. Besides, at home she hardly ever went to bed before midnight, usually kept company by a ton of work she brought home from the office.

Thinking about work, Kelly felt her heart falter.

She missed her office, her clients, her condo. She missed them with a passion. In the Houston Galleria area she heard the sounds of traffic, not owls. She shivered and wrapped her robe tighter around her. Something hot to drink always seemed to soothe her. Not this evening, however. Although she had made a cup of her favorite flavored coffee and took several sips of it, she still felt unsettled.

She lay back and closed her eyes, only to find the image

of Grant Wilcox unexpectedly imprinted on the back of her lids. Instead of freaking out, she let her mind have free reign—first, picturing him again in his flannel shirt and tight, faded jeans, covering a body most men would die for, then wondering what made him tick.

Why did she care?

So he was better than average looking in his rough, sexy way—she'd already conceded that. His features were carved with decisive strokes, and he had a killer smile and dimples to go along with that amazing body.

He had that muscled, yet loose-limbed agility that most big men didn't possess. She could picture him working outdoors shirtless, mending a fence, felling timber, or doing whatever he did.

Suddenly, her mind jumped ship and she imagined him without his jeans. No underwear, either.

The image didn't stop there. Next came the vision of the two of them together, naked…

Stop it! She told herself. What had gotten into her?

She was so traumatized by her thoughts, she couldn't even open her eyes. So what? No one knew what was going on inside her head. Those erotic, mental meanderings were hers and hers alone and would bring harm to no one.

Wrong.

This was a dangerous mind game she was playing—examining her life, including her loneliness and her need to be accepted and loved. Still, the images wouldn't let go—of mouths, tongues, entwined, of kisses that sucked out the soul.

The phone proved merciful to her, ringing with a jar-ring clarity just then. Lurching up, heart palpitating and drenched in sweat, Kelly let go of a pent-up breath.

"God!" she whispered, mortified and confused. Loosening her robe, she reached for the receiver.

"Hey, kiddo, how's it going?"

Ruth again. Although Kelly didn't want to talk to her, she had no choice. Perhaps her cousin's laughter was the antidote she needed to gather her scattered wits about her.

"How was the rest of the day?"

"Are you sure you want to know?" Kelly asked, a tremor in her voice.

"Uh-oh, something happen?"

"You might say so."

"Hey, I don't like the sound of that." Ruth paused. "Okay, did the help quit?"

"No way. They love me."

"Whew. That's a relief. If you knew how hard it was for me to find those two, you'd be relieved, too."

"I am. They're great."

"So, if the place is still standing and you're selling the goods, what could be so bad?"

Kelly cleared her throat. "Do you know a farmer by the name of Grant Wilcox?"

Ruth laughed. "First off, he's no farmer. He's a forester."

"Whatever."

"They aren't the same, cousin dear."

"That's a minor point, but I'll concede."

"Girl, he's the hunk I was telling you about. Surely you figured that out."

"I guessed as much."

"So what do…did…you think?"

If only you knew. "He's okay."

"Just okay?" Ruth practically screeched. "I'm not believing you. He's had every female in the county and sur-rounding ones try to get him down the aisle." She paused with a laugh. "Without success, I might add."

"That's too bad. You of all people know I'm not inter-ested in being with a farmer, for God's sake." Kelly found herself squirming on the sofa.

"Forester."

Kelly ignored that. "What he is is a country bumpkin who probably prefers to hug trees rather than women." She paused. "No offense intended."

"None taken," Ruth replied with more laughter. "I know how you feel about the country. Or should I say the woods?"

"They're one and the same to me."

"Uh, right. So back to Grant. What's up with him?"

Kelly cleared her throat one more time, then told the un-varnished truth, leaving nothing out.

Afterward, there was silence on the other end of the line, then Ruth whooped like a banshee. "Oh, my God, I wish I'd been there to see that."

"You mean you're not furious at me?" Kelly asked in surprise.

"For being clumsy as a lame duck?"

"I have no leg to stand on," Kelly said, "and no pun in-tended."

Ruth whooped again.

Kelly simply held her silence, confused about her cousin's reaction. "It sounds like you think he deserved what he got?"

"Not at all," Ruth said, her voice still dripping with humor. "It's just that he of all men—the county stud—got burned where it hurts most."

"Ruth! I can't believe you said that."

"Well, isn't that what you did?"

"He had on jeans, Ruth. Surely—"

"When it come to scalding liquid, jeans ain't that thick. You can bet his gonads took a hit."

"I guess they did," Kelly admitted in a meek voice.

"Let's just hope, for the sake of gals still chasing him, that his pride is just burned and not charred."

"Ruth, I'm going to strangle you when I see you."

Her cousin's giggles increased.

"You're making me feel awful."

"Honey, don't worry about it," Ruth said. "Grant's a survivor. He'll be fine. He may never come back in the shop, but hey, that's the way it goes. Other than emptying hot coffee in customers' laps, how's business?"

Later, after they had talked at length about the shop, Kelly finally made her way back into the kitchen, then heard a knock on the door. She stopped midstride, then turned around and headed back to the living room. Frowning, she opened the door, only to receive the shock of her life. Her mouth gaped open.

Grant stood on the porch with flowers in hand.

Before he said anything, she felt his gaze roam over her.

She tried to swallow, but it seemed her tongue had grown too large and was about to choke her.

"It's obvious you're not expecting company." He shifted his feet. "But may I come in, anyway?"

Three

Kelly felt her breath grow shallow. Of course he couldn't come in. There was no reason for him to be here. Certainly no reason for him to come in.

Yet she continued to stand with the door open, her common sense beginning to crack. Surely she wasn't going to give in to this insanity.

She wasn't even dressed, for heaven's sake. She had nothing on under her robe, but at least it was made of thick terry cloth, impossible to see through.

Grant cocked his head and grinned. "These flowers are sure hankering for some water. I don't know how much longer they're going to survive."

Kelly shook her head and smiled. "I noticed they are a little droopy."

"See, I knew we were bound to agree on something."

She gave him an exasperated look. "Did anyone ever tell you that you're full of it?"

"Yep," he said.

That nonchalant honesty was followed by a chuckle, a deep belly chuckle that sent Kelly's already hammering pulse skyrocketing. It amazed her that this man aroused her sexual nature where others hadn't. And not from their lack of trying, either.

Even so, she hadn't looked at men through any eyes except passive ones for a long time.

So why was *he* different?

Kelly didn't know. For more reasons than one—none of which she cared to analyze, especially with him camped on Ruth's porch as if his boots had been embedded in concrete—he frightened her.

"How 'bout I promise just to stay long enough for you to put the posies in water." It wasn't a question, though his raised eyebrows made it one.

Realizing her common sense had deserted her, Kelly stood back and gestured with her hand.

Grinning, Grant removed his hat and, in two long strides, was across the threshold. Kelly closed the door and followed him, managing to keep a safe distance between them, but giving him a once-over in the process.

Not only did he look great in another pair of faded jeans and a blue T-shirt that exactly matched his eyes, but his height and the broadness of his shoulders seemed to dwarf the room, making it much too small for both of them.

With her pulse still hammering much harder than it should have been, Kelly wanted to move farther away, but knew it wouldn't do any good. There was no place to go that would put enough space between them.

"Got a vase?" he asked, that grin still in place.

"Uh, I'm sure Ruth has one around here somewhere."

"Maybe you ought to go and look."

A short tense silence followed, before she stated, "Maybe I should."

He chuckled again. "Hey, I'm harmless. Really and truly."

Kelly raised her eyebrows and smiled. *Sure you are—like a rattlesnake on a mission.* The cure for that was to keep her wits sharpened. She reached for the flowers. "Have a seat while I look for a vase."

"Sure you don't need any help?" he asked, handing them to her.

"I'm sure," she said, with more sharpness than she intended. But jeez, this man was getting under her skin, and the worst part about it, she was giving him carte blanche to let that happen, especially when she knew he'd deliberately let his hand graze hers. Light though the touch was, it left her quivering with awareness.

She finally located a vase, filled it with water and crammed the flowers into it. She then made her way back into the living room, setting the vase on a nearby table. He was bending over the fireplace, stoking the dying embers of the fire back to life.

No question he did have one cute rear end. And right now, she was privy to staring at it without his knowledge Then, realizing what she was doing and the track her mind was taking, she shook her head violently and said, "Thanks for the flowers."

He straightened and whipped around, his gaze narrowed on her. For a long moment, their eyes met and held. Finally Grant's gaze slid away, and she breathed a sigh of relief. His being here was simply not going to work if she didn't get control of her scattered emotions. God, she was acting like a teenager in the grip of hormones, for heaven's sake.

"It's a peace offering," he said, rubbing a chin that had the beginnings of a five o'clock shadow, which only added to his attractiveness.

"If that's the case, then I should be showing up on your doorstep."

"Actually, it was just an excuse to see you again." He paused and looked directly at her. "Any problem with that?"

Yes! "You certainly don't mince words," she said, stalling for time. Now was the perfect opportunity to tell him she wasn't interested in him, or any man, for that matter. Instead, she heard herself say, "Do you want to sit down?"

"I'd like nothing better, but are you sure that's what you want?"

"No," she said in a slightly unsteady voice, "I'm not sure of anything right now."

He plopped down on the sofa and concentrated on the fire while she sat on the edge of the chair adjacent. "I didn't offer you anything to drink," she said inanely.

"A beer would be nice."

She stood. "Ruth has some in the fridge."

"I don't like to drink alone."

"I have my coffee."

His belly chuckle followed her all the way to the kitchen. With her heartbeat still out of sync, she fixed the drinks and returned to the room. Meanwhile, he'd sprawled his long lets out in front of him. Unconsciously, she eyed his powerful thighs and the bulge behind his zipper.

When she realized where she was staring, she whipped her gaze up, only to find him watching her with heat in his eyes. She took a deep breath, but it didn't help. Both her face and lungs felt scorched.

He really should go.

She eased back down in the chair and watched as he took a swig of his beer. After setting the bottle on the table beside him, he said, "What brings someone like you here?"

Kelly gave a start. "Someone like me?"

"Yeah, a real classy lady who looks and acts like a fish out of water."

"My cousin needed my help, and I came to her rescue."

"Nothing's that simple."

"Perhaps not."

He reached for his beer and took another deep swig. "But that's all you're going to tell me. Right?"

"Right," she said bluntly, though she felt a smile tug at her lips.

"So you're either carrying a lot of baggage or a lot of secrets, Kelly Baker. Which is it?"

"I'm not telling."

"If you're not willing to share, how are we going to get to know each other better?"

She didn't know if he was smiling or smirking. She suspected the latter. "Guess we're not."

"Man, you know how to pull the rug right out from under a fellow." He stood, lifting his shoulders up and down as if to stretch, before stoking the fire once again. That motion called attention to his sexual agility and charisma once again. God, the man just oozed it.

"You know the fact that you will barely talk to me makes me more curious than ever," he said.

The tension heightened.

"You know what they say about curiosity." She interlaced her fingers.

"Yeah, it killed the cat." He grinned and the atmosphere eased.

"So what about you?" she asked, watching him plop back down on the sofa.

"What about me?"

"I bet you're not willing to open your life to a stranger."

He shrugged. "What do you want to know?"

She started to say, *everything,* then caught herself. "Whatever you're comfortable telling me."

"Hell, if I have anything to hide, I don't know it."

"Everyone has secrets, Mr. Wilcox."

His features turned grim. "Mr. Wilcox? You gotta be kidding me."

Her face burned. "I don't know you well enough to be on a first-name basis."

"Bullshit. The fact that you got me hot the first time I saw you puts us on familiar territory."

"Funny," Kelly retorted, though she knew her face was beet-red.

The lines around his mouth deepened, suggesting he was about to grin. "All right, Grant," she said.

"Ah, now that's better." He polished off his beer, then got back on the subject. "I guess the most important thing about me is that I have trouble staying in one place."

"Why is that?"

"Army brat. My dad was constantly on the move, so we didn't stay in one place long enough to put down roots and form long-lasting relationships.

"Are you an only child?"

"Yep. Both my parents are dead."

"Mine, too."

"Ah, be careful now, or you'll tell me something personal."

She glared at him and he laughed; then continued, "It was only when I attended Texas A & M University that I learned what settling down meant. That was tough for a roamer like me, until I met my best friend, Toby Keathly.

"Toby was majoring in forestry at A & M, and since I also loved being outside, we bonded. I ended up majoring in forestry myself and spent all the time I could with Toby in East Texas, where he grew up.

"With the money I had inherited from my parents, after graduation I purchased several hundred acres in Lane County and built the log cabin where I now live. Soon after that, I formed my own company, and traveled around the world. And now, with the signing of this new contract for cutting timber, I'm as content as a pig can be."

"That's quite a story," Kelly said.

"It's my boring life in a nutshell."

She laughed without humor. "There's nothing boring about you."

"Coming from you, I'll take that as a compliment."

"There's one thing you left out."

"Oh?"

"Your personal life. Women."

"Not much to tell there, either. What experience I've had with them taught me one important thing."

"And what was that?"

"They like men who can offer them security—home,

family, steady job, the whole package—a package that's as foreign to me as some of the countries in which I've lived."

"Do you really believe that?" He sounded like a throwback from the 1950s.

He paused and gave her a look. "Now you're meddling."

"Ah, so when push comes to shove, I'm not the only one with secrets, or is it baggage?"

"Touché!"

That word was followed by an awkward silence, then he rose. "Guess I'd better be going. It's getting late."

She didn't argue, although she experienced a twinge of disappointment she couldn't believe she was feeling about this impossible man.

"Thanks for the beer," he said at the door, turning to face her.

"Thanks for the flowers."

"Wilted and all, huh?"

He was so close now that his smell assaulted her like a blow to the stomach, especially when she noticed that his blue eyes were centered near her chest. She glanced down and saw that her robe had parted.

Before she could catch her next breath or move, the tip of his finger was trailing down her neck, her shoulder, not stopping until he had grazed the exposed side of her breast. Her mind screamed at her to push him away, but she couldn't. She flinched, not from embarrassment but from the lust that stampeded through her, holding her rooted to the spot.

His eyes darkened as he leaned toward her. In that second she sensed he was going to kiss her, and she was powerless to stop him. He moaned, then crushed his lips against hers; she sagged into him, reveling in his mouth, which was both hungry and urgent, as though if he didn't get it all now, he wouldn't get another chance.

When they finally parted, their breathing came in rapid spurts. Her emotions, at that moment, were so raw, so terrifying, that all she could do was cling to the front of his shirt.

"I've been wanting to do that since I walked through the door of the coffee shop," he rasped.

She wanted to respond, but couldn't. She didn't know what to say.

Grant spoke again, "Look, I'm leaving now, but we'll talk later." He peered down at her with anxious, searching eyes. She seemed on the edge, and he sensed that more than his kiss had propelled her there. "You're okay, right?"

No, I'm not all right!

She swallowed, then nodded. After he had left, Kelly had no idea how long she stood in a daze before she made her way to bed, where she lay across it and sobbed her heart out.

How could she have let her guard down like that, betray her husband—the love of her life—by letting this stranger kiss her? What had come over her? She didn't want to expose her heart ever again for fear of the pain and hurt she knew it could bring. She had promised herself that. And it was so important for her to keep that promise.

The sad part was she didn't know how to right the wrong she had just committed.

Grant had just finished chopping and stacking more wood that he didn't need. But who cared? If swinging an ax made him feel good and kept his frustrations at bay, then that was a-okay.

Unfortunately, his manual labor had not worked out as planned. He couldn't get Kelly off his mind even though he hadn't seen her in two days. He could still smell and feel her soft skin, as if his flesh had absorbed hers. Actually, he could damn near taste it.

That type of thinking could get a man in big trouble, because it had to do with dependency, need and becoming emotionally connected to a woman he barely knew. With Kelly Baker that was out of the question. She wasn't going to be around for long, it seemed, and he could tell she had too damn many secrets.

Still, that one kiss had turned him inside out, made him feel higher than a kite. Who was he kidding? It had made him want more. He couldn't get her breasts off his mind. Even though he'd only managed to peek at the side of one and barely touch it, he knew it would be as firm and delicious as a newly ripened peach.

Just thinking about tasting that white flesh made his mouth water.

Careful, man, he told himself. You'd best put the brakes on or you'll scare her off for sure. If he ever expected to see her again he'd have to take it easy, use finesse. Even then, she wouldn't be a pushover.

Yet he'd seen the desire in her eyes, felt the heat radiate from her body. She wanted him, too, only she might not want to admit it. Therein lay the problem. But he had no intention of giving up. If he weren't mistaken, underneath that veneer of ice was a hot, explosive woman.

While she was here, why not test the waters and find out?

With that question weighing heavily on his mind, he cleaned up his mess, then made his way into the cabin, where he showered, dressed, then grabbed a beer. The bottle was halfway to his mouth when he heard a loud rap on the door. "It's open," Grant called out.

Seconds later, his foreman and friend, Pete Akers, entered, his weathered face all grins.

"Wanna beer?" Grant asked without preamble.

Pete's grin spread as he quickened his pace. "Thought you'd never ask."

Once the foreman had his beverage in hand, they made their way back into the great room and sat near the roaring fire.

"Damn, but it's colder than Montana out there."

"How would you know?" Grant asked, giving Pete a sideways glance. "You haven't ever been out of East Texas, much less to Montana."

"Makes no difference." Pete's tone was obstinate. "I know cold when I feel it."

"Then get your bald head over here by the fire."

Once Pete had done just that and sat down, they quietly sipped their beers, both content with their own thoughts.

"What's with all that wood?" Pete finally asked. "Looks like you cut enough wood for an Alaskan winter. And here it is nearly March."

"So you noticed?"

Pete quirked a thin brow and gave Grant a penetrating look. "How could I not?"

Grant shrugged. "Guess I just needed to work off some excess energy."

This time both of Pete's brows went up. "Surely you're not stressed about anything, not when things are all going your way."

"Can't argue about that." He wasn't about to mention his fixation with the new woman in town, so he stuck to business. "Buying that tract is something I never thought would happen. And I think it'll pay off handsomely."

"Put your company on the map is the way I see it," Pete commented.

"Hopefully. In the meantime, I got a whopping lot of bills to pay at the bank. Don't forget that. As you know, the timber wasn't cheap—neither was that new equipment I had to buy."

Pete blew out his breath. "I know. When you put things in perspective, I guess you've got a helluva good reason to be stressed."

"*Stressed* is probably the wrong word," Grant admitted with a frown. "Actually, I'm excited and confident that this tract will turn a profit and get me out of debt. So update me." He set his empty bottle down and gave his foreman a straight look.

"I've already placed both crews."

"Equipment and all?"

"Yep," Pete said in an animated voice, as though proud of that accomplishment.

"Have you found another foreman?"

Pete frowned. "I thought maybe you and me together could handle it. You know how I am about hiring people I don't know."

"But you know everyone around these parts."

"That's why I ain't hiring nobody." Peter cocked his head. "Get my drift?"

"That'll work, especially since none of the other tracts are cuttable right now due to the poor conditions."

"Let's hope the rain continues to hold off."

"It will. I'm convinced my luck has changed and all for the better. So where did you put the log sets?" Grant asked, back to business.

"I put one crew on the northwest side next to the county road and the other on the south end next to the old home place."

"I'll work the south end," Grant said, knowing it would be the most difficult site to cut.

"The saw heads are already buzzing and it looks like we're going to be able to get twelve to fourteen loads per day."

"Man, if we do that for six weeks to two months, then I'd be on easy street for sure."

Grant grinned and raised his hand. Pete hit it in a high-five just as Grant's cell phone rang. Frowning, he reached for it, noticing that the call was from Dan Holland, the landowner who had sold him the timber.

"What's up, buddy?" Grant asked without mincing words.

"I'm afraid we got a problem."

Four

Did he regret the kiss?

Probably.

Kelly figured that was the reason she hadn't seen him today. Of course, she didn't know for a fact. As always, her mind was her own worst enemy, taking off like a runaway train, imagining all sorts of crazy things.

Since she'd been in charge of the shop, she'd seen Grant only *once*. He hadn't been a regular customer so why would he stop in again?

The truth was, she couldn't stop thinking about the kiss. If only she hadn't let that happen, she'd be just fine. But she'd made an unwise choice, and choices had consequences. She wanted to see him again, even though she kept reminding herself that would be foolish.

Kelly's life was back in Houston. She would soon be

gone from Lane, Texas. More to the point, she couldn't wait to get back to her *real* job, and to the challenge it offered.

"Kelly, phone for you."

Jerking her mind back to reality, she smiled at Albert, went into the small office and picked up the receiver. It was her boss, John Billingsly.

"How's it going?" he asked in a pleasant tone.

"Do you really want to know?" Though she had a deep respect for John and thought of him as a friend as well as a boss, he wasn't exactly high on her fan list now. After all, if it weren't for him, she wouldn't be stuck here.

His sigh filtered through the line. "You know I do, or I wouldn't have asked."

"Actually, things are going better than I thought they would down here, though I hate to admit that."

He chuckled. "I know you're still unhappy with me."

"And will be for a long time." Although Kelly had spoken bluntly and truthfully, there was no rancor in her words.

"You know how much I care about you, Kelly. I only want what's best for you."

"I know." And she did. At times she sensed he would like to be more than her boss, yet he'd never once crossed that professional line. She thought there was more to his feelings than he had ever expressed, however.

"So just stay put for a while longer," John said, "to give your body and mind a chance to completely heal. That's all I'm asking."

"Do I have a choice?"

"No," he said in a soft but firm tone.

She knew he was right, though she was loath to admit

that. Both John and Dr. Rivers, her psychiatrist, had told her that, but it was John who had made a believer out of her. He hadn't exactly threatened the security of her job, but he had certainly threatened her pending promotion, a position she wanted badly.

She remembered that day so well. He had called her into his corner office. When she'd taken a seat, John had gotten up, come around his desk, sat in the chair closest to her and taken her hand. "Look me in the eye and tell me you're not struggling?"

Kelly couldn't. Tears clogged her vision as her shoulders began to shake. "Have I hurt the firm? If I have, I'm so sorry."

"I won't lie and say you haven't made some bad decisions and choices recently, because you have. But I think you know that yourself. You haven't damaged the firm— not yet. That's what we're trying to avoid."

"Thank God." Kelly had hung on to his hand and squeezed it.

"You have a chance to become a partner in this firm," John said, "but only if you get control of your emotions and become the attorney we know you can be."

But that's the person I was before my daughter and husband were killed by a drunk driver, she'd wanted to scream.

As if John had read her thoughts, he'd added, "You have to come to grips with your loss."

"I have," Kelly cried, jerking her hand out of his. She resented being patronized, as if she was a child. She dug her fingers into her palms. She couldn't believe this. She was Kelly Baker, firm overachiever. She had brought into the firm some of its biggest and best clients. Shouldn't that count for something? Apparently not, because at the first sign of trouble they wanted to toss her away like a piece of garbage.

Her conscience suddenly rebelled, reminding her that she was blowing John's words way out of proportion. Deep down, she knew he and the company were firmly on her side.

"No, you haven't faced your loss," he said softly, patiently. "Far from it, and that's the problem. You've buried your pain and heartache in your work. Now, four years after the fact, the headache you never faced, or dealt with openly, is doing a number on you. It's taking its toll on your emotions and your health. We both know you're on the brink of having a complete breakdown."

She hated to admit that he was right, but he was.

Push had come to shove and she could no longer fool herself into thinking she and everything around her was just fine.

"I know your cousin needs help, Kelly," John said into the growing silence. "Go and help her. New surroundings, new people, new job…" He paused with a lopsided smile. "Although I can't imagine you serving coffee or food, you'll give it you all, like you do everything else you tackle."

She forced a smile. "I can't imagine that either, but it looks like you've given me no choice."

"That's right," John admitted in a stern voice.

Because her throat was too full to speak, Kelly had leaned over and kissed him on the cheek, then walked out. That had been three weeks ago. Three of the longest weeks of her life.

"Kelly, are you still there?" John asked into the silence now.

"Yes. Sorry. Actually, I was just rehashing our last conversation."

"That's good, because nothing has changed on this end."

"I know." She heard the break in her voice but hoped he hadn't. She wanted to keep her dignity at all costs.

"You get back to work. I'll talk to you again soon."

The second she replaced the receiver and walked back into the dining area, Kelly pulled up short. Grant was walking in the door with a scowl on his face.

Her heart dropped to her toes. She'd been right; he wasn't glad to see her. Then why was he here? Simple. He wanted some food or coffee. Maybe both.

"You look surprised to see me," he said in a pleasant enough tone, however, his big body striding toward a table.

Today he was dressed a little more formally than he had been before. He had on jeans and boots, of course, but his shirt was smooth cotton, not flannel, and instead of his hard hat, he had on a black Stetson, which he removed.

"Actually, I am," Kelly said with honesty once she found her tongue. After that she didn't know what to say, which was totally unlike her. But then she reminded herself she'd just recently kissed this man's mouth with hot, heady passion, which had and still did unnerve her to the core.

When he'd walked by her, she'd gotten a whiff of his scent—fresh and good, as if he'd just gotten out of the shower. That added to her unnerved state.

Feeling her face flame, Kelly turned away. She hadn't had thoughts like that since her husband died. "Would you care for something to drink?" she finally asked. "Or eat?"

"Coffee'll do."

"Are you sure you want me to serve it?" She made herself ask that with a smile hoping to lighten his mood. Probably another foolish move.

The scowl on his face softened and he actually grinned, which affected her heart again. God, she had to get hold of herself.

"Sure, though notice I'm sitting real close to the table."

She smiled again.

This time he didn't reciprocate. That scowl reappeared, even fiercer than before.

Feeling as though she were treading in deep water, Kelly got his coffee and carefully placed the mug in front of him. "You seem upset." A flat statement of act. If it had to do with her, she wanted to know it.

"Yeah, but not at you." His eyes met hers.

She felt a flush steal into her face.

He leaned forward and said in a low, husky voice, "You look so damn good, if I had my way, I'd grab you right now and kiss you until you begged me to stop. Even then, I'm not sure I would."

His provocative statement took her aback so much that all she could do was stand there speechless while a flush of heat charged through her body.

"Do you have a minute?"

"Sure," she said, uneasy that she was going to hear something she didn't want to.

He pulled out the chair adjacent to him and indicated that she sit.

"Let me get a cup of coffee first. I'll be right back." Once she'd returned and sat down, they remained silent while taking several sips out of the big mugs. Finally she said, "Something's happened."

Grant's brows bunched together and he sighed. "You got that right."

"Want to talk about it?"

"I'm looking for a good attorney. Know any?"

Kelly's heart skipped a beat, but she kept her calm facade in place. *Did she ever!* "With all your business dealings, I'm surprised you don't have one."

"I do, but unfortunately he's out of the country. And his partner's an idiot."

Kelly's eyebrows rose, but she simply said, "Okay."

"Sorry. That's not exactly true. Let's just say we don't see eye to eye on things."

Kelly merely nodded, then asked, "Why do you think you need an attorney?" If he didn't want to tell her, he didn't have to, but apparently he wanted someone to talk to or he wouldn't have said anything to begin with.

"Dan Holland, the landowner I bought the timber from, just called me and dropped a friggin' bombshell."

"Oh?"

"Yeah, and one of the worst things about it is that I thought he was my friend."

"Friendship and business are two different things, Grant. You should know that."

"I do know that, dammit. Still, in a small town, a man's word is as good as his signature. And I had both from Dan."

"So what's changed?" Kelly pressed, sensing his tempter building to no good end.

"He wants my crews to stop cutting timber."

"And the reason?"

"Some crap about an illegitimate half brother showing up out of the blue and wanting a say in the deal Dan and his brothers had just made with me."

Kelly was not only shocked but puzzled. "And your friend's buying that story and wants to stop the deal?"

"Hook, line and sinker. He said that if Larry Ross— that's the guy's name—turns out to be legit, then he has a right to be included."

"Sounds ludicrous."

"It's more than that. It's crazy as hell."

"So what was your response?" Kelly asked.

"I told Holland he was nuts if he let some bozo he's never seen before waltz in and make that kind of claim, and not tell him to take a freakin' hike."

"I find it unbelievable that he didn't," Kelly said, shaking her head in dismay.

"Dan said he'd never seen me this upset."

Kelly's eyes widened. "I have a feeling that was the wrong thing to say."

"You're right. I told him if he thought I was upset now, just wait. He ain't seen nothing yet. At the moment, I was as calm as the Pope taking a nap."

Kelly shook her head. "What a mess."

"There's more," Grant said. "Dan defended this Ross character, saying that his dad had been a womanizer, that it was possible he'd had an affair and Larry Ross could be the product of that affair.

"And apparently the woman, Ross's mother, said that she'd kept quiet long enough, swearing to her son that Lucas Holland was definitely Ross's daddy and that Ross should get anything and everything that was entitled to him."

Kelly gave him a pointed look. "And your response?"

"Hogwash."

Her lips twitched.

Grant blew out a long breath. "I told him that's just too pat, too hokey. Ross is his problem, not mine. And if he is legit or not has zip to do with me. We have a deal that is on the up-and-up—signed, sealed and delivered."

"He didn't see it that way, right?"

"You got it. Apparently Larry Ross has threatened to file an injunction to stop my operation, claiming his family doesn't have the right to sell the timber without his signature."

Kelly was aghast and it showed.

"This is crazy, because at the time Dan didn't even know this guy existed. But this Ross character evidently doesn't care.

"So I told Holland to give me my money back. An injunction could wipe me out financially."

"What was his response?" Kelly asked, becoming more appalled by the second. She felt her brain churning as it hadn't in three weeks. Grant was right. He needed an attorney ASAP.

"He said he couldn't do it, that his brothers had left it up to him to do the investing, and he'd put all the money in non-liquid assets."

"That man's a piece of work."

"I said that's your problem, not mine. Of course Dan whined that we could work something out, that all he's asking of me was to suspend operations for several days until this mess could be straightened out."

"I hope you told him sorry, no can do."

"That's exactly what I told him. His comeback was that I was being unreasonable. So I asked him what if the shoe were on the other foot? Would he be so eager to give in? His answer was no, so I told him the simple solution was to borrow the money against his assets and pay the creep off."

"If he'd gone for that," Kelly said, "we wouldn't be having this conversation.

"Right again," Grant stated. "You know, Kelly, friend or no friend, a deal's a deal. I kept my end of the bargain, and I expect him to keep his. Dan got pissed and assured me I hadn't heard the end of this.

"If it's a fight he wants, then, by God, that's what he's gonna get. I *will* cut *my* timber."

"Maybe I can help."

Grant looked startled. "You?"

"That's what I said." Kelly kept her tone low and even.

He laughed. "How? Use your waitress skills and dump hot coffee in his lap?"

Kelly knew he was trying to be funny. But to her, his comment was anything but that. Forcing a sugary smile, she stood and said, "I agree that my waitress skills are lacking. But when I'm practicing law, I'm a damn good attorney."

Grant went pale, as if she'd just cut his throat.

"*You're* an attorney?" His laughter rang through the shop.

Five

He should've kept his mouth shut. Laughing at Kelly hadn't been smart, especially when he was backed into a corner and she had offered to help. But the thought of her being an attorney had never occurred to him. He'd just thought she was a pretty shoulder to cry on.

Kelly Baker, Esquire. It was hard for him to grasp that.

Grant slapped his forehead and cursed, calling himself every derogatory term he could think of and more. But kicking his backside after the fact didn't do any good. The only way to right this wrong was to tuck his tail between his legs and get down on bended knee. That thought made his eyebrows shoot up. Wouldn't that be a sight to behold, him on his knees in front of a woman?

At this point, he was ready to do whatever it took to get him out of this mess. But it wouldn't be easy. He'd almost rather face a grizzly than Kelly; probably have a better chance of winning.

He compressed his lips. He'd been tempted to call Ruth and find out what type of attorney Kelly was.

Then he'd decided that might set off another kind of fire he didn't want any part of. Ruth might think he had an ulterior motive, like a personal interest in Kelly or something, which couldn't be further from the truth.

Liar.

Grant winced. His conscience was at work again, pricking him, keeping him on the straight and narrow. He'd kissed her, dammit. But that was as far, and as personal, as things had gone. Which was not to say he didn't want more, he did.

Her breasts. They were driving him wild. What little he'd seen of them made him want much more.

"Dammit, Wilcox," he muttered tersely. He had to delete those erotic thoughts of her from his mind, or they would cripple him businesswise. Perhaps it had been too long since he'd been with woman. But everything about Kelly made him like he hadn't in eons.

But to get involved with her in any way would be like sticking his hand in a hornet's nest, expecting to get badly stung.

Still, if Kelly were truly a lawyer—and people didn't lie about things like that—he'd screwed up by laughing at her. He gritted his teeth and fisted his hands in disgust.

He should've known there was more to her than met the eye. Right off, he'd figured her for a classy lady. And when she'd refused to tell him anything about herself, he'd picked up on the fact that she had too damn many secrets. He just hadn't guessed *that* one.

Solution?

Suck up to Kelly big time.

Unfortunately, she didn't appear to be the type where groveling would work. Still, he had to try. What did he have to lose? He smiled.

He knew she wasn't indifferent to him. Their wanting each other had been mutual; he'd swear to that. Like magnets, they had been drawn to one another. And that kiss—God, when he'd put his hot, open mouth on hers...

Enough, Wilcox, he told himself, getting up from his desk and heading to the kitchen. He'd spent far too much energy on Kelly Baker. She'd either help him or she wouldn't.

Grant peered at his watch, then groaned. He'd lollygagged around the house for far too long. He should already be at the site. No. He should be at Kelly's.

He grabbed his hat just as his cell rang.

"Where are you?" Pete asked.

From the sound of his foreman's voice, Grant knew something was amiss. "At home."

"You'd best get your ass here pronto."

Grant's stomach clenched. "What's going on?"

There was silence for a moment, then his foreman stated, "Just get here."

Thirty minutes later, Grant whipped his truck into his usual parking spot at the edge of the log set and knew immediately what had Pete in such a dither. The sheriff's car was parked in front of one of the large pieces of equipment. The crew was huddled close by, talking quietly among themselves.

Pete looked as if he was about to punch Sheriff Sayers in the nose.

"Good morning, Amos," Grant said calmly, after easing out of his truck and striding toward the two men, determined to diffuse the highly charged situation.

Amos Sayers was a tall string bean of a man with glasses and big ears.

"Good morning, sir," Amos responded, with an obvious change in tone and attitude following Grant's arrival.

After handshakes, a short, uncomfortable silence ensued. Amos was the first to break it. "You're going to have to shut down."

"I haven't seen anything in writing," Grant said with a show of self-confidence.

Amos slapped a piece of paper into Grant's hand. "Well, you have now."

He didn't even bother to look it. "You're really shutting me down?"

"I don't have any choice." Amos's booted foot pawed the dirt. "I'm just carrying out the judge's order."

"So you are."

"Then you're going to comply with the injunction?" Amos asked, his tone unsure. "And suspend operations?"

A shocked-looking Pete muttered, "I hope to hell you're not going to let this young whippersnapper here dictate to us."

"You want to go to jail?" Amos demanded, his confidence blooming.

Pete shook his head violently.

"Didn't think so."

Amos pawed the dirt once more, then looked straight at

Grant. "Again, I'm sorry about all this, sir." Then he walked back to his car and got in.

"What are you going to do?" The foreman asked in a bleak tone.

"Get a lawyer and get us working again."

"What about the one you've used for years?"

"He's out of the country."

"Got another one in mind?" Pete asked.

"Yep."

Pete gave him a strange look, then said flatly, "You'll call me?"

"As soon as I know something."

Pressing his mouth into a thin line, Grant jumped back in his truck and drove off. He knew what he had to do, but he damn sure didn't have to like it.

Would this day ever end? Kelly asked herself. It was only ten o'clock on Monday morning and she was bored out of her mind. Yesterday hadn't been too bad because she'd been so tired. She had stayed in her lounging pj's most of the day, dozing off and on between reading a murder mystery and watching television.

Today, however, was a different story. She wished the shop wasn't closed on Mondays. One day off in this hole-in-the-wall town was enough. Two in a row was more than she could take.

More depressed than ever, Kelly walked to the window and stared out at the cold, cloudy world. It seemed there was more gloomy weather lately than sunny. But then it was late February, she reminded herself. It wasn't supposed to be warm and uplifting.

Yet in Texas, it could easily have been a beautiful eighty degrees on this very day. Sighing, she turned from the window, walked back to the chair and sat down, pulling her legs under her. After staring blankly at the wall for a while, she reached for her purse nearby, pulled out her wallet and watched it fall open to her pictures.

Her husband's was the first one she saw. Eddie truly had been tall, dark and handsome. More than that, he'd been a sweet, gentle man who had adored her and their daughter, Amber.

Even though Kelly stared at his face now as she had in person so many times in the past, it was hard to remember how it had felt when he'd touched her. She knew she had loved him profoundly at one time, but she couldn't remember what that was like, either. Everything about him had faded with time.

Not so with her daughter. As she looked at her picture, a piercing pain robbed Kelly of her next breath. Her precious baby. Her beautiful child. Her Amber, with her small face smiling up at her. Knowing that she would never see her again, never touch her again—even after four years—was unthinkable.

Unbearable.

Yet the finality of leaving her child in the cold, dark ground was the reality that had finally caught up with Kelly and driven her close to the edge of insanity.

Taking a deep, shuddering breath, she forced a smile through the tears now streaming down her face. She remembered so well the very day that picture had been taken. Amber had just turned three and she'd gotten that dress for her birthday. It was pink and frilly and girlie, just like

Amber. Even though she had bright red curls all over her head, the pink was perfect on her.

Kelly had nestled a pink bow among those curls, but it hadn't been easy. "Be still, squirt blossom," she had told her squirming daughter. "It'll only take a second."

That had been true. The second Amber had scrambled off her lap, she had jerked the ribbon out.

"You little toot, you," Kelly had said, scooping her up, positioning her on her lap and going through the process one more time.

That time the ribbon had stayed put, but only because Kelly had promised Amber an ice cream cone if she'd leave it in. Even at three, her child was smart enough to know a bribe when she heard one, and was smart enough to hold Kelly to it.

Amber had demanded two cones, though in a sweet voice and with her beautiful smile.

If Amber had lived, she would have been as lovely on the inside as she'd been on the outside. She'd had her father's gentle nature. When Amber looked at anyone with those big, dark brown eyes, their hearts had melted into a puddle.

Suddenly a sob caught in Kelly's throat and she slammed the wallet shut. She raised her head determined not to drown in her tears, then stood up. She hadn't had a spell of self-pity like this in quite some time. Homesickness and boredom were to blame, she told herself. Being all alone.

And Grant Wilcox with his condescension and dismissal. She couldn't leave him out.

She had composed herself and wiped the tears from her face when she heard a knock. "Oh, brother," she muttered, wondering who it was.

Kelly opened the door and felt her mouth go slack. Grant Wilcox stood squarely in front of her.

"I know the shop's closed," he said in a sheepish tone, "but I thought you might serve some crow here. Is that true?"

Six

Kelly was mystified that Grant had sought her out away from the shop again. He actually seemed embarrassed, a state that didn't fit with this forester and his killer dimples.

When he'd kissed her that night, she had noticed those tantalizing dents in his cheeks. Thank goodness she had managed to put them out of her mind. She didn't care about Grant Wilcox, she reminded herself quickly. He'd insulted her. Today of all days, she wasn't in the forgiving mood, which she saw as a good thing. This man was obnoxious, sexist—and had gotten too far under her skin.

To her dismay, he remained there.

Standing in front of her, propping his shoulder against the door post, he looked hot. And lethal. His hair, a bit shaggy for her taste, looked as freshly laundered as he did, dressed in jeans that adhered to his body in all the right places, a white shirt that flattered his dark blue eyes, and boots that made him seem taller and more brawny than usual.

She had to admit, whether she'd first thought he was Farmer Brown or not, he was one fine specimen.

Go figure.

Feeling unwanted color creep into her cheeks, Kelly turned slightly, hoping he wouldn't see her reaction to her thoughts. And the idea he might read them was more mind-boggling.

"Is the inside off-limits?" he asked in his deep sexy voice, putting an end to the silence.

"That depends."

"On what?" he asked.

"I haven't decided yet."

"I can handle that."

"Actually, I'm thinking," she said in a slightly husky tone before clearing her throat.

Although a tentative smile teased his lips, Grant refrained from saying anything that might shatter the fragile truce between them. Smart fellow, Kelly thought, One stray word, and she would've sent him away without a qualm.

"I guess it's okay for you to come in," she finally said with a sigh.

As before, once he had crossed the threshold into Ruth's small living room, everything seemed to shrink. His body warmth was something Kelly had hoped to avoid, but she couldn't. He crowded her.

He was just a big man, something she wasn't used to, she reminded herself. It was no big deal—if she didn't make it one. Eddie had been of much smaller stature.

"You didn't answer my question," Grant said, remaining on his feet.

Since she'd asked him in, her manners rose to the surface. "If you'd like, you can sit down."

He gave a shrug, then said, "Thanks. Don't mind if I do."

Kelly remained standing, thinking that gave her some leverage, which was ludicrous, she knew. No matter: she wasn't ready to sit and welcome him as an invited guest. Not yet, anyway.

"You still haven't answered my question," he pressed.

"That's because I don't recall it."

She wasn't fibbing either, not entirely. Seeing him at her door had been such a shock that what he'd said had flown right out of her mind.

"I asked if you were serving crow?"

Despite herself, Kelly felt her lips relax into a smile. "We definitely have it on the menu at the shop."

"For jerks like me, huh?"

"If the shoe fits…" Again she found herself smiling, then forced herself to grow sober. She didn't intend to cut this roughneck any slack. Although he hadn't offended her as much as she'd pretended, her reaction had put much-needed space between them. She thought about him too much for her peace of mind.

"In my case, the shoe definitely fits. And snugly, too."

"If you say so." His apology made no difference. She had no intention of rescuing him. There were plenty of lawyers in this area as competent as her—more so, probably.

Besides, the less she had to do with this man, the better. She must've had temporary mind loss to have offered to help him in the first place, especially when work was the last thing she was supposed to be thinking about.

"Will you accept my apology?" he prodded, appearing

to have hunkered down comfortably in the sofa close to the roaring fire, which gave the room a cozy feel.

Kelly shrugged. "Okay, apology accepted."

She saw his mouth tense, but only for a second, then it went slack and a sheepish look stole over his face. "Something tells me my apology fell far short of its target." His eyes delved into hers.

Rebelling against that magnetic pull, she stiffened. "Hey, give it a rest. You've apologized and I've accepted. The end."

Grant rubbed his chin. "That's what I'm afraid of, which means I'm going to have to do some major kissing up."

"Why would you even bother?" Kelly asked, remaining upright, suddenly tired of this conversation. Elements of her Houston lawyer persona were returning. She knew she should be hospitable and offer him something to drink, but if she did, that might mean he'd hang around. Even though she was definitely lonely and feeling sorry for herself, this man was hardly the one she'd choose to comfort her.

Heaven forbid.

"I have to have an attorney."

"But not me."

"Yes, you."

"How can you be so sure of that?"

"Because you're the most accessible," he said without hesitation. "And I need—*needed*—legal counsel yesterday."

"If nothing else, at least you're honest."

"So what do you say?"

"You don't even know what kind of law I practice."

"Does it matter?"

"Sure, it does. For all you know, I might be just a tax lawyer."

"Are you?"

"No."

Grant spread his hands. "Enough said."

Suddenly irritated at him and his reasoning, Kelly shook her head. "I'm not supposed to be working."

A puzzled look came over his face. "Why? You get disbarred or something?"

"No, I didn't get disbarred or something," she said with forced patience."

As if he realized he'd once again opened his mouth and inserted his big foot, he said in a sincere tone, "Look, I'm sorry. But there's something about you—" He broke off abruptly, as if he feared eating more of that shoe leather.

Kelly had no qualms about finishing the sentence. "That makes *you* say and do things you otherwise wouldn't say or do?"

"Yeah. How did you know?"

"Maybe I feel the same way."

The fact that she admitted that tidbit seemed to shock him. It shocked her, too, actually. The less personal she kept things between them the better off she would be. In fact, the sooner she got rid of him, the better.

"I'll beg if I have to," he said, peering at the fire, then back at her.

His eyes were narrowed and unreadable, but she sensed a desperation in his big body she hadn't noted before. He probably thought that if he apologized, she'd capitulate.

He was wrong. One more time.

"Begging's off-limits here."

He smiled wryly. "How about kneeling?"

She kept a straight face, but it was hard. "That's off-limits, as well."

"You don't cut a man much slack do you?"

"Only if he deserves it."

Color slowly drained from his face. "I was an ass. I've already admitted that. But if you really can't help me, then I'll leave and not bother you again."

Suddenly Kelly felt guilty. Why was that? Perhaps deep down she was dying to do something, *anything,* that pertained to law. And fighting an injunction would be simple compared to what she was used to—at least if the judge was not some old crusty curmudgeon who thought he was God in this neck of the woods.

She wouldn't be surprised if that was the case. If so, then she would be dead in the water as far as wielding any influence. Country and city lawyers mixed like oil and water. Still, she yearned to give the case a shot. Anything other that serving pie and coffee.

"The fact you haven't kicked me out yet gives me hope."

She heard a touch of little-boy eagerness in Grant's tone and it got to her. Dammit, *he* got to her. If only he wouldn't look at her like that. And even though she couldn't define what she meant by *that,* she recognized desire in a man when she saw it. And though that made her uncomfortable, it also made her feel like a woman for the first time in a long while.

"Would you care for something to drink?"

Grant's head popped back up. She'd surprised him again. Good. He didn't need to be sure of her. Then she chastised herself for caring what other women thought about him.

"Still have some beer?"

"I think so."

"It's okay if you don't."

"I'll see."

A few minutes later she returned with two opened bottles of beer. Although it was obviously Ruth's choice of drink, Kelly could barely tolerate the stuff. But today, she decided to join him.

They sipped in silence for a few minutes. Surprisingly, Kelly felt herself relax. Until now, her nerves were all twisted inside. She attributed that change to the beer, even though she'd only had two sips. Still, it didn't take much for her to feel its effects. That was why she seldom drank. With that thought, she set her bottle on the table in front of her and watched as he tossed his head back and chugged down half of his at one time.

Maybe he wasn't as comfortable or sure of himself as he'd like her to think.

"I've been shut down."

Kelly blinked. "Pardon?"

Grant blew out a breath, then finished his beer. "To put it in simple terms, my crews are not allowed to cut the timber I bought."

"So that guy did get an injunction?"

"Yep."

"Have you spoken to him yourself?"

"Not yet. Right now, I probably need to stay as far away from him as possible in order not to rip his head off his shoulders."

"I'd say that's smart." Kelly couldn't keep her sarcasm at bay, though she didn't doubt for a moment that Grant

Wilcox was serious and capable of doing exactly what he set out to do—even if he had to harm another person.

She shuddered inwardly. What was she considering getting herself into?

"So are you going to help me?" Grant had straightened and moved his big body closer to the edge of the sofa.

She sat across from him and held her silence, all the while gnawing on the inside of her lip. She knew she'd regret what she was about to do, but she was going to do it anyway. But not for him, she told herself. Her efforts were purely self-serving.

Regardless of what her doctor said, she needed a challenge or she would wither and die, even though her time here was short-lived. Serving food and beverages was simply not cutting it. Hadn't that recent crying jag proved that?

"I'm making no promises, understand," Kelly said at length, "but I will advise you on what legal advice you need."

Grant blew out a relieved breath. "Thank God."

"Don't be thanking him yet. And certainly not me."

"Uh, right."

"You'll have to indulge me. I'm a good attorney, but I'm not familiar with the timber industry or anything pertaining to it. I just know that trees are cut in the woods and used for a lot of things—building homes, paper products." She paused with a slight grin. "Including toilet paper."

He laughed, then explained in careful detail a little of how his industry worked and his part in the process. "I find landowners willing to sell some of their timber. I buy those standing trees, cut them, then sort them by size and quality.

Once that's done, the wood is hauled to contracted mills, where they're processed and shipped worldwide."

"So unless you cut, the company loses—big."

"I am the company," Grant stressed. "And as I mentioned before, this could ruin me financially."

Kelly nodded. "Go on."

"My payments on my equipment, now sitting idle in the woods, run over fifty thousand a month."

Kelly gasped.

"Oh, I haven't finished yet," Grant said. "And because I had spent my cash on tracts of timber that aren't loggable right now thanks to the wet weather, I had to borrow money to buy this large tract."

"So how much is your equipment and timber altogether?"

"Close to a hundred thou a month. So you see why I have to settle this matter now," Grant added in a harsh tone. "When my crews aren't working, I have zero dollars coming in."

"That makes sense."

"I can't let Holland *or* this Ross guy get by with this tomfoolery. If I don't get back to cutting soon—" He broke off, his features contorted.

He didn't have to finish the sentence. Owing that kind of money could be a financial death sentence for a businessman if the notes weren't paid. And that wasn't even talking about paying the bank *on time*.

"All right," she conceded, "I'll see what I can do."

He looked cautiously relieved. "You will?"

"That's what I said, but again, I'm making no promises."

"Don't worry, you'll be compensated."

"That's the least of my worries."

Grant cleared his throat, then said, "Thanks. I really appreciate you doing this."

Kelly merely nodded, and a silence fell between them.

He was the first to break it. "Do you mind me asking you something?"

"That depends."

"It has nothing to do with me."

That should've been warning enough to nip the conversation in the bud right then, but she didn't. "Ask."

"Were you crying?" Grant paused and angled his head. "You looked so incredibly sad."

Kelly stiffened, forgetting her crying jag just moments before he had knocked on her door. She was sure the remnants of it were still visible. She must look a sight— nose red and eyes all bloodshot. And some of her makeup was probably streaking her cheeks.

But what did her looks matter? She certainly wasn't trying to impress him. Not in that, way in any case..

"I was thinking about my husband and child."

He looked dumbfounded while a suffocating silence fell over the room.

Then he said, with harsh surprise, "You're *married?*"

Seven

"I'm not," she said with in a faltering voice, turning her face away from his intense, inquiring eyes.

Although he appeared more perplexed that stunned now, but he didn't say anything. Instead, he continued to stare at her. She wanted to avoid that piecing gaze at all costs, but she couldn't seem to avert her eyes.

At times it seemed that he had the power to see straight through her. No man had ever affected her that way. But again, he wasn't just any man—something she'd sensed from the first moment she'd seen him.

She had to handle this situation with the utmost care, as though she was holding the most fragile glass object. Inside, that was exactly how she felt—fragile to the breaking point.

"Kelly?"

She didn't remember him calling her by name before,

not in that low and slightly sexy voice, causing her heart to turn over. Fighting for composure, she drew a deep breath that she hoped would clear her head and get her through these next terrible moments. He wouldn't be there much longer. Then she could relax.

Or could she?

She had agreed to help get him out of his present jam, which meant she would be seeing much more of him, certainly more than she'd ever intended.

Terrific. But whose fault was that? She couldn't blame Grant. He hadn't forced her to make a commitment to help him. If the truth be known, she was thrilled that he'd asked for her advice. Not because of who he was but because she would be working, doing the thing she loved best in the world—practicing law. She couldn't believe how much the idea exited her.

"Hello?"

"Sorry," she muttered, feeling heat flood her face.

"Don't be sorry. I just didn't want you to forget I was here."

She almost laughed at that. That wasn't about to happen, not when his big body dominated the premises, and the fresh scent of his cologne drove her senses wild. But she wasn't about to tell him that or even hint at it. The sooner she got rid of him, the sooner she could collect herself.

Until the next time she saw him.

"Look, forget I mentioned your family or why you were crying. I stepped out of line. It's obviously none of my business."

Unexpectedly, and to her mortification, tears suddenly

welled up again in her eyes. This time Kelly wasn't quick enough to turn her face before he saw them.

"Hey, is there something I can do to help you?" Grant asked rather awkwardly, that sexy roughness still in his voice. "After all, you agreed to save my bacon. Maybe I could return the favor."

"I don't think so," she whispered, frantically blinking the tears from her eyes. How embarrassing to break down in front of a man who was practically a total stranger. Not only did that make her angry, it frightened her. She had come here to regain control of her emotions, to heal, so she could return to work and be the crackerjack attorney she once was.

At this rate, she was going to be in worse shape when she returned than when she left Houston. And with her once-sharp wits dulled, too.

Boredom. That was the problem. She didn't have enough to keep her mind occupied or challenged. But thanks to this man and his unfortunate business situation, now she did. Although it appeared to be a simple case, it had to do with lawyering, and she was grateful for the opportunity.

Then why wasn't she smiling instead of crying?

When she'd gathered her wits about her one more time, she found Grant's gaze still trained on her. For a second their eyes met, and to her dismay, a spark of electricity leaped between them.

Good Lord. She caught her breath and she held it for what seemed the longest time. This couldn't be happening.

She sensed he'd been zapped by that same spark and was thinking about it as he cleared his throat, then reached for his hat and made a move to leave.

The words spilled out. "My husband and child were killed in an automobile accident."

He stopped abruptly. Silence once again overtook the room.

Kelly guessed that was a good thing, because she was too flabbergasted to say anything else. She was too flabbergasted to even budge. She felt frozen inside and out. What on earth had possessed her to blurt that out? He'd already apologized for intruding in her life, which meant they had moved past her tears and he'd been getting ready to leave. Why had she said anything?

Now, she had opened that can of worms again, leaving herself totally vulnerable to him. Her eyes swept tentatively back to his. As she'd suspected, his gaze were definitely probing, his blue eyes so dark they looked black.

"That's a tough one," he finally said in a strained voice.

"Yes," she whispered, "it was. It nearly killed me—emotionally, that is."

"I'm sure it did. What happened?"

Kelly took a shaky breath. That was when Grant reached over and touched her hand, only to quickly withdraw his when the sparks once again zapped them both.

"You don't have to answer that," he stated, clearly shaken.

"It's the same story you've heard about a million times," Kelly said in a dull voice. "A drunk driver, a teenager, veered into their lane and hit them head-on. The kid was speeding and they all were killed instantly."

"God, I'm sorry."

"Me, too."

Another silence stretched.

"When did it happen?"

"Four years ago."

Grant didn't respond, but she could see the wheels turning in his mind. Like everyone else, he was thinking she should be over the tragedy by now, that she should've pulled herself and her life back together.

"I know what you're thinking," she said with strength in her voice.

Grant raised his eyebrows. "Oh? And just what would that be?"

"That I should be through wallowing in self-pity."

"Actually, I was thinking just the opposite."

She gave him a startled look.

"Yeah, I was wondering how the hell you kept your sanity and still functioned, especially as an attorney."

His answer so surprised her that her mouth dropped open. "Time," she finally said. "I didn't believe my shrink when he told me that, but I do now. Time is the greatest healer of all."

"Yet you're not completely healed."

"No, and I never will get over what happened. That's why I'm here."

"So now I know one of your secrets," he said in a gentle voice.

"Oh, I'm sure others are wondering about me, too, since I stick out like a sore thumb in the shop."

"Hey, you're doing just fine..." Grant paused, then smiled. "Except when you have a coffee cup in hand. Then you become a mite dangerous."

"A lethal weapon, right?" she added wryly.

"I can only speak for myself."

They both smiled before sobering once again.

"Was your child a boy or girl?" he asked.

"A girl. Her name is…was Amber."

"I like that."

"My husband's name was Eddie. He was an attorney also, but for another firm."

"Sounds like the perfect all-American family."

"We were," she said with another catch in her voice.

"We don't have to talk about this anymore if you don't want to. It's your call."

"My doctor says that talking is exactly what I should do. Not talking about it and pushing the pain deep down inside me is what's caused me to crash and burn."

"I'd say that's a bit strong."

"What?"

"To say you've crashed and burned. It seems to me you pretty much have it all together."

She averted her gaze. "You're wrong. I'm far from having it all together. Just ask my boss."

When she heard the bitterness in her voice, Kelly tamped down the pain, then faced Grant again.

Sympathy filled his eyes, and for some reason, that made her angry. She didn't want his pity. She wanted his… Before that thought could mature, she slammed the door shut on it.

This was all too crazy; she had no idea what she wanted, especially from this man who had her mind and body going in all kinds of crazy directions. If she weren't careful—

"So that's why you're here?"

Kelly forced her mind back on track. She had started this in-depth inquiry into her life and she might as well finish it once and for all. "Yes. I wasn't working up to par, so my boss suggested I take a leave of absence."

"You didn't agree." Grant made it a flat statement of fact.

Kelly licked her bottom lip. She watched as his eyes concentrateD on the movement of her tongue. Refusing to acknowledge the feeling that shot through her, she said, "Not at first, but then I realized they were right. I really hadn't ever grieved for my family. I had just shoved the pain so far down inside me that it couldn't surface."

"Only one day it did. Unexpectedly."

"Exactly. I stayed at home for several weeks, during which I cried and pitched hissy fits. I also threw and broke things, but at least I was facing the pain. Then out of the blue, Ruth called, and here I am."

"Only not for long."

Her smile was empty, without humor. "The day Ruth returns, I'm leaving."

"This one-horse town's not for you, huh?"

"Those are your words, not mine."

"Still, that's the way you feel."

Kelly shrugged, hearing the slight censure in his voice. Too bad. Whether she liked it here or not wasn't any of his business. Yet in all fairness to him, she had vented to him. To turn around and insult him was not her usual *modus operandi*.

"Look, I didn't mean—"

Grant held up his hand, his mouth turned down. "Hey, you don't owe me an apology. At one time, I felt the same way."

Kelly's eyes widened.

"As you already know, I haven't always lived here."

"So you said, but you seemed to have found your perfect niche."

"In other words, it didn't take me long to turn into a country bumpkin."

Kelly felt herself flush. "I didn't mean—"

"Sure you did, and that's all right. I love these woods and all the people in them."

She didn't say anything else, knowing if she did, it would probably be the wrong thing. "What if you run out of trees to cut around here?"

"That won't happen."

"Really?"

He chuckled, then leaned forward.

Kelly got another whiff of his cologne, which once again assaulted her senses. She tried to pretend that it didn't bother her, but it was getting harder and harder by the minute. This man needed to go, especially since that hot kiss they had exchanged was very much on her mind. And if she even let herself think about how she'd felt when his finger grazed her breast, she'd be in big trouble.

"This area is a forester's haven," he said, jerking her back to reality. "I don't think I'll ever run out of trees."

"That's a plus for you."

"No matter, I love it here and hopefully won't ever have to leave it."

"I understand about that," Kelly said, vigor returning to her voice. "I love the city and never plan to leave it."

He cocked his head and gave her an assessing look. "I learned never to say never a long time ago."

"Does that include marriage?" Now why had she asked that? She was appalled at herself. She didn't care if he had been married, or if he'd ever get married, for that matter. Just because he'd kissed her with sound and fury didn't warrant digging into his personal life. "Sorry, that's none of my business."

"No problem." He shrugged with a grin. "I'm not

opposed to marriage, now that I've settled down in one place. I guess I just haven't run across the right filly with the right stuff."

A feeling of disgust suddenly swept through her. The right filly, huh? Such talk reminded her once again that she had absolutely nothing in common with this man and was wasting her time carrying on a personal conversation with him. He was going to be her client, nothing more.

As if he realized the climate in the room had changed, Grant stood slowly, that notable smirk appearing on his lips. "I've taken up enough of your time now."

Walking slightly behind him to the door, she couldn't help but notice his swagger which more than did justice to the tightest and best looking male behind she'd ever seen. Realizing the turn her thoughts had taken, Kelly sucked in her breath and muttered a dirty word.

"You say something?" he asked, turning at the door.

"No," she forced a smile.

His lips twitched, then grew serious, "You're still going to help me with the injunction, right?"

She thought a minute. "Are you sure you want me, since my firm certainly doesn't have much confidence in me at the moment?"

"You know better than that." Grant's tone as gruff.

She hesitated again.

"You can't jump ship on me now," he said.

"I told you I'd do what I could, and I intend to keep my word." She paused. "I just hope you won't be sorry."

"Oh, I won't be sorry," he murmured huskily, looking at her as if he could eat her up.

No, she told herself, don't let him mess with you like

this. Her feelings were purely physical. If she ignored them, they would go away.

"You know what I'd like to do about now, don't you?" The husky pitch has grown deeper.

That tightening in her chest increased, as if she were about to have a heart attack.

When she simply stood and stared at him, he added, "I'd like to kiss the hell out of you."

Then why don't you? she almost blurted out, and then sanity returned. Taking a steadying breath, she said, "I don't think that's a good idea."

"Me, either." He paused, raking hot eyes over her. "Because once I got started I couldn't stop with a kiss."

Kelly continued to stand unmoving, blood beating like a drum in her ears.

Putting his hat on, Grant tipped it, then cleared his throat, "I'll see myself out."

Once the door closed behind him, Kelly forced her legs to move to the sofa. She sank down and clutched her stomach, her mind and body reeling.

What had she gotten herself into?

Eight
<u></u>

"Got a minute?"

Grant scowled hearing the voice of his banker, Les Rains. "Got lots of 'em. Why?"

"Let's meet for coffee."

"Where?" Grant asked, hoping it wouldn't be at the Sip 'n Snack.

"Sip 'n Snack, Where else is there in this town."

Grant sighed inwardly. "See you shortly." He cut off his cell phone and headed in that direction.

As much as he'd like to see Kelly, he was reluctant to do so—even if it was all business. He enjoyed being around her far too much, and that bothered him. The last person he needed to see right now was the woman who pushed his buttons—in more ways than one. However, he'd best get used to it, since she was going to represent him. She *was* the only lawyer in town, like it or not.

All the more reason to keep his guard up. She had too much baggage to suit him. No way did he want to compete, *wouldn't* compete, with memories of a dead man and child. Entering a relationship where that was a factor would be suicidal on his part.

He figured no other man would ever live up to her husband. Hell, Grant didn't even want to try. When and if he married, and that was a big *if,* he'd envisioned his wife as a beautiful woman who would love the outdoors, same as he. She would work a garden alongside him, would even can fruits and vegetables. The thought of Kelly Baker doing any of those things brought a smirk to his lips.

Nope. She wasn't the woman for him. Yet he'd have to admit she was hot, and she made him hot. And tempted though he might be, it would serve him best to keep their relationship purely business. Not to mention that when their business was concluded and Ruth got back, Kelly would be heading out of Lane.

Grant had no intention of letting her take his heart with her, leaving a hole in his life as big as a crater.

No, sir. He was smarter than that.

A few minutes later, he walked into the Sip 'n Snack. Les Rains, was already seated with a cup of coffee in front of him. At first Grant didn't see Kelly, then she walked through the swinging doors behind the counter. When she spotted him, she pulled up short.

Their eyes met for what seemed an interminable length of time, then she nodded and headed in the direction of a table where a couple had just sat down. He figured she'd get to him next. But there was no hurry; the second he'd walked, her sweet perfume had surrounded him. He dared not look down, but he knew his manhood had probably risen to the occasion.

"You'll remember her the next time you see her."

Grant narrowed his eyes on his banker, whose face was as round as his body. Les wasn't fat; he was stout as a bull moose due to his daily workouts at a nearby gym. He said it kept him sane after dealing with crazies all day. Grant didn't envy him in the least dealing with people, especially about money. He'd much rather fool with equipment and trees. They were so much easier; they didn't sass back.

"What are you talking about?" Grant asked in a rough tone as he pulled out a chair and sat down.

Les snorted. "The way you were looking her over. What gives? You know her or something?"

"Sort of."

Les looked at Grant in sheer disbelief. "You can do better than that, my friend."

"What if I don't want to?"

Les grinned. "You looked like you could eat her with a spoon if you had one."

"Okay, so she's easy on the eyes. And I'm not dead, you know. So...?" Grant deliberately left his question open-ended.

Les's grin widened. "I was beginning to wonder. It's been such a long time since I've seen you with a woman or even heard you talk about one, for that matter."

"I'm too busy working."

"That's a crock."

Grant shrugged.

"Who is she, anyway?" Les asked. "And what's she doing here?"

"She's Ruth's cousin, Kelly."

"Ah, so it's Kelly, huh?"

Grant glared at his friend. "Go to hell."

"Hey, I don't blame you for giving her the once-over. Man, she's a knockout, not someone you'd ever figure would work in a place like this even if it is kind of classy for Lane."

"Ruth got in a bind and she's subbing for her."

"Whatever works."

Grant kept his mouth shut, preferring to watch Kelly as she took coffee and pastries to the table across from them. Today she had on a pair of black lowcut jeans, a wide belt, and black turtleneck sweater. Some kind of sparkly earrings dangled from her ears. Les was right; she was a knockout, especially today. Her outfit accentuated all the positives.

Before she saw him lusting after her, Grant averted his gaze. While the conversation between Les and him lagged, Kelly appeared at their table.

"Morning," she said in a slightly husky voice.

Grant looked up at her, and for a millisecond, their gazes locked again. "Morning to you."

"Coffee?"

"The strongest."

Kelly nodded. "I'll be right back."

Once she'd served them and left, Les chuckled. "Again, what's with you two? I saw the way *she* looked at you. Something's going on, but if you don't want to tell me, that's all right."

"Thank you," Grant said his voice loaded with sarcasm.

Les merely grinned.

"She's an attorney, actually."

Les's smile fled. "Her? An attorney?"

"That's what I said." Grant's tone was terse and low.

"Why is she here, then?"

"That's another story and frankly, it's none your business."

"Is that so?"

"Yes."

"I'm assuming you've made it yours, though."

Grant almost strangled on a smothered curse. "You just don't know when to give up or shut up, do you?"

"Nope."

"She's going to help me get the injunction lifted since Matt's out of the country. Are you satisfied now?"

"Way to go. I've never thought Matt was worth his salt, by the way."

Grant ignored Les's comment about his attorney. It didn't matter, anyway. Getting his men and equipment back on the job was all that counted. He sure hoped Kelly could do that. He was dying to ask if she'd started working on his case yet, knowing that she probably hadn't since they had just discussed it last evening. Still, he was impatient as hell.

Each wasted second cost him time and money.

Hopefully, she'd get started this evening. Therefore he had no intention of bothering her at home, though he wanted to. And that "want to" didn't have a thing to do with his case, either.

"So has she done anything for you yet?" Les asked.

"Not yet, I'm sure."

"She needs to get the lead out."

Grant frowned and was about to respond when Kelly showed up with a full pot of coffee. Once again, he felt his heart race just because she was near him. Damn. He'd better get a grip on his libido and his emotions.

"Need refills?" she asked, her gaze moving between them.

"No thanks," Les said. "Maybe later."

She nodded, then turned and walked off. Grant couldn't help but watch the sway of her cute derriere. He had to literally stifle a groan; he'd like nothing better than to grab that rear, swing her around and plant a kiss on those full, moist lips.

Forcing his mind off her took all the willpower he possessed, but he did it. The stakes were too high to dally.

"You're still in my corner on the money issue, aren't you?" Grant asked, his cup close to his mouth.

"I'll buy you as much time as I can," Les responded. "But the other powers that be aren't going to be as lenient." He paused. "If this mess takes a while to fix, that is."

"I understand," Grant said, feeling a churning in his gut he didn't like. "That's why I'm glad we talked. I need to keep Kelly posted on what's going on."

They talked shop a bit longer before Les finished his coffee and left. Grant walked up to the counter and perched on one of the stools. Kelly had her back to him, but then, as if she realized someone was looking at her, she whipped around. A veil fell over her face and eyes, making both totally unreadable.

"I just wanted to say bye and ask you to call when you know something."

She gave him a lame smile. "I will."

Their eyes held a moment longer, then he got up and walked out, his emotions suddenly so raw, so frightening, he cursed all the way to his truck.

Nine

After doing research on Ruth's computer, using the law library to search cases similar to Grant's, Kelly decided the county courthouse was her next stop. Wellington, the county seat, was just twenty miles away.

So the following day, once the coffee shop was closed to customers, she'd drove there and filed a motion to lift the injunction, in order to get Grant back in operation ASAP.

She wasn't sure what would happen. If Larry Ross was from around these parts, Judge Winston might extend the injunction rather than lift it—simply because in small towns, the good ol' boy network was almost always alive and well.

That wasn't fair, nor was it just, but she'd learned long ago that the United States legal system had huge holes in it. Still, it was the best and the most fair in the world, and she was proud to play a part in it.

Now, as she returned to Lane and was about to pull into Ruth's drive, she braked suddenly.

His truck was in front of the house.

For a second Kelly's sat immobile, her breath coming in quick sputs. Then she finally settled back to near normal.

Why did Grant have such an adverse affect on her? He made her think, and behave in a manner totally foreign to her.

But despite her attraction to him, Kelly remained firm in her conviction not to get involved with another man. The cost was too high. Friendship had been enough.

Until she'd met Grant.

Sure, he drove her crazy with his chauvinistic statements and devil-may-care swagger. But not only had he made her aware of her body, he had reawakened desires she'd thought were long dead and could never be resurrected. *Dead?* Ha! Was she ever wrong. The key, however, was not to give in to those desires, to be strong-willed and strong-minded. She had always considered herself both.

Now Kelly guessed, in the light of this new challenge, parked at her doorstep she'd see what kind of stuff she was made of.

With her limbs shaking far more than they should, she got out of the car. Grant met her halfway, his face looking as it had that day when he'd talked about Larry Ross—like a thunderhead ready to erupt. She squared her shoulders for bad news.

"Where the hell have you been?" he demanded in a harsh tone.

Taken aback at his sudden attack, Kelly's eyes widened. At the same time, perplexed anger shot through her. "Excuse me?"

"You heard me."

Her composure slipped. "How dare you talk to me that way?"

"How dare you just disappear."

"Hey," she retorted. "I don't have to account to you."

Grant muttered a foul word, than rubbed the back of his neck, as though buying time to regain control of his frustration and his temper. "Look, I didn't mean to go on the attack."

"Well, you did."

"Kelly—"

She ignored the pleading in his voice. "Get out of my way."

"Where are you going?"

"Inside the house, away from you." Kelly's eyes and tone were as frigid as she could make them. "No man talks to me like that and gets away with it. Certainly not one I barely know."

As if Grant realized he'd made a huge mistake with his confrontation, he gave her a contrite look. "Look, I'm sorry. Really sorry."

Kelly wrestled with her conscience. She would love to tell him to take a hike, actually to go to hell, but instead stated "I'm afraid 'sorry' won't cut it."

"I was worried, that's all."

She gave him an incredulous look, then wondered why she didn't simply skirt by him, go inside and put an end to this nonsense. Perhaps it was the desperate look in his eyes, or the fact that he was so darn attractive in his black Stetson, jeans, white shirt and boots. Not to mention his smell…as always, his cologne tickled her senses, making her slightly dizzy.

Damn him.

She took a steadying breath, then demanded, "Worried about what?"

"You."

"Me?" This time her tone was incredulous. "Why would you be worried about me?"

Where Grant's face was once heightened with color, it was now devoid of it. "I don't know. When you weren't at the shop or here, I thought maybe you'd—" He broke off and gave his neck a hard rub. "Hell, I don't know what I thought."

"I'm not leaving, Grant. I told you I would help you and I will."

She watched his entire body seemingly go into meltdown.

When he finally spoke, there was a desperate note in his voice. "But time is critical."

"I know that," she said, with as much patience as she could muster, especially when she still felt anger at his harsh display of emotion. Eddie had been such a gentle man, one who rarely got upset. Apparently it didn't take much to set this man's rockets on fire.

Because that thought actually excited her, her anger deepened. At herself.

"I spoke to my banker, and the bank's really nervous about the amount of money I owe," Grant added to the silence. "And when they found out about the injunction slapped against me, that added insult to injury."

"It's not as bad as it could've been," Kelly said. "While you were getting so bent out of shape, I was actually working on your behalf. I just got back from Wellington, where I filed a motion to lift the injunction."

Grant's features suddenly registered relief and remorse

before he said, "If you'd like to kick my rear, I'll be glad to bend over."

"Something tells me that wouldn't do any good."

She knew she'd scored a point because he flushed.

Then out of the blue, he asked, "Do you have anything to do right now?"

Kelly frowned "No, but—"

"Ride with me to the site, will you? Pete's out of town, and I need to check the equipment before it gets dark. On the way, you can fill me in on the details of your trip to Wellington."

Kelly's frown deepened. "I'm really not dressed for the woods." Actually, she was dressed in a pair of jeans, a camisole and jacket. It was just her delicate shoes that were all wrong.

"Hey, it doesn't matter. You don't have to get out of the truck unless you want to."

She threw up her hands in defeat. "I'd have better luck arguing with a stump than with you."

He grinned. "Stumps and I have a lot in common."

Kelly rolled her eyes. "Funny."

The second she crawled into the truck, which smelled like Grant, Kelly tensed. You'd think she would have learned not to get into intimate situations with him. Agreeing to help him was probably the most asinine thing she'd done in a long time.

Yet she'd so wanted to sink her teeth back into the practice of law. So far, she'd loved every minute of handling this easy case. Just walking into the courthouse earlier had given her a high like nothing else could. For a while she had meandered down the halls, inhaling that particular odor that only courthouses have.

No doubt about it, just serving coffee and grub was getting to her. But then, so was Grant. At the moment, the former was by far the safest to her peace of mind.

As if he picked up on her uneasiness, he faced her and said, "I promise to be on my best behavior."

"That's funny, too," she stated ironically.

"Hey, relax," he said as he turned on the engine and pulled away from the curb. "I know how you feel about the woods, but I promise you'll be safe."

Right now she wasn't worrying about the woods, but she couldn't tell him that.

"So did you talk to Judge Timmons?" he asked, drawing her attention back to him. She stared at his profile. Even that looked good.

"As a matter of fact I did, only he's not the judge hearing your case."

"That's a relief. I hear he can be a real pain."

"He was nice enough to me."

Grant shot her a glance. "You're a good-looking woman and he's a known ladies' man."

"Him? He must be in his eighties."

Grant laughed. "That old codger can apparently still romance according to the gossip mill, anyway."

She turned so he wouldn't see her smile.

"Sorry, didn't mean to embarrass you."

She cut her gaze back to him. "I'm not embarrassed. It's just the thought of him and a woman—" She broke off, now embarrassed at what she was about to say.

Grant tossed his head back and laughed. "I couldn't agree more."

A short silence followed his laughter, then he asked, "So

if Timmons isn't the one who issued the injunction, why did you spend time with him?"

"He and the founder of our firm go way back. Our paths just happened to have crossed and he asked me who I was—you know how a stranger sticks out—and we visited for a minute."

"So who's hearing my case?"

"Judge Winston, and I know zip about him, except that the injunction is temporary, which is definitely in your favor. Otherwise, this could drag on indefinitely."

Grant's features contorted. "That can't happen."

"Oh, but it can. However, that's what I'm trying to prevent. Hopefully, I can get a quick hearing date. At that time Winston will either enforce the injunction, limit it or strike it."

"When can you get this hearing?"

"We're on the docket for the end of next week."

Grant's features darkened. "Is that the best you could do?"

Clearly, Grant wasn't up on the typical schedules of the court. She flung him a chastising look. "Under the circumstances, you should be a little more grateful." There was an intentional sting to her voice."

Grant tugged at the corner of his lip. "You're right, I should say thank you very much for all your efforts on my behalf."

"A simple thanks will suffice."

Nothing else was said as Grant maneuvered his pickup onto a road leading to a cleared area filled with stacks of logs. Several pieces of huge equipment were parked there as well. She had never seen a logging site before. Curiosity getting the better of her, she commented. "Looks like most of the wood's already been cut."

"Hardly. We've barely started. What you're seeing is a log set. For each site, we clear a place where we stack the wood and store the equipment."

Grant got out of the vehicle. She did, too.

He looked at her through hooded eyes. "I thought you weren't getting out."

"I changed my mind."

"Suit yourself, but be careful."

She paused. "Are there snakes around?"

He gave her an indulgent smile, which unexpectedly made her heart turn over. "It's too cool for them to be out. Stump holes are your worst enemy. So watch your step."

"I'm sticking close to you."

Looking around, Grant said, "I don't see the skidder. I need to check on it."

Kelly peered about at the growing shadows among the thickets of trees still standing, and shivered. "Not without me, you aren't."

He laughed. "Come on, but again, take care."

Although she was careful not to touch him, she walked as closely as she could without doing so. "What are those markings on the trees?" she asked.

"Those are the ones to be cut."

She casts her eyes around. "Now I see. There seem to be tons left."

"Now you know why time is so critical. If we don't cut, no one makes any money. Not me, not the crew, not the bank."

"Ouch!" Kelly cried, feeling her right foot sink into a hole and turn.

Grant's hand shot out and caught her before she dropped

to her knees. Then he squatted to check her ankle. "You twist it?" he asked, his voice rough with concern.

Kelly put her weight on it, but kept her hand on his shoulder for support. "Don't think so," she responded in an unsteady voice. The incident frightened the frijoles out of her. What she didn't need was a broken or sprained ankle.

"I see the skidder," Grant said in that same rough tone. "Come on, let's get you back to the truck."

Twenty minutes later, Grant whipped the truck into Ruth's drive. During the ride, neither had said much. Kelly had wanted to ask him more questions about the job, but since he didn't seem to be in a talkative mood, she had kept her silence. Besides, her ankle felt tender, which made her furious at herself. If she'd remained in the vehicle, that episode wouldn't have happened.

Still, no real harm had been done, she assured herself. After a hot, soaking her body in hot water with Epsom salts she'd feel much better.

"Wait and I'll help you out," Grant said after he'd killed the engine.

"I'm okay. I can walk on my own."

He merely shrugged, but came around to open the door nonetheless. Good thing, too, because when she stood and put weight on her foot, she winced slightly. His hand shot out once again and grasped her arm.

"Thanks," she said, "but I'm sure it's okay. I guess I'm just a little paranoid."

"That's a good thing," Grant muttered.

Before she realized what was happening, he had swept her in his arms and carried her into the house. "I'm sure your ankle will be fine," he said roughly. "What about the rest of ya? Where?" he asked in a tight voice, stopping in the middle of the living room. "Sofa or bedroom."

She didn't dare look at him for fear of what he might read in her eyes. Every nerve in her body seemed on high alert, aware of being held so tightly in his arms.

When she kept her silence, he muttered, "How about here, on the sofa?"

His tone was low and husky, making it difficult to hear him. Her own throat was so constricted, she could only nod as he placed her on the cushions.

Then he seemed to freeze, He didn't withdraw his hands or move his face, which was as close as her next heartbeat.

Ten

Her breath caught. He was going to kiss her again, and she wasn't about to stop him. In fact, it was all she could do not to reach up and pull his head down to her lips, the ache inside her was so strong.

Then, to her astonishment and disappointment, Grant drew back. "Let me take a look at your ankle and foot," he said in a strangled voice.

Before she could react, he was on his knees in front of her, removing her casual shoe and trouser sock. She stilled herself not to react when he ran callused fingers over her foot and ankle, pressing gently around the slightly swollen area.

Though his eyes were smoldering when he finished, he let go of her foot. "It's going to be okay. Nothing's broken."

"So you think it's just bruised?"

"Yep," Grant responded. "Only slightly, it seems. But let's see how you do standing on it."

She complied and did just fine, though his hand supported her. "It's a bit tender, but otherwise okay. As long as it's not broken, I can deal with the situation."

Grant straightened. "Maybe I should help you to the bedroom, anyway."

She averted her gaze. "I'll be fine on my own."

"I'm not going to pounce on you, Kelly.'

"I know that." Her tone was sharp. She didn't know why that made her mad, but it did. Was she disappointed because he hadn't pounced?

Yes!

"Just wanted to clear the air in case there was some doubt."

"I think you'd best go." When she felt her chin begin to wobble, she turned away. Surely she wasn't going to become emotional because she really didn't want him to leave?

He cleared his throat. "You're right, I should."

"I hope you don't mind seeing your way out," she forced herself to say, still not looking at him.

She heard him move toward the door, but suddenly felt the sofa sink beside her. Her gaze whipped around at the same time a groan ripped through Grant. He reached for her, hauled her against him, and then, his eyes dark with desire, ground his hard, moist lips to hers.

It was just like she'd imagined. Lost in the moment's ecstasy, Kelly could only cling to him, returning kiss for kiss, knowing full well how quickly the situation could explode out of control, but not caring.

"I didn't mean for this to happen," he'd whispered

between hot, frantic kisses, leaning his heavy body half over hers so her breasts were pressed to his hard chest.

"Me, neither," she admitted breathlessly, continuing to cling to him as if she'd never let him go.

He looked deep into her eyes. "Want me to stop?" His voice sounded like rough sandpaper.

"Do you want to?"

"God, no."

"Then don't." How could she have said these words, especially to a man who wasn't her husband? Easy, she told herself. Her body had betrayed her.

Grant adhered his mouth to hers once again, pushing her back into the cushions. Then they both went a little wild, delving, probing and sucking with such hard, wet passion that Kelly felt as if the top of her head might come off. She knew if he dared touch her breasts or another intimate place, she would have an orgasm.

That was when he did just that.

With another groan, he pulled back, and without removing his gaze from hers, he pulled the straps of her camisole off her shoulders, then down her arms. Instantly, her breasts spilled in front of him. His eyes widened and he muttered, "So beautiful, so beautiful."

Kelly was powerless against the waves of feeling that pounded through her when his tongue bathed first one nipple, then the other. That was enough to do exactly what she'd feared—bring on a hard orgasm.

While the throbbing between her thighs went on and on, he buried his lips against her neck and whispered, "Oh, Kelly, I ache for you."

He reached for her hand and placed it on the protruding mound behind his zipper.

That movement was the catalyst that whipped her back to reality.

Without warning, she dragged her mouth off his, and with unsteady arms, pushed him away, placing some much-needed distance between them. But still she couldn't find breath enough to collect herself. She could only remain unmoving, continuing to feel the way his lips and tongue delved, probed, and sucked, leaving her mindless and aching.

"Kelly," he muttered roughly into the silence. "I—" His voice halted, as if he couldn't find the words to go on.

They stared at each other out of unreadable eyes, then he got up and stood in front of the fireplace.

"If you expect an apology, you can forget it," he said in a strained voice.

"I don't want an apology."

He blew out a breath. "Good."

"Although it wouldn't be wise to make a habit of this sort of thing."

A grin of sorts twisted his lips. "I rather enjoyed it myself."

She cut him a wry look. "That's my point."

He sobered. "I read you loud and clear, but I don't have to like it."

"Me, neither, but we both know—" She broke off abruptly.

He finished the sentence for her. "That this can't go anywhere."

"Right. We have no future together." Her voice was barely audible now. She was so shaken from how he had affected her, her insides still on fire. If he were to reach for her again, she would be a goner. She lowered her head to hide her thoughts.

"Kelly, look at me," he said in a gentle tone.

She didn't know why she complied but she did.

"I want you as much as you want me. Probably more," he stated. He paused, his eyes dipping south.

Automatically, hers followed suit, and her chest tightened. The bulge behind his zipper was there for the world to see.

"What can I say?" He shrugged with a lopsided smile. "He has a mind of his own."

Kelly felt color sting her face and she focused elsewhere. She shouldn't be embarrassed by what he'd said, but for some reason she was. After all, she'd been married for years. She hadn't been modest, or a prude, nor was she now. Maybe her discomfort was because the discussion was *so* personal between two people who barely knew each other.

Grant released a ragged breath, then said, "If I leave, are you sure you'll be okay?" He paused. "With your foot, I mean."

"It'll be fine," Kelly said with more conviction than she felt.

Still he hesitated. "Then I guess I'll go."

She heard the reluctance in his voice, but didn't acknowledge it.

Once Grant reached the door, he swung around and gave her another long look, then added, "Thanks for going with me."

"Thanks for taking me," she responded in a tight voice.

"Right," he muttered, then walked out, closing the front door behind him.

* * *

So how had it happened again?

Last night's intimacy was the first thing that crossed Kelly's mind when she woke the following morning. Even though she hadn't wanted to get any more involved with Grant, life didn't always go according to plan. Hadn't she learned that the hard way a long ago? In this case, however, no real harm was done.

Both she and Grant were grown-ups, of sound mind and body, with no ties, which made it perfectly okay if they shared a kiss or two.

Kelly winced. Only it had been more than that, she admitted, feeling a tremor along her nerves. They had engaged in a physical dance at its best. The kisses on both her breasts and lips had been hot, deep and personal, as if she and Grant had been trying to reach each other's souls.

Shuddering, Kelly glanced at the clock, then climbed out of bed, and headed for the bathroom. However, her progress was slow because of her foot, as well as thoughts of Grant.

Why did he have to taste so good? Always. And feel so good? She had never even thought about those things when it came to Eddie. What was the difference?

Feeling those erotic thoughts of Grant were somehow a betrayal of her late husband, Kelly lunged off the dressing stool, only to wince at the pain in her foot. She then made her way to the closet, donning a pair of paisley slacks, a camisole and jacket, as the February air remained quite chilly for Texas.

She peered into the mirror one more time, positive there would be tangible evidence that something different had happened to her—overly flushed cheeks, a glow in her eyes, something that would give away the fact that she and Grant had made love with their lips.

Nothing seemed changed.

Confident her secret was safe, Kelly went into the kitchen and made herself a cup of tea, hoping that would settle her nerves as well as revive her composure.

Then she phoned to set up an appointment with Larry Ross's attorney, Taylor Mangum. She hadn't told Grant her plans because they might not come to fruition. But if she was going to save him from bankruptcy, she had to move quickly.

As she finished her tea and peered into the empty cup, she wished she could do the same with Grant—empty her mind of him. She couldn't seem to do that. Brooding over her infatuation with him, however, wouldn't solve her problem.

The panacea for that was to keep busy.

Grabbing her purse, Kelly made her way out the door, dreading her next, unavoidable encounter with Grant.

He should've kept his hands—*and his mouth*—to himself, but he hadn't so there was no point in berating himself over something he couldn't change.

As soon as Ruth returned, Kelly Baker would be out of these woods as if her coattail was on fire. He couldn't blame her, either. He more than understood, because he felt the same way about the city. If the shoe had been on the other foot and he'd had to do a friend a favor—say in Houston—he'd be counting the days until he could haul his butt back to the country.

Then why did the thought of her leaving depress him?

He couldn't deal with the question, much less the answer. If he dwelled on that, it would send his thoughts back to the way she'd kissed him—like he'd tasted so good she could just eat him up.

When their lips had been burning each others and she'd sucked on his tongue, he'd wanted to rip off every stitch of her clothing, unzip his fly, lift her onto his lap and have her ride him until they were both exhausted.

If she hadn't pulled away when she did, Grant was afraid he might have totally lost control and done that very thing, which could have screwed up everything. She was his lawyer! Why couldn't he remember that.

His cell phone rang, thankfully putting an end to his torturous thoughts. It was Pete.

"Where are you?"

"Headed to Holland's," Grant said. "Thought I told you."

"You didn't, but that's okay."

"What's up?"

"Nothing. That's the problem. The crews are getting restless as hell, Grant. They're even talking about walking out."

Grant wasn't surprised, yet it upped his blood pressure and made him that much angrier at the situation. "That's why I'm headed to Holland's, to pressure him into talking to that so-called illegit brother."

"Good luck."

"Meanwhile," Grant added, "we still have Kelly working on the legal end. Tell the men to give it just a few more days. We'll get everything straightened out."

"Keep me posted."

Pete ended the conversation just as Grant reached the Holland ranch. As luck would have it, Dan was working on his driveway. He stopped and leaned on his shovel while Grant got out of his pickup and strode up to him.

"Nothing's changed," Dan said, an edge to his voice.

"I want to talk to Ross."

"I don't think that's a good idea. As a family, we've decided we're doing the right thing by settling this matter in court."

"That's all well and good for your family," Grant said with gushing sarcasm, "since you've got my money and invested it. While I, on the other hand, am left with nothing."

Dan's face lost its color. "I know it doesn't seem fair that we're sitting on easy street and you're struggling, but—"

"Cut the condescending crap, Holland, and get some balls. Get your brother out of the picture. You'll be doing the right thing by holding up your end of the deal. You took my money, I'm holding *you* accountable for this mess."

"I know, and I *feel* responsible."

"Then let's avoid a court hearing. Settle this between us."

"If only I could."

"Look, man, you're destroying my company. You've got me hung out to dry."

Holland's features remained stoic. "Trust me, I'm sorry about that, but I have no choice but to stick to my plan. My brothers feel the same way."

"If you ask me, you're all a bunch of fools for letting this so-called half brother hoodwink you."

Holland stiffened his back and glared at him.

Grant was tempted to deck him on the spot. Instead, he tightened his lips and glared back.

Then Dan muttered, "Oh, no," gazing past Grant's shoulder.

Grant swung around and watched as a man he'd never seen walked around the house toward them. Adrenaline shot through Grant's veins as he realized without asking who the man was.

This was turning out to be a good day, after all. "Well, well, if it isn't old Larry himself."

"Don't start anything, Wilcox," Dan warned.

"Or what?"

"You'll be sorry."

"I'm already sorry I ever did business with you."

Dan opened his mouth, only to slam it shut as Larry Ross stopped beside him. As if he sensed the tension in the air, he didn't say anything. He just bounced his eyes between Grant and Dan.

Ross was tall, but thin and pale, as though he needed some vitamins or a hefty helping of red meat. Or both. Grant figured if push came to shove, he could best the man with one hand tied behind his back. Hopefully it wouldn't come to that. But Grant wasn't making any promises to himself or anyone else. He'd do what was necessary to get his crews back cutting the timber he'd paid for.

"Grant Wilcox, Larry Ross," Dan said reluctantly.

Larry stiffened visibly. "I don't have anything to say to you."

"That's too bad, because I have plenty to say to you." Grant's voice was sharp and cold, though he didn't raise it.

"I don't have to listen to you, either."

"Says who?" Grant purposely egged him on for the sheer hell of it.

"My attorney."

"Look, why can't we be civil about this? Man to man. And keep the court out of it?"

"I'm happy working through the court."

Grant took a step forward. Ross backed up, fear written in the grooves in his face, as though he knew he was out-manned. "I suggest you settle this beef with your family really quick—like today. If not, I'll be back and I can promise you, you won't be happy to see me."

With that, Grant turned, jumped back in his truck and took off, his fingers gripping the steering wheel until his knuckles turned paper-white.

He knew his words meant nothing. Tearing that anemic-looking fellow from limb to limb wouldn't do anything but make Grant feel better.

Unless Kelly came through in the courts, he was dead in the water.

Eleven

"We're about to close, but if there's something I can get you, I'll be glad to."

"I came to see you, honey."

Kelly moaned silently. The last thing she needed was a last-minute customer, especially not one who came specifically to see her. Most people in this town didn't even know her, though she had to admit that was slowly changing. Discounting Grant, she had actually begun to make a few friends among her customers.

However, she didn't recall ever seeing this little old lady. If so, she would not have forgotten her. Talk about an unusual character; the tiny woman slowly making her way deeper into the shop was something else, especially for Lane.

She had to be in her late eighties if she was a day. Yet it was obvious she did everything in her power to disguise her age, from puttying up the cracks in her face with too much makeup, to wearing looped earrings that were almost bigger than her entire face.

No one could ignore her clothes either. She had on a pair of jeweled pants, a jeweled blouse, and jeweled jacket. She was so bright Kelly needed sunglasses to block the glare.

What a character.

"Through looking me over?" the woman asked without rancor.

Kelly was mortified and knew that it showed.

The woman waved a hand that sported long, thin fingers and heavily painted nails. "Don't worry about it, honey," she said with a chuckle. "Everyone's jaw drops when they first meet me—strangers, that is. Around here, everyone knows I'm crazy but harmless."

Kelly knew this offbeat woman might be harmless, but she sure didn't think she was crazy.

"By the way, I'm Maud Peavy." She reached out her hand and shook Kelly's. "Folks around here call me Ms. Maud. But I'll answer to near about anything."

Kelly laughed. "Well, Ms. Maud, I have to tell you up front you're my kind of lady. Kudos to you for still staying stylish at your age."

"Listen, honey, we never get too old to take care of ourselves. Remember that, will you?"

"My grandmother used to tell me the same thing."

"You fixin' to close, right?" Maud asked.

"That I am."

"Any plans?"

Kelly thought for a moment, then said, "No. Just go back to Ruth's, I guess."

"Come home with me instead."

Kelly blinked in astonishment.

Maud laughed. "Haven't you heard I'm famous for my homemade tea cakes?"

"Actually I haven't."

Maud frowned. "I'm kinda disappointed in my friends." As suddenly as the frown appeared, it vanished. "Surprises are good, too. So know that you're in for a real treat and don't even know it." She leaned her head that had very little hair left on it.

What surprised Kelly was that she didn't wear a wig to offset that flaw since she was so style conscious.

As if she read Kelly's mind, Maud patted the top of her head. "Doctor told me I couldn't wear my wig for a while. I've had some kind of crud in my scalp." She shook her head. "You know how these doctors are. If you don't do what they say, then they won't see you anymore."

Kelly hid a smile, never having had that experience, but then she wasn't from a postage-stamp-size town where the people acted and did things differently than in the city.

"So are you coming?" Maud asked, noisily clearing a frog from her throat.

"Of course. But would you mind if I went to Ruth's first and got comfortable? I also have a phone call to make."

"Take your time, honey. That'll give me the opportunity to whip up a fresh batch of tea cakes and put them in the oven."

"Mmm, that sounds heavenly."

"Honey, when you taste one, you'll think you died and entered those pearly gates."

Kelly laughed outright, and it felt so good, so liberating, it gave her cause for serious thought. Maybe her doctor had been on target when he'd forced her to take a leave of absence from the firm. Rarely had any spontaneous laughter erupted there.

Maud gave her directions to her house, then said, "I'll see you shortly," before making her way back to the door.

A short time later Kelly had changed her shoes and clothes. For her own secret pleasure, she removed both bra and panties, since her warm-up suit was thick and showed no signs of her nudity underneath.

Already feisty Maud had been good for her, giving her the courage to be herself and to do something a bit outrageous, if you will, without worrying about what someone else would think.

Fifteen minutes later, she walked in Maud's modest home. The old lady had yelled from the kitchen telling her the door was open.

The wonderful aroma of freshly baked cake stopped Kelly in her tracks, and she inhaled deeply. She hadn't smelled anything this good since her grandmother had died. Although Grammy never made tea cakes, she did have a specialty of her own—a pound cake made with coconut, extra eggs and butter. It never failed to melt in Kelly's mouth. She suspected that would be the case with Maud's tea cakes.

"The flavor of the day will be plain ones," the eccentric woman announced as Kelly strolled into the small, cluttered kitchen. "I want you to taste the real thing first. Later, I'll put icing some."

Kelly smiled. "Beggars can't be choosers."

"Pooh, you're no beggar, just malnourished. You're skin

and bones!" Maud nodded toward the table. "Just dump that stuff out of the chair onto the floor and have a seat."

Kelly smiled and did as she was told, placing the pile on top of the things already in the opposite chair.

Maud turned and faced her, leaning against the kitchen cabinet near the sink. She had on an apron, and a bandanna tied around her head. A smudge of flour almost covered one rouged cheek. Her new friend was definitely a sight, Kelly thought. But she wouldn't have missed this adventure for anything.

None of her cohorts at the firm would believe her if she told them about this eccentric woman, so she wouldn't even bother. Even if they did believe her, her lawyer friends might look down their noses at Maude. Suddenly Kelly squirmed in her seat. At one time, she probably would have, too.

"So whatcha want to drink?" Maud asked. "Tea, coffee, milk, half-and-half?"

"Half-and-half?" Kelly's eyes widened on Maud. "You mean people actually drink that with your cookies?"

"Of course, honey. But let's get something straight. What you're about to honor your mouth with are not cookies. They are authentic tea cakes. No one besides me has the recipe."

"Will you ever share your recipe?"

Maud thought about that. "Don't know yet. Haven't decided who's worthy of it, although Ruth has begged me to let her bake and sell them."

Kelly chuckled. "Only you won't."

"Hell no, then people wouldn't come to my house. They'd go to Sip 'n Snack." Maud came a little closer, then lowered her voice as though someone else might hear. "She's sorta my competition."

Kelly giggled. "Ah, so I get it now. You like the company."

"I love company. Fills my otherwise lonely days to the brim."

"Seems like you're one of a kind, Maud Peavy."

Maud smiled, then peered so hard at Kelly she almost squirmed in her seat. "Most people think you're kind of stuck on yourself, you know."

Oh, great.

"I'm sorry they feel that way," Kelly responded, for lack of anything better to say. That out-of-the-blue statement set her back a bit, yet she wasn't surprised at the assessment. But in defense of herself, she felt as if she'd been tossed onto another planet and expected to fit right in. Well, life didn't happen that way.

"Only they're wrong. You're nice," Maud said, breaking Kelly's train of thought. "In fact, you're real nice. And pretty as a picture, too."

"Thanks," Kelly said, feeling a flush steal into her cheeks, though she was unable to figure out why. There was just something about this town, these people that baffled her, yet intrigued her, too. Especially this kind and eccentric soul.

"I know Grant thinks you're pretty, too."

Kelly went still. "You know Grant?" Silly question, she told herself. Everyone knew everyone in this town, even their personal business.

Maud chuckled. "When he leaves the woods most days, this is the first place he hits. He can scarf down a dozen of my cakes in one sitting."

"I don't doubt that."

Maud paused and narrowed her eyes. "I understand you're trying to help him get back to work, you being a lawyer and all from one of those fancy firms."

"I don't know about my firm being fancy, but I am trying to help him."

"I'm glad. He's my most favorite person in the world."

That statement shocked Kelly. Rough Grant and bejeweled Maud were *friends?* "Is he related to you?"

"No. I love him like he was, though. All my family's dead. Even when they were alive, most of 'em weren't fit to know or kill."

Kelly laughed. "Most people would never admit that."

"I understand you lost your family," Maud said, her face and tone now sober. At one time Kelly would've been offended that her business had been bandied about town. Now it didn't seem to matter. Had she changed that much since coming to Lane?

Perhaps.

"I lost a great husband and precious daughter."

"I'm so sorry. You deserve better."

"Thank you. But life can kick you in the teeth," Kelly whispered, purposely biting into another tea cake. "Oh, my gosh, this is heavenly."

Maud grinned as she poured Kelly a cup of half-and-half. "You never said what you wanted to drink, so I made the choice." She winked. "You won't regret it."

Kelly laughed and merely shook her head.

"So, how do you and Grant get along?" Maud asked in a crisp voice, changing the subject.

Kelly was taken aback, giving Maud carte blanche to keep on going. "I think he kind of likes you."

Though flustered and frustrated at the turn in the conversation, Kelly didn't alter her benign facade. Curiosity, however, got the better of her and prompted her to ask, "Did he tell you that?"

"Didn't have to. I know him better than he knows himself."

Cool it, Kelly, she warned herself, feeling color return to her face. This old woman was smarter than a fox in a hen house. And if she was on a fishing expedition for herself, or whomever else, Kelly wasn't about to bite the hook.

"So how do you feel about him?" Maud asked bluntly, placing a plate of hot tea cakes in front of her. For a moment Kelly couldn't respond; she was too eager to snatch a cake and eat it.

"Go ahead, dig in." Maud chuckled. "We can talk about Grant after you've had your fill of my delicacies."

Even as she reached for another cake, Kelly almost blurted out that Grant was off-limits. But she knew she'd be wasting her time and her words. This woman marched to her own drummer and would say exactly what she pleased, when she pleased.

"Can you help him?" Maud asked after they had both consumed their fair share of the cakes.

"I certainly hope so."

Maud looked pensive. "That boy's worked so hard to get where he is, sacrificed so much, that I'd hate to see it all go down the drain now."

"That's what I'm hoping to prevent."

The old woman nodded. "Good girl."

This time Kelly chose to change the subject, but not before drinking the last of her milk. "I don't think I've ever tasted anything as good as these cakes."

"See, I told you so."

"No wonder Ruth is itching to sell your goodies."

"Not going to happen," Maud said again, "though I'm flattered. Besides, Ruth's doing great with her thing. Right?"

"As far as I can tell, she is." Kelly shrugged. "But then you know I'm like a fish out of water. Selling coffee and soup isn't my forte."

"Then why are you here?"

"I came to help Ruth out."

Apparently Grant hadn't said anything more about her problems, just about Eddie and Amber. Kelly's estimation of him shot up a notch, but that didn't mean anything special, she assured herself hurriedly. He was just someone she'd met in this town whom she'd agreed to help. Nothing more, nothing less.

Even though she'd just met Maud, she felt like she could open up to her as a friend. "I almost had a nervous breakdown," Kelly admitted.

Maud reached out and covered her hand. "You did right by coming here, young lady. This country air and us country folk will help you heal."

Sudden tears rose in Kelly's eyes. She blinked them back. "I never thought of it like that, but maybe you're right. A change of venue just might do the trick."

"Sometime I'd like to see a picture of your family."

Kelly reached into her purse for a tissue. "Sometime I'll show you one."

Maud smiled. "I like you, Kelly Baker. I like you just fine."

"And I like you."

"You come see me anytime you want," Maud said

staunchly. "You'll always be welcome. And if you can't sleep, I'm at my best at three in the morning."

Kelly laughed and reached for another tea cake even though her stomach felt as if it was going to pop. But she didn't care. She didn't know when she'd get another opportunity to visit Maud. She expected Ruth to return sooner than later.

And she couldn't forget about Grant's case. She had her work cut out for her on it.

"I've got a batch ready for you to take home," Maud said, interrupting her thoughts.

"What about me?"

Kelly froze.

Not so Maud. Upon hearing Grant's voice she whirled around, walked over and gave him a big hug. Kelly, looking on, hoping her mouth wasn't gaping, watched as the old woman almost disappeared into his big body.

"I've told you about sneaking in," Maud scolded, punching him in the chest. "That's not nice."

"I always just walk in."

Maud sniffed. "It's different today. I'm entertaining a very distinguished guest."

Feeling embarrassed, Kelly rose and said, "Come on, Maud, give me a break."

"Sit back down, young lady," she ordered. "You're not going anywhere."

"Yes, she is," Grant said with ease.

"Oh, no, she isn't."

Kelly stared at one then the other, undecided who she wanted to strangle first. "Actually, I'm going home."

"I'm cooking steaks," Grant said, his gaze locked on her, freezing her in place. "I thought you might come over and we'd discuss the case."

"Good idea," Maud said in a cheery voice, facing Kelly. "You could use some meat on those bones."

Although Kelly steamed inside, she wouldn't hurt Maud's feelings for anything. Grant, however, was a different matter. "What I have to say can be said over the phone."

"So you do know something?" Grant asked in an eager tone.

"I spoke with Larry Ross's attorney."

"Sounds like you two have a lot to talk about." Maud walked over to Kelly and kissed her on the cheek. "Go on with him, honey. It'll be all right. He'll have to answer to me if he doesn't treat you right."

"Maud, you're meddling again," Grant said in a kind but stern voice.

Kelly felt trapped. For some crazy reason that she didn't even understand, she wanted to go with Grant. The thought of spending another evening alone didn't bear thinking about. Yet the thought of spending it with *him* didn't bear thinking about, either.

"I can't stay long," she said in a rather stilted voice.

Grant shrugged. "It's your call."

"Wonderful," Maud said with a Cheshire cat smile. "You two run along now and tend to business. I'll talk to you both later."

Kelly looked at Grant, who winked, then motioned for her to go ahead of him. She could always leave, she reminded herself, if things didn't go her way. Maybe that was the problem. When it came to Grant, things rarely went her way.

With insides quivering, she walked with him out the door into the twilight, feeling his eyes track her every step.

Twelve

"So how was your steak?"

Kelly smiled, then stretched until she felt Grant's eyes, with fire in them, peruse her body. Although they hadn't had anything to drink, she suddenly felt dizzy, as if she'd consumed a glass of strong wine.

That kind of feeling was exactly why she shouldn't have accepted his invitation to dinner. But what choice had she had? Maud and Grant had ganged up on her. If she'd made a stink about not joining him, Maud would have certainly read more into Kelly's refusal than was there.

A no-win situation!

She had wanted to have dinner with Grant. The second he'd walked through Maud's door, every nerve in Kelly's body had awakened. They were still in that state, though he'd made no effort whatsoever to touch her. Throughout the preparation of dinner—from grilling the steaks and corn, to making the salad—he'd been the perfect gentleman and host.

Yet every time they came within touching distance, she reacted inside. Her nerves tightened that much more. She sensed his reaction was the same as she'd caught him throwing her several smoldering looks when he didn't think she was watching.

Now that dinner was over and, at her insistence, the kitchen tidied, they were now seated in his rustic living room. A fire was burning and a romantic Alan Jackson CD was playing on the stereo system.

A perfect place and a perfect night for making love.

Horrified, she reined in her raw thoughts. If she didn't hurry and get back to Houston, she was going to be in big trouble.

"You're not talking?"

Kelly cut her eyes toward him and saw the humor lurking around his mouth and eyes. She heard it in his voice, too. "And you think all lawyers talk too much, right?"

"Yep. Except the one sitting on the sofa beside me."

Kelly smiled. "I guess my mind was wandering. But to answer your question, the steak was delicious as was everything else."

"Good." His gaze rested on her for a heartbeat. "I wanted you to enjoy."

"Well, you accomplished your goal."

Small talk. That was all they were doing, trying to ignore the sexual tension closing in around them.

"We need to talk," she finally said.

"Yeah, we do," Grant replied with a sigh as though disappointed that the erotic spell was broken.

"I spoke to Ross's lawyer, Taylor Mangum, today."

Grant sat a little straighter. "And?"

"I told him that I was calling out of courtesy to ask him to convince his client to take a voluntary DNA test."

Grant slapped his palms together. "Way to go. That would knock this issue in the head one way or the other."

"I went on to tell Mangum," Kelly added, "that if Ross refused, I would file a motion with the court to force him to take the test, proving whether he is or is not an heir."

"Go on." Grant's tone held rigid excitement.

"Mangum said he'd talk to his client, but doubted he'd comply."

Grant's features darkened. "Why wouldn't Mangum insist that he take it?"

"No sweat off his back whether he does or doesn't," Kelly acknowledged. "The longer this strings out, the more money Mangum makes."

Grant cursed. "Is that what all lawyers are about—making money?" Then, as if he realized what he'd said and to whom, he muttered another curse, then said, "Sorry, didn't mean that."

"Yes, you did, but that's okay. You're right. Money is what some lawyers are all about. Me, too, but I also care about doing what's right for my clients and for justice."

Grant smiled at her. "That firm's damn lucky to have you. I hope they know that."

She merely nodded, feeling tears press against the back of her eyelids. One minute this man was a rough forester with no class, and the next a smooth-talking man with tons of class. Perhaps that was what attracted her: he was an enigma.

"If Ross is legit like he claims, then why would he resist?"

"Taking a DNA test for whatever reason is frightening to most people, thanks to the horror stories in the media about how DNA and other tests are horribly misused and abused."

"So if he refuses, which Mangum suspects he will, how long will it take to get the matter heard in court?"

"Depends on how soon we can get on the docket."

"Damn," Grant muttered. "This whole legal thing moves far too slow to suit me. The bank could call in my note before I ever get inside a courtroom."

"Maybe not. Remember the injunction hearing is next week." Kelly injected a light note in her voice. "Who knows, maybe Ross will jump at the chance to take a DNA test."

"I doubt that, if for no other reason than to spite me and take delight in shutting me down permanently."

"Have you talked to him?"

"Yep."

"That wasn't smart."

Grant rubbed his jaw. "It's just one of those quirky turns of fate." Then he told her how he'd run into Larry Ross at Dan Holland's house.

"As long as you didn't take a swing at him, I think we're okay."

"You have no idea how much I wanted to deck him."

"Oh, I think I do." Kelly felt her lips twitch.

Grant gave her a sheepish grin before his features sobered once again.

"Like I said, try not to beat up on yourself," Kelly said,

her tone encouraging. "We might get lucky and Winston might force Ross to take the test."

"You think?"

"That's a possibility. Most judges don't like people who waste their time, and if one simple swab in the mouth will settle a case, then he or she usually won't hesitate to order it."

"Again, it's just getting to that courtroom." Grant's tone was harsh with disgust. "Meanwhile, I'm hanging out to dry."

"Surely your friend at the bank won't let them foreclose."

"We'll see." Grant then filled her in on his conversation with Les.

Afterward, they sat in silence for a few minutes, each of them gazing at the fire as though mesmerized by the glowing flames.

Grant finally reached over, took her hand and pulled her up. She lifted astonished eyes to him, her thoughts distracted from the case.

"Let's dance," he whispered, drawing her against his chest.

Alabama was singing, "If I Had You," a song that Kelly had heard on a C & W channel several times and liked very much. In fact, she'd considered buying the CD, only she hadn't taken the time.

"I guess I should ask if your ankle's up to boot scootin'?"

"My ankle's not a problem."

Grant began to move, and she with him, step for step.

"Mmm," he said, two-stepping her around the wooden floor. "For a city girl, you know how to move."

"Country and western dancing's really not my thing," Kelly said in a breathy voice, her head reeling for more reasons than one. She loved being held in his arms, his body grazing hers, especially when he twirled her.

Careful, Kelly, she warned herself silently, feeling her past rise up and intrude on this moment, threatening to plunge her into bitter sorrow. No matter; she didn't want him to let her go. Her breathing was becoming ragged and fast.

"You couldn't prove it by me," he said, his own voice sounding foreign, as if his throat was scratchy. "You're smooth as glass."

"You're just trying to make me feel good," she whispered.

"Oh, honey," he said, peering down at her, "that's a given. You feel so damn good I don't want to let you go."

That should've been the signal that it was time to call a halt to this craziness and go to Ruth's. Instead, Kelly continued to dance with him through several more songs. It was the last one, "There's No Way," that was the culprit that slowed them to a crawl. Before she knew it, they were belly to belly, hip to hip, then he was grinding his lips to hers.

Still, their bodies moved in time to the music while he explored her lips with his mouth.

Finally Grant withdrew, and while not dancing per se, they swayed as one.

"I should go," Kelly said in a barely audible voice.

"Why?"

"Because."

"Because why?" Grant's own voice was raspy.

Because I'm frightened of what you're doing to me, how you make me feel, as if I'm losing myself. "I—" she began, only to be interrupted.

"Stay with me. Please. You want me and I want you."

"I do. I do."

And she did. And she felt no shame for that, either. It

had been so long since she'd felt a man's mouth, tongue and hands on her body. She knew without a doubt that Grant would be that kind of lover. It would be all or nothing with him.

Was that wrong? Was *she* wrong? No, not if she could keep her heart out of the equation and enjoy making love for what it was—a release for her mind and body.

Could she do that? Maybe not. At this point she didn't know, nor did she care. Tomorrow she might be consumed with remorse and regret. But not tonight, not when she ached so desperately for him.

As if to settle the argument going on inside her head, Grant boldly placed her hand on his swollen manhood. Then he placed his hand on her swollen breast.

When Kelly didn't remove either, he added, "That's about as good as you can get between two people."

And it was.

She wanted him to quench that fiery hunger raging inside her so badly she couldn't even speak.

"You're so lovely," Grant whispered, as he stopped and slowly unzipped her warm-up jacket. When he saw she was braless, he drew in a breath and his eyes widened. "Again, so beautiful. So perfect."

He touched her breasts, first one then the other. Kelly felt her knees buckle under the tender assault, especially when he lowered his lips and sucked and kept on sucking.

After that, they'd shed their clothes posthaste, then knelt together on the thick rug in front of the fire, lips locked in a kiss as hot as the flames licking their naked bodies.

Then Grant laid her down and began licking her flesh, starting with her breasts and working his way downward.

When he reached the apex of her thighs, he paused and looked at her, a question in his eyes.

Caught up in the heat of the moment and the need to have him any way she could get him, Kelly didn't utter a word. Taking her silence as consent, he lowered his head and used his tongue until orgasm after orgasm pelted her.

No! she cried silently. She didn't want to feel this emotional intimacy with this man. This was a matter of the heart. Even if she wanted to, she couldn't give hers. It had been taken long ago by her husband, and she couldn't betray that love.

Yet she couldn't stop Grant's tongue, nor did she want to.

After moaning and thrashing, she whispered, "Please," digging her fingers in his flesh and urging him up and over her.

"Oh, baby, baby," he groaned, thrusting his hardness into her wet softness. Then he pounded flesh against flesh until they both cried out.

When they were drained, he rolled her over on top of him. They lay like that until their heartbeats calmed.

She had felt him in every part of her—even her heart.

She felt as though his heart and mind were inside her as well-merged with her soul. This was more than sex. That was exactly what she wanted to avoid. When she went back to Houston, she intended to leave fully intact, heart included. Leaving it behind was *not* an option.

Following a satisfied sigh, Grant eased her off him. Then he turned her so they were face-to-face. "That was incredible. *You're* incredible."

"So are you," Kelly managed to say around the lump in her throat, pulling back and looking at his body from head to toe, taking in the hard muscled chest, his hair in all the right places, his steely legs.

"You're perfect," she declared.

"You're unbelievable. I want you again. Now."

"Now?"

He nodded.

Without hesitation, she straddled him, then paused and stared down into his dazed eyes. "You like?"

"I could get addicted to this, to you," he said in a voice that sounded as if he was hurting.

Hadn't she already risked enough of her heart for this man? Kelly's answer, however, was to move slowly, then fast, then faster, riding him until they both froze in ecstasy.

Then with one last cry, she fell on top of him, their hearts beating as one.

Thirteen

Kelly was the first to awaken. For a moment she was completely disoriented, but then it hit her: she was at Grant's house. She was on the floor—in front of a fire that was barely alive. Had she been there all night? Yes. The incredible magenta-colored sunrise peeping through the window bore testimony to that. For a moment the beauty of it took her breath away. It was one of the loveliest sights she had ever seen.

She'd never glimpse that in the city, she told herself.

Then she peered at Grant who was either still asleep or pretending to be. Either way, he wasn't stirring, but he needed to be. And so did she. The coffee shop had to be opened. While Doris and Albert could certainly unlock the doors, they were unwilling to work at the front unless an emergency occurred.

And this was no emergency.

Yet Kelly didn't move. She felt too warm and comfortable. *Too loved*. Panic knotted her stomach, then she relaxed. Making love was not the same as *being* in love, she reminded herself. Hence, she didn't intend to agonize over last night.

She had enjoyed every second of their hot and passionate lovemaking. It had been an incredible experience. Grant was a perfect lover. Even better than Eddie, she admitted with only a prick of conscience.

And she had unashamedly loved Grant back. As she'd realized, they were grown-ups and didn't have to justify their actions to anyone. Neither was married and neither had a significant other.

So why weren't they a match made in heaven?

"My, but you look like you have the weight of the world on your shoulders."

Kelly had been so lost in thought she hadn't been aware Grant had awakened and was watching her. "I'm okay," she said with a tentative smile, wondering about his take on last night.

Instead of answering her silent question right off, he merely drew her closer to his naked body, making sure the afghan was securely wrapped around them, warding off the chill.

"I loved every second of being inside you," he finally whispered in her ear, as he outlined it with the tip of his tongue.

Shivers darted through her. "I loved it, too."

He placed a hand between her legs which sent several more shivers through her. "You have the most gorgeous body."

"When I can find time, I work out at a gym near the

firm." Kelly could barely talk; her throat was simply too tight, especially as his hand was gently moving up and down her inner thigh, pausing in all the right places.

"I can tell."

"Tell what?" she asked inanely.

Grant chuckled, obviously aware he had rattled her and that she wasn't making much sense.

"No regrets?"

Kelly took a deep breath, knowing without asking what he was referring to. "No regrets."

"Me, either."

A short silence followed.

"I didn't hurt you, did I?"

Her heart fluttered. "No, not really."

"You gotta be a little sore."

In spite of herself, Kelly felt color creep into her cheeks, which, under the circumstances, was ridiculous. She was glad he couldn't see her face.

Grant pulled her even closer, leaving no doubt that he was as full and hard as she was wet. "You haven't been with anyone since your husband died?"

"No." Her throat constricted.

"I still can't comprehend how it would be to have a family one day the next no one." He paused and clasped one of her hands in his. "You're a strong woman, Kelly Baker."

His voice had grown so thick and husky Kelly could barely hear him.

"And I admire the hell out of you," he added.

"Please don't say that. If you only knew." Her voice broke.

Sensing how distressing this subject was to her, Grant

pulled her tight against him, positioning himself between her thighs. She gulped silently and didn't move.

He tongued her ear again. "I could get used to this."

"To...to what?"

"Waking up with you in my arms. But I'd prefer a bed."

She heard the smile in his voice and it warmed her heart. Too bad there were so many differences between them. He was a wonderful lover, only she wasn't looking for a lover. She wasn't looking for a man, period....

Her purpose in Lane was to heal her mind and her body, then to return to the work she loved—in the city.

"What are you thinking about?" Grant asked in a whisper.

"How close I came to losing my mind."

"Like I told you before, I don't know how you even functioned." He paused. "You're way too hard on yourself."

"There's something you don't know about me."

"It doesn't matter."

"It does to me."

"So you want to tell me?"

She nodded. "I sort of lied to you."

"I'm listening."

"The time I took off work, I actually spent in a special care facility." She couldn't bring herself to say the word *institution*. Her stomach roiled at the thought.

"And you see that as something to be ashamed of?"

"Yes, I guess I do."

"Well, I say bully for you for admitting you needed help and getting it."

"I really had no choice. When the firm sent me home that first time, I fell apart. Although I was going to a counselor, that wasn't cutting it. I went on crying jags, pitched hissy fits, threw things. That's when I realized I was totally out of control, and checked myself into the facility."

"Oh, baby, I'm so sorry," Grant whispered his mouth against her neck.

She shivered.

"Shh, it's okay. You're going to be just fine. In fact, you're going to be more than fine. You've got what it takes—trust me on that. You'll end up putting that firm on the map."

Kelly turned in his arms and faced him, knowing tears were cascading down her cheeks. With a groan, he carefully and slowly licked the tears as they fell from her eyes.

"You're a remarkable woman. Don't ever forget that." He tapped her on the nose. "I bet one day God will give you another child."

"No he won't, because I don't intend to marry again."

"Never say never."

She ignored that and asked, "What about you?"

"What about me?"

"Don't you ever long for a permanent home?"

"I got one." His voice was lower than husky. "If I'm not mistaken, you're in it right now."

She scrutinized him noticing his bittersweet smile. "You know what I mean."

"Sure do," he drawled. "A home in suburbia with a wife, and two point three children and a dog."

"If that's the way you want to define it, yes, that's what I mean." She paused intentionally, then said, "I assume you never long for that."

"I can't say I haven't thought about it. But long for, no, I guess I haven't."

"Which means you haven't ever been wild about a woman."

"I had one serious relationship," Grant said painfully.

"What happened?" Kelly pressed, giving in to her need to pry.

"It didn't work out."

She waited for him to elaborate.

Grant sighed, as though he knew he had no choice but to say more. "She wanted me to join her dad's company in Dallas."

"Bottom line, she didn't want to live in rural America?"

"You got it."

Kelly listened for any bitterness in his tone, but found none. "What about the others?"

"We either drifted apart or became just good friends."

"Looks like you've never felt the need to make a commitment to marriage."

"Guess not. At least not enough to make it happen."

They were silent for a long moment.

"However, under different circumstances, you, Kelly Baker, could change my mind."

Though Kelly was taken aback, she rebounded. "But the circumstances are what they are and we can't change them."

"Right." Grant muzzled his lips against hers. "But this isn't a fantasy—your body next to mine—which means I'm going to act out a portion of my fantasy right now."

Wiping out all thought of a future that was never to be, Kelly sighed, slipped her leg over his thigh, sighed again as he entered her.

Simultaneously, their cries rent the air.

* * *

"Top of the morning to you, Ms. Baker."

"Good morning, Mr. Mangum."

"My, but aren't we formal," Kelly said with a tinge of sarcasm, and then felt bad about her lack of professionalism.

"I guess that's because what I have to tell you is formal." Mangum paused and cleared his throat. "More or less."

"Your client refuses to take a DNA test." She didn't ask a question.

"That's right and I think that's a wise decision."

"We'll see if the judge agrees with you."

"Good luck, young lady."

Kelly didn't bother to answer the condescending jerk. She simply hung up, and this time her lack of professionalism felt damn good.

Mangum's call had caught her between the breakfast and lunch rush, although she couldn't say she'd been all that *rushed*. Business was off a tad, and she hoped that had nothing to do with her. The townsfolk loved Ruth and missed her smile and her ability to chat with them. They obviously had no qualms about telling Ruth anything and everything about their lives.

With Kelly it was different. She didn't know the customers, though she'd tried to learn the regulars' names and felt she'd done an adequate job of that. Still, she had a long way to go before she became the people person Ruth was. But then, she had never wanted to be.

Hopefully she would soon be packing her car and heading back to Houston. *Without Grant.* Suddenly a sick feeling invaded her stomach. She got up from the chair in

Ruth's tiny office and walked to the window and peered out at the sunshine.

A perfect day for Grant to be in the woods. She knew he was going stir-crazy because he wasn't there. Right now, she had done all she could. The next move was the court's.

She wondered what he was doing at this particular moment. Was he thinking about her?

Kelly drew a trembling breath. Since she'd left his house, she'd thought of little else. Their coming together had been incredible, and even now, as much as he'd loved her body from end to end and everywhere in between, she craved more.

Had Grant turned her into a sex fiend? She laughed at the thought.

After Eddie's death and before she'd met Grant, she hadn't cared if a man ever touched her again, much less made love to her. Now, after a long lapse, she was addicted.

Too bad. She'd just have to get over her addiction, go through detox of a different kind, because she was going back to Houston *alone.*

She had survived the worst possible trauma that could happen to anyone. As Grant had pointed out, she was still functioning, albeit not as well as she could be. But she was getting there.

Returning to Houston and to her firm was what she wanted most. A thrill of anticipation shot through her. Starting to handle Grant's case had reminded her that she loved being a lawyer—and couldn't wait to return to work.

If only she didn't feel a pinch of sadness at the thought of leaving Lane. She didn't want to feel anything for this small town or any of the people who lived in it. Unfortunately, she did. She really liked Ms. Maud. Since she'd visited the old lady, Kelly could see them becoming close. And those tea cakes. They were to die for. She couldn't imagine not ever eating another one.

Besides Maud, there were other customers she'd come to know and like.

Then there was Grant. She couldn't imagine leaving him. But she knew when the time came, she could and *would* do it.

And never look back.

Fourteen

"It won't be long now."

"So you're about to wrap things up in Montana and head back to the woods of East Texas, huh?"

Ruth laughed. "That's right, so try and contain yourself. I know you're jumping through hoops to get back to Big H."

Not necessarily, Kelly was tempted to say, but didn't for fear of the questions that would follow. No doubt Ruth would be shocked.

"It's been an experience, I'll admit," Kelly said.

"Lordy, I can't wait to hear all about it. I'm still amazed you agreed to do it in the first place."

"Me, too, but you know I really didn't have a choice except to leave Houston."

"Yes, you did," Ruth countered bluntly. "You could've opted to rent a cabin on the beach or used a lawyer friend's condo in New York to rest and relax. You didn't have to help me out."

"That's where you're wrong. One good deed deserves another. No matter what I do, it'll never be enough to repay you for what you did for me when I needed you the most four years ago."

"Let's not go down that road again. You don't owe me anything."

"Whatever."

"So how are things?"

Kelly brought her up-to-date as best she could, even telling her about Grant's troubles and their professional relationship—but not their personal one.

"I'm glad you're helping him. If he doesn't get out of that jam, it'll ruin him."

"If I have anything to do with it, he's not going to lose that timber."

"You go, girl. If anyone can straighten out those local yokels, it's you."

"Whoa, you're talking about your friends here."

Ruth laughed again. "Hey, the country has their share of idiots, too, you know."

"Oops, have to run," Kelly said with a chuckle. "Customers are coming. There's money to be made."

"I'm all for that. Talk to you later. But I'll see you sooner than later."

That conversation had taken place two days ago, and since then, Kelly had been working like crazy in the shop. It seemed like a new bout of cold weather had made people hungrier than usual, because business was better than ever.

It was after this morning's rush Kelly pondered the fact

she hadn't seen Grant since they'd had made love at his place. She hadn't even told him that Larry Ross had refused to take a DNA test. But she suspected he knew that wouldn't be news to Grant.

Still, it bothered her that she hadn't seen or talked to him.

Did he have regrets about his involvement with her? Probably not, because he knew she would be leaving soon. They had enjoyed a steamy night of lovemaking, which they both had needed, and that was that.

No regrets.

No commitments.

No future.

Perfect scenario.

She knew that was pure baloney, or she wouldn't be so anxious about his absence. And angry to boot. How dare he make love to her with such passion, then ignore her? She didn't need this aggravation in her life right now. She'd come here to de-stress rather than stress.

"Grr," Kelly muttered under her breath, just as the phone rang.

It was Maud. "Come over, Kelly. Right away!"

Maud was lying in a fetal position on the sofa in her cottage, out like a light.

Kelly added another blanket to the one already on the old woman before sitting back down in the chair near the fire. She had been with Maud for over an hour now, ever since they had returned from Dr. Graham's office.

Maud, of course, had pitched a fit at the thought of going to a doctor. But when Kelly had arrived at her house and found the old woman acting bizarre, as if she'd had a seizure or light stroke, grave concern had given Kelly the courage to force Maud into action.

"Am I going to die?"

Kelly whipped her gaze from the fire to Maud who had propped herself up on the pillow.

Pity washed though Kelly, but she didn't let it show. "Absolutely not. You're going to be just fine as long as you do what Dr. Graham tells you."

Maud frowned. "Tell me again what's wrong with me."

"Your blood sugar is out of whack. As long as you keep tabs on it and keep it in check, then you shouldn't have any more of these spells."

"Honest?"

"Honest." Kelly leaned forward and stared deeply into Maud's eyes. "Unless you disobey the doctor and eat your tea cakes."

Maud's chin wobbled just like it had at the doctor's office. "You mean I can never have another tea cake?"

"Never is a long time."

"But I'm a long time old," Maud countered.

Kelly smiled, leaned over and kissed her on the cheek. "Don't worry about that right now. Just behave yourself, and before long, I'll bet you'll can at least nibble on your delicacies. That's better than nothing."

Maud grabbed Kelly's hand and pulled it up to her bony cheek. "You're a good girl, Kelly Baker. I just wish you didn't have to leave us and go so far away. I'm going to miss you."

Surprisingly tears pooled in Kelly's eyes. "I'm going to miss you, too, Maud. A lot."

"Then don't go."

Kelly gently disengaged her hand. "I have to. My job, my life, my friends—they're all in Houston."

"What about me, Grant, Ruth? Aren't we your friends?"

Kelly's heart faltered. "Sure you are, and I plan to keep in touch."

"Hogwash."

Kelly was taken aback. "Be quiet and rest or I'm going to call Dr. Graham and tattle."

"Tattle all you want," Maud said with some of her spunk. "I want to talk to you about Grant."

Kelly kept her emotions under wraps. "There's nothing to talk about." She wished she meant that. There was actually lots to talk about, and that was the problem. But to dwell too much on Grant now would dredge up the precarious intimacy between them. She didn't want to go there.

"Of course there is." Maud struck out her tongue. "Only the both of you are apparently too stubborn to see it."

Kelly tried to downplay the seriousness of the moment by smiling, then saying, "You're just miffed because you want to play matchmaker and it isn't working.

"I may be old, young lady, but I'm not blind, nor am I deaf."

"I never said you were either."

"Sure you did," Maud said in an argumentative tone. "But if—"

"Thanks," Kelly interrupted with a smile. "How 'bout we change the subject."

Maud gave her a hard look, but then complied, especially as her eyelids were drooping. Kelly remained awhile longer, then finally slipped out of the cottage, her heart heavy.

* * *

The outdoors was Grant's salvation. Always had been and always would be. Tromping through the woods had a miraculous way of clearing his head and his soul. Today was no exception.

He still couldn't believe his equipment and crew remained idle. Even though it had only been a few days since he'd been shut down, to him it seemed like an eternity. He wasn't depressed or anxious. He was downright angry.

How had things gone from good to bad in such a short time? And not just on the work front.

Kelly.

He didn't know what to do about her. She had snuck in the back door of his heart and set up camp. He didn't love her. He wasn't there yet, not by any stretch of the imagination. But he sure cared about her and ached right now to make love to her again.

She was hot and willing, a rare combination in a woman. Soon, though, she would be gone for good. While that thought was unbearable, he had no solution to the problem.

Even if he'd wanted it, a long-distance romance never worked. He knew that when she left, things would be finished between them. She'd go back to her job in the big city while he stayed with his in the woods.

City girl and country boy? The two just weren't compatible. More than that, he wasn't interested in a relationship. He'd been alone so long now, he liked his life the way it was. He didn't see a need for a permanent change, except it sure was nice to have a beautiful woman in his bed.

Grant grimaced, then reminded himself there were

worse things than doing without—such as being saddled with a wife who was as different from him as day was from dark. But had he reached the time in his life where he might do something like fall for a woman?

He hoped the hell not.

Besides, there were lots of women willing to warm his bed. Problem was he hadn't cared enough to invite them into it. Then Kelly Baker came into his life.

Who would've ever guessed he'd become smitten with her?

"Damn," Grant muttered, as he continued his trek through the woods. Nearing the log set, he walked over to a large tree that was marked to be cut.

Suddenly he yearned to do just that. The very thought of operating equipment and harvesting trees was exhilarating. But just as quickly as his eagerness grew, it chilled. If he got caught, he'd end up in jail—something he could *not* afford in more ways than one.

Still Grant didn't move, continuing to lean against the tree. That was when he heard it. He shouted when something crashed through the underbrush in the opposite direction. His head and ears perked up. His eyes perused his surroundings, but he saw nothing. The forest became quiet again. Then he felt a searing pain in his shoulder.

Whipping his head down he watched in horror as blood saturated his thick shirt. Grant's stomach roiled and he slid to his knees.

He'd been shot.

Fifteen

Kelly couldn't stop pacing the floor in the surgery waiting room. Her legs simply wouldn't cooperate and remain still enough for her to sit down.

"You're going to wear yourself and the carpet out, you know," Pete drawled. He was kicked back in a chair, his legs sprawled out in front of him.

There were other people in the room, but as a whole the place was fairly empty, which gave Kelly the freedom she needed to pace.

"I know," she admitted, pausing for a moment, "but my insides feel like they're turned inside out."

Pete raised his eyebrows, as if to ask what was going on with her and Grant. He was far too intuitive, so she'd best be on guard. But that was hard when she was so obviously anxious.

When an excited man had come through the door of the coffee shop an hour ago and announced there had been an accident in the woods, that Grant Wilcox had been shot, Kelly took action.

She had told Doris she was headed to the hospital in Wellington, then she'd called Pete. She had arrived at the E.R. just as Grant's gurney was being wheeled down the hall toward surgery.

When Grant had seen her, he'd said to the attendant, "Wait a minute."

Feeling as though her heart was going to literally jump out of her chest, Kelly had stopped beside the stretcher. Before she could speak, however, she'd had to force air into her lungs. "What...what happened?"

Despite the pain she knew he was in, his gaze on her had softened. "Some idiot shot me in the shoulder, which is no big deal."

She gasped. "No big deal! How can you say that when you're headed to surgery?"

"It could have been my heart."

While that sobering comment certainly put things in perspective, Kelly still didn't see getting shot as minor. Men and their logic.

"Ma'am, we have to go."

Grant had reached out, grabbed her hand and peered deep into her eyes.

She'd squeezed his hand tightly, then let it go. "I'll be waiting."

"I'll see you soon." He'd winked.

By the time she made it to the waiting area, Kelly's throat was too full to speak. And there sat Pete, who merely looked at her through inquisitive eyes. Neither said anything. If she had wanted to, she could've made her way to a corner and let the tears flow, but that wouldn't do any good.

Grant was going to be just fine, she told herself with firm conviction. He'd be out of surgery in no time and would be as good as new.

The idea that her stomach was a tight ball of fear was ridiculous. Suddenly she froze again.

Love.

In connection with Grant? No way. That could not be. It wasn't possible. She couldn't have been so foolish as to have fallen in love with this woodsman.

Only she knew that she had. Before Kelly's knees gave way, she eased into the nearest chair, which just happened to be next to Pete.

"Thank goodness," he said with a halfhearted grin, "you're finally sitting down."

She tried to smile, but it wouldn't happen.

Pete reached over and awkwardly patted her hand. "He's going to be fine. He's a tough old bird. It'll take more than a bullet to the shoulder to get him down."

She nodded, unable to share with him her heart's secret—the real reason she was so upset. She'd fallen in love with a man with whom she had no future.

"Now, if he loses his right to cut the timber on Holland's land—" Pete's voice broke off and a pained expression crossed his face. "That would be worse than him getting shot in the shoulder."

Kelly rallied. "He's not going to lose his timber."

"How can you be so sure?"

"I think Judge Winston will do the right thing."

Pete's thin lips turned downward. "Man, I hope so. I still can't believe that bastard Ross—" He stopped and cleared his throat. "Uh, excuse me, ma'am."

Kelly shook her head. "No apology necessary. Remember I work with a group of male attorneys. Trust me, I've heard worse."

"Trust me, I could have called him worse, too."

They both smiled, then fell silent again.

"Don't you think the doctors have had time to finish working on him?"

"Nah," Pete said, crossing his sprawled legs. "By the time they prep him and all, it takes more time than you think."

Kelly knew that, having had more experiences in surgery waiting rooms with family and friends. But this was different. This was the man she had just realized she loved.

Her stomach somersaulted, and she felt sick. What was she going to do? *Nothing,* her heart cried. What could she do? The answer was clear. She would go on with her life just as he would go on with his.

Doing different things in different places.

"You care about him, don't you?"

She saw no reason to hedge any longer. "Yes, I do."

"I'm glad. He's been alone too long."

An alarm went off inside her head. "Look, don't think—"

Pete held up his hand, stopping her words. "I don't think anything, ma'am, so don't go making a mountain out of a molehill."

"Call me Kelly."

"Okay, Kelly. All I'm saying is that since you've been here, I've seen a difference in Grant—a good difference, I might add. If that good only lasts a little while, that's better than nothing."

"I still can't believe he never married." She shouldn't be delving into Grant's life behind his back, especially under these circumstances. But despite Grant's explanation, it still mystified her that he'd remained single all these years.

Pete smiled. "He's too damn picky. When it comes to women, that is."

"That doesn't tell me a lot," Kelly said, making small talk in hopes of keeping her mind off of what was happening in surgery.

"He likes living in the sticks."

"Then that's where he should stay."

"And he sure as hell likes his independence."

"He should keep it." Kelly said those words with a sinking heart, then hated herself for feeling this way. Whatever she'd been fishing for hadn't materialized. Grant was who he was, and he wasn't about to change.

Certainly not for her.

They heard someone clear his throat behind them, and Kelly and Pete whipped around. "Ah, Amos," Pete said, rising. "Come join us."

Instantly, Kelly knew who this tall stringbean of a man was. He'd been in the coffee shop a couple of times. She stood and, out of courtesy, shook his hand, though her heart was pounding hard.

Kelly didn't think he'd made an appearance for appearance sake. She knew he had something to say. He looked uncomfortable, fiddling with the hat he held in his hand. He seemed to avoid looking at her, choosing to keep his gaze glued on Pete.

"Sheriff, was Grant's shooting deliberate?"

Kelly's blunt question seemed to take both men aback.

Pete's eyes narrowed, while Amos shifted from foot to foot. Then the sheriff's face cleared and he actually smiled, which seemed to tempered his nervousness.

"Uh, we're not sure, ma'am."

Kelly's mouth turned dust-dry, and her eyes widened in horror. "You mean…" Her voice shriveled into nothing.

"I figured it was some damn hog hunter, or a kid taking target practice," Pete commented in a grave voice. "The idea that someone might intentionally shoot at Grant never entered my mind."

Kelly let out her pent-up breath and shook her head, still too horrified to speak. Things like this just didn't happen to people she knew, especially someone she cared about, for heaven's sake."

After licking her dry lips, she said, "He could have easily been—" She broke off, unable to say the word *killed*.

"We know, ma'am," the sheriff said softly, respectfully. "It's a God thing. That's the way I see it." Changing the subject, he added, "Let Grant know the investigation's taking top priority."

"If someone did take a shot at him," Pete said in a harsh tone, "I pity the poor dumb son of a bitch when you find him. Grant will be out for blood."

"Look," Amos said, rubbing his chin, "we're doing a thorough investigation. We will find out who's responsible. As soon as we know something, we'll be back in touch." He paused and cleared his throat again. "Meanwhile, how's Grant?"

"We don't know yet," Pete said before Kelly could respond.

Amos left shortly thereafter, leaving behind a tense silence.

Kelly's eyes kept veering to the O.R. door and she was finally rewarded. A tall, bald man dressed in surgery greens entered the room.

"Ms. Baker?"

She and Pete both stood expectantly.

"I'm Dr. Carpenter, and Grant's fine. We removed the bullet without a problem." He paused and wiped his forehead. "He did, however, lose quite a bit of blood so I'm keeping him overnight."

"You mean he might have gone home otherwise?" Kelly asked in an astounded tone.

"Home, yes, only we don't recommend he go alone." The doctor looked troubled. "When he awakens, something tells me he's not going to like that."

Pete chuckled. "You can say that again. He'll be pitching a fit to get out of here."

"May I see him?" Kelly asked.

Dr. Carpenter nodded. "He's in recovery, but because it's not real busy, I'll let you sit with him."

"Thank you, sir," Kelly said with heartfelt relief, even though she realized she was adding another nail to her emotional coffin.

Leaving Pete behind, she followed the doctor.

"It's about damn time I'm getting out of this place."

"You only had to say overnight," Kelly said in a soothing, even tone, trying to calm Grant.

"That was one night too many."

Kelly wanted to tell him to stop his bellyaching, but she kept silent. She knew the pain medication had probably worn off and he was feeling discomfort. That would make anyone grouchy, especially someone who wasn't used to pain.

Once they were in her vehicle, Kelly turned on the engine then didn't move. Grant faced her and said, "Pete told me my getting shot might not have been accidental."

"That's right," she stated, telling him about the conversation with the sheriff.

"If you ask me, that's a stretch."

"Amos didn't sound that sure."

"Hunters, legal and illegal, have always been a burr in a forester's butt," Grant said. "We've learned to keep our distance."

"So you think it was a hunter?"

"Or a kid playing with his daddy's gun."

"That's what Pete said."

They were both quiet for a moment, then Grant added in a grave tone, "Are you thinking what I'm thinking?"

She cut a look at him. "That Larry Ross might be the culprit?"

Grant's expression was grim. "Yep. We're on the same page. If it was deliberate, then he's the only one I can think of who would benefit from my demise."

"But when you really think about it rationally," Kelly said, "that's ludicrous. First, what would he have to gain, and second, how could he expect to get away with it? I'm sure he's the number-one suspect."

Cold fury glinted in Grant's eyes. "If it wasn't an accident, then he sure as hell is mine."

"You'll just have to be patient and let the law work."

"And not take matters into my own hands." Grant's voice was icy-cold. "Is that what you're saying?"

"Absolutely, but then you know that."

"Don't be too sure." Grant paused for a moment, then changed the subject, his tone becoming thick and husky. "I understand I'm going home with you."

Kelly's hand stilled on the gearshift as desire leaped in his eyes. She swallowed, then said in a slightly unsteady voice, "Let's get two things straight—its not *my* home and *you're* going straight to the spare bedroom."

"Aw, shucks," he said.

She glared at him before backing out of the parking lot.

"Just because my arm's out of commission doesn't mean anything else is."

"Speaking of your arm, how is it?

"Believe it or not, it doesn't hurt all that much. In fact, I can even move it up and down without much pain."

"Still, you don't have complete control of it," Kelly stressed. "My fear is that one wrong move could rip open the stitches. Then you'd be in a heap of trouble."

Grant shrugged, his mouth in a pout. "I think you're overreacting, but go on and drive. I'm just jerking your chain. I promise I'll be a good boy."

He paused and she felt his smoldering gaze on her. "But I won't promise for how long."

Deciding it was best not to respond to that, Kelly steered the car into the street. "I need to stop by the coffee shop for a second and check on things."

"Take your time. I'm not going anywhere."

"By the way, have you heard anything from the sheriff?"

"Nope, not yet. But if I don't real soon, I'll be rattling his chain."

Kelly tended to business then, fifteen minutes later, drove to Ruth's driveway. She and Grant were about to go inside when she heard another vehicle pull in behind her. She turned around, and her jaw dropped.

John Billingsly? What on earth is he doing here?

"Who is that?" Grant asked in a slightly irritated tone, as if he realized something was not quite right.

"It's...my boss."

Sixteen

She was stunned to see John Billingsly in Lane, Texas, especially on a Monday, one of the busiest days at the firm. The fact that Grant was standing next to her giving John the once-over through narrowed eyes didn't help any.

Clearing her throat, Kelly made the appropriate introductions. Then John, looking slightly uncomfortable, said, "It appears I've come at a bad time."

"Not as far as I'm concerned," Grant said in an offhand manner, waving his good arm. "I'll leave you two alone." He paused, facing John. "Nice to meet you."

John nodded. "Same here."

Once Grant had disappeared inside, Kelly simply stared at her boss, thinking how tired he looked. Even so, that didn't detract from his handsomeness. He was tall, with broad shoulders, a thatch of silver hair and a killer smile.

She couldn't forget about that. Or what a great voice he had, which was one of the reasons he commanded so much respect in the courtroom.

"So what brings you here?" she asked. Then, as if she needed to qualify that question so he wouldn't think she was rude, she added, "Of course, I'm glad to see you."

John gave her a half smile. "I'm sure you are, but not as glad as I'd like you to be."

Kelly flushed. "I don't know what you mean."

"Oh, I think you do." John nodded toward the door. "What's with him?"

"He's a friend who just got out of the hospital."

John's eyes probed, as if searching for the whole truth.

She ignored that gaze and said, "You're actually a sight for sore eyes, as I'm dying to know how things are at the firm." She hoped her tone was cool and even because inside she was shaking.

"Then let's go somewhere and talk. Lunch, perhaps. I want to know how you're doing, then I want to bring you up-to-date on the firm. We have a couple of cases coming up that have your name on them."

"That's great."

He raised thick eyebrows. "Is that all you have to say?"

Kelly did some mental tap dancing while sweat pooled under her breasts. "I'd love to visit with you over lunch, only now's not a good time.

"Are you due back at the shop?"

"Actually, it's closed today."

John lifted his eyebrows in question, as if to ask why she couldn't leave. When she didn't answer, he murmured, "Looks like I shot myself in the foot by coming without calling first. I'm assuming it has something to do with the guy in there." He inclined his head toward the door.

"That's only partly true," Kelly said with conviction. "How about we sit on the porch swing and talk?"

After all, it was a nice day, and she couldn't just send him back without spending some time with him. The fact that he'd come to see her was a big deal, and she had to treat it as such. Her job was her life; if her boss wanted to see her, then she'd be a fool not to accommodate him. Besides, Grant could take care of himself for a while.

Once they were seated, John smiled at her. "You seem good."

"I am," she answered, with a sincere smile of her own. "You were right. I needed to get away. Only I have a confession to make."

"Oh?"

"I've been doing a little work."

"On a case?"

She nodded, then explained.

"You'll get no flack from me. I think it's great that you're dabbling in the law again and feeling good about it."

She gave him a big smile. "I'm so glad you approve, even though I haven't won the case yet."

"You will," he said with conviction.

"Thanks. Your confidence makes me feel even better."

"So when can we expect you back?"

"Just as soon as my cousin returns."

A relieved expression crossed John's face, making him look less tired. "What about him?"

Kelly didn't pretend to misunderstand the emphasis

behind this question, though she wasn't about to answer it. "What *about* him?"

John merely shrugged. "Okay, so you don't want to talk about him. I can accept that."

"While you're at it, accept that I can't wait to get back to work."

John reached out and squeezed her hand. "Everyone misses you, including myself. We can't wait to have you return."

"Thank," Kelly said, feeling tears gather in her eyes. "You don't know how much that means to me."

He rose. "I'm going now, but we'll talk later."

"Thanks for coming. I'm just sorry—"

John held up his hand. "No apology necessary. Again, I should've called first." He smiled with a wink. "I'll see you soon."

Kelly smiled in return, giving him a thumbs-up. "You can count on that."

She waited until he was back in his BMW and on the street before she made her way into the house. Closing the door, where she paused and leaned back against it. That was when she noticed Grant hadn't made it to Ruth's spare bedroom, but instead had crashed on the sofa. He appeared to be sound asleep.

She fixed her gaze on him, thinking how good he looked, especially now that the deep lines around his eyes and mouth were relaxed. Yet she sensed a vulnerability about him that tore at her heart. Between his job situation and this mishap, he was mentally and physically stressed. Even though he hadn't let on, she knew he'd probably like to bite a tenpenny nail in two.

She was tempted to walk over and rub Grant's cheek with the back of her hand for the sheer pleasure of simply touching him. Every time she saw him she *wanted* to touch him. But since that kind of "touching" had no future, she kept her hands to herself.

Especially since their lives remained worlds apart and always would.

Pulling her thoughts off Grant before she did something she would regret, Kelly forced herself to think about John and what had just taken place between them.

She remained a bit shell-shocked from his unexpected appearance. While she had wanted to spend time with him, she hadn't felt good about leaving Grant, thinking of the doctor's comments. For a second, she'd actually been pulled in two directions. She wasn't sure she'd made the right choice, either.

Now, as she shoved away from the door and made her way quietly past the sofa so as not to awaken Grant, she took a deep breath, trying to calm her rattled nerves. Why did life have to be so complicated? She was at the end of the sofa when her hand was grabbed.

Wide-eyed, she swung around and saw that Grant was sitting up, her hand clasped in his.

"You...you startled me," she said in a halting voice. "I thought you were asleep."

"I was just resting."

Their gazes locked together like magnets. Then he peered down at her left hand, and back up at her face. "I expected you to be gone with your boyfriend."

Tugging her hand free, she shoved it into her jean pocket. "He's not my boyfriend," she said tersely. "He's my boss. But then you know that."

"He's got a thing for you."

"So what if he does?"

Now why had she said that? Perhaps to make Grant jealous? For what purpose? Grant didn't love her. He felt only lust. Without commitment. And right or wrong, she had enjoyed every minute of being the focus of that lust.

"Ah, so you're keeping the poor bastard dangling."

She saw red. "What I'm doing is none of your business."

"You're damn straight, it's not," he agreed in a harsh tone as he got to his feet. "Nothing you do is my business and nothing I do is yours." Their eyes met again in a clash of wills. "Right?"

"Right," she said defiantly, holding herself together by a mere thread.

"I feel like hell. I'm going to bed."

When she heard the door to the guest bedroom close, Kelly sat on the sofa, her insides churning. If she ever thought he loved her, his words had just proved her dead wrong.

She grabbed a pillow, buried her face in it and sobbed.

"You look all tuckered out, girlie."

"I am, Maud."

"Before I came, I took some tea cakes out of the oven. Why don't you come by and have some?"

"Thanks, but no thanks. I'm going home to soak my tired bones in the tub. I'll take a rain check, though."

"You sure? I'll be glad to go home, get them and bring them to you."

"Don't you dare. I'm simply too pooped to eat anything right now."

"Okey-dokey. I'll see you later, then."

Thank goodness Maud hadn't probed. Usually, she wouldn't take no for an answer. Now that she had gone, Kelly breathed a sigh of relief, thankful the day was over. Business had remained exceptionally good. People had been in and out all day.

Except Grant.

She hadn't seen him in a couple of days. The night he'd spent in Ruth's spare room had been a short one. She'd awakened at five o'clock the next morning to check on him only to find him gone. She had no idea when he'd gotten up and left. She needed to talk to him, too, as she'd gotten the court hearing moved to the day after tomorrow.

As a result of his absence, Kelly didn't know which she wanted to do more—shake him or kiss him. She couldn't stop thinking about that hot night of passion they shared. But it was best this way, she knew. Best that he stayed away. Best that he was in no condition to touch her.

"We're leaving, Kelly," Doris said, poking her head through the swinging door.

"Me, too. See you guys in the morning."

Kelly had the door locked and was about to get in her car when Grant's pickup pulled up beside her.

"Climb in and let's go for a ride."

The idea that he was ordering her around didn't even register. The fact that he was driving did, however. "What are you doing behind the wheel?"

"I got one good hand."

"Grant Wilcox, you're nuts. You could have a wreck and kill yourself or someone else."

"Are you coming?"

"No."

"Please."

When he looked at her like that, her good sense seemed to go by the wayside, and she couldn't deny him anything, much less time. They had so little of it left that each moment seemed precious.

"Only if you let me drive."

"Have you ever driven a truck?"

"No."

He laughed, got out, then made a sweeping gesture with his good arm. "It's all yours."

Once Kelly got behind the wheel, she simply sat there, feeling his eyes on her. When she faced him, a teasing smile radiated from his lips and eyes. "It's easy driving, actually. It's just like a car, so let's go."

After adjusting the seat and the rearview mirror, she started the engine.

"Hang a right here," Grant said when she had maneuvered onto the street. "We're headed to Wellington. I have a piece of equipment in a mechanic shop that I need to check on."

"That reminds me," Kelly said. "We go to court day after tomorrow on the DNA test."

"That's great. I just know that bastard Ross is lying through his pearly whites."

"What if he's not?"

"Then I'm sunk," Grant said flatly. "My only recourse is to turn around and sue Holland to get my money back."

"Unless the judge orders Holland to give Ross his fair share of the timber money."

"Can he do that?"

"Judges are little gods." Kelly smiled without humor. "They can do anything they want to."

Grant raised his head. "Then let us pray."

The rest of the drive passed in silence, though Kelly was conscious of Grant occupying the seat next to her. She ached to touch him. The few times their gazes tangled, she saw the same smoldering desire in his. She simply gripped the steering wheel tighter and told herself to keep her distance, that dallying with him would only leave her hurting.

Once they reached the city limits of Wellington, Grant directed her to the equipment dealer. She waited in the truck while he went inside and attended to business.

"It's not ready yet," he said, climbing in the cab. "Which is probably a good thing, because it's going to cost megabucks to get it out. Bucks that I don't have right now."

It was on the tip of her tongue to say that she'd loan him the money, but Kelly thought better of it after looking at his grim features. Her instinct told her he wouldn't accept money from her.

"Where to now?" she asked. "Back to Lane?"

"Yep, unless you want to grab a bit of early dinner."

"I'd rather head back."

"That's fine with me."

They were just out of Wellington, on a side road when she saw the most beautiful house she could have imagined. Constructed of white stone, it nestled among huge trees and lush shrubs, though it didn't look unkempt. On the contrary, it looked peaceful and inviting. So intrigued was Kelly with it, that she actually slowed the truck.

"What a lovely place," she said in awe.

"You gotta be kidding."

Kelly stopped the truck and faced him. "What's that supposed to mean?"

He shrugged. "I'm just surprised that you'd think any house outside of a subdivision was pretty."

"Well, this is about as close to country living as I'd like."

"Even at that, I doubt you'd be happy. People from the city just don't belong here."

Guess that told her. Kelly's eyes flashed fire at her dismissal. "Do you intentionally try to make me angry, or does it just come naturally?"

He swore. "I don't think that calls for an answer."

The remainder of the drive was done in hostile silence. When they arrived at Ruth's place, Kelly bounded out of the truck and made her way inside. Grant grabbed her arm and swung her around to face him.

"Look, I'm sorry. I should've kept my mouth shut."

"Yes, you should have."

"Would you buy it if I told you I was under a lot of stress?"

"No."

"Didn't think you would." He rubbed his jaw. "Would you buy this? What if I told you I wanted to make you hate me so that I wouldn't want to kiss you every time you came near me?"

Blood beat with hammer force in her ears.

"Oh, to hell with it," Grant muttered, placing his good hand against her shoulder and backing her against the wall, his breathing harsh and erratic.

Within seconds, he was grinding his lips to hers.

If she hadn't been propped up, she would have melted into a puddle on the floor. Yet she gave back as good as she got, wrapping her arms around his neck, reveling in the feelings he evoked in her.

"God, I want you so much it's killing me." His voice sounded desperate.

"I want you, too," she whispered with an ache, loving him with a full and complete heart.

"I mean here." His eyes, staring into hers, were as hot as his lips had been. "Now."

"Now? What...what about your shoulder?"

"You let me take care of that," he growled.

Without further words and without taking her eyes off him, she unzipped his jeans, releasing his erection. He in turn shoved her blue jean skirt up and jerked her thong down. Kelly stepped out of them just as his strong hand cupped one cheek of her buttocks.

As if she knew exactly what he had in mind, she circled his neck with her arms. Then using all her strength, she sprang up and clasped her legs around him.

Entering her swift and hard, he groaned, "Oh, Kelly, Kelly."

Seventeen

She leaned over him, her fingers delving into the hairs on his chest, playing in them. At some point they had ended up in Kelly's bed, though she had no recollection of the particulars. After that heady session against the wall, her mind had gone on hiatus.

Only not for long. As soon as they reached the bed, their lovemaking started all over again. At first she was mindful of his shoulder, but it became apparent that his wound didn't diminish Grant's passion. It was as if they couldn't get enough of each other's bodies. She wanted him with the same intensity as he wanted her.

What had come over her? True, she was in love with Grant. But then, she'd been in love with her husband, too. With Grant it was different. He tapped into a part of herself she hadn't known existed—a wild side.

Exciting?
Yes.
Crazy?
Yes?
Dangerous?
Yes.
Permanent?
No.

Even though her heart wrenched at that thought, Kelly still didn't want to move away from his warm body, didn't want *not* to touch him. Her fingers were having a field day running over his chest and stomach.

And lower.

Groaning, Grant looked up at her with fire in his eyes. She was resting on an elbow, and knew her own eyes burned with that same fire. Neither of them bothered to turn off the lamp in the bedroom. Not so with Eddie. Their lovemaking had been done in the dark.

"What are you thinking about?" Grant asked in his low, brusque voice.

"Eddie. My husband."

Grant hesitated, then asked in a resigned voice, "What about him?"

"Although we really loved each other, our lovemaking was never wild or passionate. That's so clear to me now."

Grant's eyes darkened, then he said, "Thank you for telling me that. You have no idea how humble or how good that makes me feel." He paused to kiss her. "I've never made love to any woman like I've made love to you. The spark, fire, whatever you want to call it, just wasn't there." He paused again. "Maybe that's why I never married."

Those last words hung in the air for a long moment, creating a stifling tension.

Feeling sad for a reason she refused to admit, Kelly replaced her fingers with her lips, first tonguing his nipples until they were as rigid as hers.

"Mmm, that feels so good," he said in a guttural tone.

"This should feel even better." Using her tongue, she moved lower, down the middle of his flat stomach to his belly button, where she delved and sucked.

He moaned and squirmed as she moved even farther south. When she reached his swollen manhood, she paused and looked at him, gauging his reaction. He had raised himself onto his elbows and stared back at her, his eyes heated and glazed.

"It's…it's your call," he said in a croaking voice.

She lowered her lips onto the soft head and sucked. And sucked some more.

"Oh, Kelly," he cried, "yes, yes."

She climbed over him, sinking onto that hard shaft. Shortly, their moans turned into cries that filled the room.

How could she ever let him go? That question that went through Kelly's mind when she finally lay beside him, exhausted but satisfied, and happy beyond her wildest dreams.

"Kelly, it's John."

Her heart raced. "It's good to hear from you again."

"Same here. Having said that, I'll come straight to the point."

"Why not?" she replied a bit breathlessly. Something was up. She could tell by his crisp tone.

"You remember me mentioning the firm had a couple of cases with your name on them?

"Of course."

"Well, we're about to take them on, and we want you in on the sessions from the get-go, which means we need you here ASAP."

"Oh, John, I'd like nothing better than to say I could leave now, but I can't, though I am expecting my cousin back any day now."

A deep sigh filtered through the line. "We'll hold off as long as we can." He paused. "How's your case going?"

"It should be resolved soon."

"Good. So it won't prevent your returning to Houston when your cousin gets back." He paused again, this time longer. "You remember our talk about a partnership?"

How could she forget *that?* "I do."

"Well, if you ace these new cases, you'll be a shoo-in."

"I don't know what to say, except thanks." Kelly heart was really racing now.

John chuckled. "That's enough. Keep me informed."

"I will, and thanks again for calling."

Once she'd replaced the receiver, Kelly laughed and hollered, "Yes!"

She had made her career her life, and it was finally paying off. But then, just as quickly as that excitement flared, it died. She sand into the nearest chair, her legs like jelly.

Grant.

She would be leaving Grant, wouldn't be seeing him anymore, wouldn't be trading insults with him anymore. *Wouldn't be making love to him anymore.* That couldn't be, not when she loved him.

Yet what choice did she have? He'd never said he loved her and even if he did, a future between them was impossible. He wanted one thing, and she another. And those "wants" were as far apart as the wealth of the queen of England and a starving artist.

Thinking of Grant made Kelly long for him. He hadn't been in the coffee shop all day, nor had he called her. She'd been so busy she really hadn't had time to dwell on the fact, but now that it was closing time and the afternoon loomed empty before her, she wanted to hear from him.

She wanted to see him.

Each time they were together, she fell deeper in love. The thought of leaving him appalled her; the thought of remaining appalled her, as well.

"Yahoo, toots!"

Stunned, Kelly swung around and watched as Ruth strode toward her, arms outstretched. Kelly couldn't believe her eyes. Fate. That was the only thing to which she could attribute this unexpected twist.

"When did you get home?" Kelly asked, laughing as she returned Ruth's bear hug.

"Actually, I haven't been home." Ruth's eyes gazed about, seeming to soak up everything. "This is the first place I hit."

"It's so good to see you."

Ruth giggled. "I can imagine."

"I didn't mean it that way," Kelly said seriously. "Believe me or not, this has truly been a fun experience."

"Yeah, right."

Kelly shook her head. "I'm not pulling your leg."

"Trust me, I'm glad. I was afraid you wouldn't speak to me again."

Kelly rolled her eyes. "I just hope you won't think I've destroyed your business with my ineptness."

"Hasn't happened," Ruth declared. "If you can pour coffee and sling hash, you can run this place." She chuckled, her tall, big-boned frame shaking all over and her green eyes twinkling. "Even though we both know you've never done either."

Kelly placed her hands on her hips as though insulted. "I'll have you know I've done both. Once upon a time, that is."

"Hey, I'm just teasing," Ruth said, "but you know that. Come on, let's go home and catch up on everything."

"I can't wait."

"Kelly?"

She swung back around and saw Doris holding the phone. "It's a Mr. Mangum for you."

Kelly's heart skipped a beat.

"Who's that?" Ruth asked, as if sensing Kelly's reaction.

"I'll explain later. You go on and I'll follow."

"You take your call, and I'll see to the shop," Ruth said.

Kelly closed the door to the tiny office and reached for the receiver. For Grant, this was the moment of truth. "Hello, Mr. Mangum."

"I thought I might find you here."

Grant removed his hat and strode toward Kelly, leaving Pete fiddling with a piece of equipment. "Hey, babe," he said, leaning over and kissing her.

Slightly shocked at familiarity, especially in front of Pete, Kelly felt color seep into her cheeks.

Grant chuckled. "It amazes me that you can still blush after what we've shared."

"Stop it," she muttered, though a smile lurked around her lips. "Pete might hear you."

"Nah, he's too busy playing with that loader." Grant paused. "Now, me, I'd rather play with you."

"You're impossible," Kelly retorted.

"But you love it, only you won't admit it."

"You're right, I won't."

Grant pulled a face, then grinned. "What brings you here?"

"Good news."

Grant's body stilled. "Go on."

"Larry Ross took the DNA test and failed it."

"Glory be!" Grant shouted. He tossed his hard hat in the air, then grabbed Kelly and swung her around and around. When he put her back down, she was so dizzy she clung to him.

"You used both your arms," she said in amazement.

"That's right. Happiness will do that to a guy. Plus, my arm hardly bothers me at all."

"Dr. Carpenter must be one good surgeon."

"Grant grinned. "Must be."

Pete joined them, his gaze fixed on Grant. "What the hell's going on here? I heard you hollering like a banshee."

"We're good to go." Grant slapped Pete on his arm. "At last."

Pete whooped. "You mean we can start the engines?"

"That's exactly what it means," Kelly said, laughing now that she had pulled herself back together.

"Thank you so much, ma'am," Pete said bowing in front of her.

"Get out of here," she said through her laughter.

"You want me to notify the crew?" Pete asked Grant.

"Tell 'em to report to work first thing tomorrow morning."

"Will do."

Once Pete had walked off, Grant's features sobered. "Thanks. You know I mean that."

"I know you do."

"So how did you pull it off?"

"Apparently Ross got in some financial trouble due to gambling. Because he needed money, and because he was so sure he was a legal heir, he agreed to the test." She smiled up at Grant. "As they say, the rest is history."

"Of your making," he said. "If you hadn't pushed for the DNA test, I'd still be sitting on the sidelines." He reached out, grabbed her, pulled her against him and kissed her hard and deep. "That's my thanks in action."

Breathlessly, Kelly pulled back and was about to speak when Pete cut in. "Aw, come on, you two. Give me a break."

They both shot him a grin, which he returned. "So we got Ross on the DNA, but what about your shoulder? I'm still not sure that SOB isn't responsible for that."

Grant's features turned serious. "My gut tells me he's not that stupid, but then what do I know? When I leave here, I'm stopping by to see Amos."

It was then that his cell phone rang. He looked at the caller ID and raised his eyebrows, then said, "Hey, Sheriff, your ears must've been burning." Grant listened for a minute then added, "Yeah, okay. I'll be there shortly."

"So?" Kelly and Pete asked almost simultaneously.

"Ross has been cleared. He has an ironclad alibi for the time of the shooting."

"Damn," Pete muttered.

Kelly looked at Grant. "Then who shot you? Does Amos know?"

"Yep, but he wants to talk to me about it in person."

"At least the mystery's solved," Pete said. "Just let me know the details."

When Pete had driven off, Kelly turned to Grant and said, "We need to talk."

"You bet we do. How 'bout I cook steaks tonight and you come over?"

Kelly's stomach flipped. "I'll be there."

Everything was as perfect as Grant could possibly make it. He had cleaned the house and bought flowers for the rustic dining room table. Although they looked a bit out of place, just stuck in a vase, he was proud of them, nonetheless.

The salad was made. The beer was iced down. The wine was chilled. The potatoes were baking. The steaks ready to throw on the grill.

And he was ready to see Kelly. Now and forever.

Grant's gut twisted at the word *forever.* He didn't mean that. Yes, he did, his conscience taunted back. Had he fallen in love? While that thought panicked him, he wanted to know the answer. For him, love and lust were so closely entwined it was hard to know which was which.

God, he was sweating as if he'd been blazing a trail in the woods. He had to do better than this, or she'd think he'd lost it.

A knock on the door saved him.

He opened it and Kelly walked straight into his arms,

holding on to him as though she'd never let him go, which was a-okay with him.

Finally, he pushed her back, and smiled down at her, then kissed her softly. "Good evening."

"Good evening to you," she said in a slightly winded tone.

Something was wrong; he sensed it deep in his gut. But he wouldn't push her. She'd tell him when she was ready.

"Looks like we're celebrating," she commented, moving deeper into the room.

He gave her a sheepish smile. "Pretty pitiful, aren't they?"

"If you're talking about the flowers, I think they're lovely."

"We both know that's not true, but it sounds good, anyway."

"You're impossible," Kelly declared, shaking her head.

"Sit down," Grant said with a nervousness that stunned and annoyed him. "You want wine or beer?"

"Neither right now."

His eyebrows shot up.

"I'd like to hear what Amos said. About who shot you, to be exact."

Grant shook his head. "You won't believe what I'm about to tell you."

"Sure I will. I'm an attorney, remember?"

"Some sixteen-year-old kid decided to take his rifle and do some shooting. He borrowed his dad's truck and wound up on Holland's land. When he saw a wild hog, he stalked it.

"To make a long story short, when he finally got the opportunity to shoot, he fired, but missed. Of course, the hog took off, crashing through the underbrush. That's when I hollered and the kid got scared and ran like hell.

"He was so scared that he ran into a tree, and that's what brought about the confession. He had to tell his parents about the dent in the truck and trespassing on Holland's land.

"A couple of days later his dad heard about someone getting shot. The parents then put two and two together and figured out what had happened. Voilà! Today they appeared at Amos's office."

"He could've killed you," Kelly said in a solemn tone.

"I know. Amos asked if I wanted to press charges."

"Are you?"

"Nah. The poor kid is already scared out of his wits, knowing he hurt someone. It was an accident. Plus he has his parents to contend with, and Amos said they were not happy."

"Kids," Kelly said, shaking her head. "But at least, as Amos said, the mystery is solved. And now you're well on the road to recovery."

Grant gave her a leering grin. "You got that right, which means I can ravish you with all my limbs intact."

"We need to talk first."

"I thought that's what we just did."

"About something else."

"Fine. So talk."

"Ruth's back."

Grant visibly stiffened. "As of when?"

"This afternoon around closing time."

He forced a smile. "That's good. I'm sure you're both glad about that."

A disturbing silence followed.

"You might not need anything to drink," Grant said at last, "but I sure do." He strode into the kitchen and grabbed a beer, sucked half of it down before removing the bottle from his lips.

Kelly had followed him into the kitchen, her eyes and face serious. This time his heart twisted. "When are you leaving?" he asked.

"Soon."

"I figured as much, since I've learned to read you pretty well." Grant paused. "Before you say anything else, I want to ask you something."

"Go ahead."

"Do you think there's a chance that we, you and me, could have a future together?" When she opened her mouth to say something, he raised his hand. "I know we're from two different worlds, as corny as that sounds, and I know we're as different as two people can be." He paused and rubbed the back of his neck. "But hell, those differences make life exciting, make relationships exciting."

"Grant…"

He ignored her. "If we were all alike, how boring would that be?"

"What are you saying?" Kelly asked in a small voice, her eyes scouring his face.

"Bottom line. Will you stay awhile longer…with me? Let's see where this thing goes with us."

"Grant. John called. From Houston."

The next silence was long and stifling.

"Are you going to say anything?" Kelly asked at last.

"I've had my say. It's your turn now."

"My firm wants me back ASAP."

Though Kelly didn't say anything else, Grant could tell that she was struggling. God, he wanted to hold her. In fact, he wanted to grab her, kiss her, tell her he loved her, then beg her not to go.

Instead, he stood unmoving and mute.

"And I feel like I owe them, and I owe myself. So I'm leaving tomorrow."

Grant gave her a long, hard look, then said in a drawling tone, "I guess that pretty much says it all."

"That doesn't mean—"

Grant shook his head. "Oh, I know what it means. You've decided to haul it back to Houston." He shrugged. "And I'm not about to try and change your mind."

Her face went white. "Are you telling me it's over."

"You're the big-shot lawyer. Can't you figure that out?"

They stared at each other long and hard.

"You're also telling me I should leave now, aren't you?" Kelly could barely get the question past the lump in her throat.

"Under the circumstances, I think that's probably a good idea."

Blinking back tears, Kelly pivoted on her heel and walked out the door, closing it softly behind her.

Cursing, Grant threw the bottle of beer at the fireplace. When the glass shattered everywhere, he didn't so much as flinch.

Eighteen

"Have I told you lately how proud I am of you?"

"Every day."

John smiled before plopping down in a chair in front of Kelly's desk. "I just want to make sure you're aware of what a great job you're doing and how much the firm appreciates it."

"I know, and I appreciate all your support and compliments.

"I hated you being gone, you know," John said with a frown, "but I guess in this case it was the best thing. Now that you're back, I can see that. You're sharp as a tack and as aggressive as ever."

"You're a good man, John Billingsly, and I'm so lucky to have you for a boss."

He brightened, then said in a low tone. "I...we could be more, you know. Only you're not interested, are you?"

She gave him a sad smile. "No, not in the way you mean. But I take your interest in me as the highest of compliments."

John sighed, then smiled. "It's okay. I was prepared for a no."

"I have always considered you a friend and the best boss ever."

He hesitated for a long moment, giving her such a long look that she felt like squirming in her seat.

"What?" she asked, leaning her head to one side and returning his gaze.

"You're not the same."

Kelly's chest tightened, and she staved off a sigh. "You just got through telling me—"

"I'm not talking about your work," John interrupted.

"Oh," she said, turning away, fearing he was about to enter a forbidden zone. His next words proved her right.

"When you don't think anyone's watching, you have the saddest look on your face." He paused and angled his head. "Why is that?"

"I'm fine," she lied. "Your imagination's just working overtime."

"Baloney."

"John—"

He cut her off again. "I know I'm prying, but hell, that's what friends—and bosses—do."

"It's something I have to work through."

"Is it still your family?"

She smiled. "No, not in the way you mean. Getting away actually accomplished a remarkable thing. When I think of them, which is every day, it's with the fondest and sweetest of memories instead of pain associated with loss and heartache."

"I'm so glad to hear you say that, Kelly. That's truly wonderful."

She blinked back tears. "I know."

"But," John pressed, "you're still far too sad to suit me." He paused again and leaned forward. "It's that guy, isn't it?"

Kelly stiffened. "I don't know what guy you're talking about."

"Damn straight you do."

Trying to ward off a flush that was sure to appear in her cheeks, Kelly got up, turned her back and walked to the window. The day was gloomy and cloudy just like her spirits. John was right. She was in a funk, though she couldn't afford to admit that. Even to herself.

But heavens, she missed Grant. Not only did she miss him, she ached for him. All of him. Right now, she could envision his big rugged body in the woods wearing his hard hat, jeans and boots, operating a piece of equipment or tromping among the trees, totally immersed in what he was doing. Loving every minute of it, too.

If only he loved her with the same passion he loved the woods.

"Kelly?"

She whipped around. "Sorry. My mind was just wandering."

John frowned, then stood. "If you're not going to confide in me, then I'd best get out of here." He peered at his watch. "I'm due in court in thirty minutes, and if I'm not mistaken, so are you."

"You're right." Kelly squared her shoulders, cleared her mind of everything personal and added with grit, "This is one case I don't intend to lose."

"You won't. And, as promised, that will put you in the partner arena." When he apparently didn't get the response he wanted, his frown returned. "That's what you still want, isn't it?"

"Absolutely," Kelly said with forced enthusiasm, grabbing her briefcase, "Let's go make waves."

She'd been home only a month but it seemed like six. Her eyes swept around the living room of her condo in Houston, thinking how lucky she was to have such a lovely place to come home to every day. It just didn't seem as beautiful as it had before she'd left for Lane.

Besides this luxury, she had lots of friends and exciting places to go. Houston offered so much. It was the best.

Then why wasn't she out enjoying herself with friends? It was only six o'clock. She still had plenty of time to reconsider an invitation to a dinner theater she'd turned down earlier.

However, she didn't feel like going out. After the day she'd had in court, she wanted to soak in her tub and spend the rest of the evening reading and relaxing.

Unfortunately, that wasn't happening.

Shortly after she'd turned the key in the lock, she'd found herself uptight, anxious and lonely, all of which made her furious at herself. To make matters worse, she'd received two phone calls back to back—one from Maud and one from Ruth.

They had both told her how much they missed her, and

for her to hurry back to Lane and see them. Following both conversations, Kelly had hung up the phone, broken down and cried.

Now, as she sat with her feet curled under her on the sofa, she felt like crying some more. "Stop it," she spat out loud.

She had nothing to cry about, for God's sake. She had everything in the world going for her. In addition to this lovely home, a great job and salary, she had been offered a junior partnership in the firm, as John had predicted.

Even though she hadn't officially accepted the offer, everyone knew that she would.

Everyone except herself.

The reason being she was miserable. And it was all because of Grant. Without having all the wonderful things she had in life were just that—*things*. Since she had met Grant and fallen in love with him, things no longer seemed to matter. Sure, she still wanted to practice law, but the passion for doing that and that alone was gone. Yes, she still loved her condo, but it was just somewhere to sleep. The passion for that was gone, as well.

Her passion was Grant.

Suddenly a light clicked on inside Kelly's head. She'd rather wake up every morning with Grant beside her than anything else in the world.

She lunged to her feet and backed up to the fireplace. It was impossible! Living in a small town wasn't something she could do.

Liar, her conscience whispered. She had lived there for several weeks and survived. She had even made friends, done good work and thrived in Lane. So what did that mean?

Kelly's mind reeled as she took deep, heaving breaths,

trying to settle her rapidly beating heart and fractured nerves. Then it hit her like a knock on the head. She had lost Eddie through a tragedy she couldn't control. Not so with Grant. If she lost him, it would be her fault.

Grabbing her purse, she ran out the door.

"What's with you, anyway?" Pete asked, casting Grant a hard look.

He scowled. "Nothing."

"The hell you say. You've been acting like someone poked a hot iron up your ass."

"If you weren't my friend and I didn't need you on this job, I'd *deck* your ass."

Both men glared at each other for seconds; then they both laughed.

"Sorry, boss," Pete said. "I should've kept my mouth shut."

"Yeah, you should have. But you're right, I've got lots on my mind."

"Would that 'lots' have the initials K.B.?"

Grant hesitated, not sure how much he wanted his friend to know about his personal life. But since he'd been such a pain, Grant felt he owed Pete the truth. Or part of it, anyway.

"I miss her," Grant admitted with a sigh.

"Me, too."

"Let's get back to work."

Pete nodded.

That conversation had taken place early that morning. But although Grant worked like a Trojan soldier every day to exhaust himself, nothing could prepare him for the nights, no matter how worn-out he was.

He ached for Kelly. At every turn, he smelled her, heard her laughter, felt her skin under his callused fingers. But the worst was remembering the moans she made when he made love to her. That, and all the other special things about her, drove him mad.

He loved her, dammit. He should've told her that. He bounded off the couch, went to the kitchen, and grabbed a beer. After one swig, he poured it down the sink. Getting drunk wasn't the answer. When he came out of his stupor, Kelly would still be haunting him.

It was too late, anyhow. Or was it?

He made his way back into the living room, stood there a second, then muttered, "To hell with this."

He dashed to his desk and grabbed an envelope, reached for his jacket, then walked out of the cabin.

Kelly saw him the instant she stepped outside. While her heart dropped to her toes, she pulled up short and watched like a zombie as Grant walked across the condo parking lot, stopping just short of touching her.

"What…what are you doing here?"

"Where are you going?" Grant answered with a question.

"I asked first." Her voice came out a whisper.

"I came to see you." His eyes delved into hers.

"Why?"

He rocked back on his heels and took a deep breath. "To tell you that I love you and that I'm one miserable bastard without you."

Suddenly her excitement reached a feverish pitch. "I was on my way to see you, to tell you the same thing."

Later, Kelly had no idea who moved first. It didn't

matter. Within seconds, they were locked in each other's arms. Then, laughing and kissing her, he lifted her and swung her around.

Once he put her down, he kissed her gently on the lips, then whispered, "Marry me, Kelly Baker."

At three o'clock the following morning, Kelly and Grant sat cross-legged in the middle of Kelly's king-size bed, drinking ginger ale and munching on cheese and crackers.

They had made love until both were exhausted and starving. Naked, they had made their way into the kitchen where they grabbed whatever was handy in the refrigerator, then carried it back to bed.

Now, as they stared deep into each other's eyes and drank their ginger ale, Kelly felt Grant's free hand grasp hers and squeeze. She returned the squeeze, then reached for his glass and set both of them on the bedside table.

"I love you, Grant Wilcox."

"And I love you, Kelly Baker."

"So when is the wedding?" She blinked back unplanned tears.

He traced her lips with a finger. "How 'bout tomorrow?"

Extra blood rushed into her cheeks. "I wish."

"Me, too. But just as soon as we get the legal red tape out of the way, there'll be no stopping us."

"I hope not."

Grant cleared his throat. "I never thought I could live in civilization again, but with you as my wife, I know it's possible."

With tears flowing, Kelly leaned over, kissed him then

repeated a version of his words. "I never thought I could live in the woods and practice law, but with you as my husband, it's possible. In fact, that's what I want to do."

"You love me that much that you'd consider giving all this up?" Grant's voice held awe.

"In a heartbeat."

Grant moaned deeply, and reached for her again and held her so tightly she couldn't breathe. But that was all right with her.

Finally, he pulled back and said, "I love you so much I want to crawl inside you."

"And I you."

"I have something for you." Releasing her, he leaned over and reached for his jeans.

She watched as he removed something from one of the pockets. "What it that?"

"Open it and see."

She did, then gazed at him with a puzzled expression on her face. "It's a deed, I know. But to what?"

"The house in Wellington."

She gave him an incredulous look.

"I'd heard it was up for sale, and sure enough it was," he added.

"So you bought it." Her voice was barely audible.

"Yep. For you. For us."

Kelly let out a cry and threw her arms around his neck, landing kisses all over his face.

He laughed. "I take it I did good buying it?"

"You did better than good. You did perfect."

"After you said you liked it, I called a Realtor friend and had him check out the rumors about it being on the market." Grant held up his hand. "Don't get me wrong, I had no idea you loved me, but something told me to buy that house, no matter what."

"Oh, Grant, it's wonderful And Wellington will be perfect for us—it's big enough for me to set up a practice."

"Without a doubt."

"I've always wanted to own my own firm someday."

"That day is here. Today."

"And it's a perfect place to raise a family." She waited with bated breath for his response.

His eyes suddenly misted with tears. Her heart turned over.

"I was afraid you wouldn't want another child." His voice was strained.

"Oh, but I do," she said with a tremor. "As a matter of—"

He placed his hands on her shoulders, stopping her flow of words, and gently eased her back onto the bed. "Then we'd best get started, my love, 'cause time's a-wasting."

Kelly grinned, looped her arms around his neck, drew him down to her and whispered, "I think the first one's already a done deal."

He pulled back with awe written on his face. "You...you mean—" He gulped.

She smiled with her heart and gave him a deep kiss. When she eased back, she whispered, "That's exactly what I mean."

With tears in his eyes, Grant hugged her fiercely and cried, "I love you, I love you, I love you."

"I love you, too."

* * * * *

THE TEXAN'S
FORBIDDEN AFFAIR

BY
PEGGY MORELAND

Dedicated to the memory of
David Arthur Davidson
"Babysan"
Staff Sergeant
Special Forces
United States Army
March 8, 1947 – October 6, 1971

Prologue

Older men declare war. But it is the youth that must fight and die.

—*Herbert Hoover*

June 14, 1971

It was a hell of a way for a man to spend his last night in the States. Given a choice, Larry Blair would have preferred to be curled up in bed with his wife rather than sitting in a smoke-filled bar watching his buddies get drunk.

But the Army wasn't into choices. Larry's orders were to report to San Francisco International Airport, 15 June at 0500. Five new soldiers assigned to his platoon—all Texas boys—had agreed to meet on Monday in Austin, Texas, to catch a late flight to San Francisco. There they would board yet another plane for the last leg of their journey.

Destination: Vietnam.

Larry looked around at the guys seated at the table. Fast Eddie. T.J. Preacher. Poncho. Romeo. Those weren't their real names, of course. Real names were all but forgotten two days after hitting boot camp and replaced with one better suited to the guy's personality. Since meeting up with the soldiers, Larry had lost one handle—Tex—and received another—Pops. He supposed the new one was a better fit, since he was the oldest member of the group.

He shook his head sadly. Twenty-one and the oldest. Proof enough of the youth and inexperience of the soldiers fighting this damn war.

He narrowed his eyes thoughtfully as he studied the soldiers sitting at the table, wondering if a one of them had a clue what he would be in for once he reached 'Nam.

He sure as hell did. Unlike the others, this was his second tour of duty in 'Nam. When he'd completed his first assignment, he'd re-upped for another six months. At the time it had seemed like the thing to do. In many ways Vietnam was a young man's wet dream. Whores, booze and drugs for the taking, plus the adrenaline high that came with engaging in combat and the thrill of cheating death one more day. With no family waiting for him back home, no job to return to, he'd thought, *Why not roll the dice and stay another six months?*

But during the thirty-day leave he'd received as a bonus for re-upping, he'd met and fallen in love with

Janine Porter and married her two weeks later. Now he'd give his right arm to be able to erase his name from that dotted line. He had a wife, and that was a damn good reason to stay alive.

But like they say, he thought, lifting his beer in acknowledgment of the old adage, *hindsight is twenty-twenty.*

Before he could take a sip, Romeo scraped back his chair and headed for the bar and a woman seated there. The soldiers remaining at the table immediately began laying bets as to whether or not he would score. Larry didn't bother to reach for his wallet. If what he'd heard about Romeo's reputation was true, the lady didn't stand a chance. According to the guys who'd gone through basic training with him, Romeo could charm the panties off a nun and receive them as a souvenir afterward.

A shadow fell across the table, and Larry glanced over his shoulder to find a man standing behind him.

"You soldiers headed for Vietnam?" the stranger asked.

Larry hesitated a moment, unsure of the man's purpose in approaching him. Americans' view of the Vietnam war varied, and he'd been called everything from a hero to a murderer. But he wasn't ashamed of the uniform he wore or the job he was doing for his country. And he sure as hell wasn't one to back down from a fight, if pushed.

Scraping back his chair, he stood, his head high, his shoulders square. "Yes, sir. We're catching a plane for San Francisco tonight, then shipping out for 'Nam tomorrow."

The man nodded, his expression turning grave. "Thought so. My son served in 'Nam."

Relieved that the man didn't appear to be looking for trouble, Larry asked, "What branch of the service was he in?"

"Army. Didn't wait for the draft to get him. Volunteered fresh out of high school."

"What's his name? Maybe I know him. This'll be my second tour."

"Walt Webber," the man replied, then shook his head sadly. "But I doubt you'd know him. He was killed in '68. Stepped on a mine four days before he was supposed to leave for home."

Larry nodded soberly, having heard similar stories. "I'm sorry for your loss, sir. A lot of good men didn't make it home."

The man nodded, then forced a smile and offered his hand. "I'm Walt Sr., though I reckon the *senior*'s no longer necessary."

Larry gripped the man's hand firmly in his own. "I'm pleased to meet you, sir. Larry Blair."

Walt shifted his gaze and nodded toward the others gathered around the table. "I'd consider it an honor if you'd let me buy you and your friends a drink."

Larry dragged up another chair. "Only if you'll join us."

The man's face lit with pleasure at the invitation. "Why, thank you, son. It's been a while since I've had the opportunity to spend time with any young folks."

After they were seated, Larry introduced Walt to the others, then gestured to the bar where Romeo was still sweet-talking the lady. "And that's Romeo," he explained. "He's with us, too."

"Romeo," Walt repeated, then chuckled. "Looks like the name fits."

Smiling, Larry nodded his agreement. "Yes, sir, it does."

Walt bought a round of drinks for everyone, then bought another round when Romeo returned, after losing his chance of scoring with his lady friend when her husband showed up. He received a good razzing from those who had lost money on the bet, then conversation at the table dwindled.

Walt studied the soldiers as they nursed their drinks. "You boys scared?" he asked bluntly.

Preacher, the meekest of the bunch and probably the most honest, was the first to respond. "Yes, sir," he admitted. "I've never shot a man before. Not sure I can."

"I 'magine you'll find it easy enough once those Vietcong start shooting at you," Walt assured him.

"Maybe," Preacher replied, though his expression remained doubtful.

Walt took a sip of his drink, then set it down and sighed. "Hell of a war. From what my son told me, it's like fighting ghosts. The Vietcong hit hard, then slip back over the border into the safe zone where the Americans can't touch them."

"True enough," Larry agreed. "To make matters worse, it's hard to tell who's the enemy. Old men. Women. Children. They all pose a threat, as they're just as likely to be carrying a gun or grenade as the Vietcong soldiers."

Walt nodded. "My son said the same thing. Claimed the number of casualties reported is nothing compared to the number of soldiers who've been maimed by booby traps or mines." He set his mouth in a grim line. "That's what got Walt Jr. After he stepped on that mine, there was nothing left of him but pieces to ship home."

Larry saw the shadow of sadness in the man's eyes and knew Walt was still grieving for his son. But there was nothing he could say to ease the man's sorrow. All he could do was listen.

"He was my only son," Walt went on. "Only child, for that matter. We lost his mother to cancer when he was in grade school, and with her all hope of having any more children. Walt Jr. was planning to work the ranch with me when he got out of the service. We were going to be partners." He dragged a sleeve across the moisture that filled his eyes. "Won't be doing that now."

Every soldier at the table ducked his head, obviously uncomfortable with witnessing a grown man's tears. But Larry couldn't look away. He understood Walt's grief. He may not have lost a son to the war, but he'd lost friends. Good friends. Friends whose memories he'd carry with him until the day he died.

He clasped a hand on the man's shoulder. "Your son was fortunate to have a father who cared so much for him."

Walt glanced at Larry and their eyes met, held a long moment. "Thank you, son," he said quietly, then swallowed hard. "My only hope is he knew how much I loved him. I never was one for expressing my feelings much."

Larry gave Walt's shoulder a reassuring squeeze before releasing it. "He knew," he assured him. "Words aren't always necessary."

Firming his mouth, Walt nodded as if comforted by the assurance, then forced a smile and looked around the table. "So. What do you boys plan to do when you get back home?"

Romeo shrugged. "Beats me. Haven't thought that far ahead."

"Same here," T.J. said, and the others nodded their agreement.

Walt glanced at Larry. "What about you?"

Larry frowned thoughtfully. "I'm not sure. I've never done anything but soldiering. Signed up right out of high school, intending to make a career of it." He smiled sheepishly. "But I got married a couple of weeks ago and that's changed things considerably. Army life is hard on a family. Once I finish up this tour, I'm hoping to find myself a new career, one that'll allow me to stay closer to home."

"Ever done any ranching?" Walt asked.

Larry choked a laugh. "Uh, no, sir, can't say that I have."

Walt glanced at the others. "How about y'all?"

Romeo smoothed a hand down his chest and preened. "I have. One summer, my old man cut a deal with a buddy of his for me to work on a ranch. Figured it would keep me out of trouble."

"Did it?" Walt asked.

Romeo shot him a sly look. "Depends on what you call trouble."

His reply drew a laugh from the soldiers at the table, as well as from Walt.

"Tell you what," Walt said. "Since my son can't be my partner on the ranch, why don't the six of you take his place? Everybody gets an equal share, and when I pass on, the ranch will be yours."

For a moment Larry could only stare. Was the man drunk? Crazy? Nobody just up and gave a ranch to total strangers. "Uh, that's awfully nice of you," he said hesitantly, "but we couldn't accept a gift like that."

"Why not?" Walt asked indignantly. "It's mine to give to whoever I want, and it just so happens I want you boys to have it."

Larry glanced at the others at the table, reluctant to voice his concerns out loud. "With all due respect, sir, there's no guarantee we'll make it home either."

Walt shot him a confident wink. "I'm bettin' you will." He slipped a hand into his shirt pocket and pulled out a folded sheet of paper and a pen. After spreading the paper open on the table, he began to write.

"This here is a bill of sale," he explained as he wrote. "I'm naming each one of you as part owner in the Cedar Ridge Ranch."

"But we don't know anything about ranching," Larry reminded him.

Walt waved away his concern. "Doesn't matter. I can teach you boys everything you need to know."

When he'd completed the document, he stood and shouted to the occupants of the bar, "Anybody here a notary public?"

A woman seated at a table on the far side of the room lifted her hand. "I am."

"Have you got your seal on you?" he asked.

She picked up her purse and gave it a pat. "Just like American Express. Never leave home without it."

He waved her over. "Come on, then. I need you to notarize something for me."

When she reached the table, Walt explained that he wanted her to witness the soldiers signing the document, then make it official by applying her seal. After she nodded her assent, he passed the piece of paper to T.J., who sat at his left. "Sign your name right here," he instructed, pointing.

T.J. hesitated a moment, then shrugged and scrawled his name. The piece of paper passed from man to man until it reached Larry.

Larry looked at Walt doubtfully. "Are you sure about this?"

"Never more sure of anything in my life," Walt replied. He shot Larry another wink. "I'll share a little secret with you. On the last tax appraisal the Cedar Ridge Ranch was valued at three million. Y'all knowing that you're part owners in a place like that is going to give you boys a reason to stay alive."

Three million dollars? Larry thought in amazement. He'd never seen that kind of money in his life! He puffed his cheeks and blew out a long breath, then thought, *What the hell,* and added his name to the bottom of the page.

After verifying that all appeared legal, Walt took the document and tore it into six pieces. He lined them up on the table. "Now it's your turn," he informed the notary public. "Sign your name on each and stamp 'em with your seal."

Though Larry could tell the woman was as stunned by Walt's generosity as he was, she dutifully signed her name on each slip of paper, then pulled her embosser from her purse and applied the official seal.

When she was done, Walt gathered up the pieces. "Keep this someplace safe," he instructed the soldiers as he handed each a section of the torn document. "When your tour of duty is up, you boys put the bill of sale back together and come to the Cedar Ridge and claim your ranch."

Larry stared at the scrap of paper a moment, unable to believe this was really happening. Giving his head a shake, he slipped the paper into his shirt pocket, then extended his hand to Walt. "Thank you, sir."

Smiling, Walt grasped his hand. "The pleasure's all mine." He stood and tucked the pen into his shirt pocket. "I reckon I better head for home. It's too late for an old man like me to be out." He leveled a finger that encompassed all the soldiers. "Now you boys be careful, you hear?" he warned, then grinned. "Y'all've got yourselves a ranch to run when you get home."

One

Stephanie Calloway had always prided herself on her ability to handle even the most complex situations with both efficiency and calm. As one of the most sought-after photo stylists in Dallas, Texas, those two traits were crucial to her success. On any given day she juggled six-figure budgets, kept track of prop inventories valued sometimes in the millions, and coordinated the schedules of the photographers, models and assistant stylists assigned to a particular shoot. If requested, she could transform an empty corner of a photographer's studio into a beach on the Caribbean, outfit a dozen models in swimwear to populate the space, then tear it all down and create an entirely different setting on the whim of a hard-to-please client.

So why, when faced with the task of disassembling and disposing of the houseful of items her parents had accumulated during their thirty years of marriage, did she feel so overwhelmed, so inadequate, so utterly *helpless?*

Because this is personal, she reminded herself as she looked around the den of her childhood home. Each item in the room represented a massive mountain of emotion she feared she'd never find the strength to climb.

"And standing here dreading it isn't accomplishing a thing," she told Runt, the dog at her side.

Taking a deep breath, she crossed to her father's recliner and laid a hand on its headrest. Oh, how he'd loved his recliner, she thought as she smoothed a hand over the impression his body had worn into the leather. When he wasn't out working on the ranch, he could usually be found reared back in the chair, with one of his dogs curled on his lap. He'd always had a dog tagging along with him, Runt being his most recent… and his last.

As if aware of her thoughts, Runt nudged his nose at her knee and whined low in his throat. Blinking back tears, she looked down at him and gave him a pat, knowing by his soulful expression that he was missing her father as much as she was. Runt—the name her father had given him because he was the runt of the litter—wasn't a runt any longer, she noted. The top of his head struck her leg at midthigh. Part Australian sheepdog and part Labrador retriever, he had inherited traits from both breeds, resulting in an intelligent long-haired dog with a sweet temper. But a long line of other canines had preceded him, and not all had been as endearing as Runt. Biting back a smile, she dipped her head in search of the section of frayed upholstery at the recliner's base, compliments of Mugsy—a Jack Russell terrier—and made during a chewing stage her mother had feared would never end.

The tears rose again at the thought of her mother, and she glanced over at the overstuffed chair positioned close to the recliner. Though her mother had preceded her father in death by two years, the floor lamp at its right remained angled to shed light on her hands and the endless knitting projects she worked on at night. An afghan for the church auction. A warm shawl for one of the ladies at the nursing home. A sweater for Stephanie.

Her chin trembled as she envisioned her mother and father sitting side by side, as was their habit each night, her mother's knitting needles clicking an accompaniment to the sound of whatever television program her father had tuned in at the moment.

How will I ever get through this alone? she asked herself, then sagged her shoulders, knowing she had no other choice. With no siblings to share the responsibility, the job was hers to do.

Releasing a shuddery breath, she said, "Come on, Runt," and forced herself to walk on.

They made it as far as the hallway before she was stopped again, this time by a gallery of pictures depicting her family's life. Her gaze settled on a photo of her and her father taken at a Girl Scout banquet when she was eleven. Few would guess by the proud swell of his chest that Bud Calloway was her stepfather and not her natural father. From the moment Bud had married her mother, he'd accepted Stephanie as his own and had assumed the full duties of a father. Never once in all the years that followed had he ever complained or made her feel as if she were a burden. She touched a finger to the glass, his image blurred by her tears. She was going to miss him. Oh, God, she was going to miss him so much.

Gulping back the grief, she tore her gaze away. She had taken no more than two steps when Runt stopped and growled. Linking her fingers through his collar to hold him in place, she glanced back over her shoulder. She strained, listening, and tensed when she heard the familiar squeak of hinges that signified the opening of the front door. Since she hadn't told anyone of her plans, she wasn't expecting any visitors—especially one who could get past a locked door. Mindful that burglars sometimes read the obituaries in search of vacant homes to rob, she whispered to Runt, "I hope your bite is as ferocious as your growl," and cautiously retraced her steps, keeping a firm hold on his collar.

As she approached the doorway that opened to the entry, she caught a glimpse of a man standing just inside the door. She might've screamed if she hadn't immediately recognized him. The thick sandy-brown hair that flipped up slightly at his ears, just brushing the brim of his cowboy hat. The tall, lanky frame and wide shoulders. The faded chambray shirt, jeans and scuffed cowboy boots.

No, she had no problem recognizing him. As she'd learned the hard way, Wade Parker was a hard man to forget.

Runt whined, struggling to break free. At the sound, Wade whipped his head around and his gaze slammed into Stephanie's. As she stared into the blue depths, she felt the old familiar tug of yearning and forced steel into her spine, pushing it back.

Runt wriggled free and leaped, bracing his front paws on Wade's chest.

Smiling, Wade scrubbed his ears. "Hey, Runt. How you doin', boy?"

She advanced a step, her body rigid with anger. "What are you doing here?"

The smile Wade had offered Runt slid into a frown. Urging the dog down to all fours, he gestured at the front window. "Drapes were open. Since they're usually closed—or have been since Bud's funeral—I figured I'd better check things out. Didn't see a car. If I had, I would've knocked."

"I parked in the garage," she informed him, then narrowed her eyes to slits. "How did you get in? The door was locked."

"I didn't break in, if that's what you're suggesting. Bud gave me a key after your mother passed away. Figured someone close by should have one in case anything happened to him and needed to get inside the house."

She thrust out her hand. "There's no need for you to have a key any longer. Bud's gone."

He whipped off his hat. "Dang it, Steph!" he said, slapping the hat against his thigh in frustration. "Do you intend to spend the rest of your life hating me?"

She jutted her chin. "If emotion ends with death, yes, at least that long."

Scowling, he tucked his hat beneath his arm and dug a ring of keys from his pocket. "I thought you went back to Dallas after the funeral," he grumbled.

"Only long enough to tie up a few loose ends."

He worked a key from the loop. "So how long are you planning on staying?"

"That's none of your business."

He slapped the key on her palm and burned her with a look. "Maybe not, but Bud's cattle *are.*"

She drew back to peer at him in confusion. "But I assumed Mr. Vickers was taking care of the cattle. He always helped Dad out in the past."

He snorted and stuffed the key ring back into his pocket. "Shows how much you know. Vickers moved to Houston over a year ago. When Bud got to where he couldn't do his chores himself, I offered to do them for him."

Her eyes shot wide. "*You* worked for my father?"

"No," he replied, then added, "Not for pay, at any rate. I offered, he accepted. That's what neighbors do."

She stared, stunned that her father would accept anything, even a favor, from Wade Parker. "I…I had no idea."

"You might've if you'd ever bothered to come home."

She jerked up her chin, refusing to allow him to make her feel guilty for not visiting her father more often. "Dad and I talked on the phone three or four times a week."

He snorted. "That was mighty nice of you to squeeze him into your busy schedule."

His sarcasm rankled, but before she could form a scathing comeback, he held up a hand.

"Look," he said, suddenly looking tired. "I didn't come here to fight with you. I only came to check on the cattle."

She wanted to tell him that she didn't need his help, that she would take care of the livestock herself. But it had been years since she'd done any ranch work, and she wasn't at all sure she could handle the job alone.

She tipped up her chin. "Hopefully I'll be able to free you of that obligation soon. When I finish clearing out the house, I'm putting the ranch on the market."

He dropped his gaze and nodded. "Bud said he didn't think you'd keep the place."

She choked a laugh. "And why would I? I have no use for a ranch."

He glanced up and met her gaze for a long moment. "No, I doubt you would." He reached for the doorknob, preparing to leave. "Have you talked to Bud's attorney?"

She trailed him to the door. "Briefly. We're supposed to meet after I finish clearing out the house." She frowned. "Why do you ask?"

He lifted a shoulder as he stepped out onto the porch. "No reason. If you need anything—"

"I won't."

Her curt refusal dragged him to a stop at the edge of the porch. Dropping his chin, he plucked at the brim of his hat as if he had something to say but was having a hard time finding the words. Seconds ticked by, made longer by the silence, before he finally spoke.

"Steph…I'm sorry."

Scowling, she gave Runt's collar a firm tug to haul him back inside and closed the door without replying.

As far as she was concerned, the apology came years too late.

Wade exited the barn and headed for the house, exhausted after the long hours he'd put in that day. No, he mentally corrected. His exhaustion wasn't due to the amount of time he'd worked or the effort expended. His weariness was a result of his run-in with Steph. The woman frustrated the hell out of him and had for years.

He knew it was his fault she felt the way she did about him, but what the hell had she expected him to do? He'd made a mistake—a big one—and had tried his best to rectify it by doing what was *right*. In doing so, he'd hurt Steph. But dammit, he'd suffered, too. He wondered sometimes if she realized how much.

As he neared the house, music blasted from the open windows, the bass so loud it reverberated through the soles of his boots and made his teeth ache. Stifling a groan, he made a quick detour to his toolshed. He wasn't in the mood for another argument and he knew if he went inside now he was bound to wind up in one. Meghan called that junk she listened to hip-hop. He considered it trash and had forbidden her to play it. Unfortunately she hadn't docilely bowed to his wishes. Instead she'd screamed and cried, accusing him of ruining her life—which was nothing new, since she accused him of that at least once a day.

He slammed the door of the toolhouse behind him and succeeded in muffling the sound of the irritating music only marginally. Sinking down on an old nail keg, he buried his face in his hands. How the hell was a father supposed to deal with a rebellious daughter? he asked himself miserably. If Meghan were a boy, he'd take her out behind the woodshed and give her a good spanking, the same as his father had when Wade had disobeyed the rules. A few swats on the behind had made a believer out of Wade, and he figured it would Meghan, too…if he could bring himself to spank her.

Groaning, he dropped his head back against the wall.

When had his life gotten so screwed up? he asked himself. There was a time when his daughter had idolized him, thought he all but walked on water. Not so any longer. In fact, she'd told him on more than one occasion that she hated his guts and wished she could go and live with her mother. There were days when he was tempted to pack her bags.

He shook his head, knowing full well he'd never allow Meghan to live with Angela. Hell, that was why he'd fought so hard for custody of his daughter in the first place! Angela wasn't fit to be a mother. Even the judge, who historically ruled in favor of mothers, had recognized Angela's deficiencies and awarded Wade custody of Meghan.

No, Wade wasn't going to allow Meghan to browbeat him into letting her go and live with her mother. He'd deal with her rebellion, the same as he'd dealt with every other stage of her development. But damn, he wished there was someone to share the responsibility with, someone he could at least talk to about his problems with his daughter! He'd give his right arm to be able to sit across the table from his mom and dad right now and seek the wisdom of their years and experience as parents.

But his parents were gone, he reminded himself, victims of a random murder, according to the police. Random or not, his parents were dead, and the carjacker who had killed them was currently sitting on death row.

He'd taken the loss of his parents hard—and inheriting the millions they'd left him had in no way softened the blow. If anything, it had only made things worse. He had been twenty-two at the time of their deaths and living on his own. After he'd buried his parents, he'd gone kind of crazy and done some things he wasn't too true proud of. He'd quickly discovered that when a man has money to burn, there's always somebody around offering to light the match. *Bottom-feeders,* his dad would've called them. Folks who thrived on another person's misery.

He still wasn't sure what it was that had made him realize he was traveling on a fast train to nowhere. But one morning he'd looked at himself in the mirror and was ashamed of what he'd seen. In a desperate attempt to put his life back together, he'd pulled up roots and bought the ranch in Georgetown, hoping to make a fresh start.

Less than two months after the move, he'd met Steph. He hadn't been looking for romance the day he'd delivered the bull to the Calloway ranch. In fact, romance had been the furthest thing from his mind. But it was on that fateful day that he'd met his neighbors' daughter, home for summer break between semesters. He remembered when Bud had introduced her to him how her smile had seemed to light up her entire face, how her green eyes had sparkled with a sense of humor and innocence that he'd envied. And he remembered, when he'd shaken her hand, how delicate yet confident her fingers had felt in his. By the time he'd left several hours later, he had been head over boot heels in infatuation and already thinking of ways to see her again.

From their first date on, they'd spent almost every waking minute together. With a ranch to run, Wade hadn't had a lot of time to spare for formal dates. But Steph hadn't seemed to mind. She'd ridden along with him when he'd needed to check his fences, sat with him in the barn through the night when his mare had foaled. She'd brought him lunch to the field when he was cutting hay and sat with him beneath the shade of an old oak tree, laughing and talking with him while he ate.

When summer had come to an end and it was time for her to go back to college, he had stood with her parents and watched her drive away, feeling as though a boulder were wedged in his throat. Before the first week was out he knew he couldn't live without her. That very weekend he'd taken his mother's wedding ring out of the safe where he'd kept it and headed for Dallas to propose.

In his mind's eye he could see Steph as she'd looked that day. He hadn't told her he was coming, and when she'd spotted him standing in the parking lot of her apartment complex, her eyes had widened in surprise, then she had broken into a run, her arms thrown wide. With a trust and openness that warmed his heart, she'd flung herself into his arms and he'd spun her around and around. He remembered the way she'd tasted when he'd kissed her, the weight of her in his arms. And he could still see the awe in her expression when he'd given her the ring, the love and tears that had gleamed in her eyes when she'd looked up at him and given him her answer. It was a memory he'd carry with him to his grave.

But dwelling on the past wasn't going to help him deal with his daughter, he told himself. Knowing that, he braced his hands against his thighs and pushed himself to his feet and headed for the house, already dreading the ugly scene that awaited him.

* * *

Stephanie didn't give another thought to her encounter with Wade Parker. As she'd learned to do with any unpleasantness, she blocked it from her mind and focused instead on something more productive—in this case, cleaning out her parents' home. It helped to know that the sooner she finished the job, the sooner she could leave Georgetown and close this chapter of her life once and for all.

She had started with the dining room, thinking that, as the only formal room in the house, it would hold fewer personal possessions, fewer memories. Wrong! After two days spent purging and packing, she'd already filled all the storage boxes she'd brought with her from Dallas…and emptied two boxes of tissues mopping her tears. It seemed everything held a memory, from her mother's silver tea service to the chipped ceramic Cookies for Santa plate that had graced their hearth every Christmas for as far back as Stephanie could remember.

Fully aware that this job was going to be tough, she had attempted to disassociate herself from the personal aspects attached to it by applying an organizational tool she'd picked up while watching HGTV. She had created three areas—Keeper, Trash and Donate—and set to work.

Sadly, after two days of what she'd considered cold-blooded sorting, the Keeper stack of boxes towered over the other two.

Promising herself that she would be more ruthless in her decision making, she tried to think where she could find more boxes. She was sure there were probably some in the attic, but the attic had always given her the willies.

Unfortunately the only other option was driving into town, and that prospect held even less appeal. Thirteen years later, and she still felt the sting of the pitying glances from people she'd once counted as friends.

With a sigh of resignation she turned for the hallway and the narrow staircase at its end, with Runt tagging along at her heels. It took some muscle to open the door at the top of the stairs, and once inside, her knees turned to rubber when she was confronted with the sheet-draped objects and cobwebs that filled the space.

She remembered well the last time she'd entered this room. She'd been ten years old and sent there by her mother to retrieve a box of canning jars. While searching for the requested box, one of the sheets had billowed as if someone was trying to fight free from beneath it. Convinced that she was about to be attacked by a band of killer ghosts, she'd run back down the stairs screaming bloody murder. Though her mother had assured her there were no such things as ghosts, from that day forward Stephanie had refused to step foot in the attic again.

Narrowing her eyes, she studied the sheet-draped objects, trying to remember which one had frightened her that day. *That one,* she decided, settling her gaze on a hump-shaped object in the corner. Determined to confront her fear and dispel it, she murmured a firm, "Stay" to Runt, then marched across the room and lifted the sheet.

Half expecting a ghost to come flying out, when nothing but dust motes rose in the air, she gave a sigh of relief and flung back the sheet to expose an old steamer trunk. Never having seen the trunk before, intrigued, she lifted the lid. Another sheet, this one free of dust, protected the truck's contents. Beneath it she found a variety of boxes, each tied with string. Her curiosity piqued, she selected the largest box and sat down on the floor, anxious to see what was inside. After removing the lid, she folded back the tissue paper.

She clapped a hand over her heart. "Oh, my God," she murmured as she stared at the Army uniform folded neatly inside. Sure that it was her father's, she gently lifted the jacket and held it up to examine it more closely. A name tag attached above the breast pocket read Sgt. Lawrence E. Blair.

"Oh, my God," she whispered, awed by the sight.

Unaware that her mother had saved anything that belonged to her biological father, she shoved the box aside and pulled out another. After quickly untying the string, she lifted the lid. Bundles of letters, each bound with pink ribbon faded to a dusty rose, filled the space. She thumbed through the envelopes, noting that each was addressed to Janine Blair. Though the months of the postmarks varied, all were mailed in the same year, 1971. Stunned by her discovery, she pulled out another box, then another, and found more letters in each.

She stared at the stacks of letters scattered around her, unable to believe that her mother had never told her of their existence. Was it because the memories were too painful? she asked herself. Or was it because her mother had chosen to bury the memories of her first husband along with his body?

She knew her parents' marriage had been impulsive, spawned by him leaving for the war. She remembered her mother telling her that he'd shipped out for Vietnam just two weeks after they were married. But Stephanie really didn't know much else about her natural father—other than his name, of course, and that he had been killed in the war. She remembered asking her mother once if she had any pictures of him, and she'd claimed she hadn't.

Wondering if her mother had secreted away pictures along with the letters, she pushed to her knees and dug through the box until she found what looked to be a photo album. Hopeful that she would find pictures of her father inside, she sank back down and opened the book over her lap.

The first photo all but stole her breath. The picture was a professional shot of a soldier and probably taken after he'd completed his basic training, judging by his buzzed haircut. He was wearing a dress uniform and had his hat angled low on his forehead. The name tag above the breast pocket identified him as Lawrence E. Blair.

He looks so young, was all she could think. And so handsome. She smoothed her fingers over his image. This is my father, she told herself and waited for the swell of emotion.

But she felt nothing. The man was a stranger to her. Her *father*, yet a complete stranger.

Emotion came then, an unexpected guilt that stabbed deeply. She should feel something. If she didn't, who would? His parents had preceded him in death. Her mother—his wife—was gone now, too. There was no one left to remember him, to mourn for a life lost so young.

Along with the guilt came another emotion—resentment toward her mother. *Mom should have shown me this trunk,* she thought angrily. She should have made sure that I knew my father, that his memory lived on in my heart. He had courageously served his country and fathered a child he'd never seen. Surely he deserved more than a trunk full of memories tucked away in an attic.

Firming her jaw, she pushed to her feet and began gathering up the boxes. She would read the letters he left behind, she told herself. She'd get to know him through his correspondence and the album of pictures. She wouldn't let his memory die. He was her father, for God's sake, the man who had given her life!

Two

Later that night, as Stephanie passed through the kitchen dragging the last bag of trash she'd filled that day, the house phone rang. She didn't even slow down. It was her parents' phone, after all; anyone who wanted to speak to her would call her on her cell.

Ignoring the incessant ringing, she strong-armed the bag through the opening of the back door, then heaved it onto the growing pile at the foot of the steps. Winded, she dropped down on the top step to catch her breath.

Although the sun had set more than an hour before, a full moon lit the night sky and illuminated the landscape. From her vantage point on the porch she could see the roof of the barn and a portion of the corral that surrounded it. Beyond the barn stretched the pastures where the cattle grazed. Though she couldn't see the cattle, she heard their low bawling and knew they were near. Runt let out a sharp bark, and she winced, feeling guilty for having banished him to the barn. But it was for his own good, she told herself. She'd seen a mouse earlier that day and had set out traps. Runt, God love him, had already activated two—due to his curiosity or greed, she wasn't sure which—and had a bloody nose to prove it.

Knowing that spending one night in the barn wouldn't hurt him, in spite of the pitiful look he'd given her when she'd penned him there, she let the peacefulness of her surroundings slip over her again.

Though raised on the ranch, she'd spent her adult years surrounded by the big-city noises of Dallas and had forgotten the depth of the quiet in the country. Closing her eyes, she listened closely, separating the sounds of the night: the raspy song of katydids perched high in the trees, the closer and more melodious chirping of crickets. A quail added its plaintive call of "bob-white" to the chorus of music, and she smiled, remembering the first time she'd heard the call and asking Bud who Bob White was and was that his mommy calling him home.

Enjoying the quiet and the pleasant memories it drew, she lay back on the wooden planks of the porch and stared up at the sky, letting her mind drift as she watched the clouds float across the face of the moon.

Her earliest memories were rooted here on this ranch, she thought wistfully. Prior to her mother marrying Bud, she and her mother had lived with her mother's parents in town. Stephanie had vague recollections of that time, but she wasn't sure if they were truly hers or a result of images she'd drawn from stories her mother had shared with her of those early years. A natural storyteller, her mother had often entertained Stephanie with tales of when Stephanie was a little girl.

But she'd never told her any that had included Stephanie's father.

The resentment she'd discovered earlier returned to burn through her again. Why, Mom? she cried silently. Why didn't you tell me anything about him? Why did you refuse to talk about him when I asked questions? Was he funny? Serious? What kind of things did he enjoy? What were his fears?

Her cell phone vibrated, making her jump, and she quickly sat up, pulling it from the clip at the waist of her shorts. She flipped up the cover to check the number displayed on the screen and recognized it as Kiki's, her assistant.

Swiping at the tears, she placed the phone to her ear. "Kiki, what are you doing calling me?" she scolded good-naturedly. "You're supposed to be on vacation."

"Vacation?" Kiki repeated. "Ha! Being stuck at home with three-year-old twins isn't a vacation, it's a prison sentence!"

Laughing, Stephanie propped her elbow on her knee, grateful for the distraction Kiki offered from her whirling emotions. Five foot nothing, Kiki had flaming red hair that corkscrewed in every direction and the personality to match it. Talking to her was always a treat. "Don't you dare talk about my godchildren that way. Morgan and Mariah are angels."

"Humph. Easy for you to say. You haven't been locked up in a house with them all day."

"Wanna trade places?" Stephanie challenged. "I'd much rather be with the twins than doing what I'm doing."

Kiki made a sympathetic noise. "How's it going? Are you making any progress?"

Stephanie sighed wearily. "None that you'd notice. I had no idea my parents had so much stuff. I've spent three days in the dining room alone and I'm still not done."

"Found any hidden treasure?"

Stephanie thought of the trunk in the attic and the letters and photos she'd found hidden inside. "Maybe," she replied vaguely, unsure if she was ready to talk about that yet.

"Maybe?" Kiki repeated, her voice sharpening with interest. "Spill your guts, girl, I'm desperate for excitement."

Chuckling, Stephanie pushed the hair back from her face and held it against her head. "I doubt you'd find a bunch of old letters and a photo album that belonged to my father all that exciting."

"You never know," Kiki replied mysteriously. "Bud could've had a wild side we weren't aware of."

"They weren't Bud's. They belonged to my real father."

There was a moment of stunned silence. "Oh, wow," Kiki murmured. "I forget that Bud had adopted you."

"I do, too, most of the time, which is what I'm sure Mom intended."

Although Stephanie wasn't aware of the bitterness in her tone, Kiki—who never missed anything—picked up on it immediately.

"What gives? You sound majorly ticked."

"I'm not," Stephanie said defensively, then admitted grudgingly, "Well, maybe a little." She balled her hand into a fist against her thigh, struck again by her mother's deception. "I can't believe she never told me she saved any of his things. She kept it all hidden away in a trunk in the attic."

"Why?"

"How would I know? She just *did*."

"Bummer," Kiki said sympathetically, then forced a positive note to her voice. "But, hey, the good news is you found it! Have you read any of the letters yet?"

Stephanie had to set her jaw to fight back the tears that threatened. "No, but I'm going to read every darn one of them. Somebody's got to keep his memory alive."

"Are you okay?" Kiki asked in concern. "You sound all weepy—and you *never* cry."

Stephanie bit her lip, resisting the urge to tell Kiki everything, from the resentment she felt over her mother's deception to seeing Wade again. "I'm fine," she assured her friend. "I'm just tired."

"Cleaning out your parents' home is hard enough, and now you gotta deal with all this heavy stuff about your dad. Do you want me to come and help?"

Stephanie smiled at the offer, knowing Kiki would drop everything and drive to Georgetown if asked. She was that kind of friend. "No, I can handle it. But thanks."

"Well, I mean it," Kiki assured her. "You say the word and I'm there."

Stephanie chuckled, imagining how much work they'd get done with the twins underfoot. "Thanks, but I've got everything under control. You just caught me at a weak moment. Listen," she said, anxious to end the call before she caved and begged Kiki to come. "It's getting late. I'd better go. Give the kids a kiss for me, okay?"

"I will. And take things slow," Kiki urged. "If it takes

you longer than two weeks to finalize things there, so what? The advertising industry won't collapse without us. Once you get back home, we can work doubly hard to make up for any time lost."

Stephanie pressed her fingertips to her lips, fighting back the tears, realizing how lucky she was to have a friend like Kiki.

"Thanks, Kiki," she said, then added a hasty goodnight and disconnected the call before Kiki could say anything more.

Within fifteen minutes of ending the call with Kiki, Stephanie was in bed, propped up on pillows, the bundles of her father's letters piled around her. She'd already sobbed her way through two and was reaching for a third when the house phone rang. She angled her head to frown at the extension on the beside table. It was the second time the phone had rung since she'd talked to Kiki, and the sound was beginning to grate on her nerves.

Since her parents were a decade or more behind technology and didn't have caller ID installed on their phone line, she couldn't check to see who was calling. And she wasn't about to answer the phone just to satisfy her curiosity. At this hour, she doubted the caller would be a telemarketer, which meant that one of her parents' friends had probably heard that she was at the house and was calling to offer his or her condolences over the loss of Bud.

Considering her current emotional state, Stephanie was afraid that one kind word would send her into a crying jag she wouldn't be able to stop.

After the fifth ring, the ringing stopped. With a sigh

of relief Stephanie sank back against pillows and opened the letter over her propped-up knees.

Dear Janine,

It's been a crummy day. Rain, rain and more rain. Sometimes it seems like it's never going to stop. This is the third day we've been guarding this LZ (that's Landing Zone to you civilians), and everything I own is sopping wet–including my underwear. Ha-ha.

I got your letter before I left camp. The one where you asked about getting a dog? Honey, that's fine with me. In fact, I'd feel better knowing you have something (not someone!) to keep you company while I'm gone. What kind do you want to get? Make sure it's something that'll make a good guard dog. Not one of those sissy poodles. They are about as useless as tits on a nun.

"Tits on a nun?" she repeated, then choked a laugh. Obviously her father *had* possessed a sense of humor. Pleased to discover that small detail about his personality, she settled in to read more.

Have I told you that I love you? Probably about a million times, but it's worth repeating. I miss you so much it hurts.

Stephanie placed a hand over her heart, knowing exactly how he must have felt. She'd experienced that depth of feeling only once in her life, and though it was more than a decade ago, she remembered it as if it were

yesterday. A love so powerful it was a physical pain in
her chest. Even now, after years with no contact,
thoughts of Wade would occasionally slip unbidden
into her mind and she would experience that same deep
ache. Thankfully all she had to do was remind herself
of what a jerk he'd turned out to be and the feeling
would disappear as rapidly as it had come.

She gave her head a shake to clear the distracting
thoughts and focused again on the letter, picking up
where she'd left off.

*I know I probably shouldn't tell you that because
it'll only make you sad, but it's the truth. I'd give
anything to be holding you right now. Sometimes
at night I close my eyes real tight and concentrate
real hard on imagining you. A couple of times I
swear I thought I even smelled you. Crazy, huh?
But it's true. That perfume you wear really turns
me on. Remind me to buy you a gallon of it when
I get home!*

*I better sign off for now. It's getting so dark I
can't see, and we can't turn on so much as a flashlight when we're out in the field because it might
give our position away. Man, I'll be glad when
this damn war is over!*
Yours forever,
Larry

Stephanie stared at the letter a long time, trying to
absorb the words he'd written and what he'd revealed
about himself through them. It was obvious that he'd
loved her mother very much and was concerned for her

welfare. Had her mother's feelings for him equaled his for her? Unsure of the answer, pensive, she refolded the letter and selected another from the pile.

Dear Janine,
I'm going to be a daddy?

Stephanie sat bolt upright, her eyes riveted on the words, realizing that she was holding the letter her father had sent after learning that her mother was pregnant. She squeezed her eyes shut, afraid to read any more. What if he was disappointed that her mother had gotten pregnant so soon after their marriage? Even mad? He may not have wanted any children.

"Please, God, let him have wanted me," she prayed fervently, then opened her eyes and read on.

Whoa. That's some pretty serious sh** to throw on a guy when he's halfway around the world. Don't think I'm not happy about it, because I am! I'm just disappointed that I'm stuck over here and not there with you. The good news is, if my calculations are right, I should be home by the time our baby is born.

"Oh, God," Stephanie murmured and had to stop reading to wipe her eyes. He not only had wanted her, he'd been looking forward to being home in time for her birth. The irony of that was simply too cruel for words. Blinking hard to clear her eyes, she scanned to find her place and began to read again.

Are you feeling okay? I know women sometimes throw up a lot in the beginning. I sure hope you're not one of those who stays sick for nine months. Are you showing yet? That's probably a crazy question, since you can't be that far along. I'll bet you look really sexy pregnant!

Man, I can't believe this! Me, a daddy! It's going to take a while for this to really sink in. As soon as I get home, we're going to have to find a place of our own. I'm really glad that you're there with your parents so they can take care of you while I'm gone, but when I get home I want you all to myself! Does that sound selfish? Hell, I don't care if it does! I miss you like crazy and don't want to share you with anybody, not even your mom and dad!

We'll need a place with lots of room, because I want a whole houseful of kids. We never talked about that, but I hope you do, too. I don't want our baby growing up without any brothers or sisters the way I did. Believe me, it can get pretty lonesome at times.

You mentioned in your letter that, for my sake, you hope it's a boy. Honey, I don't care what we have. I'll love our baby no matter what.

Preacher just walked by and I told him our good news—I hope you don't mind. He said to tell you congratulations. Remember me telling you about Preacher? He's the one who didn't think he could shoot a man. So far he's squeaked by without having to. I'm worried that if it ever comes down to shoot or die, he won't be able to

pull the trigger. I try my best to keep an eye on
him, but it's hard to do that when things get
really hot, with enemy fire coming at us from
every direction.

I better sign off for now. I've got to find
somebody who's got a pass to town and see if
he'll bring me back a box of Cuban cigars. I've
got some celebrating to do!
Love forever,
Larry

Unable to keep the tears in check any longer, Stephanie dropped her forehead to her knees and wept. She
cried for a life lost so young, for the brave young man
who'd worried about his friend and was willing to put
his friend's safety above his own.

And she cried selfish tears at the injustice of never
having gotten to know her father, tears of anger at her
mother for not sharing her memories of him with her.

And she cried for the love her father had felt for her
mother, a love that he had carried to his grave with him,
a love snuffed out before it had had time to fully bloom.

And when she would've thought there were no tears
left, she cried for her own lost love and the dreams
she'd once built around Wade Parker and the life they
might have shared together. A love, like her father's, that
was snuffed out before it could fully bloom.

Muttering curses under his breath, Wade slammed
the door of his truck behind him and cranked the engine.
He wasn't in the mood to go chasing across the coun-
tryside playing the Good Samaritan. Not when his head

was still aching from going three rounds with his daughter over the proper attire for a girl her age.

Swearing again at the reminder of the argument, he stomped the accelerator and aimed the nose of his truck for the highway. Like he had a clue about women's fashion, he thought irritably. But he knew one thing for certain: no daughter of his was going out in public wearing a shirt cut six inches above her belly button and jeans that rode so low on her hips they barely covered her privates!

Where did kids come up with these crazy ideas anyway? he asked himself, then snorted, already knowing the answer. Television, that's where. And the worst were those asinine reality shows. Hell, there was nothing real about a one of 'em! And even if there was, what was the fun in *watching* reality when all a person had to do to experience it firsthand was get off his or her duff and take a stroll outside?

Feeling his blood beginning to boil again, he forced his fingers to relax from the death grip he had on the steering wheel and refocused his mind to the problem at hand. And Steph *was* a problem, whether she was aware of it or not. And thanks to a telephone call from a complete stranger, she was now *his* problem. He supposed he could've refused the lady's request that he check on Steph, but then he would've had to live with the guilt—and he was already carrying a full load. He didn't know how long he was going to be required to make atonement before he was able to clear his conscience of what he'd done to Steph. Judging by the fact that he was driving down the road in the middle of the night, when he should've been sacked out in bed, it appeared it wasn't going to be anytime soon.

He'd thought a phone call would be the easiest and least aggravating method of accomplishing the duty dumped on him. Forget that he'd already tried to call her once that evening, on his own volition, and hadn't received a response. Still, he'd tried again—twice, to be exact. Receiving no answer either time, there was nothing to do but make the drive to the Calloways' ranch and make sure she was all right. For all he knew, she could've fallen off a ladder and broken a leg and was unable to get to the phone.

As he pulled to a stop behind her SUV, he noticed that the windows on the house were dark. Good, he thought smugly and strode to the door. He hoped she was in bed and he awakened her, so that he could ruin her sleep, the same as she was ruining his. He knocked, then waited a full two minutes before knocking again. When he still didn't receive a response, he frowned, wondering if she really had injured herself. Though he figured she was going to be madder than a hornet with him for using it, he lifted a hand above the door and felt along the ledge for the key Bud kept hidden there. Finding it, he dealt with the lock and pushed open the door.

"Steph?" he called as he stepped into the entry. "Are you here?" He waited a moment, listening, and frowned when he didn't hear a reply.

"Steph," he called again and flipped on the overhead light.

God almighty, he thought in dismay as he looked around. The place looked as if a tornado had passed through it! Boxes were stacked on the floor and against the wall. In the dining room, the doors of the china cabinet stood open, its shelves stripped bare. Sheets of newspaper draped the back of the chairs and littered the floor, and more boxes lined the walls. The table itself was covered with stacks of dishes and whatnots a foot deep.

Shaking his head, he turned for the den. Not seeing any sign of Steph amongst the debris in that room, he continued down the hall. A muffled sound came from the rear of the house, and he followed it to the door of what he knew was her old childhood bedroom. Opening the door a crack, he peeked inside and found her sitting on the bed, her face buried in a pillow she held on her lap.

He hesitated, not wanting to disturb what he assumed was a private moment of grief. But the heart-wrenching sound of her sobs pulled him into the room.

"Steph?" he said quietly. "Are you okay?"

She snapped up her head, exposing a face streaked with tears. She stared, her face pale and her eyes wide, as if she were looking at a ghost.

Realizing too late that he'd probably scared her half to death, he held up his hands. "I didn't mean to scare you. I called a couple of times, and when you didn't answer, I was worried you might've hurt yourself and couldn't get to the phone."

She turned her face away, swiping at the tears. "I'm fine. I wasn't in the mood to talk to anyone."

She wasn't physically hurt, that much was obvious, but as to being fine, he had his doubts. If her swollen eyes were any indication, it appeared she'd been crying for hours and wasn't through yet.

He shifted from one foot to the other, anxious to get out of there but reluctant to leave her in her current emotional state. "I can hang around for a while, if you want," he offered hesitantly.

"That's not necessary."

Though she kept her face turned away, he heard the tears in her voice and knew she was still crying. Silently cursing her stubbornness, he crossed the room and sat down on the edge of the bed.

"I know you're missing Bud," he said gently. "I miss him, too."

She kept her face turned away but shook her head. "It—it's not Bud." She hitched a breath and lifted a hand in which she held what appeared to be a letter. "It's from my f-father."

He stared at the back of her head in confusion. Had she lost her mind? Bud *was* her father. "Bud left you a letter?" he asked, hoping to snap her back to her senses.

She shook her head in frustration. "N-not Bud. M-my *real* father."

He hesitated a moment, then reached for the phone. "Maybe I should call a doctor."

Before he could lift the receiver, she clamped her hand over his wrist.

"I don't need a doctor," she said through bared teeth. "Bud was my *step*father!" Releasing her grip on him, she fell back against the pillows and covered her face with her hands.

Wade stared, trying to make sense of what she'd said. "Bud adopted you?"

Though she kept her face covered, she bobbed her head, letting him know he'd assumed correctly.

He slowly unwound his fingers from the receiver. "But…who's your real father?"

"Larry Blair." Drawing in a deep breath, she dragged her hands from her face. "He—he was killed in Vietnam."

Wade rubbed a hand across the back of his neck. "I always assumed Bud was your father."

"Which is obviously what my mother wanted."

He drew back to peer at her, surprised by the venom in his voice. "And what's that supposed to mean?"

She pushed a foot against one of the bundles scattered over the bed. "These are all letters from my father. I found them, along with a photo album, in the attic."

"So? What does that have to do with your mother?"

"I never knew they existed! She never told me."

Stunned by her level of anger, he tried to think of a logical explanation to offer. "Maybe she did and you forgot."

"Oh, no," she said, shaking her head in denial. "I didn't forget. I distinctly remember asking her if she had a picture of him and her claiming she hadn't saved any of his things. She never wanted to talk about him. Ever." She banged a fist against her thigh, her eyes filling with tears again. "She lied to me. My own mother *lied* to me!"

He held up a hand. "Now, don't go assuming the worst. Could be she was only trying to protect you."

"From *what?*" she cried, her voice rising in hysteria. "My heritage? From the opportunity to know the man who fathered me?"

"No, from being hurt." He tipped his head toward the letter she clutched. "Obviously reading his letters has upset you. Your mother probably knew they would and wanted to save you the pain."

"She had no right. He was my father, for God's

sake! Can you imagine what it's like not knowing anything about your father? To know that he died without ever seeing you? He was excited when Mom told him she was pregnant with me." She thrust the letter in front of his face and shook it. "It says so right here. He *wanted* me!"

Reluctant to comment one way or the other for fear of setting her off again, he said vaguely, "I'm sure he did."

She dropped her hands to her lap, her shoulders sagging dejectedly. "Never mind. You wouldn't understand. I'm not even sure that I do."

She dragged in a long breath, then released it and forced a polite smile. "I appreciate you coming to check on me, but there's no need for you to stay any longer. I'm fine."

As badly as Wade would've liked to hightail it out of there and leave her to wallow in her misery alone, there was no way in hell he could do that. Not and be able to live with his conscience later.

"No rush. I can stick around for a while."

She flattened her lips, all sign of politeness gone. "Then let me make myself a little clearer. I don't want you here."

He lifted a shoulder. "I guess that makes us even, 'cause I don't particularly want to be here either."

She tossed up her hands. "Then make us both happy and *leave!*"

He shook his head. "Can't. Leavin' might make me happy, but I suspect it's not gonna help you any."

Her eyes narrowed to slits. "Wanna bet?"

He hid a smile, having forgotten how feisty Steph could get when riled. Seeing her exhibit that particular trait made him realize that he'd succeeded in getting her mind off her sadness for a while. Pleased with himself, he bumped his shoulder against hers, making room for himself to sit beside her on the bed.

"What do you think you're doing?" she asked incredulously as he stretched his legs out alongside hers.

He folded his hands behind his head. "Gettin' comfortable. Looks like you're needin' to unload some emotional baggage." He lifted a shoulder. "Since I'm willin' to listen, I figure I might as well make myself comfortable."

She rolled to her knees, her eyes dark with fury as she faced him. "If and when I think I need a shrink, I'll hire one."

Ignoring her, he picked up an envelope and pulled out the letter it held. "What branch of the service was your father in? Navy?"

"Army," she snapped. "And you're not staying."

He scanned a few lines and glanced over at her. "Have you read this one yet?"

She folded her arms across her chest and pressed her lips together.

He bit back a smile. "I'll take that as a no. Probably best if you didn't," he advised and slipped the pages back into the envelope. "There are some things about her parents' life that a daughter is better off not knowing."

She snatched the envelope from his hand and pulled out the letter. He watched her eyes widen as she skimmed the first page.

"I tried to warn you," he said, trying not to laugh.

Her cheeks flaming, she stuffed the pages back into the envelope. "You did that on purpose," she accused.

He opened his hands. "How was I supposed to know

that letter was gonna have graphic descriptions of your parents' sex life?"

She burned him with a look before burying the letter at the bottom of the stack. "You could've just set it aside and said nothing. Saying what you did was the same as daring me to read it."

"You'd have gotten around to reading it eventually," he reminded her. "I was just trying to save you the embarrassment." He cocked his head and frowned thoughtfully. "Do you think it's really possible to do it in a—"

She held up a hand. "Please. I don't need that particular visual in my head."

"Why were you crying?"

She blinked at the sudden change of subject, then let her hand drop. "I don't know," she said miserably. "It's just all so sad. There's no one left but me to remember him, yet I know nothing about him."

He picked up a bundle of letters and bounced them thoughtfully on his palm. "And this is how you plan to get to know him?"

"It's all I have."

He studied the bundle a moment. "I guess you know you're setting yourself up for a lot of pain." He shifted his gaze to hers and added, "And probably an equal share of embarrassment. What he wrote in these letters was meant for your mother's eye, and hers alone."

She nodded tearfully. "I realize that, but this is all I have that was his. Reading his letters is my only way of learning about him."

His expression grave, he set the bundle aside. "I want you to promise me something."

"What?"

"Promise that you'll call me whenever you feel the need to talk."

"No, I—"

He pressed a finger against her lips, silencing her. "You helped me through a hard time after I lost my parents. I think I deserve the chance to even the score."

He could tell that she wanted to refuse his request, but she finally dropped her chin to her chest and nodded. He figured she was only agreeing so she could get rid of him, but that was okay. He knew how to make sure she kept her end of the deal.

With that in mind, he swung his legs over the side of the bed and picked up an empty box from the floor. Using the length of his arm, he raked the bundles of letters inside.

Her mouth gaped open. "What are you doing?"

He hitched the box on his hip—and out of her reach. "Helping you keep your promise. Every afternoon, when I come over to feed the cattle, I'll drop off a bundle of letters for you to read. After I'm done feeding, I'll stop back by and check on you. That way I'll know if you're honoring your promise."

"What will seeing me prove?"

"One look at your face and I'll know whether or not you need to talk."

She opened her mouth, then clamped it shut, obviously realizing it was useless to argue with him.

His job done for the moment, he turned for the door.

"Wait!"

He stopped and glanced over his shoulder to find her eyeing him suspiciously.

"How did you get inside the house? I made you return the key Bud gave you."

"I used the one he kept hidden above the front door."

Her eyes shot wide. "You knew about that?"

He lifted a brow. "Oh, I think you'd be amazed at all I know."

Three

The next morning Stephanie stormed around the house, stripping pictures off the walls and stacking them against the wall in the dining room. It was the only packing she trusted herself to do while in a blind rage.

She couldn't believe she'd agreed to Wade's ridiculous arrangement. Having him dole out her father's letters to her was demeaning enough, but then to be subjected to his perusal so that he could judge her mental and emotional state was masochistic! She didn't want to share her thoughts and feelings with him. She'd die a happy woman if she never had to *see* him again!

Hearing his truck stop out front, she groaned, then set her jaw and marched to the door. Before he could even knock, she yanked open the door, snatched the bundle of letters from his hand and slammed the door in his face, turned the lock. Pleased with herself for outsmarting him, she hurried to the den and settled into her mother's chair.

She had just pulled the ribbon, releasing the bow that held the stack of letters together, when the hair on the back of her neck prickled. Sensing she was being watched, she glanced toward the doorway and nearly jumped out of her skin when she found Wade standing in the opening.

He dangled the house key between two fingers. "Nice try," he congratulated her. "Too bad it didn't work."

His smile smug, he slipped the key into his pocket, letting her know in his not-so-subtle way that attempting to lock him out in the future would be a waste of her time, then touched a finger to the brim of his hat in farewell.

"I'll be back as soon as I finish feeding the cattle," he called over his shoulder before closing the door behind him.

Mentally kicking herself for not thinking to remove the hidden key, Stephanie scooped up the scattered letters and rapped them into a neat stack on her lap. She should have known that a locked door wouldn't stop Wade Parker. The man could all but drip sugar when it suited him and rivaled Attila the Hun when he wanted his way.

Her smile turning as smug as the one he'd gifted her with while dangling the key in her face, she plucked a letter from the top of the stack. Well, two can play this game as well as one, she told herself as she smoothed open the creased pages. She knew how to compartmentalize her emotions, if and when the situation required it. When Wade returned to check on her, he'd find her dry-eyed and busy packing. She wouldn't give him any reason to think she needed to "unload," as he'd referred to her emotional state the previous night.

Confident that she could outsmart him, she began to read.

> *Janine,*
> *Have you ever had the feeling that everybody in the world is going crazy and you're the only sane person left? That's how I feel right now. I swear, a couple of guys in my unit have gone nuts. If they're not drunk, they're smoking grass—or worse.*
>
> *Out in the field, we work as a unit and depend on each other to stay alive. But these guys are so out of it most of the time, I can't trust them to cover my back. I tried talking to them, told them the booze and drugs were messing with their heads and that they were going to get us all killed if they didn't cut that crap out. They just laughed and called me an old man and worse. Hell, I don't care what they call me. I just don't want their stupidity getting them—or any of the rest of us—killed.*
>
> *Sorry. I didn't mean to go off like that and I sure as heck don't want to make you worry. Sometimes I just need to unload—*

Stephanie pursed her lips at the word *unload*, wishing her father had chosen a term other than the one Wade had used to describe her need to talk. Giving the pages a firm snap, she began to read again.

> *but there's nobody that I can talk to about this stuff. If I go to the lieutenant, I'll feel like a rat for squealing and probably get my buddies in trouble.*
> *Enough of this. Telling you about it isn't going*

to change things any. How are you feeling? Has the morning sickness passed yet? How much weight have you gained? And don't worry about those extra pounds. It just gives me more to love! Have you thought of any names yet? If it's a boy, we could name him William, after my father, and call him Will for short. And if it's a girl, I've always liked the name Stephanie. I knew a girl once—not a girlfriend, just a friend—named Stephanie, and she was really cool. Stephanie Blair. How does that sound?

Better go. The chopper is due soon to pick up the mail, and I want this letter to be on it when it takes off.
Love forever,
Larry

Stephanie carefully refolded the letter and slipped it back into the envelope. He had named her. Her father, not her mother, had chosen her name. She quickly sniffed back the emotion that realization drew.

See, she told herself proudly as she slid the letter beneath the last on the stack without shedding a tear. She could do this. She'd read a letter all the way through without falling apart, and one that had the potential to set her off on a crying jag. Confident that she had a handle on her emotions, she pulled the next letter from the stack.

Dearest Janine,
We lost one of the guys in our unit yesterday. North Vietcong were spotted in our area, and our

unit was sent out to verify the report and to find out how many there were and how much firepower they packed. We'd been out two days without seeing any sign of the enemy and were ready to head back, when all hell broke loose.

We were near an old bomb crater and we made a run for it so we could form a defense and radio for a chopper. We managed to hold them off until aircraft could get there to give us cover from above. Just as we spotted the chopper coming in, somebody realized that Deek, one of the new guys in our unit, was missing.

We only had seconds to get into that chopper and get the hell out of there. There were still two of us on the ground—me and T.J.—when all of a sudden there was this sound like an Indian war whoop, followed by machine-gun fire. I glanced to my left and there was Deek, standing on the edge of that crater like he thought he was John Wayne, blasting away with his machine gun. I yelled for him to get down, but it was too late. The Vietcong had already spotted him.

He took the first hit in the neck, and that was probably what killed him. He took about twenty more before his body slid behind the rim of the crater and out of their sights. T.J. and I dragged him to the chopper and brought him back to base. I imagine his parents have gotten word by now. I just hope they never know that he was stoned out of his mind when he died.

Sometimes there's no satisfaction in saying "I told you so." That's the case with Deek. If he'd listened to me and stayed clear of drugs, he might be alive today. Of course, he might've caught one anyway. That's the hell of it. You never know when your number is gonna come up.

In some ways, I owe Deek my thanks. Watching him die changed my life. I was awake most of the night, thinking back over mistakes I've made in the past, and I've come up with a plan. In the future, I'm not going to be so slow about telling people what I think or how I feel about them. I'm going to be more open to new ideas and less judgmental of those I don't agree with. And I'm going to be quicker to forgive. You never know when you're going to run out of time to make things right.

I love you, Janine.

Larry

Stephanie lowered the letter and stared blindly at the wall, numbed by the vivid scene her father had described. She couldn't imagine what horrors he must have witnessed in Vietnam. Deek's death was probably only one of many he had witnessed during the eighteen months he'd spent overseas.

How did a person deal with that? she asked herself. What kind of emotional scars did it leave him with? And how did he ever sleep at night without being haunted by the memories?

She laid a hand over the page, thinking of the effect her father had claimed that Deek's death had had on his life. If he'd lived, what kind of man would he have been? she wondered. Certainly a wiser one, judging from the things he'd seen and the lessons he'd learned. Sadly he'd never had the chance to put into action his plan to improve his life even more.

Her eyes sharpened. But she could, she realized. She could take the things he'd planned to do and incorporate them into her own life. It would be a way of honoring her father, a way of giving his life purpose. It would be a means of making him a part of *her* life.

Wade stood in the doorway quietly watching Stephanie. She wasn't sobbing her heart out, which he considered a good sign. But she wasn't dancing a jig either. Her forehead was pleated, as if she were absorbed in some deep thought. And there were creases at the corners of her eyes and mouth, as if whatever she was thinking about was either sad or depressing.

"Did you finish reading the letters?"

She jumped, then placed a hand over her heart and released a long breath. "I didn't hear you come in."

Dragging off his hat, he stepped into the room. "Sorry. Next time I'll give a holler." He dropped down on the arm of the recliner. "So? How'd it go?"

Averting her gaze, she lifted a shoulder and drew the ribbon back around the stack of letters. "Okay, I guess. I only read two."

"Two?" he repeated and glanced at his watch. "They must've been long ones—I was gone almost an hour."

"Not long. Heavy."

"Oh," he said in understanding but offered nothing more. If she wanted to talk, he'd listen, but he wasn't going to force her to say anything she wasn't ready or willing to share.

Her expression growing pensive, she framed the stack of letters between her hands. "He was only twenty-one when he died," she said as if thinking aloud. "Yet he'd probably seen and experienced more than men twice his age."

"Yeah, I imagine he had."

She glanced up and met his gaze. "In the last letter I read, he wrote about a guy in his unit who was killed." Wincing, she shook her head. "It was awful just reading about it. I can't imagine what it must have been like to be there and witness it firsthand."

"War's no picnic. Ask any veteran."

Lowering her gaze, she plucked guiltily at the ribbon that bound the letters. "I'm ashamed to admit it, but most of my knowledge of war is purely historical. Dates, battles, the political ramifications. The kind of thing you learn in a classroom. And since I've never been a fan of war movies or novels, I've never had a visual to associate with it before." She shuddered. "And to be honest, I think I preferred it that way." She glanced up, her expression sheepish. "I guess that makes me sound like an ostrich, huh? Wanting to keep my head buried in the ground?"

Wade thought of his daughter and the current problems he was having with her and shook his head. "No. Innocence is a hard thing to hold on to in today's world. What with all the graphic and gruesome TV shows and movies being shown, I consider it a miracle that you've managed to hold on to even a smidgen of your innocence."

"Innocent? Me?" She choked back a laugh and shook her head. "I think I lost my innocence about the age of six, when Tammy Jones told me there was no Santa Claus."

He clapped a hand over his heart. "Please," he begged, "tell me it isn't so."

Hiding a smile, she set the bundle aside and drew her legs beneath her. "I didn't say there *wasn't* a Santa Claus. I was only repeating what Tammy told me."

He dragged an arm across his forehead in an exaggerated show of relief. "Whew. You scared me there for a minute. I'm counting on Santa bringing me the new Kubota tractor I've been lusting after."

"A tractor?" she repeated, then rolled her eyes. "Men and their toys."

"A tractor's not a toy," he informed her. "It's a machine."

She flapped a dismissing hand. "Whatever."

"Okay, Miss Smarty-Pants. What is Santa gonna bring you?"

She blinked as if startled by the question, then tears filled her eyes.

Wade swallowed a groan, realizing that with Bud gone, this would be her first Christmas alone—an actuality he'd just brutally reminded her of. Dropping to a knee, he covered her hand with his. "I'm sorry, Steph. I wasn't thinking."

Keeping her face down, she shook her head. "It's not your fault. I just…hadn't thought that far ahead."

Hearing the sadness in her voice and knowing he'd put it there made him feel about as low as a snake. In hopes of making it up to her, he caught her hand and pulled her to her feet. "Tell you what," he said. "As punishment for sticking my foot in my mouth, I'll give you an hour of slave labor. Haul boxes, carry out the garbage. You name it, I'm your man."

He sensed her resistance, but then she surprised him by giving her head a decided nod.

"All right," she said. "But remember, this was your idea, not mine."

Stephanie didn't know what had possessed her to accept Wade's backhanded offer of help…or maybe she did.

I'm going to be quicker to forgive. You never know when you're going to run out of time to make things right….

It was one of the ways her father had planned to change his life…and one of the changes Stephanie would have to make in her own if she was going to honor her father's memory by adopting his plan.

But could she forgive Wade? *Truly* forgive him?

She gave her head a shake as she placed the wrapped platter inside the box, unsure if that was possible.

"What pile does this go in?"

Pushing the hair back from her face, she looked up to see what Wade was holding. "Oh, wow," she murmured and reached to take the round of white plaster from him. "I haven't seen that in ages."

He hunkered down beside her. "What is it?"

"Don't you recognize fine art when you see it?" she asked, then smiled as she smoothed her hand across the shallow indentations in the plaster. "I made this in Bible school. Our teacher poured plaster in a pie pan, then had us press our hands into it to leave a print."

He placed his hand over the one impressed in the plaster. "Look how little that is," he said in amazement. "Mine is three or four times the size of yours."

She gave him a droll look. "I was five years old when I made that. I've grown some since then."

"Mine are still bigger." He held up his hand. "Put yours against mine," he challenged. "Let's see whose is bigger."

She hesitated slightly, reluctant to make the physical connection, then took a bracing breath and placed her palm against his. The warmth struck her first, followed by the strength she sensed beneath the flesh. She closed her eyes as awareness sizzled to life beneath her skin, from the top of her head to the tips of her toes.

"A good three inches longer," he boasted, pressing his fingers against hers. "Maybe more. And the breadth of my palm is at least two inches wider." He shifted his gaze to hers, then frowned and peered closer. "Steph? You okay? Your face is all red."

Of course it is, she wanted to tell him. Her body felt as if it were on fire and her mind was spinning, churning up memory after memory of what his hands could do to drive a woman out of her mind.

Dragging in a breath, she forced a smile. "Just a little dizzy. That's all." Flapping a dismissive hand, she laughed weakly. "I guess I've been pushing myself too hard to get all this done." She attempted to withdraw her hand, but he slid his fingers between hers, locking them together. Startled, she glanced up and met his gaze. In his eyes she saw the same awareness, the same need that burned behind her own. Unable to look away, she stared, slowly realizing that he was going to kiss her.

"Steph…"

At the last second she turned her face away and shook her head. "No. Don't. Please. I—"

"You what?"

Gulping back tears, she met his gaze. "I don't want you to kiss me. What happened before...I can't forget that."

She saw the anger that flashed in his eyes.

"Can't or won't?" he challenged.

Shaking her head, she dropped her gaze. "It doesn't matter. The result is the same."

He clamped his fingers down hard over her hand. "It may not matter to you, but it does to me. For God's sake, Steph! All that's in the past. Why can't you let it go?"

She snapped her gaze to his, furious that he would think it was that easy. "Because it hurts," she cried, fisting her free hand against her chest. "All these years later, and it still *hurts*."

He stared, the muscles in his face going slack. "You still care," he murmured, as if awed by the realization.

She shook her head wildly and tried to pull her hand free. "I don't. I *can't*."

He clamped his fingers tighter over hers, refusing to let her go. "You may not want to, but you can't deny what I see, what you feel."

A tear slipped past her lid and slid down her cheek.

"Aw, Steph," he said miserably. "I never meant to hurt you. That's the last thing I wanted to do. I asked then for your forgiveness and you refused." He dropped his gaze and shook his head. "Maybe that was asking too much of you. Could be it still is." He lifted his head to meet her gaze again, and she nearly wept at the regret that filled his eyes. "I know I destroyed whatever chance we ever had of being together, but couldn't we at least be friends?" He gave her hand a pleading squeeze. "Please, Steph? Is that too much to ask?"

She wanted desperately to tell him yes, it was too much to ask, to scream accusations and shoot arrows of blame until his heart was filled with as many holes as hers had been.

But she found she couldn't. And it was more than her desire to carry out her father's pledge of granting forgiveness that kept her from exacting her revenge. It was the pleading in his eyes and the sincerity in his voice that reached out and touched a place in her heart she'd thought could never be breached again.

But she wouldn't let him hurt her again. She couldn't. She would try her best to be his friend—but nothing more.

Drawing a steadying breath, she squared her shoulders. "I suppose we can try."

He stared a long moment, as if not trusting his ears, then dropped his chin to his chest and blew out a long breath. "Well, at least that's a start." Releasing her hand, he picked up the plaster disk of her handprint. "So what's it going to be? Trash, keep or donate?"

Grateful that he seemed willing to put the emotional scene behind them, she blinked to clear the tears from her eyes, then frowned as she studied the piece he held. Sagging her shoulders, she pointed to the pile marked Trash. "I'll probably hate myself later, but pitch it."

"If you want it, keep it."

Shaking her head, she picked up a china cup to wrap. "I'm already going to have to rent a storage facility as it is."

"But if it's special…" he argued.

"That's just it. Everything's special!" She placed the wrapped piece in the box, then waved a hand at the stuff piled around the room. "There isn't anything here that doesn't have a memory attached to it." She rocked to her knees and plucked a crystal bowl from the dining room table. "Take this, for instance. It belonged to my mother's mother. Mom told me that her mother always used it to serve her special fruit salad whenever they had company. Mom used it for the same thing. She even used the same fruit salad recipe her mother had always used." She opened a hand in a gesture of helplessness. "How do you throw away a piece of history like that?"

Wade picked up a piece of newspaper from the floor and handed it to her. "You don't. You either add on a room to your house or rent another storage building."

Stephanie frowned as he picked up another piece of paper and began to wrap it around the plaster handprint. "What are you doing? I told you to pitch that."

"A piece of art like this?" Shaking his head, he leaned to place it in the box with the china. "No way. That thing is priceless."

Tears filled her eyes as she watched him tuck the wrapped handprint into the box. It was such a simple thing, silly really, a kindness he was probably not even aware of. Yet his refusal to throw away a souvenir from her childhood put another crack in the armor she'd placed around her heart.

Fearing he'd do something else to widen the crack even more, she quickly wrapped paper around her grandmother's bowl. "What time is it?"

He glanced at his wristwatch. "One thirty-five."

She tucked the bowl into the box and stood, dusting off her hands. "Which means you've more than ful-filled your hour of slave labor."

"I can stay a little longer, if you want."

"Uh-uh." She turned him around and gave him a push toward the door. "Though I really appreciate all you did and hate losing the extra set of hands, I know darn good and well you've got work of your own to do."

"Yeah," he said, glancing at his wristwatch again. "I do."

At the door he stopped and looked back at her. "Steph, I'm glad we're going to be friends again."

She had to swallow back emotion before she could reply. "Yeah. Me, too."

Stephanie gave up and opened her eyes to stare at the dark ceiling. She'd tried everything to lull herself to sleep. She'd counted sheep, hummed the mantra from the yoga class she attended twice a week. She'd even gotten up and made herself a warm glass of milk to drink. Nothing had worked. Her mind still refused to shut down.

He would've kissed her. That one thought kept circling through her mind over and over again, keeping her awake. If she hadn't turned her face away, Wade would've kissed her. A part of her wanted to rail at the heavens that he would have the nerve to even try. Another part wished desperately that she had let him.

And that was what was keeping her awake. The fact that she still wanted his kiss. How pathetic. What woman in her right mind would knowingly and willingly subject herself to that kind of pain again?

Groaning, she dug her fingers through her hair as if she could tear thoughts of Wade from her mind. But that didn't help either. It just made her head ache even more.

Dropping her arms to her sides, she stared at the ceiling again, praying that sleep would come soon.

Runt growled, and she tensed, listening. Not hearing anything, she slowly dragged herself to a sitting position and leaned to peer at the rug beside the bed, where Runt slept.

"What is it, Runt?" she whispered. "Did you hear something?"

In answer, he rose and crossed to the door, the click of his nails on the wooden floor sounding like gunshots in the darkness.

Stephanie swung her legs over the side of the bed and hurried to stand beside the dog. "Is someone out there?" she whispered to Runt.

Whining low in his throat, he lifted a paw and scratched at the wood.

Though the dog couldn't see her face in the dark, she gave him a stern look. "If this is nothing more than you wanting to go outside to relieve yourself, I'm going to be really mad," she warned.

He barked once, sharply.

"Oh, Runt," she moaned, wringing her hands. "I really don't need this right now."

When he continued to whine and claw at the door, she gathered her courage and slowly opened the door a crack to peer out into the hall. Not seeing anything out of the ordinary, she opened the door wider. Runt pushed past her legs before she could stop him and shot down the hall, barking wildly. Stephanie's blood turned to ice as images of burglars and mass murderers filled her mind. Remembering the shotgun Bud kept behind the door in the laundry room, she crept down the dark hallway. As she passed through the kitchen, she whispered an impatient, "Give me a minute" to Runt, who was scratching at the back door and whining.

After locating the shotgun and checking to see that it was loaded and the safety was securely in place, she returned to the kitchen. She curled her fingers around the knob. "I'm right behind you," she murmured nervously to Runt, then opened the door.

The dog took off like a shot for the barn, his shrill bark sending shivers down her spine. She hesitated a second, trying to decide whether or not to grab a flashlight. Deciding that she couldn't shoot the gun and hold a flashlight, too, she ran after him.

A thick layer of storm clouds blanketed the sky, obliterating whatever illumination the moon might have offered. Stifling a shudder, Stephanie lifted the shotgun to her shoulder and moved stealthily toward the barn, keeping her finger poised on the trigger while keeping her ear cocked to the sound of Runt's barking.

A flash of lightning split the sky, making her jump, and was followed moments later by an earthshaking rumble of thunder. Silently vowing to murder Runt if this turned out to be a wild-goose chase, she quickened her step.

When she was about forty feet from the barn, Runt suddenly quit barking. Frowning, she strained, listening, but could hear nothing over the pounding of her heart. Tightening her grip on the shotgun, she flipped off the safety and tiptoed to the barn's dark opening.

Bracing a shoulder against the frame to steady her aim, she yelled, "Come out with your hands up!" in the deepest, meanest voice she could muster.

"Steph?"

She jolted at the sound of the male voice, then squinted her eyes against the darkness, trying to make out a shape. "Wade?" she asked incredulously. "Is that you?"

"Yeah, it's me."

The overhead lights flashed on and she squinted her eyes, momentarily blinded by the bright light. When her eyes adjusted, she saw Wade walking toward her. Runt trotted at his heels.

She didn't know whether to pull the trigger and shoot them both for scaring the daylights out of her or crumple into a heap of weak relief. Deciding murder was beyond her, she put the safety back on, lowered the shotgun and resorted to using her tongue as a weapon.

"What in blue blazes are you doing out here in the middle of the night?" she shouted at Wade. Before he could answer, she turned her fury on Runt. "And you," she accused angrily, "carrying on like burglars are crawling all over the place. You're supposed to protect me, not scare me to death. I have a good mind to take you to the *pound.*"

Wade dropped a protective hand on the dog's head. "Don't blame Runt. It's my fault. I should've known he would hear me and kick up a fuss."

"Hear *what?*" she cried. "I was awake and I never heard a thing other than Runt barking." Realizing the oddity in that, she whipped her head around to look outside, then swung back around to face him. "Where's your truck?"

"At home. I walked."

"You *walked* all the way over here?"

He shoved his hands in his pockets and shrugged. "Couldn't sleep, so I figured I'd check on a heifer that's about to calf. She's young," he explained further, "and Bud was worried about her having trouble with the birth. I penned her when I was here earlier, so I could keep an eye on her."

"You walked," she repeated, unable to get beyond the incredibility in that one statement.

"It's not that far. Not if you cut through the woods."

She pressed the heel of her hand against her forehead and shook her head in disbelief. "I can't believe you did that. There's no telling what kind of varmints are hiding out in there."

He hid a smile. "I didn't run into a single grizzly or mountain lion."

She dropped her hand to frown. "Big surprise, since neither have been seen around here in fifty years or more. But there are coyotes and rattlesnakes," she reminded him, "and they can be just as dangerous."

When he merely looked at her, she rolled her eyes. "Men," she muttered under her breath. "If you cracked open the heads of the entire gender, you might come up with enough brains to form one good mind."

Lightning flashed behind her, followed by a deafening boom of thunder that made her jump.

Chuckling, he took the shotgun from her and caught her arm. "Come on," he said, tugging her along with him. "You better get back to the house before the bottom falls out of the sky."

She hurried to match her steps to his longer stride. "What about you? How will you get home?"

"The same way I came. I'll walk."

She dug in her heels, dragging him to a stop. "But you'll get soaked!"

He shrugged and nudged her into a walk again. "I've been wet before. I won't melt."

The words were no sooner out of his mouth, then the bottom of the sky did open up and rain poured down in torrents.

He grabbed her hand and shouted, "Run!"

Stephanie didn't need persuading. She took off, slipping and sliding on the wet grass, as Wade all but dragged her behind him. He reached the back door a step ahead of her and flung it open. Stephanie ducked inside and flipped on the light and was followed quickly by a drenched Runt. Wade brought up the rear, stripping off his hat and propping the gun against the wall before closing the door behind him.

"Man!" he exclaimed, dragging a sleeve across his face to swipe the rain from it. "That's some storm."

Stephanie grabbed a couple of dish towels from a drawer and tossed one to him before squatting down to rub a towel over Runt.

"Don't try to make up to me now," she scolded as Runt licked gratefully at her face. "If not for you and your stupid barking, we'd both be high and dry instead of dripping wet."

Wade hunkered down beside her and took the towel from her hand. "Here, let me. I'm the one to blame, not Runt."

Scowling, Stephanie stood and folded her arms across her breasts. "You won't get an argument out of me." A chill shook her, and she turned for the laundry room, where she'd left a basket of clean laundry. "I'm going to change clothes," she called over her shoulder.

She quickly stripped off her wet nightgown, dried off

as best she could with a towel she pulled from the basket, then tugged on a tank top and shorts. Grabbing one of her father's T-shirts from a stack on the dryer, she returned to the kitchen.

She offered the T-shirt to Wade. "It probably won't fit, but at least it's dry."

"Thanks." With a grateful smile he took the T-shirt and began to unbutton his shirt one-handed.

Stephanie didn't intend to watch but found she couldn't look away, as with each short drop of his hand to the next button, more and more of his chest was revealed. She knew from the summer they'd spent together, he often worked bare-chested. As a result, the skin he bared was as tanned as that on his face and hands, and the soft hair that curled around his nipples and rivered down to his navel had been bleached blonde.

By the time he reached the waist of his jeans and gave the shirt a tug, pulling his shirttail from beneath it, her mouth was dry as dust. Embarrassed by her reaction to such an innocent sight—and fearing he would notice his effect on her—she quickly turned away. As she did, the lights blinked out.

"Oh, great," she muttered. "Now the electricity is off."

"There's a candle on the shelf to the right of the sink."

Already on her way to fetch it, Stephanie shot him a frown over her shoulder. "I know where the candles are kept."

"Sorry."

As she struck a match and touched the flame to the wick, she frowned. The fire flickered a moment, then caught, tossing shadows to dance across the room.

Turning, she held the candle up and eyed Wade warily as he tugged Bud's T-shirt over his head. "How do you know so much about everything around here?"

He glanced up, then set his jaw and pulled the T-shirt down to his waist. "You may have shut me out of your life, but your parents didn't choose to do the same."

"You mean, you— They—"

"Yep, that's exactly what I mean." He stooped to pick up the towel he'd dried Runt with, then stood to face her. "Your mother was a little slower to forgive than Bud, but I think she finally realized I'd done the only thing an honorable man could've done in a situation like the one I was caught in."

Afraid she would drop it, Stephanie set the candle-holder on the table and pressed a hand to her stomach, suddenly feeling ill. "But they never said a word. Never so much as mentioned your name to me."

He tossed the wet towel into the sink. "That was out of respect for you, knowing it would upset you."

She dropped her face to her hands. "I can't believe this," she said. "How could they *do* that to me?"

"Oh, come on, Steph," he chided gently. "They didn't do anything to you." When she didn't respond, he crossed to pull her hands down, forcing her to look at him. "You know your parents loved you. They'd never do anything to hurt you."

"But they forgave you!" she cried. "Knowing what you had done to me, they still forgave you."

"One has nothing to do with the other," he argued.

When she opened her mouth to voice her disagreement, he silenced her with a look.

"They forgave me for what I'd done," he told her

firmly, "but not for the pain I caused you. I don't think they were ever able to forgive me for that."

She tossed up her hands. "What else was there to forgive?"

"Getting a woman pregnant and having to marry her."

Stunned, Stephanie stared, unable to believe that hearing him voice his transgression could have the same debilitating effect as it had when he'd confessed it to her so many years before.

Before she could cover her ears, refusing to hear any more, he caught her hands and held them, forcing her to hear him out.

"I never loved Angela. That's not something I'm proud of, considering, but it's true. I loved *you*, Steph, with all my heart and soul. Your parents knew that and knew, too, how much it cost me to lose you." He tightened his grip on her hands. "But don't hold their kindness to me against your mom and dad. Without them—" he dropped his chin to his chest and slowly shook his head "—I don't know how I would've survived it all."

Heaving a sigh, he gave her hands a last squeeze and turned away. "I guess I'd better go so you can get to bed." He stooped to give Runt's head a pat. "You might want to take a couple of candles with you to your bedroom," he said, the suggestion directed to Stephanie. "The electricity might not come back on until morning."

She watched him cross the kitchen, her throat squeezed so tight she could barely breathe.

I loved you, Steph, with all my heart and soul.

Out of everything he'd said, that one single statement filled her mind, obliterating all else.

He made it to the door before she found her voice.
"I loved you, too."

His hand on the knob, he glanced back.

The tears clotting her throat rose to fill her eyes.
"And you broke my heart."

Four

Wade stood, paralyzed as much by the desolation that etched Stephanie's face as by what she had just said. This was the woman he'd loved—still loved, if he was honest with himself—and, by her own admission, he'd broken her heart. He'd known he had—or at least had assumed that was the case—but it cut him to the bone to hear her say the words and see, this many years later, how much she still suffered from his infidelity.

He hadn't been able to comfort her then. How could he, when she wouldn't let him past her front door?

But he could now.

In two long strides he was across the room and had her face gathered between his hands. "I'm so sorry, Steph." He swept his thumbs beneath her eyes, swiping away the tears. "I never wanted to hurt you. I swear, if there'd been any other way…"

Realizing how inadequate the apology sounded, even to his own ears, he tightened his hands on her face, desperate to make her believe him. "You didn't deserve what I did to you. The sin was mine. You had no part in it, yet you paid a price." He swallowed hard. "But I paid, too, Steph. If you want the truth, I'm still paying."

He saw the flash of surprise in her eyes, the hope that rose slowly to glimmer in the moisture.

Helpless to do anything less, he lowered his face and touched his lips to hers. It wasn't a passionate kiss. A mere meeting of lips. But to Wade it was like coming home after a long stay away. He withdrew far enough to draw a shuddery breath, then wrapped his arms around her and pressed his mouth more fully over hers. He felt the shiver that trembled through her, swallowed the low moan that slid past her lips. With a groan he clamped his arms around her and opened his mouth over hers.

Her taste rushed through him like a swollen river, flooding him with memory after memory that he'd struggled for years to forget. The feel of her lying naked in his arms, the almost greedy race of her hands over his flesh. Her catlike purr of pleasure vibrating against his chest, the moist warmth of her laughter teasing his chin.

Rock-hard and wanting more of her, he hooked a hand beneath her knee, lifted and drew her hard against his groin. But it wasn't enough. Not nearly enough. With his mouth locked to hers, he backed her up against the wall and leaned into her, pinning her there with his body. Filling his hands with her rain-dampened hair, he held her face to his and took the kiss deeper still, until his breath burned in his lungs and his veins pumped liquid fire, until every cell in his body throbbed with his need to take her, to make her his again.

Bracing his hand in a V at her throat, he dragged his lips from hers. "I want you, Steph," he whispered and rained kisses over her face, her eyelids, across the hollows of her cheeks. "I want to make love with you." He pushed a knee between her legs and buried his face in the curve of her neck to smother a groan as her heat burned through his thigh.

Though he knew her need equaled his, he sensed her hesitancy in the tremble of hands she braced against his chest and feared he was pushing her too fast, too hard.

Drawing in a long breath to steady himself, he dragged his hand from her throat to cover her breast. Beneath his palm he could feel the pounding of her heart.

"Remember how good we were together?" Closing his fingers around her fullness, he gently kneaded. "I always loved your breasts." He lifted the one he held and warmed it with his breath. Humming his pleasure when her nipple budded beneath the thin fabric, he flicked his tongue over the swollen peak.

She arched instinctively, thrusting her breast against his mouth. He nipped, suckled, nipped again, but quickly became frustrated by the fabric that kept him from fully touching her, tasting her. "I want you bare," he said, then looked up at her, seeking her permission.

She gulped, nodded, then dropped her head back against the wall on a low moan as he eased her tank top down far enough to expose her breast. The candle behind him tossed light to flicker over her flushed flesh—the knotted bud, the pebbled areola that surrounded it, the lighter skin stained with the blush of desire. Mesmerized by the sight, he opened his mouth over her nipple, drew her in.

As he suckled, teasing her nipple with his tongue and teeth, he sensed her growing need in the hands she gripped at his head, her impatience in the fingers she knotted in his hair. Anxious to satisfy both, he released her and swept her up into his arms.

Leaving the candle behind in the kitchen, he made his way through the dark house, his familiarity with her parents' home guiding his steps. Once inside her bedroom, he pushed the door shut with his foot, in case Runt decided to follow, and continued on to her bed. He laid her down, then stretched out alongside her.

In the darkness he couldn't see her face, didn't need to in order to know that somewhere along the short walk from the kitchen to her bedroom her hesitancy had returned. He could all but feel the years that lay between them, all the days and months, stacked one on top of the other, in which she had clung to her resentment toward him, shored up a wall around her heart that he had only just begun to believe he could tear down. He had the power to seduce her. He knew that. He'd proven it in the kitchen only moments before. But he couldn't allow his physical needs to destroy whatever chance he might still have with her.

Placing a hand on her cheek, he turned her face to his. "You'll never know how much I've missed you," he said softly. "How many nights I've dreamed of touching you and holding you like this." He drew in a deep breath, anxious to make her understand how he truly felt. "But it's so much more than the sex. I've missed *you*, Steph. Your laughter, your smile. The way you always seemed to know exactly what I needed, whether it was a swift quick in the seat of the pants or a tight hug of encouragement. The hours we spent talking. And the times we spent in silence, content just to be together."

He caught her hand and drew it to his lips. "I'd be lying if I said I didn't want you right now. But more than the sexual release and pleasure that would give me—hopefully both of us—I need *you*. Back in my life, back in my heart. When we make love again, Steph, I want you to want me as much as I want you. I don't want there to be any regrets."

He heard her breath hitch and he swept his thumb across her cheek to catch the tear that fell. "Don't cry, Steph." He slipped his arm beneath her and drew her to him, tucking her head beneath his chin. "Just let me hold you. That's all I'll do, I swear, is just hold you."

Steph awakened and stretched her legs out, while wisps of sensations and emotions floated through her mind. Her eyes still closed, she separated each, naming them. Warmth. Tenderness. Comfort. Security. Lust. She stiffened at the latter and tried to remember if she'd had a dream that would explain why she'd wake with that particular thought on her mind.

Wade, she realized slowly as the events of the previous night returned. He'd aroused her with his seductive words, his lips, his touch. Even as she remembered the way his mouth had felt on her breast, the tremble of desire he'd drawn, she had to squeeze her thighs tight against the ache that throbbed to life deep in her womb.

She remembered, too, the trepidation that had grown inside her with each step he'd taken that had brought them closer to her bedroom. *Distrust.* It was such an ugly and debilitating word, one that she had lived with for far too many years. But as hard as she'd tried to banish it from her mind, it was always there in her sub-conscious, keeping her from giving her heart to any man—even, it seemed, the one responsible for planting the seed inside her in the first place.

But he'd claimed that he had suffered as much as she. And, if he was to be believed, he was still suffering. Remembering how he'd pulled her into his arms, telling her that he wanted only to hold her, she closed her eyes and gave herself up to the warmth and sense of security she'd found there.

Stiffening, she flipped her eyes open, suddenly wide-awake. Was he still here with her? she wondered. In her bed? Holding her breath, she dropped a hand behind her and groped. When her fingers met only cool sheets, she slowly brought her hand back to curl beneath her cheek, swallowing back the disappointment at finding him gone.

And why would you be sad about that? she asked herself. You should be relieved that he left. You don't need this, she reminded herself. You've got enough drama going on in your life without adding Wade to the mix.

With a sigh she flipped back the covers, preparing to get up, but froze when a piece of paper fluttered up from the pillow next to hers and drifted slowly out of sight on the far side of the bed. Making a dive for it, she flattened her stomach against the mattress and caught it before it hit the floor. Her heart in her throat, she sat up, bracing her back against the headboard and read.

Good morning, Sunshine. Sorry to leave without waking you, but you were sleeping so soundly I hated to disturb you, figuring you needed the rest. I'll be back around noon to drop off another bundle of letters. If you want, after I check on the cattle, I can stay for a while and help you pack.
Wade

She shifted her gaze to read the first line again, and a warm glow slowly spread through her chest. *Sunshine.* It was a nickname he'd used often the summer they'd met. Surprised that he would remember the endearment, she sank back against her pillow and stared out the window, her thoughts growing pensive as she wondered where all this was going.

Judging by the passionate scene in the kitchen the previous night, she had to believe that he was hoping they could be more than friends.

But she wasn't sure she could offer him anything more than friendship. He'd destroyed her trust, hurt her more than words could ever describe. How did a person get over that kind of pain, humiliation? Was it even possible? Forgiving was one thing, forgetting another. And if she couldn't forget, what was the point in getting involved with him again? Even if she were willing to agree to a strictly physical relationship, the past would always be there between them.

She shivered, remembering the way his mouth had felt on her breast, the desperate need that had burned through her body, leaving her weak and wanting. He had been right in saying that they'd been good together. They *had* been good together—though she had to give all the credit to Wade. She'd yet to meet the man who could satisfy her the way he once had. He had always seemed to understand her needs better than she did herself, knowing what pleased her, the areas of her body that were most sensitive, when she craved speed and when she preferred a slow seduction…and when she needed him to stop altogether.

He'd recognized the latter the previous night. Without her having to say a word, he'd somehow known that at some point between the kitchen and bedroom the ugly doubts had arisen, making her question what they were doing and whether or not she should allow things to go any further. Before she had even reached a decision, he'd removed her need to do so by voicing her fears aloud and refusing to make love with her until she could do so without regret.

She drew in a shuddery breath and slowly released it. How in the heck was a woman supposed to deal with a man like that? she asked herself. One who knew her fears as well as she did, then offered her his under-standing and patience while she dealt with them?

Hearing Steph's faint call of, "The door's open," Wade stepped inside.

"I'm back here!"

Since her voice was coming from the rear of the house, he assumed by "here" she meant one of the bedrooms. Taking the shortcut through the dining room, he glanced around and was surprised to find the table was clear and all the boxes were stacked neatly against one wall.

He stuck his head into the guest room and found

her standing on a ladder inside the closet, her head hidden from view. She was wearing shorts, and the view of her long, tanned legs and bare feet put a knot of need in his groin. Puffing his cheeks, he blew out a long breath to steady himself, then tossed the bundle of letters onto the bed. "Looks like you've been busy."

"And then some," came her weary reply. She backed down the ladder, balancing a stack of shoe boxes on the palm of one hand. Reaching the floor, she steadied the stack with her opposite hand and stooped to set them on the floor. Straightening, she blew a breath at the wisps of hair that had escaped the ponytail she'd pulled her hair into, then smiled. "But I'm making progress. I finished the dining room and now I'm working in here."

He looked around at the piles that covered the floor, amazed by the amount of junk she'd unearthed. "Where did all this stuff come from?"

She hooked her thumb over her shoulder at the closet. "In there. Can you believe Mom was able to cram all that junk in that small a space?"

He picked up a doll that lay on the foot of the bed. A black hole gleamed from the space where an eye should have been, and blond hair frizzed from its scalp. He lifted a brow. "Yours?"

Smiling fondly, she took the doll from him. "This is Maddy. I wagged her around from the age of three to about seven or eight, I think."

"What happened to her eye?"

"One of Bud's dogs got a hold of her and popped it out."

"The dog get her hair, too?"

She shook her head and attempted to smooth the

wild tufts. "No, that was my doing. I thought she'd look better with a short hairstyle."

He sat down on the edge of the bed. "Remind me to never get near you when you've got a pair of scissors in your hand."

Chuckling, she laid the doll on the dresser. "Coward."

In her reflection in the dresser mirror he watched her smile slowly fade and knew by the creases that appeared between her brows that something was bothering her.

"About last night," she began uneasily.

Not wanting to have that particular discussion with her halfway across the room, he stretched to catch her hand and tugged her over to sit down beside him. "What about last night?"

She glanced at him, then away, her cheeks flaming a bright red. "I'm sure that you must think I'm giving off…"

When her voice trailed off, he bit back a smile. "Mixed signals?" he suggested.

She looked at him, then dropped her chin and nodded. "One minute I'm stiff-arming you and the next I'm, well, I'm—"

"Melting into a puddle of rapturous joy at my feet?"

She shot him a frown. "I wouldn't go so far as to say *that*."

Chuckling, he slung an arm around her shoulders and hugged her to his side. "No need to get your panties in a twist. I was just trying to make you laugh so you'd relax a little."

She shot to her feet to pace. "That's the problem. It's way too easy to relax around you. So much so that I'm letting my guard down."

"And that's a bad thing?"

She whirled to face him. "Yes, it's a bad thing! You hurt me, and I can't forget that."

"But you've forgiven me."

It was a statement, not a question, and she stared, realizing it was true. She didn't know exactly when or even why, but she *had* forgiven him.

But what was the use of forgiving if she couldn't forget? she found herself thinking again.

"Give yourself time," he suggested as if he'd read her thoughts. "And me, too," he added. He caught her hand and tugged her to stand between his legs. "I'm going to win back your trust," he told her in a tone that left little doubt that he would succeed. Holding her gaze, he brought her hand to his lips and pressed a kiss to her knuckles. "The burden is mine to prove, not yours."

She blinked back tears at the depth of his determination, the tenderness with which he'd made the promise to win back her trust. Yet she couldn't help questioning her sanity for her willingness to breathe so much as the same air as him after what he'd done to her.

Again as if reading her mind, he took her hands in his. "I'm not perfect, Steph. I've made my share of mistakes. But loving you was never one of 'em."

Her face crumpling, she sank to his knee and dropped her forehead against his. "Oh, Wade," she said miserably. "Why does everything have to be so complicated?"

He turned her face up to his. "It doesn't have to be. At least, not the part that deals with us. We were good together, good for each other. And we will be again."

She lifted her head to search his eyes and knew by the warmth she found there that he was offering her a new beginning, one that she was finding difficult to refuse. He made it sound so simple, so easy. But was it really?

"Wade—"

He touched his lips to hers to silence her. "You don't need to say anything. I'm not pushing for something you're not ready to give."

She closed her eyes, gulped. When she opened them and met his gaze, saw the warmth and understanding there, what little hesitancy that remained to hold her back slipped soundlessly away.

She lifted a hand to his cheek, her fingers trembling as she traced the lines that fanned from the corner of his eye. "You don't have to push. I'm more than ready."

He stared, as if not trusting his ears. "Are you sure?"

"Yes," she murmured and touched her lips to his.

Groaning, he wrapped his arms around her and pulled her to his chest. With an urgency that left her head spinning and her heart racing, he stripped off her blouse, her bra, then twisted her around on his lap and fitted her knees on either side of his thighs.

"Sweet heaven," he murmured as his gaze settled on her breasts. He filled his hands with their softness. "So beautiful." Sweeping his hands around to settle beneath them, he lifted and placed a kiss on each peak. He tipped up his head to meet her gaze and stroked his thumbs over her nipples. "Exactly as I remember them, perfect in every way."

Knowing it wasn't true, she shook her head. "You're a wonderful liar, but age and gravity have taken their toll."

"Perfect," he insisted, then teased her with a smile. "I think I'm the better judge."

She tipped her head, willing to concede the point,

then gasped as he closed his mouth over a nipple. Dropping her head back, she clung to his head. "Wade," she said, his name rushing out on thready sigh, then gasped again as he caught the nipple between his teeth and tugged gently. "Oh, Wade," she groaned and knotted her fingers in his hair.

Desperate to have her hands on him, she reached for his shirt and fumbled open buttons. Halfway down, she grew impatient and shoved the plackets apart and sank against him to press her lips against the middle of his chest. She inhaled once, released it with a contented sigh, then inhaled again and held the breath, absorbing his male scent.

Dizzy from it, she braced her hands against his chest and began a slow journey of exploration, smoothing her palms over the swell of muscled chest, down, her fingers bumping over each rib, then bringing her hands together at the waist of his jeans. Finding the snap, she released it and eased the zipper down.

With her lungs burning for air, her chest heaving with her attempts to fill them, she found his mouth with hers and freed his sex. It sprang from the restraining clothing and filled her hands. Marveling at the feel of silk-sheathed steel, she stroked her fingers down its length until the heel of her hand bumped the nest of coarse hair at its base. She released a shuddery breath against his lips and stroked upward, gathering her fingers at its tip and swirling her thumb over the pearl of moisture there.

With a groan he fell back, bringing her with him, and toed off his boots, his socks, then, one-handed, stripped off his jeans and underwear. Letting his clothing fall to the floor, he dragged her up his body and captured her mouth again. He kissed her with an urgency that fed her own need, yet with a tenderness that twisted her heart.

Noonday sun shone through the windows at either side of the bed, filling the room with bright sunlight. Though she would've preferred candlelight to mask the changes age had left on her body, Stephanie was grateful for the illumination, as it provided her the ability to see Wade's face, the muscled lines of his body her hands traced. With each glide of flesh over flesh, the years fell away, leaving in their place the familiarity she'd once known with this man, the ease they'd once shared.

Desperate to have him inside her again, to experience the thrill of oneness she'd once known, she wiggled out of her shorts and panties, then positioned her knees on either side of his hips. Using her hand to guide him, she dragged his sex along her folds to moisten it, then positioned the tip at her opening. With her gaze on his, she drew in a deep breath, bracing herself, then plunged her hips down and took him in.

The sensations that ripped through her stole her breath and sent brilliant shards of white to explode behind her closed lids. His name became a fervent prayer for release she whispered as she pumped her hips against his. Again and again and again, until sweat beaded her upper lip, slicked her hands, making it all but impossible to keep them braced against his chest. The pressure built inside her, fed by a rising wave of need that gathered itself into a knot in her womb.

As if sensing her readiness, her need for satisfaction, Wade clamped his hands at her hips. "Come with me," he said breathlessly, then set his jaw and squeezed his eyes shut. A low growl rose from deep inside him, then he exploded inside her, and the heat that pulsed from him sent her soaring high.

Her lungs heaving like bellows, her hands fisted against his chest, she hovered a moment, suspended on that needlelike peak of pain and pleasure, wanting more than anything to hold on in order to capture the feelings and emotions that filled her. Unable to stave off the sensations any longer, she toppled over the other side into satisfaction.

Weak, sated, she sank to his chest and buried her face in the curve of his neck, every nerve in her body quivering liked plucked strings. "Oh, Wade," she whispered, unable to find the words to express the experience.

"Was it good?"

Inhaling, she stretched her toes out and curled her feet around his sweat-dampened calves. "Oh, yeah," she said, releasing the breath on a contented sigh. "Better than good."

Before she had time to draw another breath, she was on her back and he was on top of her, his face only inches from her.

"Honey, that was nothing but foreplay. What comes next ranks right up there with fantastic."

Laughing, she laced her fingers behind his neck and brought his face down to hers. "Then show me what you've got, cowboy."

Five

The next day Wade was in his toolshed early, anxious to get his work done so that he could go and see Steph.

After selecting a wrench from those hanging on the wall above his worktable, he hunkered down in front of the baler to adjust the belt's tension. He had made only two full turns when the wrench slipped and he had to stop and swipe the perspiration from his hands—and it wasn't the heat that had made his hands slick with sweat, although his toolshed held heat like a smokehouse. It was the thoughts of Steph that kept playing through his mind.

Aware of the dangers involved in working on a piece of equipment and knowing how much they escalated if a man wasn't giving his full attention to the job, he pulled the wrench free and braced it against his thigh. He still couldn't believe they'd made love. He'd hoped they would, planned on it even, but he'd thought it would take him a lot longer to persuade her.

He didn't know what had changed her mind and really didn't care. The only thing that mattered was that she'd given herself to him willingly and without any pressure from him. Not that he would have felt any compunction on applying a little, if she'd dragged her feet too much longer. From the moment he'd seen her standing in her parents' house a week ago he'd known that his feelings for her hadn't changed. Just looking at her had had the same debilitating effect on him that it had thirteen years before. And kissing her…well, he wouldn't even go there, seeing as he couldn't even hold on to a wrench, as it was.

"Dad-dy! I'm talking to you!"

Wade glanced over to find his daughter standing in the doorway, her hands fisted on her hips. Setting the wrench aside, he dragged a rag from his pocket to wipe his hands. "Sorry, sweet cheeks. Guess I was daydreaming. Whatcha need?"

She pushed her hands into fists at her sides, with an impatient huff of breath. "I *asked* if I could spend the night with Brooke."

Eyeing his daughter warily, he stuffed the rag back into his pocket, wondering whether this overnight was on the up-and-up or a smoke screen she was spreading for her to do God only knew what. "Did Brooke's mother say it was all right with her?"

She gave him a pained look, one she'd perfected over the last year, then said through clenched teeth, "Yes. She said I could ride the bus home with Brooke after school if it's okay with you."

Knowing from experience that this could all be a clever lie Meghan was weaving in order to cover her tracks, he pulled his cell from the holster at his waist. "I'll just give Jan a call and double-check things with her."

"Daddy!" she cried. "I told you Mrs. Becker said it was okay!"

He punched in the number, then looked down his nose at her as he lifted the phone to his ear. "If it's all the same to you, I'd like to hear that from Jan."

She folded her arms across her chest and pushed her lips out in a pout. "You don't trust me."

He listened through the second ring. "The last time you asked permission to go somewhere with a girl-friend, you ended up at the pizza parlor with a guy two years older than you." When she opened her mouth to spew a comeback, he held up a hand, silencing her.

"Jan?" he said into the receiver. "This is Wade Parker, Meghan's dad."

He listened a moment, then smiled. "Doing just fine. How about yourself?"

"That's good," he replied to her response that all was well in the Becker household, then scratched his head. "Listen, Jan. Meghan was telling me about her plans to spend the night with Brooke tonight, and I wanted to make sure that was all right with you before I gave her my permission."

He listened again, then breathed a sigh of relief at her affirmative answer. "No, riding the bus home with Brooke is fine with me," he told her. "Will save you and me both from having to haul them around."

He smiled and nodded again. "Yeah, I hear you. These girls would keep us in the middle of the road if they could." Anxious to end the call before Jan got started in on the trials and tribulations of being a single parent, he said, "I'd better go. I need to write a permission note for Meghan to give the bus driver before she leaves for school." He nodded again. "You, too, Jan. And thanks."

He disconnected the call and returned his cell to its holster.

Meghan lifted a haughty brow. "Well? Are you satisfied *now*?"

Wade pulled a tablet from a slot above his worktable and scrawled a note granting his permission for Meghan to ride a different bus from school. "Better watch your mouth, young lady, or you'll find yourself spending the night at home with me."

She snatched the note from his hand and spun for the house. "And wouldn't that be fun?" she muttered under her breath.

Wade heard the sassy comeback but chose to ignore it. He'd learned the hard way to choose his battles with his daughter, and this one wasn't even worth the energy required for a skirmish.

Heaving a sigh, he braced a hand on the doorjamb and watched her stalk to the house, her long blond hair swinging from side to side with each angry stride. Twelve going on twenty-two, he thought sadly. Why couldn't kids just be satisfied with being kids? he asked himself. Why were they so hell-bent on becoming adults? Didn't they realize that being a grown-up wasn't all it was cracked up to be? Kids didn't have the responsibilities and worries that adults faced every day. Hell, this was the best time of Meghan's life! She should be enjoying herself, instead of plotting and scheming ways to do things she wasn't allowed to do. Things that she was too *young* to be doing.

He shook his head, remembering the day she'd come home sporting three holes in each ear and knowing it was too late for him to do a damn thing to stop her from doing it. And what was with this new infatuation of hers with boys two and three years older than herself?

Snorting, he dropped his hand from the door and turned back to the baler he'd been working on. He may not know what his daughter was thinking, but he knew what was on those boys' minds. And that was the problem. It wasn't so long ago that he'd been a teenage boy that he couldn't recognize a hormone-raging stud looking for a girl he could charm out of her panties when he saw one.

He shuddered at the thought of his daughter being sexually active, then set his jaw and picked up his wrench, settling it into place over a bolt. "Not on my watch," he muttered and gave the wrench a hard turn, tightening the bolt into place.

Stephanie opened the door and blinked in surprise when she saw Wade standing on the stoop, his hat in his hand. "What are you doing over here at this time of day?"

His smile sheepish, he scuffed the toe of his boot at the doormat. "I'm embarrassed to admit to being this slow, but it only just occurred to me that it's Friday night and I've got nothing to do. I thought, if you weren't busy, we might go to a movie or something."

Stephanie would've laughed if he hadn't looked so

cute standing there like a lost puppy in search of a new home. She glanced down at her bare feet and the cutoff jeans she was wearing, then at her wristwatch. Wrinkling her nose, she shifted her gaze back to his. "By the time I shower and change, whatever movie is showing would be half over."

He grimaced. "Yeah, you're probably right. I should've called first. I started to, but I figured you wouldn't answer the phone."

"I wouldn't have." Taking pity on him, she opened the door wide. "Tell you what. We can watch a movie here. If there's nothing on, I'm sure I can find a video or DVD in my parents' stash for us to watch."

"Are you sure?" he asked even as he stepped eagerly inside. "If you're busy or have other plans, I can head back home. I'm sure I can find something there to do to pass the time."

Laughing, she closed the door behind him. "I'm not busy. In fact, I was just about to put a frozen pizza in the oven. Have you had dinner yet?"

He placed a hand over his stomach, as if only now realizing he'd missed the meal and was hungry. "No, as a matter of fact, I haven't."

She glanced at him over her shoulder as she led the way to kitchen. "Is pepperoni okay?"

He tossed his hat onto the counter. "Beggars can't be choosers."

She stopped, balancing a pizza on the palm of one hand, the other curled around the handle of the oven door. "If you don't like pepperoni, I can probably scrape up the makings for a sandwich."

Chuckling, he shook his head. "Pepperoni's fine. In

fact, that's all I ever eat. It's Meghan's favorite and the only one we keep stocked in our freezer."

Stephanie's smile faded.

Wade noticed the sudden change in her expression before she turned to slide the pizza into the oven and cursed his blunder, knowing it was his mention of his daughter that had robbed her of her smile. He crossed to her and caught her hand in his. "Steph, she's my daughter. I can't pretend she doesn't exist."

She squared her shoulders and forced a smile. "I know that. And I don't expect you to pretend she doesn't exist. You just—well, you caught me off guard when you mentioned her. You having a child is not something that I care to think about."

"But…" He stopped, knowing that anything else he said would only drag up more of the past. And he didn't want to spoil the one evening he had with her rehashing his mistakes.

"How about some wine?" he asked, changing the subject. "Bud usually kept a bottle or two around, if you haven't thrown them out."

She stepped around him and gestured to the far cabinet as she headed for the sink. "Up there, and the opener is in—" She stopped, hauled in a breath, then continued on to the sink. "Well, I'm sure you probably know where to find the opener, the same as you do the wine, since you seem to know where everything else is kept."

In two long strides he was across the room and turning her around to face him. His anger melted when he saw the gleam of tears in her eyes. "Aw, Steph," he said miserably. "I thought we'd already cleared that hurdle. Yes, I was friends with your parents. And yes, I know my way around their house probably as well as I do my own. But don't let that come between us. We've got enough old baggage to sort through without having to dredge up that particular subject again."

When she kept her head down, refusing to look at him, he hooked a finger beneath her chin and tipped her face up to his. "Come on, Steph. I know you feel like we all conspired against you, but that wasn't the case at all. Your parents knew that mentioning my name in any form or fashion would only upset you, so they didn't."

She closed her hand over his and drew in a breath. "I know. And I'm sorry. Really. It's just going to take time for me to get used to…well, everything. So much went on that I wasn't aware of." She held up a hand when he started to interrupt. "Which is my fault," she said, saving him from having to tell her it was. Drawing his hand to hold between hers, she gave it a reassuring squeeze. "Now about that wine…"

He dropped a kiss on her mouth. "Frozen pizza and wine. Is there something wrong with this picture?"

"I'd say it's right on par with every date I ever had with you."

"Hey!" he cried, looking insulted. "We went on a couple of real dates."

She folded her arms across her chest. "Name one."

He shifted from one foot to the other, trying to think of one to offer, then gave her a sheepish look. "I guess I did kind of drop the ball in the date department."

Laughing, she patted his cheek. "No, you didn't. I always enjoyed the time we spent together, no matter what we were doing."

Relieved that it appeared they had weathered another

storm, he pulled out a drawer and drew out the wine opener. "Remember the time you sat up all night with me when my mare was foaling?"

"Yes. That was the first equine birth I'd ever witnessed. And hopefully my last," she added with a shudder. "That poor mare. It was hard to watch her suffer when there was nothing we could do to ease her pain."

"Breach births are seldom easy," he said as he pulled the cork from the bottle with a *pop*. "I've probably lost as many babies as I've saved. Sometimes lost the mamas, too."

While he filled two wineglasses, Stephanie set the timer on the oven. "That's the one thing I don't miss about living on a ranch," she said thoughtfully as she crossed to stand beside him. "Losing an animal always made me so sad."

"Yeah, it does me, too." He handed her a glass, then draped an arm along her shoulders. "Want to sit on the patio while we wait for the pizza to cook?"

"Good idea."

Once outside, she brushed a hand over the seats of the chairs, sweeping away the dried leaves that covered them, then sat and patted the chair next to hers. "Take a load off."

He nudged the chair closer to hers, then dropped down with a sigh.

"I love this view," she said, her smile wistful as she stared out at the pastures and the low hills beyond. "The way the sun looks at sunset, as if it's melting into the hills."

He laced his fingers through hers and settled their joined hands on the arms of their pushed-together chairs. "It is pretty. I have almost this exact same view from the balcony off my bedroom."

Her gaze still on the setting sun, she hid a smile. "I remember both the balcony and the view." She waited a beat, then added, "I also remember you spreading a blanket on the balcony one night and getting me drunk on tequila shots."

He pressed a hand against his chest. "Me?" He shook his head. "You must be mistaken. I'd never take advantage of a woman that way."

She bumped her shoulder against his. "Oh, please. And that wasn't the only time you got me drunk. I distinctly remember a case of beer and an afternoon spent skinny-dipping in the creek that runs through your hay field."

"It was hot," he said defensively. "And as I recall, you only had two of those beers."

She lifted a shoulder. "What can I say? I'm a cheap drunk."

Biting back a smile, he tapped his glass against hers. "Drink up, then. Maybe I'll get lucky again tonight."

She drew back to look at him in surprise. "How long are you planning to stay?"

"All night, if you'll let me."

She dropped her mouth open, then slowly closed it to stare. "You mean…you can stay the whole night?"

He took her glass and set it, along with his, on the patio. "Yep," he said and tugged her from her chair and onto his lap. "The *whole* night."

She continued to stare, realizing the significance in that. "Do you realize this will be the first time we will have ever slept together?"

He grasped her thigh and shifted her more comfortably on his lap. "I think you're forgetting about the night it stormed."

"No. That doesn't count because you were gone when I woke up."

He lifted a hand to her cheek and met her gaze squarely. "This one might not count either, because I'm not planning on either one of us getting any sleep."

The heat in his blue eyes burned through hers, turning her mouth to cotton and twisting her stomach into a pretzel.

The timer on the oven went off, its loud buzz signaling the pizza was done.

Unable to tear her gaze from his, she wet her lips. "Are you hungry?"

He hooked a hand behind her neck and brought her face to his. "Only for you," he said before closing his mouth over hers.

Her breath stolen, Stephanie wrapped her arms around him and clung. She felt as if she were drowning, slipping deeper and deeper into a sea of desire, its waters at first tinted a soft, muted blue, cocooning her as she drifted down. Then the water changed, became a fiery-red tempest that churned, battering her senses. The heat it produced gathered into a tight knot in her middle, then slowly spread out to every extremity, making her skin steam and her lungs burn for air.

"Wade," she gasped, remembering their dinner. "The pizza."

He slid a hand beneath her shirt, cupping a breast, and found her mouth again. "Let it burn."

Though tempted, she pushed a hand against his chest, forcing him back. "We can't. The house could burn, too."

Frowning, he pulled his hand from beneath her shirt.

"Okay, so we'll take the damn thing out." He stood, hitching her up high on his chest, and carried her back to the kitchen. "You do the honors."

With one hand locked around his neck to keep from falling, she plucked a mitt from the rack on the oven's front panel, then opened the door and pulled out the pizza. Wade angled her toward the range so that she could shove the pizza onto its flat surface.

He lifted a brow. "Satisfied?"

Locking her hands behind his neck, she gave him a coy look. "Not yet, but I'm counting on you taking care of that little problem for me."

He choked on a laugh, then turned for the door, his long ground-eating stride covering the distance between the kitchen and her bedroom in record time. Once in her room, he dumped her on her bed, then dived in after her. Hooking an arm over her waist, he rolled to his back and pulled her on top of him.

Smiling, he combed his fingers through her hair to hold it back from her face. "Now let's see what we can do about satisfying you."

"Don't you think we should get rid of some clothing first?"

He dragged his hands down her back and pushed them beneath the waistband of her shorts. "Eventually."

With the cheeks of her buttocks gripped firmly within his broad hands, he lifted his head and claimed her mouth. Stephanie surrendered with a delicious shiver, willing to follow wherever he led.

The path he chose for them was a wild one. At times treacherously steep, while at others lazy and meandering. At some point during their journey—she couldn't

remember when or how exactly—"eventually" occurred, and he peeled off their clothing, letting the
pieces fall where they may. While he explored her body,
she explored his, marveling at the muscles that swelled
and ebbed beneath her curious palms, the thunderous
beat of his heart against her lips, the soft pelt of light
blond hair that shot down his middle to the darker nest
between his legs.

Sure that no other man knew her as well as Wade,
nor could please her in so many fascinating and breathtaking ways, she gave herself up to him, to them, to the
moment. She refused to think about the yesterdays in
their lives or the worries that tomorrow might bring. She
focused only on *now*.

And when he entered her, joining his body with hers,
she squeezed back the tears of joy that sprang to her
eyes at the sense of oneness that swept over her, the
sense of rightness in being here at this moment and in
this place with this man.

And when he'd given her the satisfaction he'd promised—and hopefully received an equal measure for himself—she curled naked against his side, laced her
fingers through his over his heart and slept.

Stephanie decided that sleeping with Wade was
almost as satisfying as making love with him. Cradled
like two spoons, her back to his front, her buttocks
nudged into the bowl shaped by his groin and thighs was
truly a heavenly experience. Adding to the pleasure was
having his knee wedged between hers and his arm
draped over her waist, keeping her snugged close. It
wasn't a position that either of them had choreographed

or maneuvered into after a lot of fidgeting and adjusting. It had just…happened. Naturally.

And that made her smile.

She knew couples who struggled for years to find the perfect sleeping arrangement. Others who were still struggling. Yet she and Wade had slid naturally into this position and had slept comfortably and soundly throughout the night.

And he was still sleeping.

Careful not to wake him, she turned beneath his arm, wanting to see him…and smothered a low moan of adoration when she saw his face. Handsome awake, he was absolutely adorable when sleeping, looking more like a tousle-headed toddler than a man in his late thirties. His sandy-brown hair shot from his scalp in wild clumps and flipped endearingly just above his ears. Relaxed in sleep, his lips were slightly parted, the lower one a little puffier than the upper and all but begging for a kiss. A day's worth of stubble shadowed his jaw, chin and upper lip. Lighter than most men's, the blond stubble held the faintest hint of red.

Unable to resist, she touched her lips to his.

He flinched, blinked open his eyes, then smiled and drew her hips to his. "Mornin'."

His voice was rough with sleep, and the huskiness in it sent a shiver sliding down her spine.

"Good morning to you, too. Did you sleep well?"

He nuzzled his cheek to hers. "Like a rock. You?"

Finding the graze of his stubble on her skin unexpectedly erotic, she sighed and snuggled closer. "Never better."

Lulled by the soft stroking of his hand over her buttocks, she closed her eyes, content in the silence that settled over them.

"You never married."

She flipped open her eyes, startled by the unexpected statement. "No, I didn't," she replied, hoping he'd let the topic drop.

"Why?"

Because I never met a man who could make me forget you. That was the answer that came immediately to mind. Probably because it was the truth. But she was hesitant to admit that to him. Why, she wasn't sure, but she suspected it had a lot to do with her pride, which had suffered a mortal blow when he had broken their engagement and married someone else.

She shrugged, hoping by her nonchalance he would assume that she hadn't given the subject much thought. "I guess I just never met anyone I wanted to spend the rest of my life with."

She waited, holding her breath and praying that he wouldn't probe deeper. When he remained silent, his hand still rhythmically stroking her hip, she quietly released the breath and let her eyes close again.

"Do you think you'd want to spend the rest of your life with me?"

Her breath caught in her throat, burned there. Gulping, she slowly lifted her head to look at him. "Was that a rhetorical question or a proposal?"

Gripping her hips more firmly, he shifted her over to lie on top of him. "Since I'm not sure what *rhetorical* means, I'd have to say it was a proposal."

She searched his face, sure that he was teasing her. But

she didn't find even the slightest hint of amusement in his eyes or in his expression. His face was smooth, his eyes a clear crystal blue. If anything, he looked…expectant.

She wasn't ready for this, she thought, feeling the slow burn of panic as it began to crawl through her system. Not yet. Maybe never. She'd agreed to be his friend. They'd become lovers…but husband and wife? *Married?* She gulped as thoughts of all that marrying him would entail flashed through her mind. Giving up her home and business in Dallas. Moving into the house he'd once shared with another woman. Becoming a stepmother.

Dear God, she thought, feeling the revulsion churn in her stomach, making her feel sick. His daughter. The child, whose conception had caused a ripple effect the size of a tidal wave, ripping Wade from her arms and shattering her emotions, her very life. How could she live with that reminder on a daily basis? How could she look that child in the face every day and not be reminded of all that her birth had caused? The anger. The heartbreak. The years lost that she might've shared with Wade. The loneliness. The regret.

"Steph?"

She gulped and made herself focus on his face. Seeing the concern there, she gulped again and eased back to kneel beside him. "I don't know, Wade," she said, trying to keep the tremble from her voice. "This is so unexpected." She pressed a hand to her heart, and gulped again, knowing that *unexpected* didn't even come close to describing her reaction to his proposal. "Everything is still so…new between us. We've only just begun to get to know each other again."

He braced himself up on one elbow and caught her hand. "Nothing's new, Steph. If anything, the feelings I have for you are stronger than they were before. I love you. Always have. And you love me, too. Or at least I think you do."

She dropped her gaze, unable to deny that she did still love him. But *marry* him? Oh, God, she wanted to. More than anything else in the world. But in marrying him, she had to be willing to accept all that he brought to their relationship, including his daughter.

Deciding that she had to be honest with him, she drew in a steadying breath and lifted her head to meet his gaze. "Wade, I do love you," she said and had to stop to swallow back the tears that rose to her throat. "But there's so much more to consider than our feelings for each other."

He wrinkled his brow in confusion. "What could be more important than what we feel for each other?" He squeezed her hand. "I love you, Steph. Everything else is secondary to that."

"Even your daughter?"

He stared, his hand going lax in hers. "Steph, please," he begged. "Don't do this."

She gripped his hand hard, knowing she'd hurt him by mentioning his daughter but desperate to make him understand, to see her side. "It's not that I don't like your daughter, Wade. How could I, when I don't even know her? But she was what tore us apart. Surely you realize how difficult it would be for me to see her, live with her, and not think of that every time I looked at her."

Pulling his hands from hers, he dragged himself to

a sitting position and braced his arms over his knees. "She's just a kid. An innocent kid. You can't blame her for what happened."

"I don't…not intentionally. But she would be a constant reminder." She crawled to lay a hand over his arm, hoping that in touching him she could ease the pain her confession was causing him. "I don't want to hurt you, Wade. I would never do anything to purposely hurt you. But I can't lie to you either. Your daughter presents a problem for me, and I can't promise you that I can accept her or even feel comfortable living in the same house with her."

"But you don't even know her," he said in frustration. "If you met her, spent some time with her, you might find you like her a lot."

"That's just it. I don't want to meet her. Not yet," she added quickly. She took his hands and grasped them between her own. "We've only just begun to heal old wounds and make a new start. Maybe in time…"

He searched her face. "So that's not a definite no? I mean, about marrying me."

"It's a maybe. A really strong I-want-this-to-work-out-too kind of maybe."

He opened his knees and dragged her up his chest. "I can live with one of those kind of maybes." Smiling, he swept her hair back from her face. "You're gonna like her," he said confidently. "Once you two meet, I just know that you're going to get along great."

Six

Scowling, Wade shoved the plate of pancakes in front of Meghan. "I said no, and begging isn't going to make me change my mind."

"But, Daddy!" she cried and jumped up from the table to follow him to the sink. "It's going to be the coolest party ever. Richie's parents have hired a DJ and everything!"

He shoved his hands into the dishwater. "Richie is fifteen years old," he reminded her.

"So? I'm going to be thirteen my next birthday."

"Which is still six months away." Frustrated, he dropped the pan he was scrubbing and turned to face her. "You're too young to be running around with guys Richie's age and you're definitely too young to date. Now the answer is no, and don't ask me again."

She pushed her hands into fists at her sides. "I hate

you and I wish you weren't my daddy!" Whirling, she ran from the room, sobbing uncontrollably.

Wade braced his hands against the edge of the sink and drew in a long breath. She didn't mean it, he told himself as he slowly released the breath. She was just mad. Blowing off steam. Kids said things like that all the time to their parents when they didn't get their way.

Setting his jaw, he picked up the pan again and began to scrub. She'd get over it. It wasn't as if it was the end of the world. There'd be other parties for her to go to. Other boys for her to date.

He glanced over his shoulder to the hallway beyond the kitchen and the empty staircase that stretched to the second floor.

But damn if being a parent wasn't hell.

Stephanie tossed the tattered book on veterinary medicine into the box marked Trash.

"Hey!" Frowning, Wade shifted to dig it out. "You can't throw that away."

"Why not? I have no use for it, and the library won't accept books in that bad a condition."

He smoothed a hand over the worn cover. "But this was like Bud's bible. Passed down to him from his father. He referred to it whenever any of his livestock fell sick."

She waved an impatient hand. "Then you take it. You have more use for it than I ever will." Rising to her knees, she pulled another stack of books from the shelves, then sat down to sort them.

His forehead creased in a frown, Wade watched her, wondering how she could be so indifferent about some-

thing that had belonged to her father, a book that Bud
had cherished as much as another man might have gold.
Giving his head a shake, he turned away and placed the
book near the door so that he wouldn't forget to take it
with him when he left.

"Bud had the weirdest reading taste," he heard Steph
say and glanced her way.

Propped up on her knees, her elbows on the floor and
her chin on her fists, she read the titles imprinted on the
spines of the books stacked in front of her. "*Moby Dick,
How to Win Friends and Influence People, Mommie
Dearest.* And a couple of dime-store Westerns." She
shook her head. "Weird."

"Well-rounded," he argued.

"Weird," she repeated, then picked up the books and
dumped them in the Donate box. Dusting off her hands,
she turned for the closet. "I guess I've put off dealing
with his clothes long enough."

She opened the door and scooped up an armload of
clothing and lifted, making sure the hooks had cleared
the rod before turning and heaving the stack onto the
bed. She picked up a coat, gave it a cursory once-over,
then tossed it in the trash.

Wade dug it right back out.

She huffed a breath. "Wade, I threw that away."

"And I took it out," he informed her.

"Why? It's covered with stains and the cuffs are all
frayed."

"It was Bud's favorite."

"That doesn't make it any less a rag!"

He folded the coat neatly in half and laid it in the
Donate box.

"Wade!" Stephanie cried. "What are you doing? Nobody's gonna want Bud's old coat."

"There's nothing wrong with that coat. Just because it's seen some miles doesn't mean it can't keep a body warm. Besides, I think Bud would be pleased to know that somebody got some use out of it."

"Whatever," she mumbled, then picked up a shirt and laughed. "Oh, my gosh. Do you remember this?" she asked and held it up for Wade to see. The shirt's front sported a bold red-and-white-stripe fabric, the back a blue with white stars embroidered in neat rows. "Bud wore it to every Fourth of July parade ever since I can remember."

Wade dropped the sack of trash he'd just picked up and fisted his hands on his hips. "And I suppose you're going to throw that away, too?"

She looked at him in puzzlement. "Why would I keep it?"

"Because it was *his?* Because it was something that Bud obviously liked?"

Seeing her stunned expression, he turned away, dragged a hand over his hair, then spun back, unable to suppress the frustration he'd carried since his battle with Meghan that morning. "Do you realize that you never say *my father* or *my dad* when you refer to Bud? You say *Bud.*"

She opened her hands. "So? That was his name."

"But you never used it before! You always called him Dad, never Bud."

"What difference does it make what I call him? You know who I'm talking about."

"It doesn't make any difference to me, but it would probably make a helluva lot to Bud! Can you imagine how hurt he would be if he could hear you right now? Calling him *Bud* and throwing away the things he cherished most. For God's sake, Steph! He was your father, not an acquaintance."

Seeing her hurt expression and knowing he'd gone too far, he stopped and hauled in a breath through his nose. "I'm sorry," he said, releasing it. "I didn't mean any of that."

"Obviously you did or you wouldn't have said it in the first place."

Frustrated, he dragged a hand over his hair again, then dropped it to his side. "It's just that you seem to have forgotten that Bud was your dad. He was the one who raised you, took care of you. But ever since you found those letters, all you can talk about is your *real* dad."

"I haven't forgotten Bud," she said defensively. "I loved him. I will *always* love him. But I owe a certain allegiance to my real father, too. And the only reason I refer to Dad as Bud is for clarification. I have *two* fathers," she reminded him. "My natural one and the one who adopted me. Just because I'm determined to get to know my natural father in no way detracts from my feelings for the one who raised me."

Realizing how much he'd upset her, Wade gathered her into his arms. "I'm sorry," he murmured with real regret. "I guess I'm just a little touchy about fathers in general because of what Meghan said to me this morning."

She drew back to frown up at him. "What did she say?"

He ducked his head, reluctant to repeat his daughter's angry words. "That she hated me."

"What?" Steph cried.

"She didn't mean it," he hurried to assure her. "She

was just mad because I wouldn't let her go to a party with a guy three years older than her."

"But, Wade—"

He silenced her with a kiss. "Forget it," he said and turned away. "They're just words. And you know the old saying about sticks and stones...."

Stephanie hummed along with the song playing on the radio as she sorted through the linens she'd pulled from the closet. Most she tossed into the Donate box, as there was very little sentiment to be attached to sheets and towels. But the tablecloths, especially those crocheted by her grandmother, she placed in a separate pile, planning to keep.

"A lost art," she murmured and paused to finger the decorative filet crochet border on a set of linen napkins, trying to remember who had made them. All of the women on her mother's side of the family had done some type of handiwork. Whether it was quilting, knitting, crocheting or embroidery, each had excelled at her chosen craft and had generously shared the fruits of her labors with other family members.

"Aunt Colleen," she decided and set the napkins in the Keeper stack.

A knock on the door had her lifting her head to peer toward the front of the house. Glancing at her wristwatch, she frowned as she hurried down the hall, wondering who it could be. It was too early for Wade's daily visit, plus he'd told her he'd probably be late because he was working his cattle this morning. Murmuring a fervent prayer that it wasn't Mrs. Snodgrass, the nosiest busybody at her mother's church, she opened the door.

She lifted a brow in surprise when she found Wade standing on the porch. She sputtered a laugh. "And since when have you ever knocked?" She opened the door wider. "You're lucky I even answered the door. I almost didn't because I was afraid it might be Mrs. Snodgrass."

When he made no move to enter, she looked at him curiously and noticed the tension in his face. "Is something wrong?" she asked in concern.

"You could say that," he replied tersely, then released a long breath. "I need a favor." He gestured behind him to where his truck was parked. "Meghan's in the truck, and I'd appreciate it if you would keep an eye on her for me."

"Meghan?" she repeated, her stomach knotting in dread. "But—shouldn't she be in school?"

He set his jaw. "*Should* being the operative word. She got expelled this morning." He gave her a pleading look. "I know it's asking a lot, considering, but it would only be for a couple of hours."

"Why can't she stay at home? Surely she's old enough to leave by herself."

"I don't trust her, okay?" he said, his frustration returning. "She's already threatened to run away. If I leave her at home, the minute I'm out of sight, I'm afraid she'll haul butt."

Stephanie glanced toward the truck and tried not to wring her hands. "I don't know, Wade," she said uneasily. "What if she pulls a stunt while she's here? I wouldn't know what to do."

"You can call me. I've got my cell." Before she could think of another excuse or alternative to offer, he turned for his truck.

"Wade!" she cried, reaching out a hand as if to stop him.

But it was too late. He already had the passenger door open and a young girl was climbing down. Petite and with long blond hair styled with the sides pulled up and gathered into a clip at the crown of her head, she didn't look like the kind of person who would get expelled from school. She looked more like one of the little girls that came to Stephanie's door selling Girl Scout cookies…or at least she did until Wade took her arm and started her toward the house, and Stephanie got a look at the belligerent expression on her face.

Stephanie gulped once, then gulped again. She'd thought she didn't want to meet Wade's daughter before. Now she was sure of it.

Stephanie led the way into the den. "Would you like something to drink?"

Meghan dropped down on the sofa in a slouch. "I'm not thirsty."

Racking her brain to think what to do with the child, Stephanie saw the remote for the TV and reached for it. "How about watching some television?"

"Whatever."

Irritated by the girl's surly attitude, Stephanie slapped the remote on the coffee table in front of her. "Well, here's the remote, if you decide to. I'll be in the back, packing. If you need anything, you can find me there."

Halfway down the hall, she heard the TV click on, followed by spurts of different sounds as Meghan surfed through the channels. "Delinquent," she muttered under her breath. No wonder the child had been expelled from school. With an attitude like hers, it was amazing she was allowed to attend at all.

As she passed her bedroom door, she heard the musical peal of her cell phone and ducked inside to retrieve it from the bedside table. Checking the display, she smiled when she recognized Kiki's number.

"Hey, Kiki," she said, bringing the phone to her ear. "How's motherhood?"

"Don't ask. When are you coming home? I don't know how much longer I can take all this togetherness before I start tearing out my hair."

Laughing, Stephanie sank down on the edge of her bed. "What have the twins done now?"

"What *haven't* they done," Kiki shot back, then heaved a weary sigh. "I don't want to talk about the twins. It's too depressing. Tell me what you're doing."

Stephanie cast an uneasy glance toward the door, then stood and tiptoed to her bathroom. "Babysitting a juvenile delinquent," she whispered as she closed the door behind her.

"What? Speak up. I can't hear you."

"Babysitting a juvenile delinquent," she whispered a little louder.

"Who?"

"Wade's daughter."

"What!"

Being as Kiki was one of only a handful of people in Dallas who knew about Stephanie's past relationship with Wade, Stephanie could understand her friend's shock. "I know. Crazy, isn't it?"

"Does this mean you and Wade are…?"

She sagged down onto the commode seat. "I don't know what we are," she said miserably. "We've established a truce of sorts, but—" She glanced at the door, then turned her head toward the tub, fearing Meghan might be able to hear her, and said in a low voice, "His daughter's a problem."

"Because she's a juvenile delinquent?"

She frowned, a visual of Meghan's belligerent expression popping into her mind. "That, too," she muttered, then sighed. "But can you imagine what it would be like to have to look at her every day and know, if not for her, Wade and I would be married right now?"

"Did you tell Wade that?"

"Yes."

"Please, God," Kiki begged, "tell me you didn't."

Stephanie frowned at the dread in Kiki's voice. "Of course I did. There was no point in lying."

"Oh, no," Kiki moaned, then cried, "Steph, what were you thinking? That's his daughter, for cripes' sake! You can't tell a parent something like that. It's the same as telling him his child is ugly!"

"It is not," Stephanie replied defensively. "Besides, Wade knows she's not perfect. Heck, she was expelled from school! That's why he brought her over here in the first place."

"It doesn't matter," Kiki argued. "A parent can think or say anything they want to about his kid, but let someone else make a derogatory comment, and that same parent will fight to the death to defend the kid."

Stephanie caught her lip between her teeth. She knew that she'd hurt Wade's feelings with her refusal to meet his daughter, but what other choice had she had? He'd asked her to marry him. There was no way she could have refused his proposal without telling him why.

"He understood," she said, trying to convince herself it was true.

"Uh-huh," Kiki said doubtfully. "I'll just bet he did."

"He did," she insisted, then pushed to her feet and crossed to the window to look out. "I told him that maybe in time I would feel differently. There's still so much that he and I have to work through. Everything is so new, so—" Her eyes flipped wide and she whipped the drape back for a better view. "Oh, my God!" she cried, then whirled for the door. "Kiki, I've got to go."

"Why? What's wrong?"

"Meghan's running away!"

Before Kiki could ask any more questions, Stephanie tossed the phone onto the bed and ran out of her room, down the hall.

Once outside, she broke into a full run. "Meghan!" she shouted, racing after the girl. "Where do you think you're going?"

Meghan glanced back over her shoulder, her eyes wide in alarm, then took off at a run. Stephanie raced after her. "Meghan, stop!" she yelled.

Meghan stumbled, fell, then scrambled to her feet and ran again. Her fall, coupled with the awkward backpack she was carrying, gave Stephanie the edge she needed to close the distance between them.

With her lungs burning, her arms pumping like pistons, she knew she had only one chance to stop the girl. She dived, tackling Meghan around the legs and bringing her down.

Meghan twisted beneath her, trying to fight free. "Let me go!"

Gasping, Stephanie rocked back on her heels but

kept a firm grip on Meghan's arm. "Uh-uh. You're staying right here with me."

"You can't tell me what to do," Meghan yelled angrily. "You're not my mother."

"Thank heaven for that," Stephanie muttered under her breath, then gave Meghan's arm a yank and all but dragged her back to the house.

By the time they reached the porch, Meghan was sobbing. Setting her jaw against the heartbreaking sound, Stephanie marched her into the house and to the den. She released Meghan's arm and pointed a stiff finger at the sofa. "Sit."

Sniffling, Meghan flopped down on the sofa.

Stephanie yanked tissues from the box on the coffee table and pushed them into the girl's hand. "I don't know where you thought you were going, but I'm telling you right now that you better not pull that stunt again. Understand?"

Her chin on her chest, Meghan sniffed, nodded, then lifted her head. "Are you going to tell my dad?" she asked hesitantly.

It was Stephanie's first real good look at the child. Though dirt and tears smeared her face, she could see that she was pretty. White-blond hair hung past her shoulders and framed an oval face. Her eyes, the color of roasted chestnuts, were large, and her tear-spiked lashes were thick and long. In spite of her desire not to, Stephanie found herself searching for a resemblance to Wade but found nothing in the child's features that even remotely reminded her of Wade.

"Are you?" Meghan prodded.

Stephanie firmed her lips, refusing to be suckered by

the girl's puppy-dog look. "Your father entrusted you to my care. Your running away makes me look irresponsible, incompetent, and I don't think that's fair, do you?"

Meghan hung her head. "No, ma'am," she murmured.

Stephanie didn't know if the child's contriteness was an act to draw pity or if she really did feel badly for what she'd done. Whatever her reasons, Stephanie wasn't about to take a chance on her running away again.

"As punishment for disobeying your father's instructions, you're going to help me."

"What do I have to do?"

"Pack." Stephanie motioned for Meghan to follow her. "I've been going through the linen closet," she said tersely as she led the way down the hall. "I've already—" Realizing that Meghan wasn't following, she turned to look behind her and saw that Meghan had stopped in front of her parents' bedroom. "Meghan?" she said in frustration. "What are you doing?"

The girl turned to look at her, and Stephanie was shocked to see that her eyes were filled with tears again.

"What's wrong?" she asked in concern.

Meghan dragged a hand beneath her eyes. "It's just that I haven't been here since Mr. Calloway died and I guess I forgot for a minute, 'cause I expected to see him lying in his bed."

Stephanie gulped, knowing that this was no act. No one could fake the depth of sadness she saw reflected in the child's eyes. "Yeah, I know," she said as she walked to stand with her. "Sometimes I catch myself listening for him, especially around dinnertime."

Sliding an arm around the girl, she urged her away from the door and down the hall. "Did you visit him very often?" she asked, hoping to distract the girl from the image that must surely be stuck in her mind of Bud lying sick in bed.

Meghan lifted a shoulder. "Not too much after he got sick." She pursed her lips. "Daddy was afraid I'd wear him out with my talking."

Chuckling, Stephanie removed a stack of linens from the floor, then sat down on the floor, her back to the wall, and patted the space next to her. "Have a seat," she invited.

Meghan sank down with a youthful ease that Stephanie couldn't help envying.

"So you're a talker, huh?" Stephanie said as she began to sort through the stack of pillowcases.

Meghan stretched her legs out in front of her and tapped the tip of her tennis shoes together. "Daddy seems to think so."

"I guess you knew my mother, too," Stephanie said, curious to discover how well Wade's daughter knew her parents.

"Yeah. When I was little, sometimes she would keep me when I was too sick to go to school and Daddy had something he needed to do." She plucked absently at a thread on her jeans. "When I had chicken pox, I was itching real bad, and she made me an oatmeal bath to soak in. She was always doing nice things like that."

Stephanie had to swallow back emotion before she could reply, ashamed of the resentment she'd felt toward her mother. "Yes, she had a kind heart." Forcing a smile, she picked up one of the stacks of pillowcases she had sorted and passed it to Meghan. "These go in that box over there," she said, pointing. "The one marked Donate."

Hopping up, Meghan moved to place the linens in the box, then returned to sit at Stephanie's side again.

Feeling the child's stare, Stephanie glanced over at her. "What?"

"I was just wondering how come I've never seen you before."

Stephanie quickly looked away. "Well," she said, stalling while she tried to think of a plausible explanation to offer. "I live in Dallas and own a business there. It keeps me pretty busy."

"What kind of business?"

"I'm a photo stylist."

Meghan wrinkled her brow. "What's that?"

Stephanie set the linens she held on her lap, wondering how best to describe her job to a young girl. "You know the advertisements you see in magazines? The ones that have photographs?"

"Yeah."

"I set the scenes for the pictures. I gather all the props, set everything up, then the photographer—and the models, if any are needed—come in and the photographer takes the pictures."

Meghan stared, her eyes wide in wonder. "How cool is that!"

Stephanie chuckled. "It is a cool job. But it can also be a royal pain in the patootee."

"Patootee?" Meghan repeated, then fell over on the floor, laughing. "That's the lamest word I've ever heard."

Stephanie lifted a brow. "Beats getting my mouth washed out with soap for using the more popular expression."

Her eyes rounding, Meghan pushed up to her elbows.

"You mean, Mrs. Calloway washed your mouth out with soap?"

"She certainly did," Stephanie said with a decisive nod. "But it only took twice before I learned not to say words that she didn't approve of."

"Wow."

Amused by the girl's shocked look, Stephanie shook her head and reached for another stack of linens. "So what's your punishment for saying bad words?"

Meghan blinked, then shrugged. "There's not one."

Stephanie gave her a sideways glance. "Oh, please. Surely your father doesn't allow you to say curse words."

"He doesn't exactly *allow* me to curse, but if I slip and say something I shouldn't in front of him, he just gives me a mean look and says, 'You better watch your mouth, young lady.'"

Her impersonation of Wade was so funny Stephanie couldn't help but laugh. "Maybe I should give him some pointers I picked up from my mother."

Meghan grimaced. "Yeah, like he could be any meaner. He rags on me all the time about the way I dress and the music I listen to. And I don't *dare* have the channel turned to MTV when he's at home. If I do, he goes ballistic."

Stephanie drew back to peer at her, unsure whether she should believe her or not. "That doesn't sound like the Wade I know."

"You know my daddy?"

Realizing her mistake, Stephanie looked away and busied herself straightening linens. "He moved to the ranch next door while I was in college," she replied vaguely.

"Do you know my mom, too?"

It was all Stephanie could do to remain upright. "No, I've never met your mother. I was living in Dallas when your parents married."

"Oh," Meghan said, sounding disappointed.

Anxious to change the subject, Stephanie asked, "Are you thirsty?" She heaved herself up from the floor. "I know I am. Let's get a soda."

"Okay."

Stephanie led the way to the kitchen, with Meghan following close on her heels. Just as she stepped inside, the back door opened and Wade walked in.

"Well, hi," she said in surprise. "Meghan and I were about to have a soda. Would you like one?"

"Maybe next time." He tipped his head, indicating his daughter. "Did she give you any trouble?"

Stephanie glanced down and met Meghan's gaze. Seeing the girl's fear, she gave her a reassuring smile. "Nothing I couldn't handle."

Wade shifted his gaze between the two, his expression doubtful, then heaved a sigh and motioned for Meghan to join him. "Come on," he said, already turning for the door. "We need to go."

"Couldn't I stay here with Stephanie?" Meghan asked. "I was helping her pack."

"No, we've got—" He hesitated a moment, then said, "Company waiting."

Meghan's eyes lit with hope. "Mom's here?"

Wade pushed through the door and stepped outside without answering.

Meghan let out an excited squeal and ran after him. At the door she stopped and glanced back. "Thanks for not ratting me out."

Stephanie leveled a finger at her in warning. "Just don't make me regret it."

Meghan grinned. "I won't," she said, then charged out the door, shouting, "Hey, Dad! Wait for me!"

Stephanie tried not to think about Wade's ex being at his house.

But it was hopeless. Every time she pushed the thought from her mind, it dug a new hole and came crawling back in. Deciding that a nice hot bath was what she needed to get Wade's ex off her mind, she headed for her bathroom and turned on the tap. She was stripping off her clothes when her cell phone rang. Grabbing a towel to drape around her, she hurried into the bedroom to answer it.

"Hello," she said breathlessly.

"Were you just going to leave me hanging?"

She winced at the annoyance in Kiki's voice. "Sorry. I've been sort of busy."

"So did the runaway make good her escape?"

Remembering she'd left the water running in the bathroom, Stephanie retraced her steps. "No. I caught her. But I had to tackle her from behind and drag her to the ground to stop her."

"You've got to be kidding!" Kiki cried, then hooted a laugh. "Oh, to have been a fly on the wall and seen that."

Rather proud of her accomplishment, Stephanie buffed her nails against her chest. "It was a clever save, even if I do say so myself."

"Congratulations. Now tell me the good stuff. Why did Wade bring her to you, of all people? Does she know about you and Wade? Did she say anything about her mother? I want the dirt, so start shoveling."

Shaking her head at her friend's outrageousness, Stephanie squirted bath oil beneath the tap. "Has anyone ever told you that you're nosy?"

"Daily. Now spill."

Stephanie tested the water, then dropped the towel and climbed in. "I don't know why Wade brought her here, but I'd guess it was because he had nowhere else to take her. He was in the middle of vaccinating his cattle and couldn't keep an eye on her himself."

"Why didn't he just leave her at home? Good grief. Surely the kid's old enough to stay by herself."

"She is," Stephanie agreed. "But he doesn't trust her. He said she'd threatened to run away."

"Wow. I thought you were exaggerating when you said you were babysitting a juvenile delinquent. Obviously you were being serious."

Growing thoughtful, Stephanie lifted a toe to pop a bubble. "I may be wrong—God knows I don't have any experience with children—but I don't think she's really a bad kid. She certainly doesn't look the part. She has really long white-blond hair and the biggest eyes. She looks…well, almost angelic."

Remembering the belligerent expression on her face when Wade had first dropped her off, she added, "But she has the potential to turn bad. I got a peek of a darker side when Wade first dropped her off. Angry. Hostile. Rebellious. If he doesn't get her in hand fairly soon, I would think she could easily turn into a huge problem for him."

"Bet you five he's suffering from the Guilty Parent Syndrome."

Stephanie choked out a laugh. "The *what?*"

"Guilty Parent Syndrome. You see it all the time in divorce cases. Wade's the one who asked for the divorce, right?"

"That was the talk around town."

"Right. So he's taking heat from the daughter because she blames him for making her mother leave. He feels sorry for the kid, so he goes easy on her, trying to make it up to her. If the kid's smart—and it sounds like she is—she picks up on his guilt and plays him like a piano, and the cycle continues until—bingo!—the kid is a holy terror and totally out of control."

Shaking her head, Stephanie slid farther down into the bubbles. "You need to quit working for me and hang out a shingle. You'd make an excellent psychologist."

"Comes from all the years I spent in therapy."

Stephanie frowned. "Your mother should have been the one in therapy, not you."

"Try telling her that."

Stephanie shuddered at the thought of having any conversation with Kiki's neurotic mother. "Thanks, but I think I'll pass."

"What about the kid's mother? Wade's ex? Did the kid say anything about her?"

"Nothing specific, though she did ask if I knew her."

Kiki whistled softly. "Man, this just gets crazier and crazier. Like a soap opera."

"Tell me about it," Stephanie muttered drily. "The ex is at his house right now."

"Why? Is it her weekend to have the kid or something?"

"How would I know?" Stephanie snapped. "I just know she's there."

"Do I detect a hint of jealousy?"

"Why would I be jealous? They're divorced."

"Which doesn't mean squat. He might be through with her, but that doesn't mean she's through with him."

Since that was the exact thought that Stephanie had hoped to escape by taking a bubble bath, she remained silent, refusing to discuss it.

"Steph?"

"Yes?" she said tersely.

"Just wanted to make sure you were still there."

"I am."

"And obviously don't want to talk about his ex," Kiki deducted, then sighed her disappointment. "Okay, so tell me what you think about the kid after spending the morning with her."

"She's your average twelve-year-old," Stephanie replied, then amended, "except for the ugly rebellious streak."

"So you liked her?"

Stephanie considered the question for a moment and was surprised to find that she did like Meghan. "She's okay," she replied vaguely. "And obviously crazy about her mother."

"Which would make you the ugly stepmother if you and Wade should work things out."

Stephanie scowled, not having to stretch very far to imagine the kind of problems that could create for her and Wade. "Thanks, Kiki. I really appreciate you bringing that to my attention."

"Sorry," Kiki mumbled, then brightened. "But look

at it this way. The kid won't be around forever. She's twelve, so she should be leaving the nest in another five or six years. Then you and Wade would be alone."

If their relationship lasted that long, Stephanie thought sadly. Sharing a house with another woman's child and a bed with that child's father had the potential to destroy even the strongest of relationships.

Giving herself a shake, she said to Kiki, "There's no sense in worrying about that. Wade and I aren't married. We're just…friends."

"Steph?"

Stephanie jumped at the sound of Wade's voice, almost dropping the phone in the water. "In here," she called, then brought the phone back to her ear and whispered frantically to Kiki, "I've got to go. Wade's here."

"Friends, huh?" Kiki snorted a laugh. "I'd say you're more than friends, since you just invited him into the bathroom while you're in the tub."

"Goodbye, Kiki," Stephanie said firmly, then disconnected the phone.

Just as Stephanie leaned to lay the phone on the commode seat, Wade stepped into the bathroom. He stood there a moment, staring, then started toward the tub, unbuttoning his shirt.

Stephanie sputtered a nervous laugh. "What are you doing?"

His gaze on hers, he flipped back his belt buckle and pulled down the zipper on his jeans. "What does it look like I'm doing?"

She watched as he hooked the toe of one boot behind the heel of the other and pried it off, then lifted her gaze to his. "Stripping?" she asked meekly.

He pushed his jeans down his hips, kicked them aside. "No." He gave her a nudge and slipped into the tub behind her. "I'm bathing."

"But where's Meghan?"

He slid his arms around her waist and pressed his lips to the curve of her neck. "At home."

Since he'd claimed he didn't trust Meghan to stay alone, she had to assume her mother was there with her. Although she didn't find that thought at all comforting, Wade was with her, which had to say something about his preferences. She angled her head, giving him better access to her neck. "How long can you stay?"

He dragged his lips down to her shoulder. Nipped. "As long as it takes."

She closed her eyes, stifling a groan. "As long as what takes?" she asked breathlessly.

He turned her around to face him and sent water splashing over the edge. His blue eyes, dark with passion, burned through hers as he drew her legs around his waist. "To satisfy this hunger I have for you."

Water lapped against her body, adding to the sensations created by his erection nudging her belly. Looping her arms around his neck, she smiled as she lowered her face to his. "That might take a while."

"Yeah." He released a sigh against her lips. "That's what I'm hoping."

Later, snuggled against Wade in her bed, Stephanie found herself thinking about something Meghan had said to her that morning. "Wade?" she said hesitantly.

More asleep than awake, he hummed a lazy response.

"Meghan said something this morning that concerns me."

He groaned and buried his face between her breasts. "Please tell me she wasn't rude."

Biting back a smile at the dread she heard in his voice, she ran her fingers through his hair to reassure him. "No, though I have to admit, when you first dropped her off, she was sporting a pretty tough attitude."

Sighing, he drew his head back and placed it on the pillow opposite hers. "She's *always* sporting an attitude. That's nothing new."

"This has nothing to do with her attitude. It's something she said."

"What?"

"We were talking about cursing, and I told her that when I said a curse word, my mother would wash my mouth out with soap."

He smiled softly, as if at a fond memory. "My mom did that, too."

"Meghan said that when she says a bad word, you don't punish her."

"I damn sure do," he said defensively, then waved away Stephanie's concern. "She was pulling your leg, blowing hot air."

"I don't think so." Stephanie knew she was taking a chance on alienating Wade by discussing his daughter with him, but Meghan's comment concerned her enough that she felt she should speak her mind. "She said you only give her a mean look and tell her to watch her mouth."

His brows drew together. "So? That's the same as telling her I don't approve of that kind of talk."

Stephanie laid a hand against his chest, hoping to take the sting out of what she was about to say. "Maybe you need to be a little more firm. Let her know that in the future there will be specific consequences for bad behavior."

"And you think washing her mouth out with soap is going to keep her from cussing?" He snorted a breath. "Sure as hell didn't break me."

She pursed her lips. "Obviously not. The point is, Meghan doesn't seem to think there are any consequences for her actions. A mean look from you isn't enough of a deterrent. You need to be firmer with her. Establish rules and set specific punishments to be implemented when she breaks them."

He lifted a brow. "Oh? And how many children have you raised?"

For a moment Stephanie could only stare, his careless remark cutting deeply. "I haven't," she said and rolled away, swinging her legs over the side of the bed. "I was only offering an opinion after spending some time with your daughter."

He caught her arm, stopping her before she could stand. "Hey," he said softly. "I didn't mean that the way it sounded."

When she kept her face averted, refusing to look at him, he tugged her down to lie beside him again. "I'm sorry, Steph." He laid a hand on her cheek. "You're probably right. Maybe I am too easy on Meghan. But sometimes I just flat don't know what to do with her. You have no idea what kind of crap kids are getting into these days. Body piercings and tattoos, not to mention sex and drugs. She's twelve going on twenty-two. I try to keep a tight rein on her, hoping to keep her out of trouble. But she kicks and screams about how strict I am and threatens to run away and live with her mother. I'm afraid if I come down on her too hard, she will."

"Maybe she should live with her mother."

By the look on Wade's face, Stephanie knew she'd said the wrong thing.

"Wade," she said and reached for him, wanting to explain.

He shoved her hand aside and rolled from the bed and to his feet to face her. "You think her mother would do a better job of raising her?" he asked angrily. Without waiting for an answer, he strode to the bathroom, scooped up his clothes and returned, jerking on his jeans. "Well, let me tell you something Dr. Know-It-All," he said, pointing a stiff finger at her face. "On my worst day I'm a better parent than Angela will ever be. I fought for custody of Meghan for that very reason and won. Angela's nothing but a—" He clamped his lips together and spun for the door, pulling on his shirt.

Stephanie bolted from the bed and grabbed a robe, shrugging it on as she ran after him.

"Wade, wait!"

He didn't even slow down.

She caught up with him at the front door and grabbed his arm. When he tried to jerk free, she tightened her grip. "No," she said, her anger rising to match his. "You're not leaving until I have a chance to explain. I wasn't suggesting that you are a bad parent. Meghan's a *girl,* Wade, and a young girl needs her mother. If she were a boy, maybe it would be different. But she's not a boy. She's a *girl* and she's at an age where she needs to talk about things that she may not feel comfortable talking about with you. That's why I said what I did. I was simply suggesting that maybe she needs a mother right now more than she does a father. I wasn't suggesting that her mother is a better parent than you. How could I? I don't even know the woman."

He grabbed her arms, making her blink in surprise. "No, you don't know her. If you did, you'd understand why I've fought so hard to keep Meghan away from her. Why I insist that a court-appointed guardian be present at all times when she visits Meghan. Angela is a drug addict, a whore who'll sell herself to any man who'll give her another fix."

He dropped his hands from her arms and took a step back, suddenly looking tired, beaten. "Do you know how I know that, Steph?" he asked quietly. "I know because I was once one of those men."

Seven

Stephanie walked around in a daze the next morning, still numbed by Wade's confession. She couldn't believe he'd ever been the kind of man he'd described. Sure, when they'd first started dating, he'd told her a little about his life prior to his move to the ranch next to her parents. How he'd gone a little crazy after his parents' deaths and done some things he wasn't proud of. But Wade involved in drugs? Associating with a woman like the one he described Angela to be? She couldn't believe it. He was so straight, so *good*.

Frustrated by her inability to come to grips with the man he'd described to her, she moved to the front window and looked out. What difference does it make if he had done those things? she asked herself. He wasn't the same person he was back then. That was all in the past. He'd changed, made a fresh start. He was a good person, kind. Hadn't he looked out for Bud after her mother had died? Hadn't he comforted Stephanie when he'd found her crying over her father's letters? Hadn't he fought for custody of his daughter, wanting to protect her from the environment in which her mother lived? A man who did those things wasn't a bad person. He was good and kind.

She should've told him that, she realized with a suddenness that clutched at her chest. She shouldn't have let him walk out of her house without telling him that his past didn't matter. That he was a wonderful man, kind and generous, and that she loved him with all her heart.

She glanced at her watch and was surprised to see that it was past noon, the time that Wade usually dropped off a bundle of letters for her to read. Praying that nothing had happened at home that would have prevented him from leaving, she hurried to the front door, wanting to make sure he hadn't gone on to the barn and pastures without stopping first.

Two steps onto the porch her left foot connected with something hard, making her stumble. Catching herself from falling, she glanced down to see what she'd tripped over and found a box sitting on the porch. Her heart seemed to stop for a moment when she recognized it as the one Wade had used the night he'd carried away the bundles of her father's letters.

She stooped to pick it up, wondering why he'd left it for her to find rather than bringing it inside. And why would he drop off the entire box instead of the usual single bundle?

She gulped, afraid she already knew the answer. She'd let him leave the night before without telling him that his past didn't matter to her, without assuring him of her love. She'd even suggested he allow his daughter to live with his ex, told him that she couldn't consider marrying him because she couldn't bear the thought of living with the child who would serve as a daily reminder of the choice Wade had made and all the hurt she'd suffered at his hand.

She'd let him down. When he'd needed her most, she had denied him her love, her understanding, and instead chose to batter him with the resentment she had hoarded through the years, the bitterness she had clung to.

Her heart heavy, her eyes filled with tears of regret, she gathered the box close and went back inside.

Janine,
I don't know how I survived the year I spent in Vietnam before I met you. Your letters are what keep me going, what help me deal with the tragedy and death I see every day.

I've just about worn out the pictures of you I brought with me. I can't tell you the number of times a day I pull them out just to look at them, to remind myself that there is a world beyond the hell I'm living in right now, one where there is normalcy, laughter and love.

Sometimes it's hard to remember what it's like back home. To sleep without being afraid someone is going to slip up on you in the night and slit your throat. To walk without fear of stepping on a mine or a booby trap. To be able to eat food other than C-rations. To wear clothes that aren't all but rotting off my body.

I don't understand this war. Why people would want to kill each other. Surely there's a better way to resolve differences, to make peace between nations and keep it. The loss of lives—on both sides—is unimaginable, and that's without considering the lives of the people that are destroyed or changed forever by the loss of their loved ones.

A couple of guys I knew back home went to Canada to avoid the draft. At the time I remember thinking they were cowards for choosing to leave their country rather than fight for it. Now I'm not so sure. I still don't believe I ever would've run, even knowing what I know now. But I don't feel the same about the guys who did *choose to run. I don't consider them cowards anymore. Doing what they did took courage. Granted, it was a different kind of courage than the one required to stand and fight. But it took guts to do what they did. Leaving your home and family behind and knowing that you may never see them again… well, that takes a certain kind of courage, too. In some ways, it's the same sacrifice or chance a soldier makes when he puts on a uniform and goes to war.*

Unable to read any more, Stephanie let the letter drop to her lap and stared out the window at the darkness beyond the house. Her father had only been twenty-one when he'd written the letter, yet there was a wisdom in his words, a wealth of experience which exceeded that of most men his age. Women, too, she thought. At twenty-one she'd been in her third year of college and living in an apartment in Dallas, near the campus of Southern Methodist University, and without a care in the world. Her education was paid for by her parents, who covered her living expenses, as well, which allowed her to focus on her studies without worrying about supporting herself. The only fear she had faced was making good grades in the courses she was enrolled in, and the only tragedy she'd suffered was when Wade had broken their engagement.

The latter had been devastating and it had taken weeks, months even, for her to drag herself from the depression that losing him had plunged her into. But she hadn't resurfaced fully healed or unscathed from the occurrence. From the darkness she'd brought with her her resentment toward Wade, and used it like a talisman to keep herself from ever being hurt again.

The broken engagement had changed her life in so many ways…most not very flattering. She'd remained in Dallas but had withdrawn from her classes, which had put her a semester behind in graduating. For months she'd refused to come home, unable to bear the thought of possibly bumping into Wade and his new wife. She'd let that fear control her actions for years, making only brief visits home to see her parents and, while there, refusing to step so much as a foot outside their house.

And she'd allowed the breakup to affect more than just her family life. For more than a year she had refused to go out on any of the dates her friends set up for her. And when she had finally begun dating again, she'd kept a firm grip on her emotions, her feelings, determined to never let a man hurt her again.

But the most regrettable fallout from their breakup

was holding on to her anger with Wade and never forgiving him for hurting her. In the days immediately following their breakup she'd refused to see him or talk to him. It was easy enough to do. She'd simply monitored her phone calls and deleted the messages he'd left on her answering machine without listening to them, tore up the letters he'd sent without ever opening them.

She dropped her chin in shame as she realized the domino effect her stubbornness and bitterness had had on the people she loved most—as well as many whose lives she'd touched only briefly. By stubbornly refusing to visit her parents more often, she had foolishly robbed herself of precious time she could have spent with them. And by not granting Wade her forgiveness, she'd thought she could punish him, and all but reveled in the guilt she knew he carried.

She didn't deserve his love, she told herself miserably. He'd tried so many times to tell her he was sorry, begged her repeatedly for her forgiveness. Yet in spite of her spitefulness, when he'd found her crying over her father's letters, he'd comforted her. Offered her his ear, as well as his shoulder to cry on, when he'd insisted upon being with her when she read the letters that remained.

And what had she given him in return? she asked herself. Had she given him her forgiveness when he'd admitted making a mistake? Offered him her understanding when he'd shared with her his past? Her acceptance when he'd asked her to share his life with him and his daughter?

No, she thought, shaking her head sadly. She'd used his mistake like a battering ram to beat him with. Remained silent, horrified even, as he'd confessed to a past that still shamed him. And she'd refused his proposal to share his life with him, insisting that she needed time to come to grips with her resentment toward his daughter.

She'd promised she'd be his friend, told him that she loved him. But how could a woman who professed those things turn her back on a man when he most needed her understanding and her love?

She rose, the letter she'd been reading falling to the floor, forgotten. She had to talk to him, she told herself and hurried for the door. See him. Tell him that his past didn't matter. Grant him the full forgiveness that she'd selfishly withheld. And she would deal with her conflicting feelings for his daughter, she told herself as she climbed into her car. Perhaps even help him see that Meghan needed his discipline as much as she needed his love.

It didn't occur to Stephanie that Wade's ex-wife might still be at his house until she pulled to a stop and saw the strange car parked on the drive. For a moment she was tempted to turn around and return home. She didn't want to meet his ex, doubted she could look the woman in the face without wanting to claw her eyes out.

But she couldn't let another moment pass without sharing her heart with Wade. Stiffening her resolve, she climbed out.

In spite of the lateness of the hour, a light burned in the kitchen window. Hoping not to disturb the entire household, she walked around back. At the door she hesitated a moment, then squared her shoulders and knocked.

She jumped, startled, when the door was immediately snatched open and a woman appeared in the space.

Backlit by the overhead light in the kitchen, the woman's face was shadowed, but Stephanie had a feeling she was confronting Wade's ex-wife for the first time.

Gulping, she asked uneasily, "Is Wade here?"

"Who wants to know?"

Stephanie set her jaw at the woman's hostile tone. "Stephanie Calloway. I'm a neighbor."

The woman gave her a slow look up and down, then stepped back and shouted, "Wade! That snotty little bitch from next door is here to see you."

Stephanie stared, while shock and anger fought for dominance of her emotions. Managing to push both back, she jutted her chin and strode inside.

Wade's ex had moved to the sink and was standing with her hips braced against its edge, her lips pursed in a smirk. Bone-thin, she wore a shockingly short denim skirt and a low-cut tank top. Her breasts—obviously silicone-enhanced—were as large as grapefruits and looked totally out of proportion to her emaciated frame.

"Didn't your mother teach you any manners?" the woman snapped, making Stephanie jump. "It's rude to stare."

Her cheeks flaming, Stephanie tore her gaze away. "I'm sorry. I didn't mean to—"

"Steph?"

She spun to find Wade standing in the doorway that opened from the kitchen to the den. She sagged her shoulders, almost weak with relief at seeing him. "I'm sorry to barge in like this. I had no idea you had—"

The woman quickly shifted in front of Stephanie, blocking her view of Wade.

"Well, well, well," she said as she folded her arms

across her chest and gave Stephanie another slow look up and down. "Looks like I've screwed up your plans." She lifted a brow plucked pencil-thin and added pointedly, *"Again."*

"That's enough, Angela," Wade warned.

She kept her gaze on Stephanie and smiled. "Oh, I don't think so. In fact, I haven't even gotten started good yet. I've wanted to give this lady a piece of mind for years."

"Angela," he warned again and took a step toward her.

"What's wrong, sugar?" Though her eyes were fixed on Stephanie, her question was directed at Wade. "Afraid I'll say something you don't want Miss Goody Two-shoes to hear?"

Wade lunged and caught Angela's elbow, whirled her around. "I said enough, Angela," he said, then released her and pointed a stiff finger at the hall and the stairs beyond. "Now go upstairs before you make me do something we'll both regret."

She shoved her face within inches of his. "You can't tell me what to do. Not anymore. I followed your orders for six long years, while you tried to shape me into what you considered the perfect wife. Well, guess what, Wade?" She opened her arms wide. "I'm not perfect and I never was. Not even while I was pretending to be the Stepford wife you wanted me to be. While you were off working, I'd drop Meghan off at day care and drive to Austin and have me a good ol' time. Those college boys really know how to party. All the booze and drugs I wanted, and all they expected from me in return was a piece of my ass."

He grabbed for her again, but she ducked to the side,

managing to dodge him. "I like drugs and the way they make me feel," she said, then smiled and dragged a fingernail down between her breasts. "And I like sleeping with a different man every night, especially one who isn't grieving over some old flame."

"I'm warning you, Angela," Wade said, his face red with rage, "either you shut up or I'll fix it so you'll never see our daughter again."

"*Our* daughter?" she repeated, then dropped her head back and laughed, the sound so evil it sent a shiver chasing down Stephanie's spine.

"Meghan isn't *your* daughter," she said. "I just told you that so you'd have to marry me. You thought you could just up and leave me in Houston, taking all your money with you." She snorted a laugh. "Well, I showed you, didn't I? You and Miss Goody Two-shoes here had your future all planned out, but I messed things up for you good, didn't I, when I showed up in town pregnant out to here."

Wade grabbed her again, and this time Angela was too slow to dodge him. He all but dragged her from the room and to the stairs, with her kicking and cursing him every step of the way.

Stephanie stood as if her feet had rooted to the floor, sickened by the ugly scene she'd just witnessed, the infidelities Angela had confessed to. She remained there, a hand pressed to her stomach, forcing herself to take slow, deep breaths until the nausea slowly faded and only one statement remained to circle in her mind.

Meghan isn't your daughter.

She closed her eyes, hearing again the vindictiveness in Angela's voice, envisioning the hate it had carved into her features as she'd hurled the confession like a knife to pierce Wade's heart.

Wade, she thought, and her gaze went instinctively to the stairs, wondering if it was true that he wasn't Meghan's father. Angela might only have said that to hurt him. To punish him for the injustices she felt she'd suffered at his hand.

As she continued to stare at the spot where she'd last seen him, Wade appeared on the stairway, his steps slow, his shoulders stooped as if he was burdened beneath the weight of the world. She started toward him, then stopped and wrung her hands at her waist, unsure what to say to him, what to do.

"Wade?" she said hesitantly.

He glanced her way, held her gaze a moment, then continued down the stairs.

She watched, her breath burning a hole in her chest as he reached the end and turned toward her.

"I'm sorry you had to listen to all that. You didn't deserve to hear any of what she said."

She shook her head, unable to push a word past the emotion that clotted her throat. Catching his hands, desperate for that contact, she gave them a reassuring squeeze. "It's not your fault. I should've called first. It never even occurred to me that she might still be here. I was so anxious to see you, talk to you, I didn't think about anything else. When you didn't come by at noon, I went outside and found the box of letters on the porch. When I saw it, I knew it meant you didn't want to see me, that you probably wouldn't be coming by anymore."

Tears filled her eyes, and she stubbornly blinked them back.

"But it wasn't until earlier this evening, after I'd read one of my dad's letters, that I realized it was all my fault. I let you leave last night without telling you how I feel. I should have told you then that your past doesn't matter to me, that I love you with all my heart and that I want to marry you."

Throughout her speech, he had listened quietly, his gaze steady on hers. And now that she was done, had said everything that was in her heart, and he still said nothing, she felt a moment's unease.

"Wade?" she asked hesitantly. "Is something wrong?"

"You didn't mention Meghan. When I asked you to marry me, you said you needed time, that you didn't think you could live in my house with her there as a constant reminder of the past."

"Yes, I did say that, but that's not a problem anymore."

"Why? Because Angela said that Meghan isn't mine?"

Numbed by the chill in his voice, the steely gleam in his eye, she shook her head. "Well, no. Of course not. I—"

Pulling his hands from hers, he took a step back. "What Angela said was true…to a point. Until the day Meghan was born, I did think she was mine. But when the nurse told me that Meghan weighed only four pounds and was considered a preemie, I knew that Angela had lied and was trying to stick me with another man's child.

"But here's a news flash for you, Steph," he continued. "It didn't matter. Not to me. Not then, and it sure as hell doesn't now. From the moment that doctor put Meghan in my arms she was mine. There was no way I was going to walk away from that baby and leave her with Angela to raise. I knew what kind of person Angela was, how she lived. And I knew that was the kind of life Meghan would have if I walked out on her. That's why when I divorced Angela I fought so hard for custody of Meghan."

Shaking his head, he took another step back, putting even more distance between him and Stephanie. "But it was more than Angela's lifestyle that made me want to keep Meghan with me. I love that girl as if she were my own. And because I love her, I would never marry a woman who didn't love her as much I do, who wasn't willing to put Meghan's happiness above her own. That's what parents do, Steph. They love their children unconditionally. Even when that child is not their own flesh and blood."

He turned and walked away.

Stephanie made the short drive home, her eyes fixed on the road ahead, her hands gripped tightly around the steering wheel. The tears were there in her throat, behind her eyes, yet she couldn't cry. She needed to. Oh, God, how she needed to.

She'd lost him. She'd allowed her resentment and bitterness to cost her a second chance to be with the one man she'd ever loved.

She didn't deserve to cry, she told herself. Didn't deserve the release it offered, the emptying of all emotion. She'd let him down. The man who had freely and generously offered to share everything he cherished most in the world—his heart, his daughter, his home— she'd let him down when he'd needed her most.

She understood now why he'd become so angry with

her for referring to Bud by his given name rather than her usual "Dad," and for what he considered her careless disregard of Bud's favorite possessions. He was bound to have seen himself in Bud, as they'd both raised daughters that weren't their own, and he'd probably feared that someday Meghan might find her real father and transfer her affection and allegiance to him, as Wade had thought Stephanie had transferred hers to her biological father.

Wade was wrong, though. Stephanie's determination to get to know her real father in no way changed how she felt about Bud. He was the only father she had ever known. He'd raised her, cared for her, loved her, and she would always love him. He was her father in every way but blood, and nothing would ever change that.

But she'd never have the chance to tell Wade that. She'd let him down, and now he was gone from her life forever.

For two days Stephanie packed like a wild woman, managing to accomplish more in that short space of time than she had in the entire previous week. Twice she saw Wade drive by the house on his way to check on the cattle, and though she watched from the window, praying with all her heart that he would stop, he passed by without so much as glancing toward the house. Each time, her heart would sink a little lower in her chest, and she would resume her packing, more determined than ever to finish the job and return to Dallas, putting as much distance as possible between her and the memories that haunted her.

On the third day, with most of the packing complete,

she placed a call to Bud's attorney and scheduled an appointment for that afternoon, then phoned a moving company and made arrangements to have the items she planned to save picked up on Friday and hauled to a storage facility in Dallas.

As she walked through the house on her way to her bedroom to shower and dress for her appointment with the attorney, an indescribable sadness slipped over her. The walls she passed were blank, save for the occasional rectangle of brighter paint where a picture had once hung. Boxes and furniture lined the walls and segmented the rooms, creating walkways that led from one room to the other. By Friday afternoon the house would be completely empty, listed for sale, and within a few short months, according to the Realtor she'd spoken to, a new owner would be moving in.

At the doorway to her bedroom she stopped and looked back down the hall, her heart breaking a little at the thought of another family living in the house she'd considered home for most of her life. Closing her eyes, she could almost hear the sounds that had once filled the house. The slam of the back door and Bud's voice as he called his standard greeting of, "When's dinner? I'm starving." The bark of the dog that always followed him in. Her mother fussing, "Wipe your feet, Bud Calloway! I just mopped that floor." The whir of the box fan that Bud kept aimed at his recliner in the summer months to keep him cool. The steady ticktock, ticktock of the clock that had sat on the fireplace mantel for more years than Stephanie could remember. Bud's soft call of, "'Night, Stephie," as he passed by her door on the way to his room.

Dragging an arm across the moisture that filled her eyes, she turned into her bedroom.

Stephanie settled in the chair opposite the lawyer's desk and offered Mr. Banks, Bud's attorney, a smile. "I appreciate you making time for me on such short notice."

He waved away her thanks. "No problem. I know you're anxious to get back to your own home and your work."

Stephanie released a long breath. "Yes, I am."

Getting down to business, Banks shuffled through the papers on his desk, then passed Stephanie a sheaf of papers he pulled from the stack. "A copy of Bud's will," he explained, then settled back in his chair, holding his own copy before him. "Most of this is standard language and the bequeaths what you'd expect, so I'll only bring to your attention the things I think might overly concern you or that you might question the validity of."

Stephanie looked at him curiously. "Why would I question anything? I'm familiar with Bud's wishes. He gave me a copy of his will shortly after Mom passed away."

Mr. Banks averted his gaze. "Well, uh—" He cleared his throat. "Well, you see, uh, Bud made a few changes."

A chill of premonition chased down Stephanie's spine. "What kind of changes?"

He flapped a hand, indicating the papers she held. "If you'll turn to page six, paragraph three." While she flipped pages, looking for the spot mentioned, he went on to explain, "As Bud's only child, you inherit everything. All stocks, bonds, insurance policies, the house and all its contents." He paused to clear his throat, then added, "But Bud left the land to Wade Parker."

Stunned, Stephanie could only stare. "He left the ranch to Wade?"

His expression grim, Banks nodded. "I know you must be shocked to learn this and I regret that it's my duty to deliver the news. I tried to get Bud to talk to you about it before he made the change, but he refused. Said he couldn't."

Stephanie choked out a laugh as the irony of the bequest set in. "No, Bud would never have mentioned Wade's name to me."

Banks leaned forward, his face creased with sympathy. "I'm sorry to be the one to tell you all this," he said with real regret. "I can only imagine how upsetting it must be for you. But I assure you, Bud was in sound mind when he made the change. I would never have done what he asked if I hadn't been absolutely sure he was sane."

Stephanie offered Banks a soft smile, hoping to ease his concern. "You needn't worry. I have no intention of contesting Bud's will. He knew that I wasn't interested in the land or in returning to Georgetown. Giving the land to Wade was his way of seeing that his ranch remained intact and wasn't cut up into a subdivision."

"He did mention that he feared that was what would happen to the place if it were ever put up for sale."

Rising, Stephanie extended her hand. "Thank you, Mr. Banks. I appreciate your concern for me. I truly do. But you can rest assured that I will honor Bud's wishes and will do nothing to stand in the way of Wade obtaining the deed to my father's ranch."

* * *

Late that night, unable to sleep, Stephanie sat on the front porch swing, slowly swaying back and forth, thinking over what Bud had done. Mr. Banks had been right when he'd assumed that Stephanie would be shocked by the discovery. She was more than shocked. She was stunned.

But that had lasted only a moment or two. She knew better than anyone how much Bud had loved his ranch, and it made perfect sense to her that he would want someone to have it who would love it as much as he had. Not that Stephanie didn't have strong feelings about the home where she was raised. She did. But she'd never made a secret of the fact that she had no desire to ever live there again. The truth was, she'd avoided coming home most of her adult life. Even though that must have hurt Bud, he had never held it against her. He'd loved her unconditionally throughout his life and, after his death, had generously left her with everything that was his, with the exception of his land.

Wade was the natural choice to receive the ranch. He would honor the gift and care for the land as much—if not more than—Bud had, and certainly more than Stephanie ever would. He'd already proved his dependability by taking care of things for Bud when Bud's health had declined, making it difficult, if not impossible, for him to do his chores himself. The gift to Wade was a large one, the value of the land alone worth probably close to a million dollars. But Wade would never sell the land to get the money it would bring. He had plenty of his own.

Closing her eyes, Stephanie examined her heart,

searching for any signs of resentment or bitterness toward Wade for receiving something that by all rights should have been hers. Oddly she felt nothing but a swell of pride that Bud had thought enough of Wade to give him something that had meant so much to him.

Sighing, she laid her head back and pushed a bare toe against the floor of the porch, setting the swing into motion again. Tomorrow the movers would come, she reminded herself, and she would be returning to Dallas and her own home.

She remembered when she'd first arrived to clean out her parents' house, she'd been anxious to close this chapter of her life once and for all and return to Dallas and her home there.

Now the mere thought of leaving made her want to cry.

Eight

Runt's sharp bark all but snatched Stephanie from a deep sleep and into a sitting position on the bed. Her heart thumping, she looked around.

"What is it, Runt?" she whispered.

He barked again, then trotted to the bedroom door.

Stephanie swung her legs over the side of the bed and grabbed her robe, pulling it on. Just as she reached the door, she heard a loud pounding.

"Steph? Open up! It's me. Wade."

Fully awake now, she flung open her bedroom door and ran down the hall, dodging boxes as she passed through the den. When she reached the front door, she fumbled the lock open, then flipped on the porch light as she swung the door wide, sure that he had come to reconcile with her.

Seeing the worry that etched his face, she wrapped

her robe more tightly around her and stepped outside. "What's wrong? Has something happened?"

"It's Meghan. She's gone. She was in bed asleep not more than four hours ago and now she's gone."

"Are you sure?"

"Of course I'm sure," he shouted impatiently. "I've searched the house, the barn, and there's no sign of her anywhere. I thought maybe she had come over here."

"Here?" she repeated, stunned that he would think Meghan would run away to her house.

Dragging a hand over his hair, he paced in front of her. "She likes you. Was mad when I wouldn't let her come back over and help you pack."

Stephanie gulped, unaware that Meghan had felt anything toward her, much less affection. Gathering the collar of her robe to her neck, she shook her head. "I haven't seen her. Have you called any of her friends."

"No. I hated to wake people up in the middle of the night until I was sure she was missing. I was so sure I'd find her here." He stopped and dropped his head back. "Oh, God," he moaned, his face contorted with what looked like pain. "She's gone to Angela's. I know she has."

Stephanie shuddered at the very suggestion, understanding Wade's concern, then set her jaw, knowing one of them had to remain calm. "You don't know that she has. Have you called Angela? Maybe she's talked to Meghan, knows where she is."

"I tried. She didn't answer, which doesn't surprise me." He scowled. "She was mad at me when she left the other day."

"How she feels about you isn't important right now,"

Stephanie reminded him firmly. "Meghan's safety is what you need to focus on. Now think. Where would she go? Who would she call?"

Wade tossed up his hands. "Hell, I don't know! When she's threatened to run away in the past, it's always been to her mother's. There isn't any other place I can think of where she'd go."

"Houston is almost three hours from here," Stephanie said, trying to think things out. "She couldn't very well walk there." Her eyes sharpened. "The bus station," she said and grabbed Wade's arm, shoving him toward his truck. "She'd probably catch a bus. Check there. Show her picture around. See if anyone remembers seeing her."

Wade dug in his heels. "But she'd have to get to town first."

Stephanie yanked open the door of his truck. "She could've walked. Hitchhiked. How she got there isn't important, and the more time you waste, the colder her trail is going to grow." She gave him a push. "Go! Find her and bring her home."

His expression grim, Wade started the ignition. "If she shows up here or contacts you—"

"I'll call you on your cell," she said, cutting him off. "And you call me if you find her."

Nodding, he slammed the door and gunned the engine and drove off with a squeal of tires.

Hugging her arms around her waist, Stephanie moved to stand in the middle of the drive and watched until his taillights disappeared from sight.

Drawing a deep breath, she turned for the house, knowing she wouldn't get a wink of sleep until she knew Meghan was safe and praying that Meghan was with one of her girlfriends and not on her way to Houston and Angela's house.

Her eyes burning from lack of sleep and her nerves tingling with worry, Stephanie walked through the house, directing the movers as they loaded the furniture and the boxes she'd marked as keepers.

Wade had called around four o'clock that morning to let her know that Meghan had bought a bus ticket for Houston and he was on his way there, hoping to intercept her before she reached Angela's. Since then, the phone had remained frustratingly silent.

She wanted desperately to call him, but each time she reached for the phone, she pulled her hand back, telling herself that he would contact her if there was any news.

Her nerves shot, she watched the movers load the last piece of furniture into the van. "I gave you the address of the storage facility, right?" she asked.

The driver patted his pocket. "Yes, ma'am. Got it right here."

She forced a smile. "Okay, then. I guess you're all set."

He lifted a hand in acknowledgment, then climbed behind the wheel while his partner hopped up onto the passenger seat on the opposite side.

With nothing left for her to do, Stephanie returned to the house and closed the front door behind her. The sound echoed hollowly in the empty house. She looked around, unsure what to do. One of the local charities had sent a truck by earlier in the day to pick up the items she had opted to donate. All that remained to signify the passing of her parents' lives was the huge pile of trash bags out back, and that, too, would be gone by morning, as she'd made arrangements with a garbage company to have it hauled off.

She'd originally planned to leave right after the moving van pulled out. Her bag was already packed and propped by the back door. But she couldn't leave now. Not with Meghan still missing. Worried that the phone company had misunderstood her instructions and shut off the phone today, rather than next week as she'd requested, she hurried to the kitchen and picked up the phone to make sure it was still working. Hearing the buzz of the dial tone, she replaced the receiver quickly, fearing she'd miss Wade's call.

"No news is good news," she reminded herself. Finding no consolation in the old adage, she began to pace—and nearly jumped out of her skin when the phone rang.

Leaping for it, she snatched the receiver to her ear. "Hello?"

"She's not at Angela's. Nobody is."

She pressed her fingers to her lips, her heart breaking at the defeat she heard in Wade's voice. "What are you going to do now?"

"I'm staying here. I know a couple of Angela's old hangouts, people she used to run around with. I'm going to make the rounds, find out if anybody has seen her."

"But what if Meghan comes back home? If you're gone, she might leave again."

"I was hoping you would go over there. Keep her there until I could get back."

"Of course I will."

"There's a key under the mat at the back door."

"I'll find it."

She started to hang up, but Wade's voice stopped her. "Steph?"

She pressed the phone back to her ear. "Yes?"

"Thanks."

Tears filled her eyes, but before she could respond, the dial tone buzzed in her ear, letting her know that he'd broken the connection.

Stephanie felt odd being in Wade's house. She was familiar with his home's layout, as she'd spent a lot of time there the summer they'd dated, but she chose to remain in the kitchen and near the phone hanging on the wall.

She made a pot of coffee to keep herself awake and drained cup after cup while sitting at the table. The clock on the oven recorded a digital time of 10:00 p.m., reminding Stephanie that she'd been at his house for over four hours.

The phone rang, startling her, and she lunged for it, catching it on the second ring.

"Hello?" she said breathlessly.

"Wade Parker, please."

Disappointed that it wasn't Wade calling, she brushed the hair back from her face. "I'm sorry, but he isn't in right now. Can I take a message?"

"No, I need to speak with him directly."

She frowned, wondering at the insistency in the man's voice. "I have his cell number. Would you like to try that?"

"I've already tried his cell. The call went straight to his voice mail. Hang on a second."

Her frown deepening, she listened, trying to make out what was being said, but whoever was on the other end of the line had covered the mouthpiece with his hand.

"Who am I talking to?"

Surprised by the question, she said, "Stephanie Calloway. I'm a neighbor."

"Just a sec."

Again the man covered the mouthpiece. Stephanie tightened her hand on the receiver, wondering if the call had something to do with Meghan.

"There's a young girl here who wants to speak to you," the man said.

The next voice Stephanie heard was Meghan's.

"Stephanie?" she said and sniffed. "Do you know where my daddy is?"

Fearing Meghan would hang up before Stephanie found out where she was, she said, "Where are you, Meghan? Your father is worried sick."

Meghan sniffed again, then said tearfully, "At the police station. In Austin."

Stephanie's eyes shot wide. A thousand questions crowded her tongue, but she couldn't ask them. Now was not the time. "Sweetheart, your daddy is in Houston looking for you."

Meghan burst into tears, and Stephanie had to swallow hard to keep from crying, too. "Meghan, listen to me," she said firmly. "Is the man with you a police officer?"

"Y-yes, ma'am."

"Let me speak to him."

"Okay. Stephanie?"

"Yes, sweetheart?"

"Will you come and get me?"

"Oh, honey," Stephanie moaned, her heart breaking at the pleading in the girl's voice. "I don't know if they'll release you to me. I'm not family."

"Please," Meghan begged and began to cry again. "I'm so scared."

"I'm on my way," Stephanie said quickly, having to raise her voice to be heard over Meghan's sobbing. "Give the phone back to the police officer so he can give me directions."

It was Stephanie's first visit to a police station…and she prayed it was her last. She supposed it could be the lateness of the hour that made the place appear so spooky, but she wouldn't bet on it. People—hoodlums, judging by their appearance—lounged outside the building and stood in loose groups in the hallway inside. Hugging her purse to her side for fear one of the thugs eyeing her would snatch it, she approached the desk.

"I'm here to see Meghan Parker," she told the officer on duty.

He looked at her, his expression bored. "You family?"

"No. A friend."

He shook his head. "We can only release her to a family member."

She bit down on her temper. "I'm aware of that, but she's just a child and she's frightened. I only want to stay with her until her father can get here."

He lifted a brow. "He's on his way? Last I heard, he couldn't be reached."

Anxious to see Meghan, she balled her hands to keep herself from throttling the man. "That's true, but I've left him a message on his cell phone and I'm sure as soon as he receives it he'll get here as quickly as he can. Now may I please see Meghan?"

With a shrug he stood and motioned her to follow him. He led her down a long hall and stopped before a door marked Interview and gave her a warning look. "Don't try sneaking her out. You'll only get yourself thrown in jail. She's a minor and can only be released to a family member."

She burned him with a look. "You needn't worry. I have an aversion to jails and have no intention of staying here a second longer than is necessary." Pushing past him, she opened the door.

Meghan was stretched out on a grouping of chairs, her face buried in the crook of her arm. She looked so small lying there. So incredibly young.

"Meghan?" Stephanie called softly.

Meghan sat up, blinked. Her eyes rounded when she saw Stephanie, then she shot off the chairs and into Stephanie's arms.

"Oh, Stephanie," she sobbed. "I was so scared you wouldn't come."

"Shh," Stephanie soothed. "There's no need to cry. I'm here and I'm going to stay with you until your dad arrives. Now why don't you tell me what happened? Why did you run away?"

Meghan's sobs grew louder. "Mom said Daddy didn't want me anymore. That I wasn't his. She told me to go to the bus station and buy a ticket to Houston. I did, but then she came to the station and got me. Said the ticket was just to fool dad. She took me to Austin and to a friend of her's house. It was awful," she cried and clung tighter to Stephanie. "People were snorting coke and doing all kinds of bad things.

"I begged her to leave. Take me somewhere else. But she wouldn't. She told me to shut up and have some fun for a change. I was so scared. These men kept looking at me all weirdlike. So I went into the bathroom and locked the door."

Stephanie stroked a hand down Meghan's hair, horrified to think of what might have happened to Meghan, the danger her mother had placed her in. "That was a very smart thing for you to do."

"I thought so, too. But then the police came and started beating on the door. Only I didn't know it was the police. I was crying and screaming for them to go away, and they beat the door down. I tried to tell the cop that I didn't want to be there, that my mother had brought me and made me stay. But he wouldn't listen. Said I had to go with him, that he couldn't leave me there alone. He made me get into the back of a police car with a couple of other people and brought me here."

Stephanie tried to block the awful images that rose in her mind. The kind of people that Meghan would've been sequestered with. The things she'd seen at that house. What might've happened to her if the police hadn't arrived when they had. Squeezing her eyes shut, she made herself focus on what Meghan was saying.

"When we got here, this woman cop brought me to this room. I gave them Daddy's name and number. She called him, but he wasn't home. So I gave them his cell number, but he didn't answer it either."

"I tried to call him, too, sweetheart," Stephanie told her. "His battery must be dead or he's out of range."

Gathering Meghan beneath her arm, she moved her toward the chairs. "But he'll come as soon as he gets the message."

Meghan sat, her eyes round with fear and fixed on Stephanie. "What if he doesn't?" Tears welled in her eyes. "Maybe he doesn't want me anymore. Mom said he didn't."

Stephanie pulled her into her arms. "That's not true. Your father loves you very much."

"But that's just it," Meghan sobbed. "He's not my father. Mom lied to him. She said she told him she was pregnant and the baby was his so he'd have to marry her."

Stephanie set her jaw hard enough to crack a tooth and hugged Meghan tighter against her chest. "I don't care what your mother told you. Wade loves you. Don't you ever doubt that for a minute."

Swearing, Wade yanked his battery charger from the adapter on his dash and hurled it out the window. Of all times for the stupid thing to break, this had to be the worst. He dragged a hand down his face and focused on the road, trying to think what to do. Seeing a gas station up ahead, he wheeled his truck into the parking lot and braked to a stop in front of a pay phone hanging on the side of the building.

Jumping out, he fished a quarter from his pocket, fed it into the slot, then punched in his cell phone number, silently praying Stephanie had called and left him a message telling him Meghan was home. When the recorded message started, asking him to leave a message, he quickly punched in the numerical code to take him directly to his voice mail. Pressing the phone to his ear, he listened. "Oh, no," he moaned and braced a hand against the wall to hold himself upright while he listened to a man, who identified himself as an Austin police officer, inform him that his daughter, Meghan Parker, was currently being held at the Austin Police Department on Seventh Street.

Wiping a shaky hand over his brow, he waited for the next message to begin.

"Wade, it's Stephanie. I talked to Meghan and she's at the Austin Police Department on Seventh Street, right off I-35. She's fine," she added quickly, "though understandably scared. I'm leaving now to go and stay with her. They won't release her to me, so you need to get to Austin as soon as possible."

Swearing, he dropped the receiver and jumped back into his truck. He was going to kill Angela, he told himself. If he ever got his hands on her, he was going to wring her lying neck. He knew she was behind this. How she'd pulled it off, he didn't know. But if Meghan was at a police station, Angela was the one responsible for her being there.

The door of the interview room flew open and Wade rushed in. He took one look at Meghan curled against Stephanie's side, then whipped his gaze to Stephanie's, the blood draining from his face.

Realizing that he thought Meghan was hurt, she shook her head. "She's fine," she whispered. "Just exhausted."

Meghan lifted her head and blinked. "Daddy?" she murmured sleepily. Tears filled her eyes when she saw Wade, and her face crumpled. "Oh, Daddy. I'm so sorry."

Wade crossed the room in two strides and gathered

her up in his arms, fitting her legs around his waist. "It's okay, baby," he soothed, then had to bury his face in her hair and gulp back his own tears. "Thank God you're all right. That's all that matters. You're safe."

Meghan clung tighter to him. "I just want to go home, Daddy. Please take me home."

"Don't worry, sweet cheeks," he assured her and headed for the door. "I've already cleared things with the police. We're good to go." He stopped at the doorway, as if only then remembering Stephanie was there, and glanced back, a brow lifted in question. "Do you need a ride?"

Stephanie rose, realizing that now that Wade and his daughter were reunited, her services were no longer needed. Though she should have been relieved that all had seemingly turned out well, she felt an inexplicable sadness.

She forced a smile. "No, I have my car."

Stephanie debated her options as she drove north on I-35 toward Georgetown, relieved to be leaving Austin behind. She was too tired to drive all the way to her home in Dallas, yet there was no place for her to sleep at her parents' house. All of the furniture had either been hauled away by the charitable group she'd donated it to or was currently sitting in a storage facility in Dallas.

Seeing a sign for a motel at the next exit, she slowed, considering stopping and getting a room. She sped up and passed the exit by, deciding that after the night she'd just spent, she needed the comfort and familiarity of her parents' home, even if it did mean she'd have to sleep on the floor.

Upon arriving, she parked beneath the shade of a tree near the back door rather than hassle with raising the garage door, Climbing out, she moaned softly as she stretched out the kinks sitting so long had left in her body. Hoping to find something she could use as bedding, she opened the rear doors of her SUV and dug through the items she kept stored there. She found a paper-thin blanket in the bag of emergency gear, tucked it under her arm, then dug around some more until she unearthed the inflatable neck pillow she used when traveling on airplanes. As an afterthought, she picked up the box containing her father's letters and headed for the house.

Once inside, she walked from room to room, feeling like Goldilocks as she searched for the most comfortable place to sleep. Deciding that the carpet in her bedroom was the cushiest, she set the box on the floor, then sank down beside it and blew up the neck pillow. Satisfied that she'd done all she could to make herself comfortable, she stretched out on her side, tucked the neck pillow beneath her cheek and drew the thin blanket up over her shoulder.

She released a long, exhausted breath, drew in another…and slept.

"Daddy?"

"Yeah?"

"Mom said that you and Stephanie used to be engaged."

Wade tensed, then forced his fingers to relax on the wand he held and twisted, closing the blinds and blocking out as much sunlight as possible from Meghan's room so that she could get some rest. "Yeah, we were."

"Mom said she broke y'all up so that you'd have to marry her."

Adding yet another item to the long list of reasons Meghan had already given him during the drive home to despise his ex, Wade crossed to sit down on the side of his daughter's bed. "In a way, I guess she did," he replied, not wanting to burden her with the details.

Tears welled in her eyes. "It was my fault, wasn't it? Because Mom was pregnant with me, you had to break your engagement to Stephanie."

He leaned to brush her hair back from her face. "No, sweet cheeks," he assured her. "The fault was mine. You had no part in it."

"You still like her, don't you? Stephanie, I mean."

He smiled sadly and drew his hand to cup her cheek. "Yeah. I guess I always will."

"You could still get married, couldn't you? I mean, it's not like you're married to Mom anymore."

He dropped his gaze, not sure how to answer. "It's more complicated than that."

She pulled herself up to sit, dropping her arms between her spread knees. "How?"

He hesitated, searching for a way to explain why he couldn't marry Stephanie that wouldn't make his daughter feel as if she were to blame. "Marriage is a big commitment," he began.

She rolled her eyes. "Duh. Like I don't already know that."

Chuckling, he scrubbed a hand over her hair. "If you're so smart, then you tell me why I *should* marry her."

"Because she's a hottie."

He choked out a laugh. "Hottie?" He shook his head. "Only a shallow man marries a woman for her looks."

"That's not the only reason," she said drily, then lifted a hand and began to tick off items. "She's smart, hip and really, really nice." She dropped her hands, her eyes filling with tears. "She came all the way to Austin to stay with me because I was scared. And she held me real tight when I cried, just like a real mom would. She made me feel safe, loved. Even knowing how bad I'd been, she didn't yell at me or anything. She was just…nice."

Wade stared, wondering if Stephanie's kindness to Meghan was a sign that she no longer resented his daughter. "Meghan?" he said hesitantly. "If Stephanie and I were to get married, she would become your stepmother. How would you feel about that?"

Meghan frowned, as if she hadn't considered that aspect, then smiled. "I think that would be really cool."

"Are you sure? Now think about this before you answer," he warned. "She'd be living in our house with us, and I'm sure she'd have her own set of rules she'd expect us to follow. Consequences, too," he added, remembering his conversation with Stephanie about cursing.

She drew back, eyeing him warily. "Gosh, Dad. You make her sound like some kind of witch."

He shrugged. "I just want to make sure that you understand that if Stephanie and I were to marry, I would expect you to give her the respect any mother deserves."

She lifted a brow and looked down her nose at him. "*Any* mother?"

He rolled his eyes, knowing she was referring to Angela. "You know what I mean."

"I will. I promise." She gave him a push. "Go and ask her. I'll bet she says yes."

He gaped. "Now?"

She flopped to her back and pulled the covers to her chin. "Why not? It's not like you have anything better to do."

He rose slowly, fighting a sudden attack of nerves. "No, I guess I don't."

Wade wasn't sure if he'd find Stephanie at her parents' house, but he figured that was as good a place as any to start his search.

He prayed it was a good sign when he found her SUV parked beneath the shade tree near the back. Unsure how she'd respond to another proposal, he crossed to the front door and knocked. He waited, shifting nervously from foot to foot. When he didn't receive a response, he lifted a hand above the door and felt along the edge for the key. Finding it, he unlocked the door and let himself in.

He glanced around and was shocked to see that the house was empty, not a stick of furniture or a box in sight. Realizing that Steph had completed the job she'd come to do and would be leaving soon made his stomach twist with dread.

Runt trotted out from the kitchen and bumped his nose against Wade's hand.

"Hey, Runt," he said and gave the dog a distracted pat as he looked around. "Where's Steph?"

In answer, the dog started down the hall. Wade followed, his hands slick with sweat, his throat dry as a bone.

At the door of her bedroom Runt dropped down on his haunches and looked up expectantly at Wade.

"Good boy," Wade murmured and gave the dog a pat as he leaned to peek inside.

Guilt stabbed at him when he saw Steph asleep on the floor with only a blanket for cover. Silently kicking himself for not thinking to ask her to come to his house when they'd left the police station, he tiptoed into the room and sank down to his knees at her side.

"Steph?" he whispered and gave her arm a nudge.

She moaned softly and pulled the blanket over her head. "Not now, Runt," she complained. "I'm sleeping."

Biting back a smile, Wade stretched out on his side to face her. Careful not to startle her, he lifted the edge of the blanket. "It's not Runt, Steph," he whispered. "It's me. Wade."

She blinked open her eyes. Blinked again, then tensed. "Is Meghan okay? Has something happened to her?"

He laid a hand against her cheek, touched by the alarm and concern in her voice. "She's fine. When I left, she was sleeping."

Obviously relieved, she closed her hand over his and let her lids drift down. "Good. Poor baby was tired."

Poor baby. Hearing her use that one endearment told Wade all he needed to know. He eased his body closer to hers. "Steph? I need for you to wake up."

"Tired," she moaned. "So tired."

"I know you are, sunshine, but there's something I need to ask you."

"Can't it wait?" she complained.

Chuckling, he placed a finger on her eyelid and forced it up. "No, it can't," he told her firmly.

Heaving a sigh, she rolled to her back and scrubbed her hands over her face. "What?" she asked wearily.

He sat up in order to better see her. "I wanted to thank you for going to Austin and staying with Meghan until I could get there. That meant a lot to me."

Yawning, she rolled back to her side and pulled the blanket over her shoulder. "You're welcome."

"Meghan sends her thanks, too."

"Poor baby," she murmured sympathetically. "I can't imagine how frightened she must have been."

Because he knew only too well the kind of horrors his ex had subjected his daughter to, Wade scowled. "Yeah, she was scared all right." Heaving a sigh, he focused on Steph's face again. "Meghan said that you were really nice to her. Held her tight, like a real mom would."

Though her eyes remained closed, a tender smile curved Steph's lips. "That's really sweet. She's a good kid."

"You think so?"

Something in his voice must have caught her attention, because Steph opened her eyes and looked up at him. "Yes, I do."

"You said before that you didn't think you could live in the same house with her. Do you still feel that way?"

Her gaze on his, she slowly pushed herself up to an elbow. "Wade, what are you saying?"

He dipped his chin, shrugged. "Meghan and I had a little talk before I came here. She seems to think we should get married."

Her eyes shot wide. "Meghan said that?"

"Yeah. Angela told her that we were engaged before,

and Meghan was worried that it was her fault that our engagement was broken."

She shifted to sit and dropped her face onto her hands. "Oh, no," she moaned. "That is so unfair, so wrong. Angela should never have said that to her. Meghan wasn't to blame."

"Don't worry. I straightened Meghan out. I told her it was my fault, that she had nothing to do with it."

She opened her hands enough to peek at him. "And she believed you?"

He lifted a brow. "What choice did she have? It's kind of hard to argue with the truth. It *was* my fault."

She dropped her hands to frown. "No, it wasn't. It was Angela's."

He lifted a shoulder. "No matter who was to blame, I don't regret the decision I made. I only have to look at Meghan and know I did the right thing."

"Oh, Wade," she said, her face crumpling. "After all that woman put you through, you never once turned your back on Meghan."

"And I never will," he said firmly. He caught her hand and squeezed. "And I hope you won't either."

Her tears welled higher. "I won't. I couldn't."

He gulped and gripped her hands more tightly. "There's something you need to know. Something that might make you angry. I probably should've mentioned it before, but I didn't think it was my place."

A soft smile curved her lips. "If it's about Bud leaving you his land, you needn't worry. I already know."

His eyes widened in surprise. "You knew?",

"I met with Bud's lawyer. He told me."

"And you're not mad?"

She shook her head. "No. Surprised, yes, but not mad. Bud willed you his land because he knew you would love it as much as he did." She sputtered a laugh. "And I wouldn't be surprised if he didn't do it in hopes it would bring us together."

Smiling, he nodded. "That sounds like something Bud would do." Growing solemn, he shifted to kneel before her and brought her hands to his lips. "Stephanie Calloway, would you do me the honor of marrying me and becoming my wife?"

She stared at him as if afraid this was a dream she would wake from.

"Will you?" he prodded.

Laughing, she flung her arms around his neck. "Yes, yes, a thousand times yes!"

He squeezed his arms tightly around her and buried his face in her hair. "I've waited so long to hear you say that," he murmured, then drew back to look deeply into her eyes. "We're going to be a family. You, me and Meghan."

A sharp bark had him glancing toward the doorway, where Runt sat, looking at him expectantly.

Smiling, he added, "And Runt." He turned to look at Steph again and the smile melted from his face. "I love you, Stephanie Calloway."

"No more than I love you, Wade Parker."

He framed her face between his hands. "We're going to make it this time. Nothing is ever going to separate us again."

"Nothing," she promised and lifted her face to his.

Epilogue

Stephanie turned her hand slowly, watching as light from the bedside lamp caught the emerald-cut diamond of her ring and made it shimmer. It was the same ring Wade had slipped on her finger almost thirteen years ago. His mother's ring. Two weeks after he'd placed it on her finger, she'd ripped the ring off and thrown it at him. Closing her eyes against the unwanted memory, she curled her fingers to her palm as if to protect the ring and silently vowed never to take it off again. Ever.

Sighing, she opened her eyes to look at the ring again, then dropped her hand and reached for the last stack of letters sitting on the bedside table. She'd read them, just as she'd promised herself she would, and only one remained before she could say she'd read them all. Slipping the last envelope from the stack, she pushed back the flap and pulled out the folded pages.

As she opened them, a torn piece of paper fell to her lap.

"What's this?" she murmured and picked it up to examine it. Finding a jumble of handwritten words on one side, she turned it over to look at the back. Impressed into the paper was a notary's seal and a woman's signature. *Helen Thompson.* Frowning at the unfamiliar name, she flipped the paper back over and tried again to make sense of the words. She quickly gave up. Whatever message was originally written on the piece had lost its meaning when the document was torn.

Hoping to find an explanation in her father's letter, she set the piece of paper aside and smoothed open the pages of the letter over her propped up knees.

Dearest Janine,
I'm enclosing part of a document that I want you to have. I have no idea if it'll ever be worth anything, but keep it somewhere safe, just in case. I never mentioned it to you before, but I honestly thought the guy who gave this to me was either crazy or drunk. Maybe I'd better explain.

The night before I left for 'Nam I was in a bar in Austin with the guys I was traveling with and this man came up to our table and offered to buy us all a drink. We invited him to join us and he told us that he'd had a son who was killed in Vietnam. It happened several years before, but I could tell the man was still grieving. Anyway, he said, now that his son was dead, he didn't have anybody to leave his ranch to and said he wanted to leave it to us. He wrote out this bill of sale, had each one of us sign it, then tore it into six pieces and gave each one of us a piece. He told us, when we got back from Vietnam, we were to put the pieces together and come claim our ranch.

Like I said, I don't know if anything will ever come of this, but I want you to have it, just in case I don't make it home. Kind of like insurance, I guess.

I've never really thought about dying, but lately it's been on my mind a lot. Maybe it's because I'm going to be a daddy. I don't know. I've been worrying how you and the baby would make it if something were to happen to me. You'd get money from the Army. I know that for sure. But what I don't know is if it would be enough to support you and the baby without you having to work. And I don't want you to have to worry about working or money or anything like that.

I want you to be able to devote yourself to being a mommy.

I hope I haven't depressed you by telling you all this. My only purpose in writing it all down is so that you can take advantage of this opportunity, if it should ever present itself. If something should happen to me, the other guys will know what to do and they'll contact you. You can trust them. They'll see that you get your fair share.

I'd better go. We're heading out early in the morning and moving to an area where there's been some trouble. The guys and I have already decided that we're going to kick butt and get this war over with so we can come home.

Love forever and ever,
Larry

Blinking back tears, Stephanie carefully refolded the letter, then picked up the torn piece of paper. Insurance, she thought sadly, turning the yellowed and ragged piece of paper between her fingers. Since Stephanie was unaware of her mother ever having received a windfall, she had to believe that her father's assumption was right. The man who had given him the piece of paper had either been drunk or crazy.

"You still awake?"

Stephanie glanced up to find Wade in the doorway. Though she'd agreed to stay in his house, she had refused to sleep in his bedroom with him until they were properly married. With his daughter in the house, she'd thought it only proper.

Smiling, she patted the spot on the bed beside her. "I was just reading the last of my father's letters."

He hopped up onto the bed and settled beside her, stretching his legs out next to hers. "So? How was it? Any new revelations?"

She frowned thoughtfully. "I don't know." She passed the torn piece of paper to him. "Take a look at this. It was inside the letter."

He studied first one side, then the other, then shrugged and passed it back. "What is it? Some kind of secret code?"

She laughed softly. "It looks like it, doesn't it?" Her smile faded and she shook her head. "He sent it to Mom and told her to keep it someplace safe. Said it was insurance, in case he didn't make it home."

He took the piece of paper back from her to look at it again, then snorted. "Sure doesn't look like an insurance policy to me."

"It's not. A man gave it to him the night before he left for Vietnam. Him and five other soldiers. It's like a deed, I guess. Supposedly his son died in Vietnam, and since he didn't have anyone to leave his ranch to, he wanted my father and his friends to have it."

He snorted a laugh. "What man in his right mad would give his ranch to six complete strangers?"

"My father thought the same thing. He said in the letter that he thought the guy had to be drunk or crazy to do something like that." Growing thoughtful, she rubbed the torn edge of the paper across her lips. "I wonder what happened to the other five men?" She glanced at Wade. "There's a chance that some of them, if not all, made it back home."

He lifted a shoulder. "You'd think so."

"Wade," she said as an idea begin to form in her mind. "Do you think it would be possible to locate those soldiers? Find out what happened to them? Maybe where they live?"

"I don't know," he said doubtfully. "That was— what?—thirty-five years ago?"

"Give or take a few months." Catching her lower lip between her teeth, she tried to think how to go about locating the men. "I could write a letter to the Army," she said, thinking aloud. "Find out the names of the men that were in Dad's unit at the time he was killed."

"Yeah," he agreed. "That would be a start."

"Wonder how many men there were?"

"In his unit, you mean?" At her nod, he shrugged. "I have no idea. A lot, I'd imagine."

She firmed her mouth in determination. "It doesn't matter. I don't care if I have to write a thousand letters, I'm going to track down the five men who have the other pieces of paper."

"You don't really think it has any value, do you? Even if the guy who gave it to them was serious, that was thirty-five years ago. A lot could have happened in that amount of time."

Smiling, she dropped a kiss on his cheek. "Doesn't matter. Not to me. The only thing I'm interested in is finding my father's friends."

"Would you mind waiting until after we're married to start your search?"

She looked at him curiously. "Why?"

He curled up close to her and nuzzled her neck. "Because I don't want anything distracting you from planning this wedding and causing a delay. Having you in my house and not in my bed is driving me crazy."

She slid down until her face was even with his. "Doesn't Meghan ever have sleepovers with her friends?"

A slow smile spread across his face as he realized what she was suggesting. "Yeah, she does. Remind me to call Jan tomorrow and set one up."

She drew back to peer at him in surprise. "Isn't that rather bold to ask if your daughter can spend the night at someone's house? Shouldn't the invitation come from Jan?"

He looped an arm around her waist and drew her to him. "Jan'll understand." His lips spread across hers in a smile. "She's a single parent, too."

* * * * *

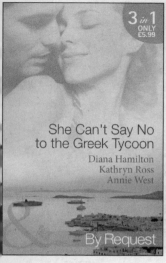
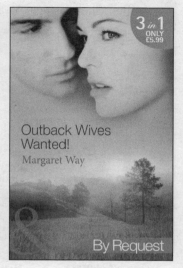

These hot-blooded, hard-hearted desert sheikhs have chosen their queens!

The Desert Sheikh's Defiant Queen

4th March 2011

The Desert Sheikh's Innocent Queen

1st April 2011

www.millsandboon.co.uk

ULTIMATE ALPHA MALES:

Strong, sexy…and intent on seduction!

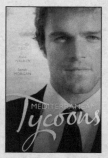

Mediterranean Tycoons
4th February 2011

Hot-Shot Heroes
4th March 2011

Powerful Protectors
1st April 2011

Passionate Playboys
6th May 2011

Collect all four!

www.millsandboon.co.uk

Nora Roberts' *The O'Hurleys*

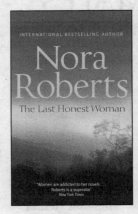

4th March 2011

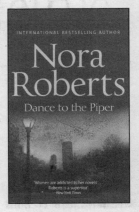

1st April 2011

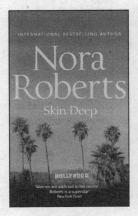

6th May 2011

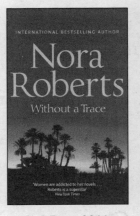

3rd June 2011

THE
Royal
HOUSE OF NIROLI

*The richest royal family in the world—united by blood
and passion, torn apart by deceit and desire*

The Royal House of Niroli: Scandalous Seductions
Penny Jordan & Melanie Milburne
Available 17th December 2010

The Royal House of Niroli: Billion Dollar Bargains
Carol Marinelli & Natasha Oakley
Available 21st January 2011

The Royal House of Niroli: Innocent Mistresses
Susan Stephens & Robyn Donald
Available 18th February 2011

The Royal House of Niroli: Secret Heirs
Raye Morgan & Penny Jordan
Available 18th March 2011

Collect all four!

www.millsandboon.co.uk

M&B

BAD BLOOD

A POWERFUL DYNASTY, WHERE SECRETS AND SCANDAL NEVER SLEEP!

VOLUME 1 – 15th April 2011
TORTURED RAKE
by Sarah Morgan

VOLUME 2 – 6th May 2011
SHAMELESS PLAYBOY
by Caitlin Crews

VOLUME 3 – 20th May 2011
RESTLESS BILLIONAIRE
by Abby Green

VOLUME 4 – 3rd June 2011
FEARLESS MAVERICK
by Robyn Grady

8 VOLUMES IN ALL TO COLLECT!

www.millsandboon.co.uk